the

john grisham
the runaway jury

arrow books

Reissued in the United Kingdom by Arrow Books in 2010

11

Copyright © John Grisham 1996

First published in the United Kingdom in 1996 by Century
First published in paperback in 1997 by Arrow books

Arrow Books
The Random House Group Limited
20 Vauxhall Bridge Road, London, SW1V 2SA

www.randomhouse.co.uk

Addresses for companies within The Random House Group Limited can
be found at: www.randomhouse.co.uk/offices.htm

The Random House Group Limited Reg. No. 954009

A CIP catalogue record for this book
is available from the British Library

ISBN 9780099537182

Typeset by SX Composing DTP, Rayleigh, Essex

Penguin Random House is committed to a sustainable future for
our business, our readers and our planet. This book is made from
Forest Stewardship Council® certified paper.

Printed and bound in Great Britain by Clays Ltd, Elcograf S.p.A.

To the memory of Tim Hargrove
(1953–1995)

Acknowledgements

Once again, I am indebted to my friend Will Denton, now of Biloxi, Mississippi, for providing much of the research and many of the stories upon which this one is based; and to his lovely wife Lucy, for the hospitalities extended to me while I was on the Coast.

Thanks also to Glenn Hunt of Oxford, Mark Lee of Little Rock, Robert Warren of Bogue Chitto; and to Estelle, for finding more mistakes than I care to think about.

ONE

The face of Nicholas Easter was slightly hidden by a display rack filled with slim cordless phones, and he was looking not directly at the hidden camera but somewhere off to the left, perhaps at a customer, or perhaps at a counter where a group of kids hovered over the latest electronic games from Asia. Though taken from a distance of forty yards by a man dodging rather heavy mall foot traffic, the photo was clear and revealed a nice face, clean-shaven with strong features and boyish good looks. Easter was twenty-seven, they knew that for a fact. No eyeglasses. No nose ring or weird haircut. Nothing to indicate he was one of the usual computer nerds who worked in the store at five bucks an hour. His questionnaire said he'd been there for four months, said also that he was a part-time student, though no record of enrollment had been found at any college within three hundred miles. He was lying about this, they were certain.

He had to be lying. Their intelligence was too good. If the kid was a student, they'd know where, for how long, what field of study, how good were the grades, or how bad. They'd know. He was a clerk in a Computer Hut in a mall. Nothing more or less. Maybe he planned to enroll somewhere. Maybe he'd dropped out but still liked the notion of referring to himself as a part-time student. Maybe it made him feel better, gave him a sense of purpose, sounded good.

But he was not, at this moment nor at any time in the recent past, a student of any sort. So, could he be trusted? This had been thrashed about the room twice already, each time they came to Easter's name on the master list and his face hit the screen. It was a harmless lie, they'd almost decided.

He didn't smoke. The store had a strict nonsmoking rule, but he'd been seen (not photographed) eating a taco in the Food Garden with a co-worker who smoked two cigarettes with her lemonade. Easter didn't seem to mind the smoke. At least he wasn't an antismoking zealot.

The face in the photo was lean and tanned and smiling slightly with lips closed. The white shirt under the red store jacket had a buttonless collar and a tasteful striped tie. He appeared neat, in shape, and the man who took the photo actually spoke with Nicholas as he pretended to shop for an obsolete gadget; said he was articulate, helpful, knowledgeable, a nice young man. His name badge labeled Easter as a Co-Manager, but two others with the same title were spotted in the store at the same time.

The day after the photo was taken, an attractive young female in jeans entered the store, and while browsing near the software actually lit up a cigarette. Nicholas Easter just happened to be the nearest clerk, or Co-Manager, or whatever he was, and he politely approached the woman and asked her to stop smoking. She pretended to be frustrated by this, even insulted, and tried to provoke him. He maintained his tactful manner, explained to her that the store had a strict no-smoking policy. She was welcome to smoke elsewhere. 'Does smoking bother you?' she had asked, taking a puff. 'Not really,' he had answered. 'But it bothers the man who owns this store.' He then asked her once again to stop. She really wanted to purchase a new digital radio, she explained, so would it be possible for him to

2

fetch an ashtray. Nicholas pulled an empty soft drink can from under the counter, and actually took the cigarette from her and extinguished it. They talked about radios for twenty minutes as she struggled with the selection. She flirted shamelessly, and he warmed to the occasion. After paying for the radio, she left him her phone number. He promised to call.

The episode lasted twenty-four minutes and was captured by a small recorder hidden in her purse. The tape had been played both times while his face had been projected on the wall and studied by the lawyers and their experts. Her written report of the incident was in the file, six typed pages of her observations on everything from his shoes (old Nikes) to his breath (cinnamon gum) to his vocabulary (college level) to the way he handled the cigarette. In her opinion, and she was experienced in such matters, he had never smoked.

They listened to his pleasant tone and his professional sales pitch and his charming chatter, and they liked him. He was bright and he didn't hate tobacco. He didn't fit as their model juror, but he was certainly one to watch. The problem with Easter, potential juror number fifty-six, was that they knew so little about him. Evidently, he had landed on the Gulf Coast less than a year ago, and they had no idea where he came from. His past was a complete mystery. He rented a one-bedroom eight blocks from the Biloxi courthouse – they had photos of the apartment building – and at first worked as a waiter in a casino on the beach. He rose quickly to the rank of blackjack dealer, but quit after two months.

Shortly after Mississippi legalized gambling, a dozen casinos along the Coast sprang forth overnight, and a new wave of prosperity hit hard. Job seekers came from all directions, and so it was safe to assume Nicholas Easter arrived in Biloxi for the same reason as ten thousand others. The only odd thing about his move was that he had registered to vote so quickly.

He drove a 1969 Volkswagen Beetle, and a photo of it was flashed on the wall, taking the place of his face. Big deal. He was twenty-seven, single, an alleged part-time student – the perfect type to drive such a car. No bumper stickers. Nothing to indicate political affiliation or social conscience or favorite team. No college parking sticker. Not even a faded dealer decal. The car meant nothing, as far as they were concerned. Nothing but near-poverty.

The man operating the projector and doing most of the talking was Carl Nussman, a lawyer from Chicago who no longer practiced law but instead ran his own jury consulting firm. For a small fortune, Carl Nussman and his firm could pick you the right jury. They gathered the data, took the photos, recorded the voices, sent the blondes in tight jeans into the right situations. Carl and his associates flirted around the edges of laws and ethics, but it was impossible to catch them. After all, there's nothing illegal or unethical about photo-graphing prospective jurors. They had conducted exhaustive telephone surveys in Harrison County six months ago, then again two months ago, then a month later to gauge community sentiment about tobacco issues and formulate models of the perfect jurors. They left no photo untaken, no dirt ungathered. They had a file on every prospective juror.

Carl pushed his button and the VW was replaced with a meaningless shot of an apartment building with peeling paint; home, somewhere in there, of Nicholas Easter. Then a flick, and back to the face.

'And so we have only the three photos of number fifty-six,' Carl said with a note of frustration as he turned and glared at the photographer, one of his countless private snoops, who had explained he just couldn't catch the kid without getting caught himself.

4

The photographer sat in a chair against the back wall, facing the long table of lawyers and paralegals and jury experts. The photographer was quite bored and ready to bolt. It was seven o'clock on a Friday night. Number fifty-six was on the wall, leaving a hundred and forty still to come. The weekend would be awful. He needed a drink.

A half-dozen lawyers in rumpled shirts and rolled-up sleeves scribbled never-ending notes, and glanced occasionally at the face of Nicholas Easter up there behind Carl. Jury experts of almost every variety – psychiatrist, sociologist, handwriting analyst, law professor, and so on – shuffled papers and thumped the inch-thick computer printouts. They weren't sure what to do with Easter. He was a liar, and he was hiding his past, but still on paper and on the wall he looked okay.

Maybe he wasn't lying. Maybe he was a student last year in some low-rent junior college in eastern Arizona, and maybe they were simply missing this.

Give the kid a break, the photographer thought, but he kept it to himself. In this room of well-educated and well-paid suits, he was the last one whose opinion would be appreciated. Wasn't his job to say a word.

Carl cleared his throat while glancing once more at the photographer, then said, 'Number fifty-seven.' The sweaty face of a young mother flashed on the wall, and at least two people in the room managed a chuckle. 'Traci Wilkes,' Carl said, as if Traci was now an old friend. Papers moved slightly around the table.

'Age thirty-three, married, mother of two, doctor's wife, two country clubs, two health clubs, a whole list of social clubs.' Carl clicked off these items from memory while twirling his projector button. Traci's red face was replaced by a shot of her jogging along a sidewalk, splendidly awash in pink and black spandex and spotless Reeboks with a white sun visor sitting just above the latest in reflective sport sunglasses, her long hair in a

5

cute perfect ponytail. She was pushing a jogging carriage with a small baby in it. Traci lived for sweat. She was tanned and fit, but not exactly as thin as might be expected. She had a few bad habits. Another shot of Traci in her black Mercedes wagon with kids and dogs looking from every window. Another of Traci loading bags of groceries into the same car, Traci with different sneakers and tight shorts and the precise appearance of one who aspired to look forever athletic. She'd been easy to follow because she was busy to the point of being frazzled, and she never stopped long enough to look around.

Carl ran through the photos of the Wilkeses' home, a massive suburban trilevel with Doctor stamped all over it. He spent little time with these, saving the best for last. Then there was Traci, once again soaked with sweat, her designer bike nearby on the grass, sitting under a tree in a park, far away from everyone, half-hidden and – smoking a cigarette!

The same photographer grinned stupidly. It was his finest work, this hundred-yard shot of the doctor's wife sneaking a cigarette. He had had no idea she smoked, just happened to be nonchalantly smoking himself near a footbridge when she dashed by. He loitered about the park for half an hour until he saw her stop and reach into the pouch on her bike.

The mood around the room lightened for a fleeting moment as they looked at Traci by the tree. Then Carl said, 'Safe to say that we'll take number fifty-seven.' He made a notation on a sheet of paper, then took a sip of old coffee from a paper cup. Of course he'd take Traci Wilkes! Who wouldn't want a doctor's wife on the jury when the plaintiff's lawyers were asking for millions? Carl wanted nothing but doctors' wives, but he wouldn't get them. The fact that she enjoyed cigarettes was simply a small bonus.

Number fifty-eight was a shipyard worker at Ingalls

6

in Pascagoula – fifty years old, white male, divorced, a union officer. Carl flashed a photo of the man's Ford pickup on the wall, and was about to summarize his life when the door opened and Mr. Rankin Fitch stepped into the room. Carl stopped. The lawyers bolted upright in their seats and instantly became enthralled by the Ford. They wrote furiously on their legal pads as if they might never again see such a vehicle. The jury consultants likewise snapped into action and all began taking notes in earnest, each careful not to look at the man.

Fitch was back. Fitch was in the room.

He slowly closed the door behind him, took a few steps toward the edge of the table, and glared at everyone sitting around it. It was more of a snarl than a glare. The puffy flesh around his dark eyes pinched inward. The deep wrinkles running the length of his forehead closed together. His thick chest rose and sank slowly, and for a second or two Fitch was the only person breathing. His lips parted to eat and drink, occasionally to talk, never to smile.

Fitch was angry, as usual, nothing new about that because the man even slept in a state of hostility. But would he curse and threaten, maybe throw things, or simply boil under the surface? They never knew with Fitch. He stopped at the edge of the table between two young lawyers who were junior partners and thus earning comfortable six-figure salaries, who were members of this firm and this was their room in their building. Fitch, on the other hand, was a stranger from Washington, an intruder who'd been growling and barking in their hallways for a month now. The two young lawyers dared not look at him.

'What number?' Fitch asked of Carl.

'Fifty-eight,' Carl answered quickly, anxious to please.

'Go back to fifty-six,' Fitch demanded, and Carl

7

flicked rapidly until the face of Nicholas Easter was once again on the wall. Paperwork ruffled around the table.

'What do you know?' Fitch asked.

'The same,' Carl said, looking away.

'That's just great. Out of a hundred and ninety-six, how many are still mysteries?'

'Eight.'

Fitch snorted and shook his head slowly, and everyone waited for an eruption. Instead, he slowly stroked his meticulously trimmed black and gray goatee for a few seconds, looked at Carl, allowed the severity of the moment to filter in, then said, 'You'll work until midnight, then return at seven in the morning. Same for Sunday.' With that, he wheeled his pudgy body around and left the room.

The door slammed. The air lightened considerably, then, in unison, the lawyers and the jury consultants and Carl and everybody else glanced at their watches. They had just been ordered to spend thirty-nine out of the next fifty-three hours in this room, looking at enlarged photos of faces they'd already seen, memorizing names and birthdates and vital stats of almost two hundred people.

And there wasn't the slightest doubt anywhere in the room that they all would do exactly what they'd been told. Not the slightest.

Fitch took the stairs to the first floor of the building, and was met there by his driver, a large man named José. José wore a black suit with black western boots and black sunglasses that were removed only when he showered and slept. Fitch opened a door without knocking, and interrupted a meeting which had been in progress for hours. Four lawyers and their assorted support staff were watching the videotaped depositions of the plaintiffs first witnesses. The tape stopped just

8

seconds after Fitch burst in. He spoke briefly to one of the lawyers, then left the room. José followed him through a narrow library to another hallway, where he barged through another door and frightened another bunch of lawyers.

With eighty lawyers, the firm of Whitney & Cable & White was the largest on the Gulf Coast. The firm had been handpicked by Fitch himself, and it would earn millions in fees because of this selection. To earn the money, though, the firm had to endure the tyranny and ruthlessness of Rankin Fitch.

When satisfied that the entire building was aware of his presence and terrified of his movements, Fitch left. He stood on the sidewalk, in the warm October air, and waited for José. Three blocks away, in the top half of an old bank building, he could see an office suite filled with lights. The enemy was still working. The plaintiff's lawyers were up there, all huddled together in various rooms, meeting with experts and looking at grainy photos and doing pretty much the same things his people were doing. The trial started Monday with jury selection, and he knew they too were sweating over names and faces and wondering who the hell was Nicholas Easter and where did he come from. And Ramon Caro and Lucas Miller and Andrew Lamb and Barbara Furrow and Delores DeBoe? Who were these people? Only in a backwater place like Mississippi would you find such outdated lists of prospective jurors. Fitch had directed the defense in eight cases before this one, in eight different states where computers were used and rolls were purged and where, when the clerks handed you your list of jurors, you didn't have to worry about who was dead and who wasn't.

He stared blankly at the distant lights and wondered how the greedy sharks would split the money, if they happened to win. How in the world could they ever agree to divide the bloody carcass? The trial would be a

9

gentle skirmish compared to the throat-cutting that would ensue if they got their verdict, and their spoils.

He hated them, and he spat on the sidewalk. He lit a cigarette, squeezing it tightly between his thick fingers.

José pulled to the curb in a shiny, rented Suburban with dark windows. Fitch took his customary place in the front seat. José too looked up at the enemy lawyers' office as they drove past, but he said nothing because his boss did not suffer small talk. They drove past the Biloxi courthouse, and past a semi-abandoned dime store where Fitch and associates maintained a hidden suite of offices with fresh plywood dust on the floor and cheap rented furniture.

They turned west on Highway 90 at the beach and limped through heavy traffic. It was Friday night, and the casinos were packed with people gambling away grocery money with big plans to win it back tomorrow. They slowly made it out of Biloxi, through Gulfport, Long Beach, and Pass Christian. Then they left the coastline, and were soon passing through a security checkpoint near a lagoon.

TWO

The beach house was modern and sprawling and built without the benefit of a beach. A white-board pier disappeared into the still and weedy waters of the bay, but the nearest sand was two miles away. A twenty-foot fishing boat was moored at the pier. The house had been leased from an oil man in New Orleans – three months, cash, no questions. It was being temporarily used as a retreat, a hiding place, a sleep-over for some very important people.

On a deck high above the water, four gentlemen enjoyed drinks and managed small talk while waiting for a visitor. Though their businesses normally required them to be bitter enemies, they had played eighteen holes of golf this afternoon, then eaten shrimp and oysters off the grill. Now they drank and looked into the black waters below them. They loathed the fact that they were on the Gulf Coast, on Friday night, far away from their homes.

But business was at hand, crucial affairs that necessitated a truce and made the golf almost pleasant. Each of the four was the CEO of a large public corporation. Each corporation was in the Fortune 500, each was traded on the NYSE. The smallest had sales last year of six hundred million, the largest, four billion. Each had record profits, large dividends, happy stockholders, and CEO's who earned millions for their performances.

Each was a conglomerate of sorts with different divisions and a multitude of products, fat ad budgets, and insipid names such as Trellco and Smith Greer, names designed to deflect attention from the fact that at the core they were little more than tobacco companies. Each of the four, the Big Four as they were known in financial circles, could easily trace its roots to nineteenth-century tobacco brokers in the Carolinas and Virginia. They manufactured cigarettes – together, ninety-eight percent of all cigarettes sold in the United States and Canada. They also manufactured such things as crowbars and corn chips and hair dye, but dig just below the surface and you'd find that their profits came from cigarettes. There had been mergers and name changes and various efforts at preening for the public, but the Big Four had been thoroughly isolated and vilified by consumer groups, doctors, even politicians.

And now the lawyers were after them. The survivors of dead people out there were actually suing and asking for huge sums of money because cigarettes cause lung cancer, they claimed. Sixteen trials so far, and Big Tobacco had won them all, but the pressure was mounting. And the first time a jury handed out a few million to a widow, then all hell would break loose. The trial lawyers would go berserk with their nonstop advertising, begging smokers and the survivors of smokers to sign up now and sue while the suing was good.

As a rule, the men talked of other matters when they were alone, but the liquor loosened their tongues. The bitterness began to ooze forth. They leaned on the railing of the deck, stared at the water, and began to curse lawyers and the American tort system. Each of their companies spent millions in Washington on various groups trying to reform tort laws so that responsible companies like themselves could be protected from litigation. They needed a shield from

12

such senseless attacks by alleged victims. But, it seemed, nothing was working. Here they were somewhere in the backwaters of Mississippi sweating out yet another trial.

In response to the growing assault from the courts, the Big Four had created a pool of money known simply as The Fund. It had no limits, left no trail. It did not exist. The Fund was used for hardball tactics in lawsuits; to hire the best and meanest defense lawyers, the smoothest experts, the most sophisticated jury consultants. No restrictions were placed on what The Fund could do. After sixteen victories, they sometimes asked, among themselves, if there was anything The Fund couldn't do. Each company siphoned off three million a year and routed the cash circuitously until it landed in The Fund. No bean counter, no auditor, no regulator had ever caught wind of the slush money.

The Fund was administered by Rankin Fitch, a man they collectively despised but nonetheless listened to and even obeyed when necessary. And they waited for him. They gathered when he said to gather. They dispersed and returned at his command. They tolerated being at his beck and call as long as he was winning. Fitch had directed eight trials without a loss. He'd also engineered two mistrials, but of course there was no proof of this.

An assistant stepped onto the deck with a tray of fresh drinks, each mixed to exact specifications. The drinks were being lifted from the tray when someone said, 'Fitch is here.' In unison the drinks shot upward then downward as the four knocked back a stiff belt.

They quickly stepped into the den while Fitch was parking José just outside the front door. An assistant handed him a mineral water, no ice. He never drank, though in an earlier life he'd consumed enough to float a barge. He didn't say thanks to the assistant, didn't acknowledge his presence, but moved to the faux

13

fireplace and waited for the four to gather around him on the sofas. Another assistant ventured forth with a platter of leftover shrimp and oysters, but Fitch waved him off. There was a rumor that he sometimes ate, but he'd never been caught in the process. The evidence was there, the thick chest and ample waistline, the fleshy roll under his goatee, the general squattiness of his frame. But he wore dark suits and kept the jackets buttoned, and did a fine job of carrying his bulk with importance.

'A brief update,' he said when he felt he'd waited long enough for the honchos to settle in. 'At this moment, the entire defense team is working nonstop, and this will continue through the weekend. Jury research is on schedule. Trial counsel are ready. All witnesses are prepped, all experts are already in town. Nothing unusual has yet to be encountered.'

There was a pause, just a little gap as they waited long enough to make sure Fitch had finished for a bit.

'What about those jurors?' asked D. Martin Jankle, the most nervous of the bunch. He ran U-Tab, as it was formerly known, an abbreviation for an old company which for years was called Union Tobacco but after a marketing cleansing was now traded as Pynex. The lawsuit at hand was *Wood v. Pynex,* so the roulette wheel had placed Jankle on the hot seat. Pynex was number three in size with sales of almost two billion last year. It also happened to possess, as of the last quarter, the largest cash reserves of any of the four. The timing of this trial was lousy. With a bit of bad luck, the jury might soon be shown blowups of Pynex' financials, nice neat columns which would indicate in excess of eight hundred million in cash.

'We're working on them,' Fitch said. 'We have soft data on eight. Four of whom might either be dead or gone. The other four are alive and expected to be in court Monday.'

'One rogue juror can be poison,' Jankle said. He'd been a corporate lawyer in Louisville before joining U-Tab, and he always insisted on reminding Fitch that he knew more about the law than the other three.

'I'm well aware of that,' Fitch snapped.

'We have to know these people.'

'We're doing our best. We can't help it if the jury lists here are not as current as other states'.'

Jankle took a long drink and stared at Fitch. Fitch, after all, was a well-paid security thug, nothing remotely near the level of CEO of a major company. Call him whatever you want – consultant, agent, contractor – fact was, he worked for them. Sure he had some clout right now, liked to swagger and bark because he was pushing the buttons, but dammit he was just a glorified thug. These thoughts Jankle kept to himself.

'Anything else?' Fitch demanded of Jankle, as if his initial inquiry were thoughtless, as though if he had nothing productive to say then maybe he should just keep his mouth shut.

'Do you trust these lawyers?' Jankle asked, not for the first time.

'We've covered this before,' Fitch answered.

'We can certainly cover it again if I choose.'

'Why are you worried about our lawyers?' Fitch asked.

'Because, well, because they're from around here.'

'I see. And you think it'd be wise to bring in some New York lawyers to talk to our jury? Maybe some from Boston?'

'No, it's just that, well, they've never defended a tobacco case.'

'There's never been a tobacco case on the Coast before. Are you complaining?'

'They just worry me, that's all.'

'We've hired the best in this area,' Fitch said.

'Why do they work so cheap?'

'Cheap. Last week you were worried about defense costs. Now our lawyers are not charging enough. Make up your mind.'

'Last year we paid four hundred bucks an hour for Pittsburgh lawyers. These guys work for two hundred. That worries me.'

Fitch frowned at Luther Vandemeer, CEO of Trellco. 'Am I missing something here?' he asked. Is he serious? We're at five million bucks for this case, and he's afraid I'm pinching pennies.' Fitch waved in the direction of Jankle. Vandemeer smiled and took a drink.

'You spent six million in Oklahoma,' Jankle said.

'And we won. I don't recall any complaints after the verdict came in.'

'I'm not complaining now. I'm just voicing a concern.'

'Great! I'll go back to the office, gather all the lawyers together, and tell them my clients are upset about the bills. I'll say, "Look, fellas, I know you're getting rich off us, but that's not good enough. My clients want you to bill more, okay. Stick it to us. You guys are working too cheap." That sound like a good idea?'

'Relax, Martin,' Vandemeer said. 'The trial hasn't started yet. I'm confident we'll be sick of our own lawyers before we leave here.'

'Yeah, but this trial's different. We all know that.' Jankle's words trailed off as he lifted his glass. He had a drinking problem, the only one of the four. His company had quietly dried him out six months ago, but the pressure of the lawsuit was too much. Fitch, a former drunk himself, knew Jankle was in trouble. He would be forced to testify in a few weeks.

As if Fitch didn't have enough to worry about, he was now saddled with the burden of keeping D. Martin Jankle sober until then. Fitch hated him for his weakness.

'I assume the plaintiff's lawyers are ready,' asked another CEO.

'Safe assumption,' Fitch said with a shrug. 'There are enough of them.'

Eight, at last count. Eight of the largest tort firms in the country had allegedly put up a million bucks each to finance this showdown with the tobacco industry. They had picked the plaintiff, the widow of a man named Jacob L. Wood. They had picked the forum, the Gulf Coast of Mississippi, because the state had beautiful tort laws and because juries in Biloxi could at times be generous. They hadn't picked the judge, but they couldn't have been luckier. The Honorable Frederick Harkin had been a plaintiff's lawyer before a heart attack sent him to the bench.

It was no ordinary tobacco case, and everyone in the room knew it.

'How much have they spent?'

'I'm not privy to that information,' Fitch said. 'We've heard rumors that their war chest may not be as loaded as advertised, maybe a small problem collecting the upfront money from a few of the lawyers. But they've spent millions. And they have a dozen consumer groups hanging around ready to pitch in advice.'

Jankle rattled his ice, then drained the last drop of liquid from his glass. It was his fourth drink. The room was silent for a moment as Fitch stood and waited and the CEO's watched the carpet.

'How long will it last?' Jankle finally asked.

'Four to six weeks. Jury selection goes fast here. We'll probably seat a jury by Wednesday.'

'Allentown lasted three months,' Jankle said.

'This ain't Kansas, Toto. You want a three-month trial?'

'No, I was just, well . . .' Jankle's words trailed off sadly.

17

'How long should we stay in town?' Vandemeer said, instinctively glancing at his watch.

'I don't care. You can leave now, or you can wait until the jury is picked. You all have those big jets. If I need you, I can find you.' Fitch set his water on the mantel and looked around the room. He was suddenly ready to leave. 'Anything else?'

Not a word.

'Good.'

He said something to José as he opened the front door, then he was gone. They stared in silence at the posh carpet, worrying about Monday, worrying about lots of things.

Jankle, his hands quivering slightly, finally lit a cigarette.

Wendall Rohr made his first fortune in the suing game when two offshore oil workers were burned on a Shell rig in the Gulf. His cut was almost two million, and he quickly considered himself a trial lawyer to be reckoned with. He spread his money around, picked up more cases, and by the age of forty had an aggressive firm and a decent reputation as a courtroom brawler. Then drugs, a divorce, and some bad investments ruined his life for a while, and at the age of fifty he was checking titles and defending shoplifters like a million other lawyers. When a wave of asbestos litigation swept the Gulf Coast, Wendall was once again in the right place. He made his second fortune, and vowed never to lose it. He built a firm, refurbished a grand suite of offices, even found a young wife. Free of booze and pills, Rohr directed his considerable energies into suing corporate America on behalf of injured people. On his second trip, he rose even quicker in trial lawyer circles. He grew a beard, oiled his hair, became a radical, and was beloved on the lecture circuit.

Rohr met Celeste Wood, the widow of Jacob Wood,

18

through a young lawyer who had prepared Jacob's will in anticipation of death. Jacob Wood died at the age of fifty-one after smoking three packs a day for almost thirty years. At the time of his death, he was a production supervisor in a boat factory, earning forty thousand a year.

In the hands of a less ambitious lawyer, the case appeared to be nothing more than a dead smoker, one of countless others. Rohr, though, had networked his way into a circle of acquaintances who were dreaming the grandest dreams ever known to trial lawyers. All were specialists in product liability, all had made millions collecting on breast implants, Dalkon Shields, and asbestos. Now they met several times a year and plotted ways to mine the mother lode of American torts. No legally manufactured product in the history of the world had killed as many people as the cigarette. And their makers had pockets so deep the money had mildewed.

Rohr put up the first million, and was eventually joined by seven others. With no effort, the group quickly recruited help from the Tobacco Task Force, the Coalition for a Smoke Free World, and the Tobacco Liability Fund, plus a handful of other consumer groups and industry watchdogs. A plaintiff's trial council was organized, not surprisingly with Wendall Rohr as the chairman and designated point man in the courtroom. Amid as much fanfare as it could generate, Rohr's group had filed suit four years earlier in the Circuit Court of Harrison County, Mississippi.

According to Fitch's research, the Wood case against Pynex was the fifty-fifth of its kind. Thirty-six had been dismissed for a multitude of reasons. Sixteen had gone to trial and ended with verdicts in favor of the tobacco companies. Two had ended in mistrials. None had been settled. Not one penny had ever been paid to a plaintiff in a cigarette case.

19

According to Rohr's theory, none of the other fifty-four had been pushed by so formidable a plaintiff's group. Never had the plaintiff been represented by lawyers with enough money to level the playing field.

Fitch would admit this.

Rohr's long-term strategy was simple, and brilliant. There were a hundred million smokers out there, not all with lung cancer but certainly a sufficient number to keep him busy until retirement. Win the first one, then sit back and wait for the stampede. Every main street ham-and-egger with a grieving widow would be calling with lung cancer cases. Rohr and his group could pick and choose.

He operated from a suite of offices which took the top three floors of an old bank building not far from the courthouse. Late Friday night, he opened the door to a dark room and stood along the back wall as Jonathan Kotlack from San Diego operated the projector. Kotlack was in charge of jury research and selection, though Rohr would do most of the questioning. The long table in the center of the room was littered with coffee cups and wadded paper. The people around the table watched bleary-eyed as another face flashed against the wall.

Nelle Robert (pronounced Roh-bair), age forty-six, divorced, once raped, works as a bank teller, doesn't smoke, very over-weight and thus disqualified under Rohr's philosophy of jury selection. Never take fat women. He didn't care what the jury experts would tell him. He didn't care what Kotlack thought. Rohr never took fat women. Especially single ones. They tended to be tightfisted and unsympathetic.

He had the names and faces memorized, and he couldn't take any more. He had studied these people until he was sick of them. He eased from the room, rubbed his eyes in the hallway, and walked down the stairs of his opulent offices to the conference room, where the Documents Committee was busy organizing thousands of papers under the supervision of André Durond from New Orleans. At this moment, at almost ten o'clock on Friday night, more than forty people were hard at work in the law offices of Wendall H. Rohr.

He spoke to Durond as they watched the paralegals for a few minutes. He left the room and headed for the next with a quicker pace now. The adrenaline was pumping.

The tobacco lawyers were down the street working just as hard.

Nothing rivaled the thrill of big-time litigation.

21

THREE

The main courtroom of the Biloxi courthouse was on the second floor, up the tiled staircase to an atrium where sunlight flooded in. A fresh coat of white paint had just been applied to the walls, and the floors gleamed with new wax.

By eight Monday a crowd was already gathering in the atrium outside the large wooden doors leading to the courtroom. One small group was clustered in a corner, and was comprised of young men in dark suits, all of whom looked remarkably similar. They were well groomed, with oily short hair, and most either wore horn-rimmed glasses or had suspenders showing from under their tailored jackets. They were Wall Street financial analysts, specialists in tobacco stocks, sent South to follow the early developments of *Wood v. Pynex.*

Another group, larger and growing by the minute, hung loosely together in the center of the atrium. Each member awkwardly held a piece of paper, a jury summons. Few knew one another, but the papers labeled them and conversation came easy. A nervous chatter rose quietly outside the courtroom. The dark suits from the first group became still and watched the potential jurors.

The third group wore frowns and uniforms and guarded the doors. No fewer than seven deputies were

22

assigned to keep things secure on opening day. Two fiddled with the metal detector in front of the door. Two more busied themselves with paperwork behind a makeshift desk. They were expecting a full house. The other three sipped coffee from paper cups and watched the crowd grow.

The guards opened the courtroom doors at exactly eight-thirty, checked the summons of each juror, admitted them one by one through the metal detector, and told the rest of the spectators they would have to wait awhile. Same for the analysts and same for the reporters.

With a neat ring of folding chairs in the aisles around the padded benches, the courtroom could seat about three hundred people. Beyond the bar, another thirty or so would soon crowd around the counsel tables. The Circuit Clerk, popularly elected by the people, checked each summons, smiled, and even hugged a few of the jurors she knew, and in a much experienced way herded them into the pews. Her name was Gloria Lane, Circuit Clerk for Harrison County for the past eleven years. She wouldn't dare miss this opportunity to point and direct, to put faces with names, to shake hands, to politic, to enjoy a brief moment in the spotlight of her most notorious trial yet. She was assisted by three younger women from her office, and by nine the jurors were all properly seated by number and were busy filling out another round of questionnaires.

Only two were missing. Ernest Duly was rumored to have moved to Florida, where he supposedly died, and there was not a clue to the whereabouts of Mrs. Tella Gail Ridehouser, who registered to vote in 1959 but hadn't visited the polls since Carter beat Ford. Gloria Lane declared the two to be nonexistent. To her left, rows one through twelve held 144 prospective jurors, and to her right, rows thirteen through sixteen held the remaining 50. Gloria consulted with an armed deputy, and pursuant to Judge Harkin's written edict, forty spectators were admitted and seated in the rear of the courtroom.

The questionnaires were finished quickly, gathered by the assistant clerks, and by ten the first of many lawyers began easing into the courtroom. They came not through the front door, but from somewhere in the back, behind the bench, where two doors led to a maze of small rooms and offices. Without exception they wore dark suits and intelligent frowns, and they all attempted the impossible feat of gawking at the jurors while trying to appear uninterested. Each tried vainly to seem preoccupied with weightier matters as files were examined and whispered conferences took place. They trickled in and took their places around the tables. To the right was the plaintiff's table. The defense was next to it. Chairs were packed tightly into every possible inch between the tables and the wooden rail which separated them from the spectators.

Row number seventeen was empty, again Harkin's orders, and in eighteen the boys from Wall Street sat stiffly and studied the backs of the jurors. Behind them were some reporters, then a row of local lawyers and other curious types. Rankin Fitch pretended to read a newspaper in the back row.

More lawyers filed in. Then the jury consultants from both sides took their positions in the cramped seats between the railing and the counsel tables. They began the uncomfortable task of staring into the inquiring faces of 194 strangers. The consultants studied the jurors because, first, that was what they were being paid huge sums of money to do, and second, because they claimed to be able to thoroughly analyze a person through the telltale revelations of body language. They watched and waited anxiously for arms to fold across the chest, for fingers to pick nervously at teeth, for heads to cock suspiciously to one side, for a hundred other gestures that supposedly would lay a person bare and expose the most private of prejudices.

They scribbled notes and silently probed the faces. Juror number fifty-six, Nicholas Easter, received more than his share of concerned looks. He sat in the middle of the fifth row, dressed in starched khakis and a button-down, a nice-looking young man. He glanced around occasionally, but his attention was directed at a paperback he'd brought for the day. No one else had thought to bring a book.

More chairs were filled near the railing. The defense had no fewer than six jury experts examining facial twitches and hemorrhoidal clutches. The plaintiff was using only four.

For the most part, the prospective jurors didn't enjoy being appraised in such a manner, and for fifteen awkward minutes they returned the glaring with scowls of their own. A lawyer told a private joke near the bench, and the laughter eased the tension. The lawyers gossiped and whispered, but the jurors were afraid to say anything.

The last lawyer to enter the courtroom was, of course, Wendall Rohr, and as usual, he could be heard before he was seen. Since he didn't own a dark suit, he wore his favorite opening-day ensemble – a gray checkered sports coat, gray slacks that didn't match, a white vest, blue shirt with red-and-yellow paisley bow tie. He was barking at a paralegal as they strode in front of the defense lawyers, ignoring them as if they'd just finished a heated skirmish somewhere in the rear. He said something loudly to another plaintiff's lawyer, and once he had the attention of the courtroom, he gazed upon his potential jurors. These were his people. This was his case, one he'd filed in his hometown so he could one day stand in this, his courtroom, and seek justice from his people. He nodded at a couple, winked at another. He knew these folks. Together, they would find the truth.

25

His entrance rattled the jury experts on the defense side, none of whom had actually met Wendall Rohr, but all of whom had been briefed extensively on his reputation. They saw the smiles on the faces of some of the jurors, people who actually knew him. They read the body language as the entire panel seemed to relax and respond to a familiar face. Rohr was a local legend. Fitch cursed him from the back row.

Finally, at ten-thirty, a deputy burst from the door behind the bench and shouted, 'All rise for the court!' Three hundred people jumped to their feet as the Honorable Frederick Harkin stepped up to the bench and asked everyone to be seated.

For a judge he was quite young, fifty, a Democrat appointed by the governor to fill an unexpired term, then elected by the people. Because he'd once been a plaintiff's lawyer, he was now rumored to be a plaintiff's judge, though there was no truth to this. Just gossip deliciously spread by members of the defense bar. In reality, he'd been a decent general practitioner in a small firm not noted for its courtroom victories. He'd worked hard, but his passion had always been local politics, a game he'd played skillfully. His luck had paid off with an appointment to the bench, where he now earned eighty thousand dollars a year, more than he'd ever made as a lawyer.

The sight of a courtroom packed with so many qualified voters would warm the heart of any elected official, and His Honor couldn't conceal a broad grin as he welcomed the panel to his lair as if they were volunteers. The smile slowly vanished as he completed a short welcoming speech, impressing upon them the importance of their presence. Harkin was not known for either his warmth or his humor, and he quickly turned serious.

And with good reason. Seated before him were more lawyers than could actually fit around the tables. The court file listed eight as counsel of record for the plaintiff, and nine for the defense. Four days earlier, in a closed courtroom, Harkin had assigned seating for both sides. Once the jury was selected and the trial started, only six lawyers per side could sit with feet under the table. The others were assigned to a row of chairs where the jury consultants now huddled and watched. He also designated seats for the parties – Celeste Wood, the widow, and the Pynex representative. The seating arrangement had been reduced to writing and included in a small booklet of rules His Honor had written just for this occasion.

The lawsuit had been filed four years ago, and actively pursued and defended since its inception. It now filled eleven storage boxes. Each side had already spent millions to reach this point. The trial would last at least a month. Assembled at this moment in his courtroom were some of the brightest legal minds and largest egos in the country. Fred Harkin was determined to rule with a heavy hand.

Speaking into the microphone on the bench, he gave a quick synopsis of the trial, but only for informational purposes. Nice to let these folks know why they're here. He said the trial was scheduled to last for several weeks, and that the jurors would not be sequestered. There were some specific statutory excuses from jury duty, he explained, and asked if anyone over the age of sixty-five had slipped through the computer. Six hands shot upward. He seemed surprised and looked blankly at Gloria Lane, who shrugged as if this happened all the time. The six had the option of leaving immediately, and five chose to do so. Down to 189. The jury consultants scribbled and X'ed off names. The lawyers gravely made notes.

'Now, do we have any blind people here?' the Judge asked. 'I mean, legally blind?' It was a light question, and brought a few smiles. Why would a blind person show up for jury duty? It was unheard of.

Slowly, a hand was raised from the center of the pack, row seven, about halfway down. Juror number sixty-three, a Mr. Herman Grimes, age fifty-nine, computer programmer, white, married, no kids. What the hell was this? Did anybody know this man was blind? The jury experts huddled on both sides. The Herman Grimes photos had been of his house and a shot or two of him on the front porch. He'd lived in the area about three years. His questionnaires didn't indicate any handicap.

'Please stand, sir,' the Judge said.

Mr. Herman Grimes stood slowly, hands in pockets, casually dressed, normal-looking eyeglasses. He didn't appear to be blind.

'Your number please,' the Judge asked. He, unlike the lawyers and their consultants, had not been required to memorize every available tidbit about every juror.

'Uh, sixty-three.'

'And your name?' He was flipping the pages of his computer printout.

'Herman Grimes.'

Harkin found the name, then gazed into the sea of faces. 'And you're legally blind?'

'Yes sir.'

'Well, Mr. Grimes, under our law, you are excused from jury duty. You're free to go.'

Herman Grimes didn't move, didn't even flinch. He just looked at whatever he could see and said, 'Why?'

'I beg your pardon.'

'Why do I have to leave?'

'Because you're blind.'

'I know that.'

'And, well, blind people can't serve on juries,' Harkin said, glancing to his right and then to his left as his words trailed off. 'You're free to go, Mr. Grimes.'

Herman Grimes hesitated as he contemplated his

28

response. The courtroom was still. Finally, 'Who says blind people can't serve on juries?'

Harkin was already reaching for a lawbook. His Honor was meticulously prepared for this trial. He'd stopped hearing other matters a month ago, and had secluded himself in his chambers, where he pored over pleadings, discovery, the applicable law, and the latest in the rules of trial procedure. He'd picked dozens of juries during his tenure on the bench, all kinds of juries for all kinds of cases, and he thought he'd seen it all. So of course he'd get ambushed during the first ten minutes of jury selection. And of course the courtroom would be packed.

'You want to serve, Mr. Grimes?' he said, trying to force a lighthearted moment as he flipped pages and looked at the wealth of legal talent assembled nearby.

Mr. Grimes was growing hostile. 'You tell me why a blind person can't be on a jury. If it's written in the law, then the law is discriminatory, and I'll sue. If it ain't written in the law, and if it's just a matter of practice, then I'll sue even faster.'

There was little doubt that Mr. Grimes was no stranger to litigation.

On one side of the bar were two hundred little people, those dragged into court by the power of the law. On the other side was the law itself – the Judge sitting elevated above the rest, the packs of stuffy lawyers looking down their nasty noses, the clerks, the deputies, the bailiffs. On behalf of the draftees, Mr. Herman Grimes had struck a mighty blow at the establishment, and he was rewarded with chuckles and light laughter from his colleagues. He didn't care.

Across the railing, the lawyers smiled because the prospective jurors were smiling, and they shifted in their seats and scratched their heads because no one knew what to do. 'I've never seen this before,' they whispered.

29

The law said that a blind person *may* be excused from jury service, and when the Judge saw the word *may* he quickly decided to placate Mr. Grimes and deal with him later. No sense getting sued in your own courtroom. There were other ways to exclude him from jury duty. He'd discuss it with the attorneys. 'On second thought, Mr. Grimes, I think you'd make an excellent juror. Please be seated.'

Herman Grimes nodded and smiled and politely said, 'Thank you, sir.'

How do you factor in a blind juror? The experts mulled this question as they watched him slowly bend and sit. What are his prejudices? Which side will he favor? In a game with no rules, it was a widely held axiom that people with handicaps and disabilities made great plaintiff's jurors because they better understood the meaning of suffering. But there were countless exceptions.

From the back row, Rankin Fitch strained to his right in a vain effort to make eye contact with Carl Nussman, the man who'd already been paid $1,200,000 to select the perfect jury. Nussman sat in the midst of his jury consultants, holding a legal pad and studying the faces as if he'd known perfectly well that Herman Grimes was blind. He hadn't, and Fitch knew he hadn't. It was a minor fact that had slipped through their vast web of intelligence. What else had they missed? Fitch asked himself. He'd peel the hide off Nussman as soon as they broke for a recess.

'Now, ladies and gentlemen,' the Judge continued, his voice suddenly sharper and anxious to move on now that an on-the-spot discrimination suit had been averted. 'We enter into a phase of jury selection that will be somewhat time-consuming. It deals with physical infirmities which might prevent you from serving. We are not going to embarrass you, but if you have a

30

physical problem, we need to discuss it. We'll start with the first row.'

As Gloria Lane stood in the aisle by row one, a man of about sixty raised his hand, then got to his feet and walked through the small swinging gate of the bar. A bailiff led him to the witness chair and shoved the microphone away. The Judge moved to the end of the bench and leaned downward so that he could whisper to the man. Two lawyers, one from each side, took their places directly in front of the witness stand and blocked the view from the spectators. The court reporter completed the tight huddle, and when everyone was in place the Judge softly asked about the man's affliction.

It was a herniated disc, and he had a letter from his doctor. He was excused and left the courtroom in a hurry.

When Harkin broke for lunch at noon, he had dismissed thirteen people for medical reasons. The tedium had set in. They would resume at one-thirty, for much more of the same.

Nicholas Easter left the courthouse alone, and walked six blocks to a Burger King, where he ordered a Whopper and a Coke. He sat in a booth near the window, watching kids swing in the small playground, scanning a *USA Today*, eating slowly because he had an hour and a half.

The same blonde who first met him at the Computer Hut in tight jeans now wore baggy Umbros, a loose T-shirt, new Nikes, and carried a small gym bag over her shoulder. She met him for the second time as she walked by his booth carrying her tray and stopped when she seemed to recognize him.

'Nicholas,' she said, feigning uncertainty.

He looked at her, and for an awkward second knew they'd met somewhere before. The name escaped him.

'You don't remember me,' she said with a pleasant

31

smile. 'I was in your Computer Hut two weeks ago looking for –'

'Yeah, I remember,' he said with a quick glance at her nicely tanned legs. 'You bought a digital radio.'

'Right. The name is Amanda. If I remember correctly, I left you my phone number. I guess you lost it.'

'Would you like to sit down?'

'Thank you.' She sat quickly and took a french fry.

'I still have the number,' he said. 'In fact –'

'Don't bother. I'm sure you've called several times. My answering machine is broken.'

'No. I haven't called, yet. But I was thinking about it.'

'Sure,' she said, almost giggling. She had perfect teeth, which she delighted in showing him. Her hair was in a ponytail. She was too cute and too put together to be a jogger. And there was no evidence of sweat on her face.

'So what are you doing here?' he asked.

'On my way to aerobics.'

'You're eating french fries before you do aerobics?'

'Why not?'

'I don't know. It just doesn't seem right.'

'I need the carbohydrates.'

'I see. Do you smoke before aerobics?'

'Sometimes. Is that why you haven't called? Because I smoke?'

'Not really.'

'Come on, Nicholas. I can take it.' She was still smiling and trying to be coy.

'Okay, it crossed my mind.'

'Figures. Have you ever dated a smoker?'

'Not that I recall.'

'Why not?'

'Maybe I don't want to breathe it secondhand. I don't know. It's not something I spend time worrying about.'

32

'Have you ever smoked?' She nibbled on another fry and watched him intently.

'Sure. Every kid tries it. When I was ten, I stole a pack of Camels from a plumber working around our house. Smoked them all in two days, got sick, and thought I was dying of cancer.' He took a bite of his burger.

'And that was it?'

He chewed and thought it over before saying, 'I think so. I can't remember another cigarette. Why did you start?'

'Stupid. I'm trying to quit.'

'Good. You're too young.'

'Thanks. And let me guess. When I quit, you'll give me a call, right?'

'I may call you anyway.'

'I've heard this before,' she said, all toothy and teasing. She took a long drink from her straw, then said, 'Can I ask what you're doing here?'

'Eating a Whopper. And you?'

'I've told you. I'm headed to the gym.'

'Right. I was just passing through, had some business down-town, got hungry.'

'Why do you work in a Computer Hut?'

'You mean, like, why am I wasting my life working for minimum wage in a mall?'

'No, but close.'

'I'm a student.'

'Where?'

'Nowhere. I'm between schools.'

'Where was the last school?'

'North Texas State.'

'Where's the next one?'

'Probably Southern Mississippi.'

'What are you studying?'

'Computers. You ask a lot of questions.'

'But they're easy ones, aren't they?'

33

'I suppose. Where do you work?'

'I don't. I just divorced a rich man. No kids. I'm twenty-eight, single, and would like to stay that way, but a date every now and then would be nice. Why don't you give me a call?'

'How rich?'

She laughed at this, then checked her watch. 'I need to go. My class starts in ten minutes.' She was on her feet, getting her bag but leaving her tray. 'I'll see you around.'

She drove off in a small BMW.

The rest of the sick folks were hastily cleared from the panel, and by 3 P.M. the number was down to 159. Judge Harkin ordered a fifteen-minute recess, and when he returned to the bench he announced they were entering into a different phase of jury selection. He delivered a strong lecture on civic responsibility, and practically dared anyone to claim a nonmedical hardship. The first attempt was by a harried corporate executive who sat in the witness chair and softly explained to the Judge, the two lawyers, and the court reporter that he worked eighty hours a week for a large company that was losing lots of money, and any time away from the office would be disastrous. The Judge instructed him to return to his seat and await further directions.

The second attempt was by a middle-aged woman who operated an unlicensed day care center in her home. 'I keep kids, Your Honor,' she whispered, fighting back tears. 'It's all I can do. I collect two hundred dollars a week, and I barely get by. If I have to serve on this jury, then I'll have to hire a stranger to keep the kids. Their parents won't like this, plus I can't afford to hire anyone. I'll go busted.'

The prospective jurors watched with great interest as she walked down the aisle, past her row, and out of the courtroom. Her story must've been a good one. The harried corporate executive fumed.

By five-thirty, eleven people had been excused, and sixteen others had been sent back to their seats after failing to sound sufficiently pitiful. The Judge instructed Gloria Lane to pass out another, lengthier questionnaire, and told the remaining jurors to have it answered by nine in the morning. He dismissed them, with firm warnings against discussing the case with strangers.

Rankin Fitch was not in the courtroom when it adjourned Monday afternoon. He was in his office down the street. There was no record of any Nicholas Easter at North Texas State. The blonde had recorded their little chat at Burger King, and Fitch had listened to it twice. It had been his decision to send her in for a chance meeting. The meeting was risky, but it worked. She was now on a plane back to Washington. Her answering machine in Biloxi was on and would remain so until after the jury was selected. If Easter decided to call, something Fitch doubted, he wouldn't be able to reach her.

FOUR

It asked questions like, Do you now smoke cigarettes? And if so, how many packs a day? And if so, how long have you smoked? And if so, do you want to stop? Have you ever smoked cigarettes as a habit? Has any member of your family, or someone you know well, suffered any disease or illness directly associated with smoking cigarettes? If so, who? (Space provided below. Please give person's name, nature of disease or illness, and state whether or not the person was successfully treated.) Do you believe smoking causes (a) lung cancer; (b) heart disease; (c) high blood pressure; (d) none of the above; (e) all of the above?

Page three held the weightier matters: State your opinion on the issue of tax dollars being used to fund medical care for smoking-related health problems. State your opinion on the issue of tax dollars being used to subsidize tobacco farmers. State your opinion on the issue of banning smoking in all public buildings. What rights do you think smokers should have? Large empty spaces were available for these answers.

Page four listed the names of the seventeen lawyers who were officially attorneys of record, then it listed the names of eighty more who happened to be in some related practice with the first seventeen. Do you personally know any of these lawyers? Have you ever been represented by any of these lawyers? Have you ever been involved in any legal matter with any of these lawyers?

No. No. No. Nicholas made quick check marks.

Page five listed the names of potential witnesses, sixty-two people including Celeste Wood, the widow and plaintiff. Do you know any of these people? No.

He mixed another cup of instant coffee and added two packs of sugar. He'd spent an hour with these questions last night, and another hour had already passed this morning. The sun was barely up. Breakfast had been a banana and a stale bagel. He ate a small bite of the bagel, thought about the last question, then answered it with a pencil in a neat, almost tedious hand – all caps printed, because his cursive was ragged and barely legible. And he knew that before dark today an entire committee of handwriting experts on both sides would be poring over his words, not caring so much about what he said but more about how he formed his letters. He wanted to appear neat and thoughtful, intelligent and open-minded, capable of hearing with both ears and deciding matters fairly, an arbitrator they would clamor for.

He'd read three books on the ins and outs of handwriting analysis.

He flipped back to the tobacco subsidy question because it was a tough one. He had an answer ready because he'd given much thought to the issue, and he wanted to write it clearly. Or maybe vaguely. Maybe in such a way that he wouldn't betray his feelings, yet wouldn't scare either side.

Many of these same questions had been used in the Cimmino case last year in Allentown, Pennsylvania. Nicholas had been David then, David Lancaster, a part-time film student with a genuine dark beard and fake horn-rimmed glasses who worked in a video store. He'd copied the questionnaire before turning it in on the second day of jury selection. It was a similar case, but with a different widow and a different tobacco company, and though there'd been a hundred lawyers involved, they were all different from this bunch. Only Fitch remained the same.

Nicholas/David had made the first two cuts then, but was four rows away when the panel was seated. He shaved his beard, ditched the pharmacy eyeglasses, and left town a month later.

The folding card table vibrated slightly as he wrote. This was his dinette – the table and three mismatched chairs. The tiny den to his right was furnished with a flimsy rocker, a TV mounted on a wooden crate, and a dusty sofa he'd purchased at a flea market for fifteen dollars. He probably could have afforded to rent some nicer pieces, but renting required forms and left a trail. There were people out there practically digging through his garbage to find out who he was.

He thought of the blonde and wondered where she might turn up today, no doubt with a cigarette close at hand and an eagerness to draw him into another banal chat about smoking. The idea of calling her hadn't crossed his mind, but the question of which side she worked for was quite intriguing. Probably the tobacco companies, because she was exactly the type of agent Fitch liked to use.

Nicholas knew from his studies of the law that it was highly unethical for the blonde, or any other hireling for that matter, to directly approach a potential juror. He also knew that Fitch had enough money to make the blonde disappear from here, without a trace, only to surface at the next trial as a redhead with a different brand and an interest in horticulture. Some things were impossible to uncover.

The one bedroom was consumed almost entirely with a king-size mattress, lying directly on the floor with nothing under it, another purchase from the flea market. A series of cardboard boxes served as the chest of drawers. Clothing littered the floor.

It was a temporary home, with the look of a place one might use for a month or two before leaving town in the middle of the night; which was exactly what he had in mind. He'd lived there for six months already, and the apartment number was his official address, at least the one used when he registered to vote and obtained his Mississippi driver's license. He had nicer quarters four miles away, but couldn't run the risk of being seen there.

So he lived happily in poverty, just another broke student with no assets and few responsibilities. He was almost certain Fitch's snoops had not entered his apartment, but he took no chances. The place was cheap, but carefully arranged. Nothing revealing could be found.

At eight, he finished the questionnaire and proofed it one last time. The one in the Cimmino case had been written in longhand, in a different style altogether. After months of practicing his printing he was certain he would not be detected. There had been three hundred potential jurors then, and almost two hundred now, and why would anyone suspect that he would be in both pools?

From behind a pillowcase stretched over the kitchen window, he quickly checked the parking lot below for photographers or other intruders. He'd seen one three weeks ago sitting low behind the wheel of a pickup.

No snoops today. He locked his apartment door and left on foot.

Gloria Lane was much more efficient with her herding on the second day. The remaining 148 prospective jurors were seated on the right side, packed tightly twelve to a row, twelve deep with four in the aisle. They were easier to handle when seated on one side of the courtroom. The questionnaires were gathered as they entered, then quickly copied and given to each side. By ten, the answers were being analyzed by jury consultants locked away in windowless rooms.

Across the aisle, a well-mannered throng of financial boys, reporters, the curious, and other miscellaneous spectators sat and stared at the crowds of lawyers, who sat and studied the faces of the jurors. Fitch had quietly moved to the front row, nearer to his defense team, with a nicely dressed flunkie on each side just waiting for his latest command.

Judge Harkin was a man on a mission on Tuesday, and took less than an hour to complete the nonmedical hardships. Six more were excused, leaving 142 on the panel.

Finally, it was showtime. Wendall Rohr, wearing apparently the same gray checkered sports coat, white vest, and red-and-yellow bow tie, stood and walked to the railing to address his audience. He cracked his knuckles loudly, opened his hands, and displayed a dark, broad grin. 'Welcome,' he said dramatically, as if what was about to follow was an event the memory of which they would cherish forever. He introduced himself, the members of his team who would be participating in the trial, and then he asked the plaintiff, Celeste Wood, to stand. He managed to use the word 'widow' twice as he displayed her to the prospects. A petite woman of fifty-five, she wore a plain black dress, dark hose, dark shoes that could not be seen below the railing, and she offered a painfully proper little smile as if she had yet to exit the mourning stage, though her husband had been dead for four years. In fact, she'd almost remarried, an event Wendall got canceled at the last moment, as soon as he learned of it. It's okay to love the guy, he had explained to her, but do so quietly and you can't marry him until after the trial. The sympathy factor. You're supposed to be suffering, he had explained.

40

Fitch knew about the aborted nuptials, and he also knew there was little chance of getting the matter before the jury.

With everyone on his side of the courtroom officially introduced, Rohr gave his brief summary of the case, a recitation that attracted immense interest from the defense lawyers and the Judge. They seemed ready to pounce if Rohr stepped over the invisible barrier between fact and argument. He didn't, but he enjoyed tormenting them.

Then a lengthy plea for the potential jurors to be honest, and open, and unafraid to raise their timid little hands if something bothered them in the least. How else can they, the lawyers, explore thoughts and feelings unless they, the would-be jurors, speak up? 'We certainly can't do it simply by looking at you,' he said with another flash of teeth. At the moment, there were no less than eight people in the courtroom trying desperately to read every lifted eyebrow and curled lip.

To get things rolling, Rohr picked up a legal pad, glanced at it, then said, 'Now, we have a number of people who've served on civil juries before. Please raise your hands.' A dozen hands rose obediently. Rohr scanned his audience and settled on the nearest one, a lady on the front row. 'Mrs. Millwood, is it?' Her cheeks reddened as she nodded. Every person in the courtroom was either staring at or straining to see Mrs. Millwood.

'You were on a civil jury a few years back, I believe,' Rohr said warmly.

'Yes,' she said, clearing her throat and trying to be loud.

'What kind of case was it?' he asked, though he knew virtually every detail – seven years ago, this very court-room, different judge, zero for the plaintiff. The file had been copied weeks ago. Rohr had even talked to the plaintiff's lawyer, a friend of his. He started with this

41

question and this juror because it was an easy warm-up, a soft pitch to show the others how painless it was to raise one's hand and discuss matters.

'A car wreck case,' she said.

'Where was the trial?' he asked sincerely.

'Right here.'

'Oh, in this courtroom.' He sounded quite surprised, but the defense lawyers knew he was faking.

'Did the jury reach a verdict in that case?'

'Yes.'

'And what was that verdict?'

'We didn't give him anything.'

'Him being the plaintiff?'

'Yes. We didn't think he was really hurt.'

'I see. Was this jury service a pleasant experience for you?'

She thought a moment, then, 'It was okay. Lot of wasted time, though, you know, when the lawyers were wrangling about this or that.'

A big smile. 'Yes, we tend to do that. Nothing about that case would influence your ability to hear this one?'

'No, don't think so.'

'Thank you, Mrs. Millwood.' Her husband was once an accountant for a small county hospital that was forced to close after being nailed in a medical malpractice case. Large verdicts were something she secretly loathed, and for good reason. Jonathan Kotlack, the plaintiff's lawyer in charge of final jury selection, had long since removed her name from consideration.

However, around the table not ten feet from Kotlack, the defense lawyers regarded her highly. JoAnn Millwood would be a prize catch.

Rohr asked the same questions of the other veterans of jury service, and things quickly became monotonous. He then tackled the thorny issue of tort reform, and asked a string of rambling questions about the rights of

42

victims, and frivolous lawsuits, and the price of insurance. A few of his questions were wrapped around mini-arguments, but he stayed out of trouble. It was almost lunchtime, and the panel had lost interest for a while. Judge Harkin recessed for an hour, and the deputies cleared the courtroom.

The lawyers remained though. Box lunches containing soggy little sandwiches and red apples were passed out by Gloria Lane and her staff. This was to be a working lunch. Pending motions of a dozen varieties needed resolution, and His Honor was ready for argument. Coffee and iced tea were poured.

The use of questionnaires greatly facilitated the selection of the jury. While Rohr asked questions inside the courtroom, dozens of people elsewhere examined the written answers and marked names off their lists. One man's sister had died of lung cancer. Seven others had close friends or family members with serious health problems, all of which they attributed to smoking. At least half the panel either smoked now or had been regular smokers in the past. Most of those smoking admitted their desire to quit.

The data were analyzed, then put in computers, and by mid-afternoon of the second day the printouts were being passed around and edited. After Judge Harkin recessed at four-thirty on Tuesday, he again cleared the courtroom and conducted proceedings on the record. For almost three hours, the written answers were discussed and debated, and in the end thirty-one additional names were removed from consideration. Gloria Lane was instructed to immediately phone these newest deletions and tell them the good news.

Harkin was determined to complete jury selection on Wednesday. Opening statements were scheduled for Thursday morning. He had even hinted at some Saturday work.

43

At eight o'clock Tuesday night he heard one last motion, a quickie, and sent the lawyers home. The lawyers for Pynex met Fitch at the offices of Whitney & Cable & White, where another delicious feast of cold sandwiches and greasy chips awaited them. Fitch wanted to work, and while the weary lawyers slowly filled their paper plates, two paralegals distributed copies of the latest handwriting analyses. Eat quickly, Fitch demanded, as if the food could be savored. The panel was down to 111, and the picking would start tomorrow.

The morning belonged to Durwood Cable, or Durr as he was known up and down the Coast, a place he'd never really left in his sixty-one years. As the senior partner for Whitney & Cable & White, Sir Durr had been carefully selected by Fitch to handle the bulk of the courtroom work for Pynex. As a lawyer, then a judge, and now a lawyer again, Durr had spent most of the past thirty years looking at and speaking to juries. He found courtrooms to be relaxing places because they were stages – no phones, no foot traffic, no secretaries scurrying about – everyone with a role, everyone following a script with the lawyers as the stars. He moved and talked with great deliberation, but between steps and sentences his gray eyes missed nothing. Where his adversary, Wendall Rohr, was loud and gregarious and gaudy, Durr was buttoned up and quite starched. The obligatory dark suit, a rather bold gold tie, the standard issue white shirt, which contrasted nicely with his deeply tanned face. Durr had a passion for saltwater fishing, and spent many hours on his boat, in the sun. The top of his head was bald, and very bronzed.

He once went six years without losing a case, then Rohr, his foe and sometime friend, popped him for two million in a three-wheeler case.

He stepped to the railing and looked seriously into the faces of 111 people. He knew where each lived and the number of children and grandchildren, if any. He crossed his arms, pinched his chin like a pensive professor, and said in a pleasantly rich voice, 'My name is Durwood Cable, and I represent Pynex, an old company that's been making cigarettes for ninety years.' There, he was not ashamed of it! He talked about Pynex for ten minutes, and did a masterful job of softening up the company, of making his client warm and fuzzy, almost likable.

Finished with that, he plunged fearlessly into the issue of choice. Whereas Rohr had dwelt on addiction, Cable spent his time on the freedom to choose. 'Can we all agree that cigarettes are potentially dangerous if abused?' he asked, then watched most of the heads shake in agreement. Who could argue with this? 'There, fine. Now since this is common knowledge, can we all agree that a person who smokes should know the dangers?' More nodding, no hands, yet. He studied the faces, especially the blank one belonging to Nicholas Easter, now seated on row three, eighth from the aisle. Because of the dismissals, Easter was no longer juror number fifty-six. He was now number thirty-two, and advancing with each session. His face revealed nothing but rapt attention.

'This is a very important question,' Cable said slowly, his words echoing in the stillness. With a pointed finger, he delicately jabbed at them and said, 'Is there a single person on this panel who doesn't believe that a person who chooses to smoke should know the dangers?'

He waited, watching and tugging at the line a bit, and finally caught one. A hand was slowly raised from the fourth row. Cable smiled, took a step closer, said, 'Yes, I believe you're Mrs. Tutwiler. Please stand.' If he was truly eager to have a volunteer, his joy was short-lived. Mrs. Tutwiler was a fragile little lady of sixty, with an angry face. She stood straight, lifted her chin, and said, 'I got a question for you, Mr. Cable.'

'Certainly.'

'If everybody knows cigarettes are dangerous, then why does your client keep making them?'

There were a few grins from her colleagues in the pool. All eyes were on Durwood Cable as he kept smiling, never flinching in the least. 'Excellent question,' he said loudly. He was not about to answer it. 'Do you think the making of all cigarettes should be banned, Mrs. Tutwiler?'

'I do.'

'Even if people want to exercise their right to choose to smoke?'

'Cigarettes are addictive, Mr. Cable, you know that.'

'Thank you, Mrs. Tutwiler.'

'The manufacturers load up the nicotine, get folks hooked, then advertise like crazy to keep selling.'

'Thank you, Mrs. Tutwiler.'

'I'm not finished,' she said loudly, clutching the pew in front of her and standing ever taller. 'The manufacturers have always denied that smoking is addictive. That's a lie, and you know it. Why don't they say so on their labels?'

Durr's face never changed expression. He waited patiently, then asked quite warmly, 'Are you finished, Mrs. Tutwiler?' There were other things she wanted to say, but it dawned on her that perhaps this was not the place. 'Yes,' she said, almost in a whisper.

'Thank you. Responses such as yours are vital to the jury selection process. Thank you very much. You may now sit down.'

She glanced around as if some of the others should stand and fight with her, but left alone, she dropped to her seat. She might as well have left the courtroom.

Cable quickly pursued less sensitive matters. He

asked a lot of questions, provoked a few responses, and gave his body language experts much to chew on. He finished at noon, just in time for a quick lunch. Harkin asked the panel to return at three, but told the lawyers to eat fast and return in forty-five minutes.

At one o'clock, with the courtroom empty and locked and the lawyers crowded tightly in bunches around their tables, Jonathan Kotlack stood and informed the court that 'The plaintiff will accept juror number one.' No one seemed surprised. Everyone wrote something on a printout, including His Honor, who, after a slight pause, asked, 'The defense?'

'The defense will accept number one.' Not much of a surprise. Number one was Rikki Coleman, a young wife and mother of two who'd never smoked and worked as a records administrator in a hospital. Kotlack and crew rated her as a 7 out of 10 based on her written answers, her background in health care, her college degree, and her keen interest in everything that had been said so far. The defense rated her as a 6, and would've passed on her but for a string of serious undesirables forthcoming further down row one.

'That was easy,' Harkin mumbled under his breath. 'Moving right along. Juror number two, Raymond C. LaMonette.' Mr. LaMonette was the first strategical skirmish of jury selection. Neither side wanted him – both rated him 4.5. He smoked heavily but was desperate to quit. His written answers were thoroughly indecipherable and utterly useless. The body linguists on both sides reported that Mr. LaMonette hated all lawyers and all things related to them. He'd nearly been killed years earlier by a drunk driver. His lawsuit netted him nothing.

Under the rules of jury selection, each side was granted a number of peremptory challenges, or strikes as they were called, which could be used to ax potential jurors for no reason whatsoever. Because of the importance of this case, Judge Harkin had granted each side ten strikes, up from the customary four. Both wanted to cut LaMonette, but both needed to save their strikes for more objectionable faces.

The plaintiff was required to go first, and after a brief delay, Kotlack said, 'The plaintiff will strike number two.'

'That's peremptory challenge number one for the plaintiff,' Harkin said, making a note. A small victory for the defense. Based on a last-second decision, Durr Cable had been prepared to strike him as well.

The plaintiff used a strike on number three, the wife of a corporate executive, and also on number four. The strategic strikes continued, and practically decimated row one. Only two jurors survived. The carnage lessened with row two, with five of the twelve surviving various challenges, two by the court itself. Seven jurors had been chosen when the selection moved to row three. Eight spots down sat the great unknown, Nicholas Easter, juror number thirty-two, who'd so far paid good attention and seemed to be somewhat palatable, though he gave both sides the jitters.

Wendall Rohr, now speaking for the plaintiff because Kotlack was deep in a hushed conference with an expert about two of the faces on row four, used a peremptory strike on number twenty-five. It was the plaintiff's ninth strike. The last one was reserved for a much-feared and notorious Republican on the fourth row, if they got that far. The defense struck number twenty-six, burning its eighth peremptory. Jurors number twenty-seven, twenty-eight, and twenty-nine were accepted. Juror number thirty was challenged by the defense for cause, a plea for the court to excuse the juror for mutual reasons without requiring either side to exhaust a strike. Durr Cable asked the court to go off the record because he had something he wished to discuss in private. Rohr was a bit perplexed, but did not object. The court reporter stopped recording. Cable handed a thin brief to Rohr and the same to His Honor. He lowered his voice, and said, 'Your Honor, we have learned, through certain sources, that juror number thirty, Bonnie Tyus, is addicted to the prescription drug Ativan. She has never been treated, never been arrested, never admitted her problem. She certainly didn't disclose it on the questionnaires or during our little Q and A. She manages to live quietly, keep a job and a husband, though he's her third.'

'How'd you learn this?' Harkin asked.

'Through our rather extensive investigation of all potential jurors. I assure you, Your Honor, that there has been no unauthorized contact with Mrs. Tyus.'

Fitch had found it. Her second husband had been located in Nashville, where he washed tractor-trailer rigs at an all-night truck stop. For one hundred dollars cash, he'd happily told all he could remember about his ex.

'What about it, Mr. Rohr?' asked His Honor.

Without a second's hesitation, Rohr said, lying, 'We have the same information, Your Honor.' He cast a pleasant glance at Jonathan Kotlack, who in turn glared at another lawyer who'd been in charge of the group which included Bonnie Tyus. They'd spent over a million bucks so far on jury selection, and they'd missed this crucial fact!

'Fine. Juror number thirty is excused for cause. Back on the record. Juror number thirty-one?'

'Could we have a few minutes, Your Honor?' Rohr asked.

'Yes. But be brief.'

After thirty names, ten had been selected; nine had been struck by the plaintiff, eight by the defense, and three had been excused by the court. It was unlikely the selection would reach the fourth row, so Rohr, with one strike remaining, looked at jurors thirty-one through thirty-six, and whispered to his huddled group, 'Which one stinks the most?' The fingers pointed unanimously to number thirty-four, a large, mean white woman who had scared them from day one. Wilda Haney was her name, and for a month now they had all vowed to avoid Wide Wilda. They studied their master sheet a few minutes longer, and agreed to take numbers thirty-one, thirty-two, thirty-three, and thirty-five, not all of whom were terribly attractive, but far more so than Wide Wilda.

In a denser huddle just a few feet away, Cable and his troops agreed to strike thirty-one, take thirty-two, challenge thirty-three because thirty-three was Mr. Herman Grimes, the blind man, then take thirty-four, Wilda Haney, and strike, if necessary, number thirty-five.

Nicholas Easter thus became the eleventh juror selected to hear *Wood v. Pynex*. When the courtroom was opened at three and the panel was seated, Judge Harkin began calling out the names of the chosen twelve. They walked through the gate in the railing and took their assigned seats in the jury box. Nicholas had chair number two on the front row. At twenty-seven, he was the second youngest juror. There were nine whites, three blacks, seven women, five men, one blind. Three alternates were seated in padded folding chairs wedged tightly together in one corner of the jury box. At four-thirty, the fifteen stood and repeated their oaths as jurors. They then listened for half an hour as Judge Harkin issued a series of stern warnings to them, and to the lawyers and parties involved. Contact with the jurors of any type or manner would result in stiff sanctions, monetary penalties, maybe a mistrial, perhaps disbarment and death.

He forbade the jurors from discussing the case with anyone, even their spouses and mates, and with a cheery smile bid them farewell, a pleasant night, see you at nine sharp tomorrow morning.

The lawyers watched and wished they could leave too. But there was work to do. When the courtroom was cleared of everyone but lawyers and clerks, His Honor said, 'Gentlemen, you filed these motions. Now we must argue them.'

FIVE

Partially out of a mixture of eagerness and boredom, and partially on a hunch that someone would be waiting, Nicholas Easter slipped through the unlocked rear door of the courthouse at eight-thirty, up the seldom-used back stairs, and into the narrow hallway behind the courtroom. Most of the county offices opened at eight, so there was movement and noise to be heard on the first floor. But little on the second. He peeked into the courtroom, and found it empty of people. The briefcases had arrived and been parked haphazardly on the tables. The lawyers were probably in the back, near the coffee machine, telling jokes and preparing for battle.

He knew the turf well. Three weeks earlier, the day after he'd received his precious summons for jury duty, he had come poking around the courtroom. Finding it unused and vacant for the moment, he had explored the alleys and spaces around it; the Judge's cramped chambers; the coffee room where the lawyers gossiped while sitting on ancient tables strewn with old magazines and current newspapers; the makeshift witness rooms with folding chairs and no windows; the holding room where the handcuffed and dangerous waited for their punishment; and, of course, the jury room.

This morning, his hunch was correct. Her name was Lou Dell, a squatty woman of sixty in polyester pants and old sneakers and gray bangs in her eyes. She was sitting in the hallway by the door to the jury room, reading a battered romance and waiting for someone to enter her domain. She jumped to her feet, whipped out a sheet of paper from under her, and said, 'Good morning. Can I help you?' Her entire face was one massive smile. Her eyes glowed with mischief.

'Nicholas Easter,' he said, as he reached for her outstretched hand. She squeezed tightly, shook with a vengeance, and found his name on her paperwork. Another, larger smile, then, 'Welcome to the jury room. This your first trial?'

'Yes.'

'Come on,' she said, virtually shoving him through the door and into the room. 'Coffee and doughnuts are over here,' she said, tugging at his arm, pointing to a corner. 'I made these myself,' she said proudly, lifting a basket of oily black muffins. 'Sort of a tradition. I always bring these on the first day, call 'em my jury muffins. Take one.'

The table was covered with several varieties of doughnuts arranged neatly on trays. Two coffeepots were filled and steaming. Plates and cups, spoons and forks, sugar, cream, sweeteners of several varieties. And in the center of the table were the jury muffins. Nicholas took one because he had no choice.

'Been making them for eighteen years,' she said. 'Used to put raisins in them, but had to quit.' She rolled her eyes up at him as if the rest of the story was just too scandalous.

'Why?' he asked, because he felt compelled.

'Gave 'em gas. Sometimes every sound can be heard in the courtroom. Know what I mean?'

'I guess.'

'Coffee?'

'I can get my own.'

'Fine then.' She whirled around and pointed to a

stack of papers in the center of the long table. 'There's a list of instructions from Judge Harkin. He wants every juror to take one, read it carefully, and sign at the bottom. I'll collect them later.'

'Thanks.'

'I'll be in the hall by the door if you need me. That's where I stay. They're gonna put a damned deputy with me for this one, can you believe it? Just makes me sick. Probably some clod who can't hit a barn with a shotgun. But anyway, I guess this is about the biggest one we've ever had. Civil, that is. You wouldn't believe some of the criminal ones we've had.' She took the doorknob and yanked it toward her. 'I'm out here, dear, if you need me.'

The door closed, and Nicholas gazed at the muffin. Slowly, he took a small bite. It was mostly bran and sugar, and he thought for a second about the sounds in the courtroom. He tossed it in the wastebasket and poured black coffee into a plastic cup. The plastic cups would have to go. If they planned for him to camp here for four to six weeks, then they'd have to provide real cups. And if the county could afford pretty doughnuts, then it could certainly afford bagels and croissants.

There was no decaf coffee. He made a note of this. And no hot water for tea, just in case some of his new friends weren't coffee drinkers. Lunch had better be good. He would not eat tuna salad for the next six weeks.

Twelve chairs were arranged neatly around the table, which was in the center of the room. The thick layer of dust he had noticed three weeks ago had been removed; the place was much tidier, and ready for use. On one wall was a large blackboard, with erasers and fresh chalk. Across the table, on the opposite wall, three large windows, from floor to ceiling, looked upon the courthouse lawn, still green and fresh though summer had ended over a month ago. Nicholas looked through a window and watched the foot traffic on the sidewalks.

The latest from Judge Harkin was a list of a few things to do, and many to avoid: Get organized. Elect a foreman, and if you are unable to do so, notify His Honor and he will be happy to select one. Wear the red-and-white Juror buttons at all times. Lou Dell would dispense these. Bring something to read during downtimes. Do not hesitate to ask for anything. Do not discuss the case among yourselves until you are instructed to do so by His Honor. Do not discuss the case with anyone, period. Do not leave the courthouse without permission. Do not use the telephones without permission. Lunch will be catered and eaten in the jury room. A daily menu will be provided each day before the trial resumes at nine. Notify the court immediately if you or anyone you know is in any way contacted with regard to your involvement in this trial. Notify the court immediately if you see or hear or notice anything suspicious which may or may not be related to your service as a juror in this case.

Odd directions, these last two. But Nicholas knew the details of a tobacco trial in east Texas, a trial which blew up after only one week when it was discovered that mysterious agents were slinking through the small town and offering huge sums of money to relatives of jurors. The agents disappeared before they were caught, and it was never learned which side they worked for, though both made heated accusations. Cooler heads laid heavy odds that it was the work of the tobacco boys. The jury appeared to have a strong sympathy bent to it, and the defense was delighted when the mistrial was declared.

Though there was no way to prove it, Nicholas was certain Rankin Fitch was the phantom behind the payoffs. And he knew Fitch would quickly go to work on his new set of friends.

He signed the bottom of the sheet and left it on the table. There were voices in the hallway, and Lou Dell was meeting another juror. The door opened with a kick and a thud, and Mr. Herman Grimes entered first with his walking stick tapping along in front of him. His wife was close behind, not touching him but instantly inspecting the room and describing it under her breath. 'Long room, twenty-five by fifteen, length in front of you, width from left to right, long table running lengthwise in center with chairs around it, nearest chair to you is eight feet.' He froze as he gathered this in, his head moving in whatever direction she was describing. Behind her, Lou Dell stood in the doorway with hands on hips and just dying to feed the blind man a muffin.

Nicholas took a few steps and introduced himself. He grabbed Herman's outstretched hand and they exchanged pleasantries. He said hello to Mrs. Grimes, then led Herman to the food and coffee where he poured him a cup and stirred in sugar and cream. He described the doughnuts and the muffins, a preemptive strike against Lou Dell, who lingered near the door. Herman was not hungry.

'My favorite uncle is blind,' Nicholas said for the benefit of all three. 'I'd consider it an honor if you'd allow me to assist you during the trial.'

'I'm perfectly capable of handling myself,' Herman said with a trace of indignation, but his wife couldn't conceal a warm smile. Then she winked and nodded.

'I'm sure you are,' Nicholas said. 'But I know there are lots of little things. I just want to help.'

'Thank you,' he said after a brief pause.

'Thank you, sir,' his wife said.

'I'll be outside in the hallway if you need anything,' Lou Dell said.

'What time should I come get him?' Mrs. Grimes asked.

'Five. If sooner, I'll call.' Lou Dell was closing the door as she rattled off instructions.

Herman's eyes were covered with dark glasses. His

hair was brown, thick, well greased, and barely yielding to gray.

'There's a bit of paperwork,' Nicholas said when they were alone. 'Take a seat there in front of you and I'll go over it.' Herman felt the table, set down his coffee, then groped for a chair. He outlined it with his fingertips, got his bearings, and sat down. Nicholas took an instruction sheet and began reading.

After spending fortunes on the selection, the opinions came cheap. Everybody had one. The experts for the defense congratulated themselves on picking such a fine jury, though most of the puffing and posturing was done for the benefit of the legion of lawyers working round the clock. Durr Cable had seen worse juries, but he'd seen much friendlier ones too. He'd also learned many years ago that it was virtually impossible to predict what any jury would do. Fitch was happy, or as happy as he could allow himself, though that didn't stop his bitching and snarling about everything. Four smokers were on the jury. Fitch clung to the unspoken belief that the Gulf Coast, with its topless joints and casinos and proximity to New Orleans, was not a bad place to be right now because of its tolerance for vice.

On the other side of the street, Wendall Rohr and his trial counsel declared themselves satisfied with the composition of the jury. They were especially delighted with the unexpected addition of Mr. Herman Grimes, the first blind juror in the history of anyone's memory. Mr. Grimes had insisted on being evaluated just the same as those 'with sight,' and had threatened legal action if treated differently. His hair-trigger reliance on lawsuits greatly warmed the hearts of Rohr and company, and his handicap was a plaintiff's lawyer's dream. The defense had objected on all imaginable grounds, including the inability to see the forthcoming exhibits. Judge Harkin had allowed the lawyers to

57

quietly quiz Mr. Grimes about this, and he assured them he could see the exhibits if the exhibits could be sufficiently described in writing. His Honor then decided that a separate court reporter would be used to type descriptions of the exhibits. A disc could then be fed into Mr. Grimes' braille computer, and he could read at night. This made Mr. Grimes very happy, and he quit talking about discrimination suits. The defense softened a bit, especially when it learned that he had once smoked for many years and had no problems being around people who continued the habit.

So, both sides were cautiously pleased with their jury. No radicals had been seated. No bad attitudes had been detected. All twelve had high school diplomas, two had college degrees, and another three had accumulated credits. Easter's written answers admitted completion of high school, but his college studies were still a mystery.

And as both sides prepared for the first full day of real trial activities, they quietly pondered the great question, the one they loved to guess about. As they looked at the seating charts and studied the faces for the millionth time, they asked over and over, 'Who will be the leader?'

Every jury has a leader, and that's where you find your verdict. Will he emerge quickly? Or will she lie back and take charge during deliberations? Not even the jurors knew at this point.

At ten sharp, Judge Harkin studied the packed courtroom and decided everyone was in place. He pecked his gavel lightly and the whispers ceased. Everyone was ready. He nodded at Pete, his ancient bailiff in a faded brown uniform, and said simply, 'Bring in the jury.' All eyes watched the door beside the jury box. Lou Dell appeared first, leading her flock like a mother hen, then the chosen twelve filed in and went to their assigned seats. The three alternates took their positions in folding chairs. After a moment of settling in – adjusting seat cushions and hem lengths and placing purses and paperbacks on the floor – the jurors grew still and of course noticed that they were being gawked at.

'Good morning,' His Honor said with a loud voice and a large smile. Most of them nodded back.

'I trust you've found the jury room and gotten yourselves organized.' A pause, as he lifted for some reason the fifteen signed forms Lou Dell had dispensed then collected. 'Do we have a foreman?' he asked.

The twelve nodded in unison.

'Good. Who is it?'

'It's me, Your Honor,' Herman Grimes said from the first row, and for a quick second the defense, all its lawyers and jury consultants and corporate representatives, suffered a collective chest pain. Then they breathed, slowly, but never allowing the slightest indication that they had anything but the greatest love and affection for the blind juror who was now the foreman. Perhaps the other eleven just felt sorry for the old boy.

'Very well,' His Honor said, relieved that his jury was able to reach this routine selection without apparent acrimony. He'd seen much worse. One jury, half white and half black, had been unable to elect a foreman. They later brawled over the lunch menu.

'I trust you've read my written instructions,' he continued, then launched into a detailed lecture in which he repeated twice everything he'd already put in print.

Nicholas Easter sat on the front row, second seat from the left. He froze his face into a mask of noncommitment, and as Harkin droned on he began to take in the rest of the players. With little movement of the head, he cut his eyes around the courtroom. The lawyers, packed around their tables like vultures ready to pounce on roadkill, were, without exception, staring unabashedly at the jurors. Surely they'd tire of this, and soon.

On the second row behind the defense sat Rankin Fitch, his fat face and sinister goatee looking straight into the shoulders of the man in front of him. He was trying to ignore Harkin's admonitions and pretending to be wholly unconcerned about the jury, but Nicholas knew better. Fitch missed nothing.

Fourteen months earlier, Nicholas had seen him in the Cimmino courtroom in Allentown, Pennsylvania, looking then much the same as he looked now – thick and shadowy. And he'd seen him on the sidewalk outside the courthouse in Broken Arrow, Oklahoma, during the Glavine trial. Two sightings of Fitch were enough. Nicholas knew that Fitch now knew that he'd never attended college at North Texas State. He knew Fitch was more concerned about him than about any of the other jurors, and with very good reason.

Behind Fitch were two rows of suits, sharply dressed clones with scowling faces, and Nicholas knew these to be the worried boys from Wall Street. According to the morning paper, the market had chosen not to react to the jury's composition. Pynex was holding steady at eighty bucks a share. He couldn't help but smile. If he suddenly jumped to his feet and shouted, 'I think the plaintiff should get millions!' the suits would bolt for the door and Pynex would drop ten points by lunch.

The other three – Trellco, Smith Greer, and ConPack – were also trading evenly.

On the front rows were little pockets of distressed souls who Nicholas was certain had to be the jury experts. Now that the selecting was done, they moved to the next phase – the watching. It fell to their miserable lot to hear every word of every witness and predict how the jury absorbed the testimony. The strategy was that if a particular witness made a feeble or even damaging impression on the jury, then he or she could be yanked off the stand and sent home. Perhaps another, stronger witness could then be used to repair the damage. Nicholas wasn't sure about this. He'd read a lot about jury consultants, even attended a seminar in St. Louis where trial lawyers told war stories about big verdicts, but he still wasn't convinced these 'cutting edge' experts were little more than con artists.

They claimed to evaluate jurors just by watching their bodily reactions, however slight, to what was said. Nicholas managed another smile. What if he stuck his finger up his nose and left it there for five minutes? How would that little expression of body language be interpreted?

He couldn't classify the rest of the spectators. No doubt there were a number of reporters, and the usual collection of bored local lawyers and other courthouse regulars. The wife of Herman Grimes sat midway back, beaming with pride in the fact that her husband had been elected to such a lofty position. Judge Harkin stopped his rambling and pointed at Wendall Rohr, who stood slowly, buttoned his plaid jacket while flashing his false teeth at the jurors, and strode importantly to the lectern. This was his opening statement, he explained, and in it he would outline his case for the jury. The courtroom was very quiet.

They would prove that cigarettes cause lung cancer, and, more precisely, that the deceased, Mr. Jacob Wood, a fine fellow, developed lung cancer after smoking Bristols for almost thirty years. The cigarettes killed him, Rohr announced solemnly, tugging at a pointed patch of gray beard below his chin. His voice was raspy but precise, capable of floating up and down to hit the right dramatic pitch. Rohr was a performer, a seasoned actor whose crooked bow tie and clicking dentures and mismatched clothing were designed to endear him to the average man. He wasn't perfect. Let the defense lawyers, in their impeccable dark suits and rich silk ties, talk down their long noses at these jurors. But not Rohr. These were his people.

But how would they prove cigarettes cause lung cancer? There'd be lots of proof, really. First, they would bring in some of the most distinguished cancer experts and researchers in the country. Yes, that's right, these great men were on their way to Biloxi to sit and chat with this jury and explain unequivocally and with mountains of statistics that cigarettes do in fact cause cancer.

Then, and Rohr couldn't suppress a wicked smile as he prepared to reveal this, the plaintiff would present to the jury people who'd once worked for the tobacco industry. Dirty laundry would be aired, right there in that very courtroom. Damning evidence was on the way.

In short, the plaintiff would prove cigarette smoke, because it contains natural carcinogens, and pesticides, and radioactive particles, and asbestos-like fibers, causes lung cancer.

At this point, there was little doubt in the courtroom that Wendall Rohr could not only prove this, but would be able to prove it without much trouble. He paused, tugged at the ends of his bow tie with all ten chubby fingers, and glanced at his notes, then, very solemnly, began talking about Jacob Wood, the deceased. Beloved father and family man, hard worker, devout Catholic, member of the church softball team, veteran. Started smoking when he was just a kid who, like everyone else back then, was not aware of the dangers. A grandfather. And so on.

Rohr got overly dramatic for a moment, but seemed to know it. He briefly covered the area of damages. This was a big trial, he announced, one of vast importance. The plaintiff expected, and would certainly ask for, a lot of money. Not just actual damages – the economic value of Jacob Wood's life, plus his family's loss of his love and affection – but also punitive damages.

Rohr rambled on a bit about punitive damages, seemed to lose his place a few times, and it was clear to most of the jurors that he was so inspired by the prospect of a huge punitive verdict that he lost his concentration.

Judge Harkin, in writing, had allowed one hour for each side's opening statement. And had promised, in writing, to cut off any lawyer who ran over. Though he suffered from the common lawyerly affliction of overkill, Rohr knew not to mess with His Honor's clock. He finished in fifty minutes with a somber appeal for justice, thanked the jurors for their attention, smiled and clicked his dentures, and sat down.

Fifty minutes in a chair with no conversation and precious little movement feels like hours, and Judge Harkin knew it. He announced a recess for fifteen minutes, to be followed by the defendant's opening statement.

Durwood Cable finished his remarks in under thirty minutes. He coolly and deliberately assured the jurors that Pynex had experts of its own, scientists and researchers who would clearly explain that cigarettes in fact do not cause lung cancer. The skepticism of the jurors was expected, and Cable asked only for their patience and open-mindedness. Sir Durr spoke without the benefit of notes, and each word was drilled into the eyes of a juror. His eyes moved down the first row, then up slightly to the second, taking in their curious gazes one at a time. His voice and stare were almost hypnotic, but honest. You wanted to believe this man.

SIX

The first crisis occurred at lunch. Judge Harkin announced the noon recess at twelve-ten, and the courtroom sat still as the jurors filed out. Lou Dell met them in the narrow hallway and couldn't wait to shuffle them to the jury room. 'Just have a seat,' she said, 'and lunch will be here in a moment. Coffee's fresh.' Once all twelve were in the room, she shut them in and left to check on the three alternates, who were kept separated in a smaller room down the hall. With all fifteen in place, she returned to her post and glared at Willis, the mentally deficient deputy assigned to stand nearby with a loaded gun on his belt and protect somebody.

The jurors slowly scattered about the jury room, some stretching or yawning, others continuing formal introductions – most making small talk about the weather. For some, the movements and small talk were stiff; demeanor to be expected from people suddenly thrown into a room with perfect strangers. With nothing to do but eat, the noon meal loomed as a major event. What were they going to be fed? Surely, the food would be decent.

Herman Grimes took a seat at the head of the table, fitting for the foreman, he thought, and was soon chatting away with Millie Dupree, a kindly soul of fifty who actually knew another blind person. Nicholas Easter introduced himself to Lonnie Shaver, the only

64

black male on the jury, and a man who clearly did not want to serve. Shaver managed a grocery store for a large regional chain, and was the highest-ranking black in the company. He was wiry and nervous, and found it difficult to relax. The idea of spending the next four weeks away from the store was frightening.

Twenty minutes passed, and no lunch appeared. At exactly twelve-thirty, Nicholas said from across the room, 'Hey, Herman, where's our lunch?'

'I'm just the foreman,' Herman replied with a smile as the room was suddenly quiet.

Nicholas walked to the door, opened it, and summoned Lou Dell. 'We're hungry,' he said.

She slowly lowered her paperback, looked at the eleven other faces, and said, 'It's on the way.'

'Where is it coming from?' he demanded.

'O'Reilly's Deli. Just around the corner.' Lou Dell didn't appreciate the questions.

'Listen, we're penned up in here like a bunch of house pets,' Nicholas said. 'We can't leave like normal people to go eat. I don't understand why we can't be trusted to walk down the street and enjoy a nice lunch, but the Judge has spoken.' Nicholas took a step closer and glared down at the gray bangs hanging over Lou Dell's eyes. 'Lunch is not going to be a hassle every day, okay?'

'Okay.'

'I suggest you get on the phone and find out where our lunch is, or I'll discuss it with Judge Harkin.'

'Okay.'

The door closed, and Nicholas walked to the coffeepot.

'That was a bit harsh, don't you think?' asked Millie Dupree. The others were listening.

'Maybe, and if it was, then I'll apologize. But if we don't get things straight up front, then they'll forget about us.'

65

'It's not her fault,' Herman said.

'Her job is to take care of us.' Nicholas walked to the table and sat near Herman. 'Do you realize that in virtually every other trial they allow the jurors to leave like normal people and go eat? Why do you think we wear these Juror buttons?' The others moved closer to the table.

'How do you know?' asked Millie Dupree from directly across the table.

Nicholas shrugged as if he knew plenty but maybe couldn't talk about it. 'I know a little about the system.'

'And how's that?' Herman asked.

Nicholas paused for effect, then said, 'I had two years of law school.' He took a long sip of coffee as the others weighed this engaging bit of background.

Easter's stature among his peers rose immediately. He'd already proved himself to be friendly and helpful, courteous and bright. Now, though, he was silently elevated because he knew the law.

No food had arrived by twelve forty-five. Nicholas abruptly stopped a conversation and opened the door. Lou Dell was glancing at her watch in the hallway. 'I've sent Willis,' she said nervously. 'Should be here any minute now. I'm really sorry.'

'Where's the men's room?' Nicholas asked.

'Around the corner, to your right,' she said, relieved and pointing. He didn't stop at the men's room, but instead walked quietly down the rear staircase and out of the courthouse. He made his way along Lamuese Street for two blocks until he came to the Vieux Marche, a pedestrian mall lined with neat shops along what was once the central business section of Biloxi. He knew the area well because it was only a quarter of a mile from his apartment building. He liked the cafés and delis along the Vieux Marche. There was a good bookstore.

He turned left and was soon entering a large, old white building that housed Mary Mahoney's, a locally famous restaurant where most of the town's legal community usually gathered for lunch when court was in session. He'd rehearsed this walk a week ago, and had even had his lunch at a table close to the Honorable Frederick Harkin.

Nicholas entered the restaurant, and asked the first waitress he saw if Judge Harkin was eating. Yes. And where might he be? She pointed, and Nicholas walked quickly through the bar, through a small foyer, and into a large dining room with windows and sunshine and lots of fresh flowers. It was crowded, but he saw His Honor at a table of four. Harkin saw him coming, and his fork froze halfway up with a meaty grilled shrimp stuck to the end of it. He recognized the face as one of his jurors, and he saw the bold red-and-white Juror button.

'Sorry to interrupt, sir,' Nicholas said, stopping at the edge of the table, a table covered with warm bread and leafy salads and large glasses of iced tea. Gloria Lane, the Circuit Clerk, was also momentarily speechless. A second woman was the court reporter, and a third was Harkin's law clerk.

'What are you doing here?' Harkin asked, a speck of goat cheese on his lower lip.

'I'm here on behalf of your jury.'

'What's the matter?'

Nicholas leaned down so he wouldn't create a scene. 'We're hungry,' he said, his anger apparent through clenched teeth and clearly absorbed by the four stricken faces. 'While you folks are sitting here having a nice lunch, we're sitting over there in a cramped room waiting on deli food that, for some reason, can't find its way to us. We're hungry, sir, with all due respect. And we're upset.'

Harkin's fork hit his plate hard, the shrimp bouncing off and tumbling to the floor. He tossed his napkin on the table while mumbling something completely

67

indecipherable. He looked at the three women, arched his eyebrows, and said, 'Well, let's go see.' He stood, followed by the women, and the five of them stormed out of the restaurant.

Lou Dell and Willis were nowhere to be seen when Nicholas and Judge Harkin and the three women entered the hallway and opened the door to the jury room. The table was bare – no food. The time was five minutes after one. The jurors stopped their chatting and stared at His Honor.

'It's been almost an hour,' Nicholas said, waving at the empty table. If the other jurors were astonished to see the Judge, their surprise quickly turned to anger.

'We have the right to be treated with dignity,' snapped Lonnie Shaver, and with that Harkin was thoroughly defeated.

'Where's Lou Dell?' he said in the general direction of the three women. Everyone looked at the door, and suddenly Lou Dell was rushing forth. She stopped cold when she saw His Honor. Harkin faced her squarely.

'What's going on?' he asked firmly, but with control.

'I just talked to the deli,' she said, out of breath and scared, beads of sweat on her cheeks. 'There's been a mixup. They claim someone called and said we wouldn't need lunch until one-thirty.'

'These people are starving,' Harkin said, as if by now Lou Dell didn't know this. 'One-thirty?'

'It's just a mixup at the deli. Somebody got their wires crossed.'

'Which deli?'

'O'Reilly's.'

'Remind me to speak to the owner of the deli.'

'Yes sir.'

The Judge turned his attention to his jury. 'I'm very sorry. This will not happen again.' He paused for a second, looked at his watch, then offered them a pleasant smile. 'I'm inviting you to follow me to Mary

68

Mahoney's and join me for lunch.' He turned to his law clerk, and said, 'Call Bob Mahoney and tell him to prepare the back room.'

They dined on crab cakes and grilled snapper, fresh oysters and Mahoney's famous gumbo. Nicholas Easter was the man of the hour. When they finished dessert a few minutes after two-thirty, they followed Judge Harkin, at a leisurely pace, back to the courtroom. By the time the jury was seated for the afternoon session, everyone present had heard the story of their splendid lunch.

Neal O'Reilly, owner of the deli, later met with Judge Harkin and swore on a Bible that he had talked to someone, a young female claiming to be with the Circuit Clerk's office, and that she had specifically instructed him to deliver lunch at precisely one-thirty.

The trial's first witness was the deceased, Jacob Wood, testifying by a video deposition taken a few months before his death. Two twenty-inch monitors were rolled into place before the jury, and a series of six others were situated around the courtroom. The wiring had been completed while the jury feasted at Mary Mahoney's.

Jacob Wood was propped up with pillows in what appeared to be a hospital bed. He wore a plain white T-shirt with a sheet covering him from the waist down. He was thin, gaunt, and pale, and took oxygen from a tiny tube running from behind his bony neck into his nose. He was told to begin, and he looked at the camera and stated his name and address. His voice was raspy and sick. He was also suffering from emphysema.

Though he was surrounded by lawyers, Jacob's face was the only one to be seen. Occasionally a small skirmish would erupt off-camera among the lawyers, but Jacob didn't seem to care. He was fifty-one, looked twenty years older, and was clearly pounding at death's door.

With prompting from his lawyer, Wendall Rohr, he shared his biography beginning with his birth, and this took almost an hour. Childhood, early education, friends, homes, Navy, marriage, jobs, kids, habits, hobbies, adult friends, travel, vacation, grandkids, thoughts of retirement. Watching a dead man talk was quite compelling at first, but the jurors soon learned that his life had been just as boring as theirs. The heavy lunch settled in, and they began to twitch and fidget. Brains and eyelids grew sluggish. Even Herman, who could only hear the voice and imagine the face, got bored. Fortunately, His Honor began to suffer from the same post-lunch sinking spell, and after an hour and twenty minutes he called for a quick recess.

The four smokers on the jury needed a break, and Lou Dell happily walked them to a room with an open window, a room next to the men's toilet, a small cubicle normally used to hold juvenile delinquents awaiting court appearances. 'If you can't quit smoking after this trial, something's wrong,' she said, in a very flat effort at humor. Not a smile from the four. 'Sorry,' she said, closing the door behind her. Jerry Fernandez, thirty-eight, a car salesman with heavy casino debts and a bad marriage, lit his first, then waved his lighter in the faces of the three women. They pulled heavy puffs and blew large clouds at the window. 'Here's to Jacob Wood,' Jerry said as a toast. Nothing from the three women. They were too busy smoking.

Mr. Foreman Grimes had already delivered one brief lecture on the illegalities of discussing the case; he simply wouldn't tolerate it because Judge Harkin was harping on it so strenuously. But Herman was in the next room, and Jerry was curious. 'Wonder if ole Jacob ever tried to quit?' he said, to no one in particular.

Sylvia Taylor-Tatum, drawing ferociously on the end of a slender, emancipated cigarette, replied, 'I'm sure we're about to find out,' then released an impressive torrent of bluish vapors from her long, pointed nose. Jerry loved nicknames, and he had already secretly tagged her as Poodle because of her narrow face, sharp protruding nose, and shaggy thick graying hair that parted perfectly in the center and fell in heavy layers to her shoulders. She was at least six feet tall, very angular, with a constant frown that kept people away. Poodle intended to be left alone.

'I wonder who's next,' Jerry said, trying to start a conversation.

'I guess all those doctors,' Poodle said, staring through the window.

The other two ladies simply smoked, and Jerry gave it up.

The woman's name was Marlee, at least that was the alias she'd chosen to use for this period of her life. She was thirty, short brown hair, brown eyes, medium height, slim build with simple clothing carefully selected to avoid attention. She looked great in tight jeans and short skirts, she looked great in anything or nothing, really, but for the moment she wanted no one to notice her. She'd been in the courtroom on two prior occasions – once two weeks earlier when she'd sat through another trial, and once during jury selection in the tobacco case. She knew her way around. She knew where the Judge kept his office and where he ate lunch. She knew the names of the plaintiff's lawyers and those of the defense – no small task. She'd read the court file. She knew in which hotel Rankin Fitch was hiding during the trial.

During the recess, she got herself cleared through the metal detector at the front door, and eased into the rear row of the courtroom. Spectators were stretching and lawyers were huddling and conferencing. She saw Fitch standing in a corner, chatting with two people she believed to be jury consultants. He did not notice her. There were about a hundred people present.

A few minutes passed. She carefully watched the door behind the bench, and when the court reporter came out with a cup of coffee, Marlee knew the Judge could not be far behind. She took an envelope from her purse, waited a second, then walked a few feet to one of the deputies guarding the front door. She flashed a comely smile and said, 'Could you do me a favor?'

He almost smiled in return and noticed the envelope. 'I'll try.'

'I've gotta run. Could you hand this to that gentleman over there in the corner? I don't want to interrupt him.' The deputy squinted in the direction she was pointing, across the courtroom. 'Which one?'

'The heavyset man in the middle, with the goatee, dark suit.'

At this moment, the bailiff entered from behind the bench and shouted, 'Court come to order!'

'What's his name?' the deputy asked, his voice lower. She handed him the envelope and pointed to the name on it. 'Rankin Fitch. Thanks.' She patted him on the arm and vanished from the courtroom.

Fitch leaned down the row and whispered something to an associate, then made his way to the rear of the courtroom as the jury returned. He'd seen enough for one day. Fitch typically spent little time in the courtroom once the juries were selected. He had other means of monitoring the trial.

The deputy stopped him at the door and handed him the envelope. Fitch was startled to see his name in print. He was an unknown, a nameless shadow who introduced himself to no one and lived under an assumed name. His D.C. firm was called Arlington West Associates, about as bland and nondescript as he could imagine. No one knew his name – except of course his employees, his clients, and a few of the lawyers he hired. He glared at the deputy without muttering a 'Thank you,' then stepped into the atrium, still staring in disbelief at the envelope. The printed letters were no doubt from a feminine hand. He slowly opened it, and removed a single sheet of white paper. Printed neatly in the center was a note: 'Dear Mr. Fitch: Tomorrow, juror number two, Easter, will wear a gray pullover golf shirt with red trim, starched khakis, white socks, and brown leather shoes, lace-up.'

José the driver sauntered over from a water fountain and stood like an obedient watchdog beside his boss. Fitch reread the note, then looked blankly at José. He walked to the door, opened it slightly, and asked the deputy to step outside the courtroom.

'What's the matter?' the deputy asked. His position was inside, against the door, and he was a man who followed orders.

'Who gave you this?' Fitch asked as nicely as was possible for him. The two deputies manning the metal detector were watching curiously.

'A woman. I don't know her name.'

'When did she give it to you?'

'Just before you left. Just a minute ago.'

With that, Fitch looked quickly around. 'Do you see her here?'

'Nope,' he answered after a cursory look.

'Can you describe her for me?'

He was a cop, and cops are trained to notice things. 'Sure. Late twenties. Five six, maybe five seven. Short brown hair. Brown eyes. Pretty damned good-looking. Slim.'

'What was she wearing?'

He hadn't noticed, but he couldn't admit it. 'Uhm, a light-colored dress, sort of a beige, cotton, buttons down the front.'

Fitch absorbed this, thought a second, asked, 'What did she say to you?'

'Not much. Just asked me to hand this to you. Then she was gone.'

73

'Anything unusual about the way she talked?'

'No. Look, I need to get back inside.'

'Sure. Thanks.'

Fitch and José descended the steps and roamed the corridors of the first floor. They walked outside and strolled around the courthouse, both smoking and acting as if they were out for a bit of fresh air.

The video deposition of Jacob Wood had taken two and a half days to complete while he was alive. Judge Harkin, after editing the fights among the lawyers, the interruptions of the nurses, and the irrelevant portions of testimony, had pared it down nicely to a mere two hours and thirty-one minutes.

It seemed like days. Listening to the poor man give his personal history of smoking was interesting, to a point, but the jurors soon wished Harkin had cut more. Jacob started smoking Redtops at the age of sixteen because all of his buddies smoked Redtops. He soon had the habit and was up to two packs a day. He quit Redtops when he left the Navy because he got married, and his wife convinced him to smoke something with a filter. She wanted him to quit. He couldn't, so he started smoking Bristols because the ads claimed lower tar and nicotine. By the age of twenty-five he was smoking three packs a day. He remembered this well because their first child was born when Jacob was twenty-five, and Celeste Wood warned him he wouldn't live to see his grandchildren if he didn't stop smoking. She refused to buy cigarettes when she shopped, so Jacob did it himself. He averaged two cartons a week, twenty packs, and he usually picked up another pack or two until he could purchase by the carton.

He'd been desperate to quit. He once put 'em down for two weeks, then sneaked out of bed at night to start again. He'd cut back a few times; to two packs a day, then to one pack a day, then before he knew it he was back to three. He'd been to doctors and he'd been to hypnotists. He tried acupuncture and nicotine gum. But he simply couldn't stop. He couldn't after he was diagnosed with emphysema, and he couldn't after he was told he had lung cancer.

It was the dumbest thing he'd ever done, and now at the age of fifty-one, he was dying for it. Please, he implored between coughs, if you're smoking, stop.

Jerry Fernandez and Poodle glanced at each other.

Jacob turned melancholy when he talked about the things he'd miss. His wife, kids, grandkids, friends, trolling for redfish around Ship Island, etc. Celeste started crying softly next to Rohr, and before long Millie Dupree, number three, next to Nicholas Easter, was rubbing her eyes with a Kleenex.

Finally, the first witness spoke his last words and the monitors went blank. His Honor thanked the jury for a fine first day, and promised more of the same tomorrow. He turned serious and launched into a dire warning against discussing this case with anyone, not even a spouse. Also, and more importantly, if anyone in any way tried to initiate contact with a juror, please report it immediately. He hammered them on this point for a good ten minutes, then dismissed them until 9 A.M.

Fitch had toyed with the idea of entering Easter's apartment before, but now it was necessary. And it was easy. He sent José and an operative named Doyle to the apartment building where Easter lived. Easter, of course, was at the time confined to the jury box and suffering along with Jacob Wood. He was being watched closely by two of Fitch's men, just in case court was suddenly adjourned.

José stayed in the car, near the phone, and watched the front entryway as Doyle disappeared inside. Doyle walked up one flight of stairs and found Apartment 312

75

at the end of a semi-lit hall-way. There was not a sound from the neighboring apartments. Everyone was at work.

He shook the loose-fitting doorknob, then held it firmly as he slid an eight-inch plastic strip down the facing. The lock clicked, the knob turned. He gently pushed the door open two inches, and waited for the alarm to either beep or sound. Nothing. The apartment building was old and low-rent, and the fact that Easter had no alarm system didn't surprise Doyle.

He was inside in an instant. Using a small camera with a flash attachment, he quickly photographed the kitchen, den, bathroom, and bedroom. He took close-ups of the magazines on the cheap coffee table, the books stacked on the floor, the CD's on top of the stereo, and the software littered around the rather fancy PC. Being careful what he touched, he found a gray pullover golf shirt with red trim hanging in the closet, and took a photo of it. He opened the refrigerator and took a photo of the contents, then the cabinets and under the sink.

The apartment was small and cheaply furnished, but an effort was being made to keep it clean. The air conditioning was either turned off or out of order. Doyle photographed the thermostat. He was in the apartment less than ten minutes, long enough to shoot two rolls of film and determine that Easter in fact lived alone. There was clearly no trace of another person, especially a female.

He carefully locked the door and silently left the apartment. Ten minutes later, he was in Fitch's office.

Nicholas left the courthouse on foot, and stopped, coincidentally, at O'Reilly's Deli on the Vieux Marche, where he purchased a half-pound of smoked turkey and a container of pasta salad. He took his time walking home, no doubt enjoying the sunshine after a day inside. He bought a bottle of cold mineral water at a corner grocery and drank it as he walked. He watched some black kids play a fierce game of basketball in a church parking lot. He ducked through a small park, and for a moment almost lost his shadow. But he exited on the other side, still sipping the water and now certain he was being followed. One of Fitch's goons, Pang, a small Asian with a baseball cap, had nearly panicked in the park. Nicholas had seen him through a row of elevated box-woods.

At his apartment door, he removed a small keypad and punched in the four-digit code. The tiny red light turned green, and he unlocked the door.

The surveillance camera was hidden in an air vent directly above the refrigerator, and from its silent perch had a complete view of the kitchen, den, and door to the bedroom. Nicholas went straight to his computer, and within seconds determined that, first, no one had attempted to turn it on, and, second, that a UAEA – unauthorized entry/apartment – had occurred at exactly 4:52 P.M.

He took a deep breath, glanced around, and decided to inspect the place. He expected to find no evidence of entry. The door appeared no different, the knob loose and easy to force open. The kitchen and den were precisely as he'd left them. His only assets – the stereo and CD's, the TV, the computer – appeared untouched. In the bedroom, he found no evidence of either a burglar or a crime. Back at the computer, he held his breath and waited for the show. He went through a series of files, found the correct program, then stopped the surveillance video. He punched two keys to rewind it, then sent it to four fifty-two. *Voilà!* In black and white, on the sixteen-inch monitor, the apartment door opened, and the camera turned directly to it. A narrow crack, as his visitor waited for the alarm to shriek. No alarm, then the door opened and a man entered. Nicholas stopped the video and stared at the face on his monitor. He'd never seen him before.

The video continued as the man rapidly pulled a camera from his pocket and began flashing away. He nosed around the apartment, disappeared for a moment in the bedroom, where he continued to take photos. He studied the computer for a moment, but didn't touch it. Nicholas smiled at this. His computer was impossible to enter. This thug couldn't find the power switch.

He was in the apartment for nine minutes and thirteen seconds, and Nicholas could only speculate on why he came today. His best guess was that Fitch knew the apartment would be empty until court adjourned.

The visit was not frightening, but rather expected. Nicholas watched the video again, chuckled to himself, then saved it for future use.

SEVEN

Fitch himself was sitting in the back of the surveillance van at eight the next morning when Nicholas Easter walked into the sunshine and looked around the parking lot. The van had a plumber's logo on the door and a fake phone number stenciled in green. 'There he is,' Doyle announced and they all jumped. Fitch grabbed the scope, focused it quickly through a blackened porthole, and said, 'Damn.'

'What is it?' asked Pang, the Korean technician who had pursued Nicholas yesterday.

Fitch leaned toward the round window, his mouth open, top lip curled upward. 'I'll be damned. Gray pullover, khakis, white socks, brown leather shoes.'

'Same shirt in the photo?' Doyle asked.

'Yep.'

Pang pressed a button on a portable radio and alerted another shadow two blocks away. Easter was on foot, probably headed in the general direction of the courthouse.

He bought a large cup of black coffee and a newspaper at the same corner grocery, and sat in the same park for twenty minutes scanning the news. He wore dark sunglasses and noticed anyone who walked nearby.

Fitch went straight to his office down the street from the courthouse and huddled with Doyle, Pang, and an ex-FBI agent named Swanson. 'We have to find the girl,' Fitch said over and over. A plan was devised to keep one person in the back row of the courtroom, one outside near the top of the stairs, one near the soft-drink machines on the first floor, and one outside with a radio. They would change posts with every recess. The flimsy description of her was passed around. Fitch decided to sit exactly where he'd sat yesterday, and go through the same motions.

Swanson, an expert on surveillance, was unsure of all the fuss. 'It won't work,' he said.

'Why not?' Fitch demanded.

'Because she'll find you. She has something she wants to talk about, so she'll make the next move.'

'Maybe. But I wanna know who she is.'

'Relax. She'll find you.'

Fitch argued with him until almost nine o'clock, then walked briskly back to the courthouse. Doyle talked to the deputy, and persuaded him to point out the girl if she happened to appear again.

Nicholas had selected Rikki Coleman to chat with over coffee and croissants Friday morning. She was thirty and cute, married with two young children, and worked as a records administrator in a private hospital in Gulfport. She was a health nut who avoided caffeine, alcohol, and, of course, nicotine. Her flaxen hair was short, cut like a boy's, and her pretty blue eyes looked even cuter behind designer frames. She was sitting in a corner, sipping an orange juice and reading *USA Today*, when Nicholas zeroed in and said, 'Good morning. I don't think we officially met yesterday.'

She smiled, something she did easily, and offered a hand. 'Rikki Coleman.'

'Nicholas Easter. Nice to meet you.'

'Thanks for lunch yesterday,' she said with a quick laugh.

'Don't mention it. Can I sit down?' he asked, nodding at a folding chair next to her.

'Sure.' She laid the paper in her lap.

All twelve jurors were accounted for, and most were engaged in quiet pockets of early morning chatter. Herman Grimes sat alone at the table, in his beloved head chair, holding his coffee with both hands and no doubt listening for wayward words about the trial. Lonnie Shaver also sat alone at the table, his eyes poring over computer printouts from his supermarket. Jerry Fernandez had gone down the hall for a quick smoke with the Poodle.

'So how's jury service?' Nicholas asked.

'Overrated.'

'Did anyone attempt to bribe you last night?'

'No. You?'

'No. It's too bad, because Judge Harkin will be terribly disappointed if no one tries to bribe us.'

'Why does he go on about this unauthorized contact?'

Nicholas leaned forward a bit, though not too close. She leaned too and cast a wary eye at the Foreman as if he could see them. They enjoyed the closeness and privacy of their little chat, the way two physically attractive people are sometimes drawn to one another. Just a little harmless flirting. 'It's happened before. Several times,' he said, almost in a whisper. Laughter erupted by the coffeepots as Mrs. Gladys Card and Mrs. Stella Hulic found something funny in the local paper.

'What's happened before?' Rikki asked.

'Contaminated juries in tobacco cases. In fact, it almost always happens, usually at the hands of the defense.'

'I don't understand,' she said, believing all and wanting much more information from the guy with two years of law school under his belt.

81

'There have been several of these cases around the country, and the tobacco industry has yet to get hit with a verdict. They pay millions for defense because they can't afford to lose the first time. One big plaintiff's verdict, and the floodgates open.' He paused, looked around, and sipped his coffee. 'So, they use all sorts of dirty tricks.'

'Such as?'

'Such as offering money to family members of jurors. Such as spreading rumors in the community that the deceased, whoever he was, had four girlfriends, beat his wife, stole from his friends, went to church only for funerals, and had a homosexual son.'

She frowned in disbelief, so he continued. 'It's true, and it's well known in legal circles. Judge Harkin knows it, I'm sure, that's why we're getting the warnings.'

'Can't they be stopped?'

'Not yet. They're very smart, and shrewd, and crooked, and they leave no trail. Plus, they have millions.' He paused as she studied him. 'They watched you before jury selection.'

'No!'

'Of course they did. It's standard procedure in big trials. The law forbids them to directly contact any prospective juror before selection, so they do everything else. They probably photographed your house, car, kids, husband, place of employment. They might have talked to co-workers, or eavesdropped on conversations at the office or wherever you eat lunch. You never know.'

She set her orange juice on a windowsill. 'That sounds illegal, or unethical, or something.'

'Something. But they got by with it because you had no idea they were doing it.'

'But you knew?'

'Yep. I saw a photographer in a car outside my apartment. And they sent a woman into the store where

I work to pick a fight over our no-smoking policy. I knew exactly what they were doing.'

'But you said direct contact was prohibited.'

'Yes, but I didn't say they played fair. Just the opposite. They'll break any rule to win.'

'Why didn't you tell the Judge?'

'Because it was harmless, and because I knew what they were doing. Now that I'm on the jury, I'm watching every move.'

With her curiosity piqued, Nicholas thought it best to save more dirt for later. He glanced at his watch and abruptly stood. 'I think I'll run to the boys' room before we get back in the box.'

Lou Dell burst into the room, rattling the door on its hinges. 'Time to go,' she said firmly, not unlike a counselor at camp with much less authority than she assumed.

The crowd had thinned to about half of yesterday's number. Nicholas scanned the spectators as the jurors sat and adjusted themselves on the worn cushions. Fitch, predictably, was sitting in the same spot, now with his head partially behind a newspaper as if he couldn't care less about the jury; couldn't give a damn what Easter was wearing. He'd stare later. The reporters had all but vanished, though they'd trickle in during the day. The Wall Street types looked to be thoroughly bored already; all were young, fresh college grads sent South because they were rookies and their bosses had better things to do. Mrs. Herman Grimes held her same position, and Nicholas wondered if she'd be there every day, hearing everything and ever ready to help her husband cast his lot.

Nicholas fully expected to see the man who'd entered his apartment, maybe not today, but at some point during the trial. The man was not in the courtroom at the moment.

'Good morning,' Judge Harkin said warmly to the

jury when everyone was still. Smiles everywhere: from the Judge, the clerks – even the lawyers, who had stopped their huddling and whispering long enough to look at the jury with phony grins. 'I trust everyone is well today.' He paused and waited for fifteen faces to nod awkwardly. 'Good. Madam Clerk has informed me that everyone is ready for a full day.' It was hard to picture Lou Dell as Madam anything.

His Honor then lifted a sheet of paper which contained a list of questions the jurors would learn to hate. He cleared his voice and stopped smiling. 'Now, ladies and gentlemen of the jury. I'm about to ask you a series of questions, very important questions, and I want you to respond if you feel the slightest need to. Also, I'd like to remind you that your failure to respond, if a response is in order, could be deemed by me as an act of contempt, punishable by a jail term.'

He allowed this grievous warning to float around the courtroom; the jurors felt guilty just for receiving it. Convinced he'd found his mark, he then started the questions: Did anyone attempt to discuss this trial with you? Did you receive any unusual phone calls since we adjourned yesterday? Did you see any strangers watching you or any members of your family? Did you hear any rumors or gossip about any of the parties in the trial? Any of the lawyers? Any of the witnesses? Did any person contact any of your friends or family members in an effort to discuss this trial? Did any friend or family member attempt to discuss this trial with you since yesterday's adjournment? Did you see or receive any piece of written material which in any way mentioned anything to do with this trial?

Between each question in this script, the Judge would stop, look hopefully at each juror, then seemingly with disappointment, return to his list.

What struck the jurors as odd was the air of expectation surrounding the questions. The lawyers hung on every word, certain that damning responses were forthcoming from the panel. The clerks, usually busy shuffling papers or exhibits or doing a dozen things unrelated to the trial, were completely still and watching to see which juror would confess. The Judge's glowering face and arched eyebrows after each question challenged the integrity of every juror, and he took their silence as nothing short of deceit.

When he finished, he quietly said, 'Thank you,' and the courtroom seemed to breathe. The jurors felt assaulted. His Honor sipped coffee from a tall cup and smiled at Wendall Rohr. 'Call your next witness, Counselor.'

Rohr stood, a large brown stain in the center of his wrinkled white shirt, bow tie as crooked as ever, shoes scuffed and getting dirtier by the day. He nodded and smiled warmly at the jurors, and they couldn't help but smile at him.

Rohr had a jury consultant assigned to record everything the jurors wore. If one of the five men happened to wear cowboy boots one day, then Rohr had an old pair at the ready. Two pairs actually – pointed toe or round. He was prepared to wear sneakers if the time was right. He'd done so once before when sneakers appeared in the jury box. The Judge, not Harkin, had complained in chambers. Rohr had a foot ailment, he'd explained, and had produced a letter from his podiatrist. He could wear starched khakis, knit ties, polyester sports coats, cowboy belts, white socks, penny loafers (either shined or battered). His eclectic wardrobe was designed to connect with those now forced to sit nearby and listen to him for six hours a day.

'We'd like to call Dr. Milton Fricke,' he announced.

Dr. Fricke was sworn and seated and the bailiff adjusted his microphone. It was soon learned that his résumé could be measured by the pound – lots of degrees from many schools, hundreds of published articles, seventeen books, years of teaching experience, decades of research into the effects of tobacco smoke. He was a small man with a perfectly round face with black horn-rimmed glasses; he looked like a genius. It took Rohr almost an hour to cover his astounding collection of credentials. When Fricke was finally tendered as an expert, Durr Cable wanted no part of him. 'We stipulate that Dr. Fricke is qualified in his field,' Cable said, in what sounded like a major understatement.

His field had been narrowed over the years, so that Dr. Fricke now spent ten hours a day studying the effects of tobacco smoke on the human body. He was the director of the Smoke Free Research Institute in Rochester, New York. The jury soon learned that he had been hired by Rohr before Jacob Wood died, and that he had been present during an autopsy performed on Mr. Wood four hours after his death. And that he had taken some photos of the autopsy.

Rohr emphasized the existence of the photos, leaving no doubt that the jurors would see them eventually. But Rohr was not ready yet. He needed to spend time with this extraordinary expert on the chemistry and pharmacology of smoking. Fricke proved quite the professor. He treaded cautiously through ponderous medical and scientific studies, weeding out the big words and giving the jurors what they could understand. He was relaxed and thoroughly confident.

When His Honor announced the lunch recess, Rohr informed the court that Dr. Fricke would be on the stand for the remainder of the day.

Lunch was waiting in the jury room, with Mr. O'Reilly himself in charge of its presentation and readily offering apologies for what had happened the day before.

'These are paper plates and plastic forks,' Nicholas said as they took their seats around the table. He did not sit. Mr. O'Reilly looked at Lou Dell, who said, 'So?'

'So, we specifically said we wanted to eat on real china with real forks. Didn't we say that?' His voice was rising, and a few of the jurors looked away. They just wanted to eat.

'What's wrong with paper plates?' Lou Dell asked nervously, her bangs shaking.

'They soak up grease, okay? They get spongy and leave stains on the table, you understand? That's why I specifically asked for real plates. And real forks.' He took a white plastic fork, snapped it in two, and threw it in a waste can. 'And what really makes me mad, Lou Dell, is that right now the Judge and all the lawyers and their clients and the witnesses and the clerks and the spectators and everybody else involved with this trial are sitting down to a nice lunch in a nice restaurant with real plates and real glasses and forks that don't snap in two. And they're ordering good food from a thick menu. That's what makes me mad. And we, the jurors, the most important people of the whole damned trial, we're stuck here like first-graders waiting to be fed our cookies and lemonade.'

'The food's pretty good,' Mr. O'Reilly said in self-defense.

'I think you're overdoing it a bit,' said Mrs. Gladys Card, a prim little lady with white hair and a sweet voice.

'Then eat your soggy sandwich and stay out of this,' Nicholas snapped, much too harshly.

'Are you gonna show your ass every day at lunch?' asked Frank Herrera, a retired colonel from somewhere up North. Herrera was short and portly with tiny hands and an opinion, so far, on just about everything. He was the only one who was truly disappointed when he wasn't elected foreman.

Jerry Fernandez had already nicknamed him Napoleon. Nap for short. The Retarded Colonel as an alternative.

'There were no complaints yesterday,' Nicholas shot back.

'Let's eat. I'm starving,' Herrera said, unwrapping a sandwich. A few of the others did the same.

The aroma of baked chicken and french fries rose from the table. As Mr. O'Reilly finished unpacking a container of pasta salad, he said, 'I'll be happy to bring over some plates and forks on Monday. No problem.'

Nicholas quietly said, 'Thanks,' and sat down.

The deal was an easy one to make. The details were wrapped up between two old friends over a three-hour lunch at the '21' Club on Fifty-second. Luther Vandemeer, CEO of Trellco, and his former protégé, Larry Zell, now CEO of Listing Foods, had discussed the basics on the phone, but needed to meet face-to-face over food and wine so no one could hear them. Vandemeer gave him the background of the latest serious threat down in Biloxi, and didn't hide the truth that he was worried. Sure, Trellco was not a named defendant, but the entire industry was under fire and the Big Four was standing firm. Zell knew this. He'd worked for Trellco for seventeen years, and had learned to hate trial lawyers a long time ago.

There was a small regional grocery chain, Hadley Brothers, out of Pensacola, which just happened to own a few stores along the Mississippi Coast. One such store was in Biloxi, and its manager was a sharp young black man named Lonnie Shaver. Lonnie Shaver just happened to be on the jury down there. Vandemeer wanted SuperHouse, a much larger grocery chain in Georgia and the Carolinas, to purchase, at whatever premium necessary, Hadley Brothers. SuperHouse was one of twenty or so divisions of Listing Foods. It would be a small transaction – Vandemeer's people had already done the numbers – and would cost Listing no more than six million. Hadley Brothers was privately

88

owned, so the deal would create virtually no attention. Listing Foods had grossed two billion last year, so six million was no sweat. The company had eighty million in cash and little debt. And to sweeten the deal, Vandemeer promised that Trellco would quietly purchase Hadley Brothers in two years if Zell wished to unload it.

Nothing could go wrong. Listing and Trellco were totally independent of each other. Listing was already in the business of owning grocery chains. Trellco was not directly involved in the litigation down there. It was a simple handshake deal between two old friends.

Later, of course, there would need to be a personnel shakeup within Hadley Brothers, one of the usual realignments inherent in any buyout or merger or whatever it was to be called. Vandemeer would need to pass along some instructions for Zell to send down the line until the right amount of pressure could be placed on Lonnie Shaver.

And it needed to be done quickly. The trial was scheduled to last for four more weeks. Week one would end in just a few hours.

After a brief nap in his office in downtown Manhattan, Luther Vandemeer called the number in Biloxi and left a message for Rankin Fitch to call him in the Hamptons over the weekend.

Fitch's office was in the back of an empty store, a five-and-dime that had closed years earlier. The rent was low, parking was plentiful, no one noticed the place, and it was just a short walk from the courthouse. There were five large rooms, all hastily built with unpainted plywood walls; the sawdust was still on the floor. The furniture was cheap, rented, and consisted primarily of folding tables and plastic chairs. The lighting was fluorescent and plentiful. The outer doors were heavily secured. Two men with guns guarded the suite at all times.

If pennies had been pinched throwing the place together, nothing had been spared in getting it plugged in. Computers and monitors were everywhere. Wires to faxes and copiers and phones ran over the floor in no apparent design. Fitch had the latest technology, and he had the people to operate it.

The walls of one room were covered with large photos of the fifteen jurors. Computer printouts were tacked to another wall. A huge seating chart was on another wall, and an employee was adding data to the block under Gladys Card's name.

The room in the back was the smallest, and it was strictly off-limits for the regular employees, though they all knew what was happening in it. The door locked automatically from the inside, and Fitch had the only key. It was a viewing room, with no windows, a large screen on one wall, and half a dozen comfortable chairs. Friday afternoon, Fitch and two jury experts sat in the dark and stared at the screen. The experts preferred not to engage in small talk with Fitch, and Fitch wasn't about to entertain them. Silence.

The camera was a Yumara XLT-2, a tiny unit capable of fitting almost anywhere. The lens was half an inch in diameter, and the camera itself weighed less than a pound. It had been meticulously installed by one of Fitch's boys, and was now situated in a well-worn brown leather satchel sitting on the floor in the courtroom under the defense table, and being covertly guarded by Oliver McAdoo, a lawyer from Washington and the only foreigner selected by Fitch to sit alongside Cable and the rest. McAdoo's job was to think strategy, smile at the jurors, and feed documents to Cable. His real job, known only to Fitch and a few others, was to walk into the courtroom each day, heavily laden with the tools of warfare, including two large, identical brown briefcases, one of which held the camera, and to sit at approximately the same spot at the defense table.

He was the first defense lawyer in the courtroom each morning. He would set the satchel upright, aim it at the jury box, then quickly call Fitch on a cellphone to get things adjusted.

At any given moment during the trial, there were twenty or so briefcases scattered through the court-room, most congregated on or under the counsel tables, but some were stacked together near the clerk's bench, some were under chairs where the lower-tier lawyers labored, some were even leaning against the bar, seemingly abandoned. While they varied in size and color, as a collection they all looked pretty much the same, including McAdoo's. One he opened occasion-ally to retrieve papers, but the other, the one holding the camera, was locked so tight that explosives would be required to open it. Fitch's strategy was simple – if, for some unimaginable reason, the camera attracted attention, then in the ensuing fracas McAdoo would simply switch briefcases and hope for the best.

Detection was extremely remote. The camera made no noise and sent signals no human could hear. The briefcase sat near several others, and it occasionally got itself jostled or even kicked over, but readjustment was easy. McAdoo would simply find a quiet spot and call Fitch. They'd perfected the system during the Cimmino trial last year in Allentown.

The technology was amazing. The tiny lens captured the width and depth of the jury box, and sent all fifteen faces, in color, down the street to Fitch's little viewing room where two jury consultants sat throughout the day and studied every slight twitch and yawn.

Depending on what was happening in the jury box, Fitch would then chat with Durr Cable, and tell him their people in the courtroom had picked up on this and that. Neither Cable nor any of the local defense lawyers would ever know about the camera.

The camera recorded dramatic responses Friday

afternoon. Unfortunately, it was frozen on the jury box. The Japanese had yet to design one that could scan from inside a locked briefcase and focus on other points of interest. So the camera couldn't see the enlarged photos of the shriveled, blackened lungs of Jacob Wood, but the jurors certainly saw them. As Rohr and Dr. Fricke worked through their script, the jurors, without exception, gawked with unrestrained horror at the ghastly wounds slowly inflicted over thirty-five years.

Rohr's timing was perfect. The two photos were mounted on a large tripod in front of the witness stand, and when Dr. Fricke finished his testimony at fifteen minutes after five, it was time to adjourn for the weekend. The last image the jurors had, the one they'd think about for the next two days and the one that would prove to be unshakable, was of the charred lungs, removed from the body and posed on a white sheet.

EIGHT

Easter laid an easy trail to follow throughout the weekend. He left the courtroom Friday, and walked again to O'Reilly's Deli, where he had a quiet conversation with Mr. O'Reilly. They could be seen smiling. Easter purchased a sack full of food and a tall beverage. He then walked straight to his apartment and didn't leave. At eight Saturday morning, he drove to the mall, where he worked a twelve-hour shift selling computers and gadgets. He ate tacos and fried beans in the food garden with a teenager named Kevin, a co-worker. There was no visible communication with any female who remotely resembled the girl they were looking for. He returned to his apartment after work, and didn't leave.

Sunday brought a pleasant surprise. At 8 A.M., he left his apartment and drove to the Biloxi small-craft harbor, where he met none other than Jerry Fernandez. They were last seen leaving the pier in a thirty-foot fishing boat with two others, presumably friends of Jerry's. They returned eight and a half hours later with red faces, a large cooler of some undetermined species of saltwater fish, and a boat full of empty beer cans.

The fishing was the first discernible hobby of Nicholas Easter. And Jerry was the first friend they'd been able to discover.

There was no sign of the girl, not that Fitch really expected to find her. She was proving to be quite patient, and this in itself was maddening. Her first little clue was most assuredly a setup for the second, and the third. The waiting was a torment.

However, Swanson, the ex-FBI agent, was now convinced she would reveal herself to them within the week. Her scheme, whatever it was, was predicated on more contact.

She waited only until Monday morning, thirty minutes before the trial resumed. The lawyers were already in place, plotting in small groups around the courtroom. Judge Harkin was in chambers dealing with an emergency matter in a criminal case. The jurors were gathering in the jury room. Fitch was down the street in his office, in his command bunker. An assistant, a young man named Konrad, who was a whiz with phones, wires, tapes, and high-tech surveillance gadgets, stepped through the open door and said, 'There's a phone call you might want to take.'

Fitch, as always, stared at Konrad and instantly analyzed the situation. All of his phone calls, even from his trusted secretary in Washington, were taken at the front desk and cleared to him by use of an intercom system built into the phones. It worked this way every time.

'Why?' he asked with a great deal of suspicion.

'She says she has another message for you.'

'Her name?'

'She won't say. She's very coy, but she insists it's important.'

Another long pause as Fitch looked at the blinking light on one of the phones. 'Any idea how she got the number?'

'No.'

'Are you tracing it?'

'Yes. Give us a minute. Keep her on the line.'

94

Fitch punched the button and lifted the receiver. 'Yeah,' he said as nicely as possible.

'Is this Mr. Fitch?' she asked, quite pleasantly.

'It is. And who is this?'

'Marlee.'

A name! He paused a second. Every phone call was automatically recorded, so he could analyze it later. 'Good morning, Marlee. And do you have a last name?'

'Yeah. Juror number twelve, Fernandez, will walk into the courtroom in about twenty minutes holding a copy of *Sports Illustrated*. It's the October 12 issue with Dan Marino on the cover.'

'I see,' he said as if he were taking notes. 'Anything else?'

'Nope. Not now.'

'And when might you call again?'

'Don't know.'

'How'd you get the phone number?'

'Easy. Remember, number twelve, Fernandez.' There was a click, and she was gone. Fitch punched another button, then a two-digit code. The entire conversation was replayed on a speaker above the phones.

Konrad raced in with a printout. 'Came from a pay phone in Gulfport, a convenience store.'

'What a surprise,' Fitch said as he grabbed his jacket and began straightening his tie. 'Guess I'll run to court.'

Nicholas waited until most of his colleagues were either sitting at the table or standing nearby, and he waited until there was a lull in the chatter. He said loudly, 'Well, did anyone get bribed or stalked over the weekend?' There were some grins and light laughs but no confessions.

'My vote's not for sale, but it can certainly be rented,' said Jerry Fernandez, repeating a punchline he'd heard from Nicholas on the fishing boat yesterday. This was humorous to everyone but Herman Grimes.

'Why does he keep lecturing us like that?' asked Millie Dupree, obviously delighted someone had broken the ice and anxious to start the gossip. Others moved in closer and leaned forward to hear what the ex-law student thought about it. Rikki Coleman stayed in the corner with a newspaper. She'd already heard this.

'These cases have been tried before,' Nicholas explained reluctantly. 'And there have been some shenanigans with the juries.'

'I don't think we should discuss this,' Herman said.

'Why not? It's harmless. We're not discussing evidence or testimony.' Nicholas was authoritative. Herman was not sure.

'Judge said not to talk about the trial,' he protested, waiting for someone to come to his aid. There were no volunteers. Nicholas had the floor, and said, 'Relax, Herman. This is not about evidence or the things we'll eventually deliberate over. This is about . . .' He hesitated a second for effect, then continued, 'This is about jury tampering.'

Lonnie Shaver lowered his computer printout of grocery inventory and eased closer to the table. Rikki was now listening. Jerry Fernandez had heard it all on the boat yesterday, but it was irresistible.

'There was a tobacco trial, a very similar one in Quitman County, Mississippi, about seven years ago, up in the Delta. Some of you may remember it. It was a different tobacco company, but some of the players are the same, on both sides. And there was some pretty outrageous behavior both before the jury was picked and after the trial started. Judge Harkin, of course, has heard all the stories, and he is watching us very closely. Lots of people are watching us.'

Millie glanced around the table for a second. 'Who?' she asked.

'Both sides.' Nicholas had decided to play it fair, because both sides had been guilty of misconduct in the other trials. 'Both sides hire these guys called jury consultants, and they come in here from all over the country to help pick the perfect jury. The perfect jury, of course, is not one that will be fair, but one that'll deliver the verdict they want. They study us before we're selected. They –'

'How do they do that?' interrupted Mrs. Gladys Card.

'Well, they photograph our homes and apartments, our cars, our neighborhoods, our offices, our kids and their bikes, even ourselves. This is all legal and ethical, but they come close to crossing the line. They check public records, things such as court files and tax rolls, in an effort to get to know us. They might even talk to our friends and co-workers and neighbors. This happens in every big trial nowadays.'

All eleven were listening and staring, inching closer and trying to remember if they'd seen any strangers lurking around corners with cameras. Nicholas took a sip of coffee, then continued: 'After the jury is picked, they change gears a little. The panel has been narrowed from two hundred to fifteen, and so we're much easier to watch. Throughout the trial each side will keep a group of jury consultants in the courtroom, watching us and trying to read our reactions. They usually sit on the first two rows, though they move around a lot.'

'You know who they are?' Millie asked in disbelief.

'I don't know their names, but they're fairly easy to spot. They're well dressed, and they stare at us constantly.'

'I thought those folks were reporters,' said Retired Colonel Frank Herrera, unable to ignore the conversation.

'I hadn't noticed,' said Herman Grimes, and everyone smiled, even Poodle.

'Watch them today,' Nicholas said. 'They usually start off behind their respective counsel. In fact, I have

97

a great idea. There's this one woman whom I'm almost positive is a jury consultant for the defense. She's about forty, heavyset with thick short hair. Every morning so far she's been on the front row behind Durwood Cable. When we go out this morning, let's stare at her. All twelve of us, just glare at her real hard and watch her unravel.'

'Even me?' Herman asked.

'Yes, Herm, even you. Just turn to ten o'clock, and stare with the rest of us.'

'Why are we playing games?' asked Sylvia 'Poodle' Taylor-Tatum.

'Why not? What else have we got to do for the next eight hours?'

'I like it,' said Jerry Fernandez. 'Maybe it'll make 'em stop staring at us.'

'How long do we stare?' asked Millie.

'Let's do it while Judge Harkin is reading us the riot act this morning. That'll take ten minutes.' They more or less agreed with Nicholas.

Lou Dell came for them at exactly nine, and they left the jury room. Nicholas held two magazines – one of which was the October 12 issue of *Sports Illustrated*. He walked beside Jerry Fernandez until they came to the door leading into the courtroom, and as they began to file in he casually turned to his new friend and said, 'Want something to read?'

The magazine was slightly pressing his stomach, so Jerry just as casually took it and said, 'Sure, thanks.' They walked through the door into the courtroom.

Fitch knew Fernandez, number twelve, would have the magazine, but the sight of it was still a jolt. He watched him shuffle along the back row and take his seat. Fitch had seen the cover on a newsstand four blocks from the courthouse, and he knew it was Marino in the aquamarine jersey, number thirteen, arm cocked and ready to drill one.

The surprise quickly gave way to excitement. The girl Marlee was working the outside while someone on the jury was working the inside. Maybe there were two or three or four on the jury who were conspiring with her. Didn't matter to Fitch. The more the better. These people were setting the table, and Fitch was ready to deal.

The jury consultant's name was Ginger, and she worked for Carl Nussman's firm in Chicago. She had sat through dozens of trials. She usually spent half of each day in the courtroom, changing places during recesses, removing her jacket, removing her eyeglasses. She was an old pro at studying juries, and she'd seen it all. She was on the front row behind the defense lawyers; a colleague sat a few feet down scanning a newspaper as the jury settled in.

Ginger looked at the jury and waited for His Honor to greet them, which he did. Most of the jurors nodded and smiled at the Judge, then all of them, every one of them including the blind man, turned and stared directly at her. A couple had smiles, but most seemed rather perturbed about something.

She looked away.

Judge Harkin trudged through his script – one ominous question after another – and he too quickly noticed that his jury was preoccupied with one of the spectators.

They kept staring, in perfect unison.

Nicholas struggled to keep from howling. His luck was incredible. There were about twenty people sitting on the left side of the courtroom, behind the defense lawyers, and two rows behind Ginger sat the hulking figure of Rankin Fitch. From the jury box, Fitch was in the same line of vision as Ginger, and from fifty feet away it was difficult to tell exactly who the jurors were staring at – Ginger or Fitch.

Ginger certainly thought it was her. She found

some notes to study while her colleague scooted farther away.

Fitch felt naked as the twelve faces studied him from the jury box. Small beads of sweat popped through above his eyebrows. The Judge asked more questions. A couple of the lawyers turned awkwardly to look behind them.

'Keep staring,' Nicholas said softly without moving his lips.

Wendall Rohr glanced over his shoulder to see who was sitting out there. Ginger's shoelaces caught her attention. They kept staring.

It was unheard of for a trial judge to ask a jury to pay attention. Harkin had been tempted before, but it was usually a juror who'd become so bored with the testimony that he'd fallen asleep and was snoring. And so he raced through the rest of his tampering questions, then loudly said, 'Thank you, ladies and gentlemen. Now we will continue with Dr. Milton Fricke.'

Ginger suddenly had to visit the ladies' room, and she scurried from the courtroom as Dr. Fricke entered from a side door and resumed his place on the witness stand.

Cable had just a few questions on cross-examination, he said politely, with great deference to Dr. Fricke. He was not about to argue science with a scientist, but he hoped to score a few minor points with the jury. Fricke admitted that not all of the damage to Mr. Wood's lungs could be attributed to smoking Bristols for almost thirty years. Jacob Wood worked in an office for many years with other smokers, and, yes, it's true that some of the destruction of his lungs could have been caused by exposure to other smokers. 'But it's still cigarette smoke,' Dr. Fricke reminded Cable, who readily agreed.

And what about air pollution? Is it possible that breathing dirty air added to the condition of the lungs?

100

Dr. Fricke admitted that this was certainly a possibility.

Cable asked a dangerous question, and he got by with it. 'Dr. Fricke, if you look at all of the possible causes – direct cigarette smoke, indirect cigarette smoke, air pollution, and any others that we've failed to mention – is it possible for you to say how much of the damage to the lungs was caused by smoking Bristols?'

Dr. Fricke concentrated on this for a moment, then said, 'The majority of the damage.'

'How much – sixty percent, eighty percent? Is it possible for a medical scientist such as yourself to give us an approximate percentage?'

It was not possible, and Cable knew it. He had two experts ready for rebuttal in the event Fricke stepped out of bounds and speculated too much.

'I'm afraid I can't do that,' Fricke said.

'Thank you. One final question, Doctor. What percentage of cigarette smokers suffer from lung cancer?'

'Depends on which study you believe.'

'You don't know?'

'I have a good idea.'

'Then answer the question.'

'About ten percent.'

'No further questions.'

'Dr. Fricke, you are excused,' said His Honor. 'Mr. Rohr, please call your next witness.'

'Dr. Robert Bronsky.'

As the witnesses were passing each other in front of the bench, Ginger reentered the courtroom and took a seat on the back row, as far from the jurors as possible. Fitch took advantage of the brief break to leave. He attracted José in the atrium, and they hurried out of the courthouse and back to the dime store.

Bronsky too was a superbly educated medical researcher who had almost as many degrees and published almost as many articles as Fricke. They knew each other well because they worked together at the research center in Rochester. Rohr took great pleasure in walking Bronsky through his marvelous pedigree. Once he was qualified as an expert, they launched into a clinic on the basics:

Tobacco smoke is extremely complex in makeup, with over four thousand compounds identified in its composition. A total of sixteen known carcinogens, fourteen alkalis, and numerous other compounds with known biological activity are included in the four thousand plus compounds. Tobacco smoke is a mixture of gases in tiny droplets, and when a person inhales, about fifty percent of the inhaled smoke is retained in the lungs, and some of the droplets are deposited directly in the walls of the bronchial tubes.

Two lawyers from Rohr's team quickly set up a large tripod in the center of the courtroom, and Dr. Bronsky left the witness stand to lecture a bit. The first chart was a list of all the compounds known to exist in tobacco smoke. He didn't name them all, because he didn't have to. Each of the names looked menacing, and when viewed as a group they looked downright deadly.

The next chart was a list of the known carcinogens, and Bronsky gave each one a brief summary. In addition to these sixteen, he said, tapping his pointing stick in his left hand, there may well be other, yet undetected, carcinogens present in tobacco smoke. And it's quite possible that two or more of these might act in combination to reinforce each other to cause cancer.

They dwelt on the carcinogens for the entire morning. With each new chart, Jerry Fernandez and the other smokers felt sicker and sicker until Sylvia the Poodle was almost light-headed as they left the jury box to eat lunch. Not surprisingly, the four of them first went to the 'smoke hole,' as Lou Dell called it, for a quick one before they joined the rest to eat.

Lunch was waiting and evidently the wrinkles had been ironed out. The table was set with china and the iced tea was poured into real glasses. Mr. O'Reilly served custom-made sandwiches to those who'd ordered them, and he opened large bowls of steaming vegetables and pasta for the others. Nicholas spared no compliment.

Fitch was in the viewing room with two of his jury people when the call came. Konrad nervously knocked on the door. There were strict orders against getting near the room without authorization from Fitch.

'It's Marlee. Line four,' Konrad whispered, and Fitch froze at the news. He then walked quickly to his office door down a makeshift hallway.

'Trace it,' he ordered.

'We are.'

'I'm sure she's at a pay phone.'

Fitch punched button four on his phone, said, 'Hello.'

'Mr. Fitch?' came the familiar voice.

'Yes.'

'Do you know why they were staring at you?'

'No.'

'I'll tell you tomorrow.'

'Tell me now.'

'No. Because you're tracing the call. And if you keep tracing the calls, then I'll stop calling.'

'Okay. I'll stop tracing.'

'And you expect me to believe you?'

'What do you want?'

'Later, Fitch.' She hung up. Fitch replayed the conversation as he waited for her phone to be located. Konrad appeared with the expected news that it was indeed a pay phone, this one in a mall in Gautier, thirty minutes away.

Fitch fell into a large, rented swivel chair and studied

103

the wall for a moment. 'She wasn't in the courtroom this morning,' he said softly, thinking aloud, tugging at the tip of his goatee. 'So how did she know they were staring at me?'

'Who was staring?' asked Konrad. His duties did not include sentry work in the courtroom. He never left the dime store. Fitch explained the curious incident of being stared at by the jury.

'So who's talking to her?' Konrad asked.

'That's the question.'

The afternoon was spent on nicotine. From one-thirty until three, then from three-thirty until adjournment at five, the jurors learned more than they cared to about nicotine: It is a poison contained in tobacco smoke. Each cigarette contains from one to three milligrams of nicotine, and for smokers who inhale, as did Jacob Wood, up to ninety percent of the nicotine is absorbed into the lungs. Dr. Bronsky spent most of his time on his feet, pointing at various parts of the human body displayed in a brightly colored, life-size drawing mounted on the tripod. He explained in great detail how nicotine causes constriction of the superficial vessels in the limbs; it raises the blood pressure; it increases the pulse rate; it makes the heart work harder. Its effects on the digestive tract are insidious and complex. It can cause nausea and vomiting, especially when one begins to smoke. Secretions of saliva and movement of the gut are first stimulated and then depressed. It acts as a stimulant on the central nervous system. Bronsky was methodical yet sincere; he made a single cigarette sound like a dose of lethal poison.

And the worst thing about nicotine is that it's addictive. The last hour – again timed perfectly by Rohr – was spent convincing the jurors that nicotine was wildly addictive, and that this knowledge had been around for at least four decades.

The levels of nicotine can easily be manipulated during the manufacturing process.

If, and Bronsky stressed the word 'if,' the levels of nicotine were artificially increased, then smokers would naturally become addicted much faster. More addicted smokers means more cigarettes sold.

It was a perfect spot to end the day.

NINE

On Tuesday morning, Nicholas arrived at the jury room early, as Lou Dell was brewing the first pot of decaf and carefully arranging the daily platter of fresh rolls and doughnuts. A collection of sparkling new cups and saucers sat near the food. Nicholas claimed to hate coffee from a plastic cup, and fortunately two of his colleagues held similar prejudices. A list of requests had been quickly acceded to by His Honor.

Lou Dell hastily finished her business when he entered the room. He smiled and greeted her pleasantly, but she held a grudge from their earlier skirmishes. He poured coffee and opened a newspaper.

As Nicholas expected, Retired Colonel Frank Herrera arrived shortly after eight, almost a full hour before they were due, clutching two newspapers, one *The Wall Street Journal.* He wanted the room to himself, but managed a smile at Easter.

'Mornin', Colonel,' Nicholas said warmly. 'You're here early.'

'So are you.'

'Yeah, I couldn't sleep. Found myself dreaming of nicotine and black lungs.' Nicholas studied the sports page.

Herrera stirred his coffee and sat down across the table. 'I smoked for ten years in the Army,' he said, sitting stiffly, shoulders square, chin up, always ready to bolt to attention. 'But I had the good sense to quit.'

'Some people can't, I guess. Like Jacob Wood.'

The Colonel grunted with disgust, and opened a newspaper. For him, the kicking of a bad habit was nothing but a simple act of willpower. Get the head straight, and the body can do anything.

Nicholas turned a page, said, 'Why'd you quit?'

'Because it's bad for you. Doesn't take a genius, you know. Cigarettes are deadly. Everybody knows that.'

If Herrera had been so blunt on at least two of the pretrial questionnaires, he wouldn't be sitting where he was now. Nicholas remembered the questions well. The fact that Herrera felt so strongly probably meant only one thing: He wanted to be on the jury. He was retired military, probably bored with golf, tired of his wife, looking for something to do, and obviously carrying a grudge about something.

'So you think cigarettes should be outlawed?' Nicholas asked. The question was one he'd posed to the mirror a thousand times, and he had all the right comebacks to all the possible answers.

Herrera slowly placed the newspaper on the table and took a long drink of black coffee. 'No. I think people should have more sense than to smoke three packs a day for almost thirty years. What the hell do you expect? Perfect health?' His tone was sarcastic, and left no doubt that he'd walked into jury service with his mind made up.

'When did you become convinced of this?'

'Are you dense? It ain't that hard to figure out.'

'Maybe that's your opinion. But you certainly should've expressed yourself during voir dire.'

'What's voir dire?'

'The jury selection process. We were asked questions covering these very matters. I don't recall you saying a word.'

107

'Never felt like it.'

'You should have.'

Herrera's cheeks flushed red, but he hesitated for a second. This guy Easter after all knew the law, or at least knew more than the rest of them. Maybe he had done something wrong. Maybe there was a way Easter could report him and get him bumped from the jury. Maybe he would be held in contempt, sent to jail, or fined.

And then another thought hit him. They weren't supposed to be discussing the case, right? So how could Easter report anything to the Judge? Seemed like Easter would risk getting in trouble himself if he went and repeated anything he heard in the jury room. Herrera relaxed a bit. 'Lemme guess. You're gonna push hard for a big verdict, lots of punitives and stuff like that.'

'No, Mr. Herrera. Unlike you, I haven't made up my mind. I think we've listened to three witnesses, all for the plaintiff, so there are many yet to come. I think I'll wait until all the evidence is in, from both sides, then I'll try to sort things out. I thought that's what we promised to do.'

'Yeah, well, me too. I can be persuaded, you know.' He suddenly had an interest in the editorials. The door burst open, and Mr. Herman Grimes entered with his walking stick tapping away in front of him. Lou Dell and Mrs. Grimes followed. Nicholas, as usual, rose to prepare his foreman's coffee, a ritual now.

Fitch stared at his phones until nine. She'd mentioned a possible call today.

Not only did she play games, but evidently she was not above lying. He had no desire to be stared at again, so he locked his door and walked to the viewing room where two of his jury experts were sitting in the dark, staring at a crooked scene on the wall, waiting for the courtroom adjustment. Someone had kicked McAdoo's briefcase, and the camera was off by ten feet. Jurors one, two, seven, and eight were out of the picture, and only half of Millie Dupree and Rikki Coleman behind her were visible.

The jury had been seated for two minutes, and so McAdoo was pinned to his seat and couldn't use his cellphone. He didn't know some bigfoot under the table had kicked the wrong briefcase. Fitch swore at the screen, then returned to his office where he scribbled a note. He gave it to a well-dressed errand boy, who dashed up the street, entered the courtroom like one of a hundred young associates or paralegals, and slipped the note to the defense table.

The camera inched to the left, and the full jury came into view. McAdoo pushed a bit too hard and cut off half of Jerry Fernandez and Angel Weese, juror number six. Fitch cursed again. He'd wait until the morning recess and get McAdoo on the phone.

Dr. Bronsky was rested and ready for another day of thoughtful discourse on the ravages of tobacco smoke. Having discussed the carcinogens in tobacco smoke, and the nicotine, he was ready to move to the next compounds of medical interest: irritants.

Rohr served up the fat pitches, Bronsky swung from the heels. Tobacco smoke contains a variety of compounds – ammonia, volatile acids, aldehydes, phenols, and ketones – and these have an irritant effect on the mucous membrane. Bronsky once again left the witness stand and walked to a fresh cutaway diagram of the upper torso and head of a human. This showed the jury the respiratory tract, the throat, the bronchial tubes, and the lungs. In this area of the body, tobacco smoke stimulates secretion of mucus. At the same time, it delays the removal of the mucus by retarding the action of the ciliated lining of the bronchial tubes. Bronsky had been remarkably adept at keeping the

109

medical jargon on a level reachable by the average layman, and he slowed a notch to explain what happens to the bronchial tubes when smoke is inhaled. Two other large, colorful diagrams were mounted in front of the bench, and Bronsky went to work with his pointer. He explained to the jury that the bronchial tubes are lined with a membrane equipped with fine, hairlike fibers called cilia, which move together in waves and control the movement of the mucus on the surface of the membrane. This movement of the cilia acts to free the lungs from virtually all the dust and germs that are inhaled.

Smoking, of course, wreaks havoc with this process. Once Bronsky and Rohr were as certain as they could be that the jurors understood how things were supposed to work, they quickly moved forward to explain just precisely how smoking irritated the filtering process and caused all sorts of damage in the respiratory system.

They went on about mucus and membranes and cilia.

The first visible yawn came from Jerry Fernandez in the back row. He'd spent his Monday night at one of the casinos watching the football game and drinking more than he'd planned. He smoked two packs a day, and he was well aware that the habit was unhealthy. Still, he needed one now.

More yawns followed, and at eleven-thirty, Judge Harkin sent them out for a badly needed two-hour lunch.

The stroll through downtown Biloxi had been Nicholas' idea, one he'd put in a letter to the Judge on Monday. It seemed absurd to keep them confined to a small room all day with no hope of fresh air. It wasn't as if their lives were in jeopardy, or that they'd be assailed by unknown conspirators if let loose on the sidewalks. Just simply put Madam Lou Dell and Willis the guard with another lethargic deputy, give them a route, say, six or eight city blocks, forbid the jurors from

110

speaking to anyone, as usual, and, well, turn them loose for thirty minutes after lunch so the food could settle. It seemed like a harmless idea, and in fact upon further reflection Judge Harkin embraced it as his own.

Nicholas, however, had shown the letter to Lou Dell, and so when lunch was being finished, she was explaining that a walk was planned, thanks to Mr. Easter, who had written the Judge. It seemed such a humble idea to receive such unbridled admiration.

The temperature was in the low eighties, the air clear and fresh, the trees trying their best to turn colors. Lou Dell and Willis led the way while the four smokers – Fernandez, Poodle, Stella Hulic, and Angel Weese – hung at the back thoroughly enjoying the deep inhaling and long exhaling. To hell with Bronsky and his mucus and his membranes, and to hell with Fricke and his gross pictures of Mr. Wood's sticky black lungs. They were outdoors now. The light, salt air, and conditions were perfect for a smoke.

Fitch sent Doyle and a local operative named Joe Boy to take pictures from a distance.

Bronsky wore thin as the afternoon progressed. He lost his talent for keeping things simple, and the jurors lost their struggle to stay tuned. The fancy and obviously expensive charts and diagrams ran together, as did the body parts and compounds and poisons. The opinions of superbly trained and hideously expensive jury consultants were not needed to know that the jurors were bored, that Rohr was engaging in a practice lawyers simply can't avoid – overkill.

His Honor adjourned early, at four, his reason being that two hours were needed to hear some motions and other things not involving the jury. He discharged the jurors with the same dire warnings, admonitions they now had memorized and barely heard. They were delighted to escape.

111

Lonnie Shaver was particularly thrilled to leave early. He drove straight to his supermarket, ten minutes away, parked in his special place in the rear, and made a quick entrance through the stockroom, secretly hoping to catch a wayward stacker napping by the lettuce. His office was upstairs above the dairy and meats, and from behind a two-way mirror he could see most of the floor.

Lonnie was the only black manager in a chain of seventeen stores. He earned forty thousand dollars a year, with health insurance and an average pension plan, and was due for a raise in three months. He'd also been led to believe he'd be promoted to the level of a district supervisor, assuming his tenure as manager produced satisfactory results. The company was anxious to promote a black, he'd been told, but, of course, none of these commitments were in writing.

His office was always open, and usually occupied with any one of a half-dozen subordinates. An assistant manager greeted him, then nodded toward a door. 'We have guests,' he said, with a frown.

Lonnie hesitated and looked at the closed door, which led to a large room used for everything – birthday parties, staff meetings, visits from bosses. 'Who is it?' he asked.

'Home office. They want to see you.'

Lonnie rapped on the door, entering as he knocked. It was, after all, his office. Three men with their sleeves rolled up to their elbows sat at the end of the table, amid a pile of papers and printouts. They stood awkwardly.

'Lonnie, good to see you,' said Troy Hadley, son of one of the owners, and the only face Lonnie recognized. They shook hands as Hadley made hasty introductions. The other two men were Ken and Ben; Lonnie wouldn't remember their last names until later. It had been planned that Lonnie would sit at the end of the table, in the chair eagerly vacated by the young Hadley,

112

with Ken on one side and Ben on the other.

Troy started the conversation, and he sounded somewhat nervous. 'How's jury duty?'

'A pain.'

'Right. Look, Lonnie, the reason we're here is that Ken and Ben are from an outfit called SuperHouse, a large chain out of Charlotte, and, well, for lots of reasons, my dad and my uncle have decided to sell out to SuperHouse. The whole chain. All seventeen stores and the three warehouses.'

Lonnie noticed that Ken and Ben were watching him breathe, so he took the news with a straight face, even offered a very slight shrug, as if to say, 'So what?' He was, however, finding it hard to swallow. 'Why?' he managed to ask.

'Lots of reasons, but I'll give you the top two. My dad is sixty-eight, and Al, as you know, just had surgery. That's number one. Number two is the fact that SuperHouse is offering a very fair price.' He rubbed his hands together as if he couldn't wait to spend the new money. 'It's just time to sell, Lonnie, pure and simple.'

'I'm surprised, I never –'

'You're right. Forty years in the business, from a mom-and-pop fruit stand to a company in five states with sixty million in sales last year. Hard to believe they're throwing in the towel.' Troy was not the least bit convincing in his effort at sentiment. Lonnie knew why. He was a witless dunce, a rich kid who played golf every day while trying to project the image of a hard-charging, ass-kicking corporate honcho. His father and his uncle were selling now because in a few short years Troy would take the reins and forty years of toil and prudence would get spent on racing boats and beach property.

There was a pause as Ben and Ken continued staring at Lonnie. One was in his mid-forties with a bad haircut and a pocket liner stuffed with cheap ballpoints. Maybe

113

he was Ben. The other was a little younger, a slim-faced, executive type with better clothes and hard eyes. Lonnie looked at them, and it was obvious it was his turn to say something.

'Will this store be closed?' he asked, almost in defeat.

Troy jumped at the question. 'In other words, what happens to you? Well, let me assure you, Lonnie, that I've said all the right things about you, all the truth, and I've recommended that you be kept here in the same position.' Either Ben or Ken nodded very slightly. Troy was reaching for his coat. 'But that's not my business anymore. I'm gonna step outside for a bit while you guys talk things over.' Like a flash, Troy was out of the room.

For some reason his departure brought smiles to Ken and Ben. Lonnie asked, 'Do you guys have business cards?'

'Sure,' both said, and they pulled cards from pockets and slid them to the end of the table. Ben was the older, Ken the younger.

Ken was also in charge of this meeting. He began, 'Just a bit about our company. We're out of Charlotte, with eighty stores in the Carolinas and Georgia. Super-House is a division of Listing Foods, a conglomerate based in Scarsdale with about two billion in sales last year. A public company, traded on NASDAQ. You've probably heard of it. I'm Vice President for Operations for SuperHouse, Ben here is regional VP. We're expanding south and west, and Hadley Brothers looked attractive. That's why we're here.'

'So you're keeping the store?'

'Yes, for now, anyway.' He glanced at Ben, as if there was a lot more to the answer.

'And what about me?' Lonnie asked.

They actually squirmed, almost in tandem, and Ben removed a ballpoint from his collection. Ken did the talking. 'Well, you have to understand, Mr. Shaver –'

114

'Please call me Lonnie.'

'Sure, Lonnie, there are always shakeups along the line when acquisitions occur. Just part of the business. Jobs are lost, jobs are created, jobs are transferred.'

'What about my job?' Lonnie pressed. He sensed the worst and was anxious to get it over with.

Ken deliberately picked up a sheet of paper and gave the appearance of reading something. 'Well,' he said, ruffling the paper, 'you have a solid file.'

'And very strong recommendations,' Ben added helpfully.

'We would like to keep you in place, for now anyway.'

'For now? What does that mean?'

Ken slowly returned the paper to the table, and leaned forward on both elbows. 'Let's be perfectly candid, Lonnie. We see a future for you with our company.'

'And it's a much better company than the one you're with now,' Ben added, the tag-team working to perfection. 'We offer higher salaries, better benefits, stock options, the works.'

'Lonnie, Ben and I are ashamed to admit that our company does not have an African-American in a management position. We, along with our bosses, would like for this to change, immediately. We want it to change with you.'

Lonnie studied their faces, and suppressed a thousand questions. In the span of a minute, he'd gone from the brink of unemployment to the prospect of advancement. 'I don't have a college degree. There's a limit to –'

'There are no limits,' Ken said. 'You have two years of junior college, and, if necessary, you can finish your studies. Our company will cover the cost of college.'

Lonnie had to smile, as much from relief as from good fortune. He decided to proceed cautiously. He was dealing with strangers. 'I'm listening,' he said.

115

Ken had all the answers. 'We've studied the personnel at Hadley Brothers, and, well, let's say most of the upper- and mid-management people will soon be looking for work elsewhere. We spotted you, and another young manager from Mobile. We'd like for both of you to come to Charlotte as soon as possible and spend a few days with us. You'll meet our people, learn about our company, and we'll talk about the future. I must warn you, though, you can't spend the rest of your life here in Biloxi if you want to advance. You must be willing to move around.'

'I'm willing.'

'We thought so. When can we fly you up?'

The image of Lou Dell closing the door on them flashed before his eyes, and he frowned. He breathed deeply, and said with great frustration, 'Well, I'm tied up in court right now. Jury duty. I'm sure Troy told you.'

Ken and Ben appeared to be confused by this. 'It's just a couple of days, isn't it?'

'No. The trial's scheduled for a month, and we're in week two.'

'A month?' Ben asked, on cue. 'What kind of trial is it?'

'The widow of a dead smoker is suing a tobacco company.'

Their reactions were almost identical and left no doubt how they personally felt about such lawsuits.

'I tried to get out of it,' Lonnie said in an effort to smooth things.

'A product liability suit?' Ken asked, thoroughly disgusted.

'Yeah, something like that.'

'For another three weeks?' Ben asked.

'That's what they say. I can't believe I got stuck,' he said, his words trailing away.

There was a long pause in which Ben opened a fresh

pack of Bristols and lit one. 'Lawsuits,' he said bitterly. 'We get sued every week by some poor clod who trips and falls and then blames it on the vinegar or the grapes. Last month a bottle of carbonated water exploded at a private party in Rocky Mount. Guess who sold 'em the water? Guess who got sued last week for ten million? Us and the bottler. Product liability.' A long puff, then a quick chew on a thumbnail. Ben was steaming. 'Gotta seventy-year-old woman in Athens claiming she wrenched her back when she allegedly reached up high to get a can of furniture polish. Her lawyer says she's entitled to a coupla mill.'

Ken stared at Ben as if he wanted him to shut up, but Ben evidently exploded easily when the topic was broached. 'Stinkin' lawyers,' he said, smoke pouring from his nostrils. 'We paid over three million last year for liability insurance, money just thrown away because of all the hungry lawyers circling above.'

Ken said, 'That's enough.'

'Sorry.'

'What about the weekends?' Lonnie asked anxiously. 'I'm free from Friday afternoon until late Sunday.'

'I was just thinking of that. Tell you what we'll do. We'll send one of our planes to get you Saturday morning. We'll fly you and your wife to Charlotte, give you the grand tour of the home office, and we'll introduce you to our bosses. Most of these guys work Saturdays anyway. Can you do it this weekend?'

'Sure.'

'Done. I'll arrange the plane.'

'You sure there's no conflict with the trial?' Ben asked.

'None that I can foresee.'

TEN

After moving along with impressive punctuality, the trial hit a snag on Wednesday morning. The defense filed a motion to prohibit the testimony of Dr. Hilo Kilvan, an alleged expert from Montreal in the field of statistical summaries of lung cancer, and a small battle erupted over the motion. Wendall Rohr and his team were particularly enraged at the defense tactic; the defense so far had tried to bar the testimony of every plaintiff's expert. Indeed, the defense had proved quite effective at delaying and attempting to bar everything for four years. Rohr insisted that Cable and his client were once again stalling, and he made an angry plea to Judge Harkin for the imposition of sanctions against the defense. The war over sanctions, with each side demanding monetary penalties from the other and the Judge so far denying same, had been raging almost since the initial suit was filed. As with most large civil cases, the subplot of sanctions often consumed as much time as the real issues.

Rohr ranted and stomped in front of the empty jury box as he explained that this latest motion by the defense was the seventy-first – 'count 'em, seventy-one!' – to be filed by the tobacco company seeking to exclude evidence. 'We've had motions to exclude evidence of other diseases caused by smoking, motions to prevent evidence of warnings, motions to prevent evidence of

118

advertising, motions to exclude evidence of epidemiological studies and statistical theories, motions to preclude reference to patents not used by the defendant, motions to exclude evidence of subsequent or remedial measures taken by the tobacco company, motions to preclude our evidence of the testing of cigarettes, motions to strike portions of the autopsy report, motions to exclude addiction evidence, motions –'

'I've seen these motions, Mr. Rohr,' His Honor interrupted when it appeared as if Rohr might name them all.

Rohr hardly missed a beat. 'And, Your Honor, in addition to the seventy-one – count 'em, seventy-one! – motions to exclude evidence, they've filed exactly eighteen motions for continuances.'

'I'm very much aware of this, Mr. Rohr. Please move along.'

Rohr walked to his cluttered table and was handed a thick brief by an associate. 'And, of course, each defense filing is accompanied by one of these damned things,' he said loudly as he dropped the brief onto the table. 'We don't have time to read these, as you know, because we're too busy preparing for trial. They, on the other hand, have a thousand lawyers billing by the hour and working even as we speak on another harebrained motion, which will, no doubt, weigh six pounds and doubtless take up more of our time.'

'Can we get to the merits, Mr. Rohr?'

Rohr didn't hear him. 'Since we don't have time to read these, Your Honor, we simply weigh them, and so our rather brief answer goes something like this: "Please allow this letter memorandum to serve as our response to the defendant's four-and-a-half-pound, typically overdone brief in support of its latest frivolous motion."'

With the jury out of the courtroom, smiles and manners and pleasant behavior were forgotten by

119

everyone. The strain was evident on the faces of all the players. Even the clerks and the court reporter looked edgy.

Rohr's legendary temper was boiling, but he had long since learned to use it to his advantage. His occasional friend Cable kept his distance without holding his tongue. The spectators were treated to a loosely controlled brawl.

At nine-thirty, His Honor sent word to Lou Dell to inform the jurors that he was finishing up a motion, and the trial would start in a few moments, hopefully by ten. Since this was the first delay in which the jurors were told to wait after being set to go, they took it well. The little groups reconvened themselves, and the idle chitchat of folks waiting against their wishes continued. The divisions were along the lines of sex, not race. The men tended to group together at one end of the room, the women at the other. The smokers came and went. Only Herman Grimes kept the same position, at the head of the table, where he played hunt-and-peck with a laptop braille computer. He had let it be known that he was up until all hours of the morning plowing through the narrative descriptions of Bronsky's diagrams.

The other laptop was plugged into a socket in a corner where Lonnie Shaver had established a make-shift office with three folding chairs. He analyzed print-outs of grocery stock, studied inventories, checked a hundred other details, and was generally content to be ignored. He was not unfriendly, just preoccupied.

Frank Herrera sat near the braille computer, poring over the closing quotations in *The Wall Street Journal,* and occasionally chatting with Jerry Fernandez, who sat across the table grappling with the latest Vegas line on Saturday's college games. The only male who enjoyed talking to the women was Nicholas Easter, and on this day he was quietly discussing the case with Loreen

Duke, a large jovial black lady who worked as a secretary at Keesler Air Force Base. As juror number one, she sat next to Nicholas, and the two had developed a habit of whispering during the trial, at the expense of almost everybody. Loreen was thirty-five with no husband and two kids, and a nice federal job which she missed not in the least. She had confessed to Nicholas that she could be absent from the office for a year and no one would care. He told her wild stories of bad deeds by the tobacco companies in trials past, and he confessed to her that he had studied tobacco litigation at great length during his two years of law school. Said he dropped out due to financial reasons. Their low voices were carefully gauged to land just outside the ear-range of Herman Grimes, who at the moment was slapping his laptop.

Time passed and at ten Nicholas went to the door and jolted Lou Dell from her paperback. She had no idea when the Judge might send for them, and there was simply nothing she could do.

Nicholas took a seat at the table and began discussing strategy with Herman. It was not fair to keep them locked up during delays such as this, and Nicholas was of the opinion that they should be allowed to leave the building, with escorts, and engage in morning walks, as opposed to those of the noontime variety. It was agreed that Nicholas should put this request in writing, as usual, and present it to Judge Harkin during the noon recess.

At ten-thirty, they finally walked into the courtroom, the air still heavy with the heat of battle, and the first person Nicholas saw was the man who'd broken into his apartment. He was out there on the third row, plaintiff's side, in a shirt and tie with a newspaper spread before him and resting on the back of the pew in front. He was alone, and he barely looked at the jurors

121

as they took their seats. Nicholas didn't stare; two long glances and the identification was complete.

For all of his guile and cunning, Fitch could do some stupid things. And sending this goon into the courtroom was a risky move with little potential benefit. What was he supposed to see or hear that would not be seen or heard by one of the dozen lawyers, or half-dozen jury consultants, or handful of other flunkies Fitch kept in the courtroom?

Though he was surprised to see the man, Nicholas had already thought about what to do. He had several plans, depending upon where the man surfaced. The courtroom was a surprise, but it took only a minute to sort through things. It was imperative for Judge Harkin to know that one of the thugs he'd been so overly concerned about was now sitting in the courtroom pretending to be just another casual observer. Harkin needed to see the face, because later he would see it on video.

The first witness was Dr. Bronsky, now in his third day but his first on cross-examination by the defense. Sir Durr started slowly, politely, as if in awe of this great expert, and asked a few questions that most of the jurors could have answered. Things changed rapidly. Whereas Cable had been deferential to Dr. Milton Fricke, he was ready to battle Bronsky.

He started with the over four thousand compounds identified in tobacco smoke, picked one seemingly at random, and asked what effect benzol(a)pyrene would have on the lungs. Bronsky said he didn't know, and tried to explain that the damage inflicted by a single compound was impossible to measure. What about the bronchial tubes and the membranes and the cilia? What did benzol(a)pyrene do to them? Bronsky again tried to explain that research could not determine the effect of a single compound in tobacco smoke.

Cable hammered away. He picked another

122

compound and forced Bronsky to admit that he couldn't tell the jury what it would do to lungs or bronchial tubes or membranes. Not specifically, anyway.

Rohr objected, but His Honor overruled on the grounds that it was a cross-examination. Virtually anything relevant or even semirelevant could be thrown at the witness.

Doyle stayed in place, out there on the third row, looking bored and waiting for a chance to leave. His assigned duty was to look for the girl, something he'd been doing for four days now. He'd loitered in the hallway below for hours. He'd spent one full afternoon sitting on a Dr. Pepper crate near the vending machines, chatting with a janitor while watching the front door. He'd consumed gallons of coffee in the small cafés and delis nearby. He and Pang and two others had been hard at work, wasting their time but satisfying their boss.

After four days of sitting in one place for six hours a day, Nicholas had a sense of Fitch's routine. His people, whether the jury consultants or run-of-the-mill operatives, moved around. They used the entire courtroom. They sat in groups and they sat alone. They came and went silently when there were short breaks in the action. They rarely spoke to one another. They would pay strict attention to the witnesses and the jurors, and the next minute they would work crosswords and stare at the windows.

He knew the man would be gone before long.

He scribbled a note, folded it, and convinced Loreen Duke to hold it without reading it. He then convinced her to lean forward, during a pause in the cross-examination when Cable was consulting his notes, and hand it to Willis the deputy, who was standing against the wall guarding the flag. Willis, suddenly awakened, paused a second to collect himself, then realized he was supposed to hand the note to the Judge.

Doyle saw Loreen hand the note over, but he didn't see it originate from Nicholas.

Judge Harkin gathered the note while barely acknowledging it, and slid it across the bench close to his robe as Cable fired another question. Harkin slowly unfolded it. It was from Nicholas Easter, number two, and it said:

Judge:
That man out there, left side, third row from front, on the aisle, white shirt, blue and green tie, was following me yesterday. It was the second time I've seen him. Can we find out who he is?
Nicholas Easter

His Honor looked at Durr Cable before he looked at the spectators. The man was sitting alone, staring back at the bench as if he knew someone was watching.

This was a new challenge for Frederick Harkin. In fact, at the moment he couldn't recall an incident even remotely similar. His options were limited, and the more he pondered the situation the fewer choices he had. He, too, knew both sides had plenty of consultants and associates and operatives lurking either in the courtroom or very nearby. He watched his courtroom closely, and he noticed a lot of quiet movement by people who had experience in such trials and didn't want to be noticed. He knew the man was likely to disappear in an instant.

If Harkin suddenly called a short recess, the man would probably vanish.

This was a terribly exciting moment for the Judge. After all the tales and rumors and lore from other trials, and after all the seemingly empty admonitions to the jury, there in the courtroom at this very moment was one of the mystery agents, a sleuth hired by one side or the other to monitor his jurors.

124

Courtroom deputies, as a general rule, are uniformed and armed and normally quite harmless. The younger men are kept on the streets to battle the elements, and trial duty tends to attract the seniors bearing down hard on retirement. Judge Harkin glanced about and his options shrank again.

There was Willis, leaning against the wall near the flag, and it appeared he had already lapsed into his usual state of semi-slumber with his mouth open partially at the right corner and saliva dripping. Down the aisle, directly in front of Harkin but at least a hundred feet away, Jip and Rasco guarded the main door. Jip, at the moment, was sitting on the back bench, near the door, with his reading glasses perched on the end of his beefy nose, scanning the local paper. He'd had hip surgery two months earlier, found it difficult to stand for long periods, and had received permission to sit during the proceedings. Rasco was in his late fifties, the youngest of the crew, and was not known for his quick movements. A younger deputy was usually assigned to the main door, but at the moment he was on the atrium side manning the metal detector.

During voir dire, Harkin had requested uniforms everywhere, but after a week of testimony the initial excitement had disappeared. It was now just another tedious civil trial, though one with enormous stakes.

Harkin took the measure of the available troops, and decided against approaching the target. He quickly scribbled a note, held it for a moment while ignoring the man, then slid it to Gloria Lane, the Circuit Clerk, who was at her small desk below the bench, opposite the witness stand. The note indicated the man, instructed Gloria to get a good look at him without being obvious, then to ease away through a side door and go fetch the Sheriff. There were other instructions to the Sheriff, but, unfortunately, they were never needed.

After more than an hour of watching the merciless cross-examination of Dr. Bronsky, Doyle was ready to move. The girl was nowhere in sight; not that he'd expected to find her. He was just following orders. Plus, he didn't like the note-passing around the bench. He quietly gathered his newspaper, and slipped unchallenged from the courtroom. Harkin watched in disbelief. He even grabbed his mounted microphone with his right hand as if he might yell at the man to stop, sit down, and answer some questions. But he kept his cool. Chances were the man would return.

Nicholas looked at His Honor and both men were frustrated. Cable paused between questions, and the Judge suddenly rapped his gavel. 'Ten-minute recess. I think the jurors need a short break.'

Willis relayed the message to Lou Dell, who stuck her head through a crack in the door and said, 'Mr. Easter, could I see you for a minute?'

Nicholas followed Willis through a maze of narrow hallways until they came to the side door of Harkin's chambers. The Judge was alone, robe off, coffee in hand. He excused Willis and locked the door. 'Please sit down, Mr. Easter,' he said, waving at a chair across from his cluttered desk. The room was not his permanent office, in fact he shared it with two other judges who used the courtroom. 'Coffee?'

'No thanks.'

Harkin dropped into his chair and leaned forward on his elbows. 'Now, tell me, where did you see this man?'

Nicholas would save the video for a more crucial moment. He'd already carefully planned the next tale. 'Yesterday, after we adjourned, I was walking back to my apartment when I stopped to get an ice cream at Mike's, around the corner. I walked in the place, then looked out, back on to the sidewalk, and I saw this guy

126

peeking in. He didn't see me, but I realized I'd seen him somewhere before. I got the ice cream, and began walking home. I thought the guy was following me, so I doubled back and took odd turns, and sure enough, I caught him tracking me.'

'And you've seen him before?'

'Yes sir. I work at a computer store in the mall, and one night this guy, same guy I'm sure, kept walking by the door and looking in. Later, I took a break and he showed up at the other end of the mall where I was drinking a Coke.'

The Judge relaxed a bit and adjusted his hair. 'Be honest with me, Mr. Easter, have any of your colleagues mentioned anything like this?'

'No sir.'

'Will you tell me if they do?'

'Certainly.'

'There's nothing wrong with this little chat we're having, and if something happens in there, I need to know it.'

'How do I contact you?'

'Just send a note through Lou Dell. Just say we need to talk without giving specifics because God knows she'll read it.'

'Okay.'

'Is it a deal?'

'Sure.'

Harkin took a deep breath and began fishing through an open briefcase. He found a newspaper and slid it across the desk. 'Have you seen this? It's today's *Wall Street Journal*.'

'No. I don't read it.'

'Good. There's a big story about this trial and the potential impact a plaintiff's verdict might have on the tobacco industry.'

Nicholas couldn't allow the opportunity to pass. 'There's only one person who reads the *Journal*.'

'Who's that?'

'Frank Herrera. He reads it every morning, cover to cover.'

'This morning?'

'Yes. While we were waiting, he read every word twice.'

'Did he comment on anything?'

'Not to my knowledge.'

'Damn.'

'Doesn't matter, though,' Nicholas said, looking at a wall.

'Why not?'

'His mind's made up.'

Harkin leaned forward again and squinted hard. 'What do you mean?'

'He should never have been picked for jury service, in my opinion. I don't know how he answered the written questions, but he didn't tell the truth or else he wouldn't be here. And I distinctly remember questions during voir dire that he should've responded to.'

'I'm listening.'

'Okay, Your Honor, but don't get mad. I had a conversation with him early yesterday morning. We were the only ones in the jury room, and, I swear, we weren't discussing this case in particular. But somehow we got around to cigarettes, and Frank quit smoking years ago and he has no sympathy for anybody who can't quit. He's retired military, you know, rather stiff and hard about –'

'I'm an ex-Marine.'

'Sorry. Shall I shut up?'

'No. Keep going.'

'Okay, but I'm nervous about this and I'll be happy to stop at any time.'

'I'll tell you when to stop.'

'Sure, well anyway, Frank's of the opinion that anyone who smokes three packs a day for almost thirty years deserves what he gets. No sympathy whatsoever. I argued with him a little, just for the sake of it, and he accused me of wanting to give the plaintiff a huge punitive award.'

His Honor took it hard, sinking in his chair a bit, closing then rubbing his eyes as his shoulders sagged. 'This is just great,' he mumbled.

'Sorry, Judge.'

'No, no, I asked for it.' He sat straight again, made another adjustment to his hair with his fingers, forced a smile, said, 'Look, Mr. Easter. I'm not asking you to become a snitch. But I'm concerned about this jury because of pressures from the outside. This type of litigation has a sordid history. If you see or hear anything even remotely related to unauthorized contact, please let me know. We'll deal with it then.'

'Sure, Judge.'

The story, on the front page of the *Journal,* had been written by Agner Layson, a senior reporter who'd sat through most of jury selection and all of the testimony. Layson had practiced law for ten years and had been in many courtrooms. His story, the first of a series, gave the basics of the issues and the specifics on the players. There was no opinion of how the trial was progressing, no guess as to who was winning or losing, just a fair summary of the rather convincing medical proof offered so far by the plaintiff.

In response to the story, Pynex' stock dipped a dollar at the opening bell, but by noon had found itself sufficiently corrected and adjusted and was deemed to be weathering the brief storm.

The story prompted a flood of phone calls from brokerage houses in New York to their analysts on the ground in Biloxi. Minutes of meaningless gossip accumulated into hours of hopeless speculation as the harried souls in New York quizzed and inquired and pondered about the only question that mattered: 'What's the jury gonna do?'

The young men and women assigned to monitor the trial and predict what the jury might do had no collective clue.

ELEVEN

The cross-examination of Bronsky ended late Thursday afternoon and Marlee struck with a fury Friday morning. Konrad took the first call at seven twenty-five, routed it quickly to Fitch, who was on the phone to Washington, then listened as it played on the speakerphone: 'Good morning, Fitch,' she said sweetly.

'Good morning, Marlee,' Fitch answered with a happy voice, his best effort at pleasantness. 'And how are you?'

'Fabulous. Number two, Easter, will wear a light blue denim shirt, faded jeans, white socks, old running shoes, Nikes, I think. And he'll bring with him a copy of *Rolling Stone,* October issue, Meat Loaf on the cover. Got that?'

'Yes. When can we get together and talk?'

'When I get ready. Adios.' She hung up. The call was traced to the lobby of a motel in Hattiesburg, Mississippi, at least ninety minutes away by car.

Pang was sitting in a coffee shop three blocks from Easter's apartment, and within minutes he was loitering under a shade tree fifty yards from the ancient VW Beetle. On schedule, Easter exited through the front entranceway at seven forty-five, and began his customary twenty-minute walk to the courthouse. He stopped at the same corner grocery for the same newspapers and the same coffee.

131

Of course, he was wearing exactly what she'd promised.

Her second call also came from Hattiesburg, though from a different number. 'Got a new wrinkle for you, Fitch. And you're gonna love it.'

Fitch, barely breathing, said, 'I'm listening.'

'When the jurors come out today, instead of sitting, guess what they're gonna do?'

Fitch's brain froze. He couldn't move his lips. He knew he wasn't expected to make an intelligent guess. 'I give up,' he said.

'They're gonna do the Pledge of Allegiance.'

Fitch shot Konrad a bewildered look.

'Got that, Fitch?' she asked, almost mocking.

'Yeah.'

Her line went dead.

Her third call went to the law offices of Wendall Rohr, who, according to a secretary, was quite busy and unavailable. Marlee understood perfectly well, but explained that she had an important message for Mr. Rohr. The message would arrive in about five minutes on the fax machine, so would the secretary be so kind as to receive it and take it straight to Mr. Rohr before he left for court. The secretary reluctantly agreed, and five minutes later found a plain sheet of paper lying alone in the receiving tray of the fax. There was no transmitting number, no indication of from where or from whom the fax came. In typed, single-spaced words in the center of the page, the message read:

WR: Juror number 2, Easter, will today wear a blue denim shirt, faded jeans, white sox, old Nikes. He likes *Rolling Stone* and he will prove to be quite patriotic.

MM

The secretary rushed it to Rohr's office where he was packing a bulky briefcase for the day's battle. Rohr read it, quizzed the secretary, then called in his co-counsel for an emergency session.

The mood couldn't quite be classified as festive, especially for twelve people being held against their will, but it was Friday and the chatter was noticeably lighter as they gathered and greeted one another. Nicholas held a seat at the table, near Herman Grimes and across from Frank Herrera, and he waited for what he thought to be a lull in the idle talk. He looked at Herman, who was hard at work with his laptop. He said, 'Hey, Herman. I have an idea.'

By now Herman had the eleven voices committed to memory, and his wife had spent hours providing matching descriptions. He especially knew Easter's tone.

'Yes, Nicholas.'

Nicholas raised his voice in an effort to catch everyone's attention. Well, when I was a kid, I went to a little private school, and we were trained to begin each day with the Pledge of Allegiance. Every time I see a flag early in the morning, I have this desire to give the pledge.' Most of the jurors were listening. Poodle had gone out for a smoke. 'And in the courtroom out there we have this beautiful flag standing behind the Judge, and all we do is sit and look at it.'

'I hadn't noticed,' Herman said.

'You wanna do the Pledge of Allegiance, out there, in open court?' asked Herrera, Napoleon, the Retired Colonel.

'Yeah. Why not do it once a week?'

'Nothing wrong with that,' said Jerry Fernandez, who had secretly been recruited for the event.

'But what about the Judge?' asked Mrs. Gladys Card.

'Why should he care? In fact, why should anyone be bothered if we stand for a moment and honor our flag?'

'You're not playing games, are you?' asked the Colonel.

Nicholas was suddenly wounded. He gazed across the table with aching eyes, and said, 'My father was killed in Vietnam, okay. He was decorated. That flag means a lot to me.'

And with that, the deal was sealed.

Judge Harkin greeted them with a warm Friday smile as they came through the door one by one. He was prepared to zip through his standard routine about unauthorized contact, and get on with the testimony. It took a second to realize they were not sitting, as usual. They remained standing until all twelve were in place, then they looked at the wall to his left, behind the witness stand, and they covered their hearts with their hands. Easter opened his mouth first and led them in a vigorous recitation of the Pledge of Allegiance.

Harkin's initial reaction was one of total disbelief; it was certainly a ceremony he'd never witnessed, not in a courtroom, not by a group of jurors. Nor had he ever *heard* of such a thing and by now he thought he'd heard or seen it all. It was not a part of the daily ritual, had not been approved by him, did not in fact appear in any manual or handbook. And so his first impulse, after the jolt, was to call them down, make 'em stop it; and they'd talk about it later. Then he instantly realized that it seemed horribly unpatriotic and maybe even downright sinful to interrupt a group of well-meaning citizens as they took a moment to honor their flag. He glanced at Rohr and Cable and saw nothing but open mouths and slack jaws.

So then he stood. About halfway through the pledge, he lurched forward and upward, his black robe floating around him, and turned to the wall, clutched his chest, and picked up the chant.

134

With the jury and the Judge honoring the Stars and Stripes, it suddenly seemed imperative for everyone else to do likewise, especially the lawyers, who couldn't chance disfavor or show the slightest hint of disloyalty. They jumped to their feet, kicking over briefcases and knocking back chairs. Gloria Lane and her deputy clerks, and the court reporter, and Lou Dell, sitting out there on the first row, far side, likewise stood and turned and followed along. The fervor lost its momentum, though, somewhere beyond the third row of spectators, and Fitch was thus fortunately saved from having to stand like a Cub Scout and mumble words he barely remembered.

He was in the back row with José on one side and Holly, a comely young associate, on the other. Pang was out in the atrium. Doyle was back on his Dr. Pepper crate on the first floor near the Coke machines, dressed like a laborer, joking with the janitors and watching the front lobby.

Fitch watched and listened in utter amazement. The sight of a jury, on its own initiative and working as a group, assuming control of a courtroom in such a manner was simply hard to believe. The fact that Marlee knew it was coming was bewildering.

The fact that she was playing games with it was exhilarating.

At least Fitch, though, had some inkling of what was coming. Wendall Rohr felt thoroughly ambushed. He was so stunned by the sight of Easter dressed precisely as promised, and holding the exact magazine, which he placed under his chair, and then leading his fellow jurymen in the pledge, that he could only mouth the remaining words. And he did so without looking at the flag. He stared at the jury, especially at Easter, and he wondered what the hell was going on.

As the final phrase '. . . and justice for all' echoed up to the ceiling, the jurors settled into their seats and, as

135

a group, looked quickly around the courtroom to assess the reactions. Judge Harkin adjusted his robe while shuffling some papers and seemed determined to act as if all juries were supposed to do the same thing. What could he say? It had taken thirty seconds.

Most of the lawyers were secretly embarrassed by the silly display of patriotism, but, Hey!, if the jurors were happy, then they were happy too. Only Wendall Rohr kept staring, seemingly speechless. An associate nudged him and they fell into a hushed conversation as His Honor raced through the standard comments and questions for the jury.

'I believe we're ready for a new witness,' the Judge said, anxious to speed things along.

Rohr stood, still dazed, and said, 'The plaintiff calls Dr. Hilo Kilvan.'

As the next expert was retrieved from a witness holding room in the back, Fitch quietly slipped out of the courtroom with José fast behind him. They walked down the street and into the old dime store.

The two jury wizards in the viewing room were silent. On the main screen, one was watching the initial questioning of Dr. Kilvan. On a smaller monitor, the other was watching a replay of the Pledge of Allegiance. Fitch hovered over the monitor, and asked, 'When was the last time you saw that?'

'It's Easter,' the nearest expert said. 'He led them into it.'

'Of course it was Easter,' Fitch snapped. 'I could see that from the back row of the courtroom.' Fitch, as usual, was not playing fair. Neither of these consultants knew of Marlee's phone calls because Fitch had yet to share the information with anyone but his agents – Swanson, Doyle, Pang, Konrad, and Holly.

'So what does that do to your computer analysis?' Fitch asked with heavy sarcasm.

'Blows it to hell.'

136

'That's what I figured. Keep watching.' He slammed the door and went to his office.

The direct examination of Dr. Hilo Kilvan was handled by a new plaintiff's lawyer, Scotty Mangrum from Dallas. Mangrum had made his fortune suing petrochemical companies for toxic torts, and now at the age of forty-two he was deeply concerned about consumer products that caused injuries and death. After Rohr, he'd been the first lawyer to pony up his million bucks to finance the Wood case, and it had been decided that he would become fluent in statistical summaries of lung cancer. In the past four years, he'd spent countless hours reading every possible study and report on the subject, and he'd traveled extensively to meet with the experts. With great care and no regard for expense, he'd selected Dr. Kilvan as the man to visit Biloxi and share his knowledge with the jury.

Dr. Kilvan spoke perfect but deliberate English, with a touch of an accent that made an instant impression on the jury. Few things can be more persuasive in a courtroom than an expert who's traveled a great distance to be there, and has an exotic name and accent to boot. Dr. Kilvan was from Montreal, where he'd lived the past forty years, and the fact that he was from another country only added to his credibility. The jury was on board long before he got around to his testimony. He and Mangrum tag-teamed through an intimidating résumé, with particular emphasis placed on the volume of books Dr. Kilvan had published on the statistical probabilities of lung cancer.

When finally asked, Durr Cable conceded that Dr. Kilvan was qualified to testify in his field. Scotty Mangrum thanked him, and then began with the first study – one comparing ratios of lung cancer mortality between cigarette smokers and nonsmokers. Dr. Kilvan had been studying this for the past twenty years at the

137

University of Montreal, and he relaxed in his chair as he explained the basics of this research to the jury. For American men, and he'd studied groups of men and women from around the world but primarily Canadians and Americans, the risk of getting lung cancer for one who smokes fifteen cigarettes a day for ten years is ten times greater than for one who doesn't smoke at all. Increase it to two packs a day, and the risk is twenty times greater. Increase it to three packs a day, the quantity smoked by Jacob Wood, and the risk is twenty-five times greater than for a nonsmoker.

Brightly colored charts were produced and mounted on three tripods, and Dr. Kilvan, carefully and without a trace of hurry, demonstrated his findings to the jurors.

The next study was a comparison of the death rates from lung cancer in men in relation to the type of tobacco smoked. Dr. Kilvan explained the basic differences in pipe and cigar smoke and the rates of cancer for American men who used those forms of tobacco. He'd published two books on these comparisons, and was quite ready to show the jury the next series of charts and graphs. The numbers piled up, and they began to blur.

Loreen Duke was the first person with the nerve to remove her plate from the table and take it to a corner where she balanced it on her knees and ate alone. Because the lunches were ordered by menu at nine each morning, and because Lou Dell and Willis the deputy and the folks at O'Reilly's Deli and anyone else involved in the serving of the food were determined to have the food on the table at the crack of noon, a certain order was necessary. A seating arrangement was developed. Loreen's seat was directly across the table from Stella Hulic, who smacked as she talked and allowed large chunks of bread to hang from her teeth. Stella was a poorly dressed social climber who'd spent most of her time in recess working desperately to convince the other eleven that she and her husband, a retired plumbing executive named Cal, possessed more than the rest. Cal had a hotel, and Cal had an apartment complex, and Cal had a car wash. There were other investments, most of which managed to pop out with the food as if both were accidents. They took trips, just traveled all the time. Greece was a favorite. Cal had an airplane and several boats.

According to widely accepted knowledge along the Coast, Cal, a few years earlier, had used an old shrimping boat to haul marijuana from Mexico. True or not, the Hulics were now flush, and it was Stella's burden to discuss it with anyone who would listen. She rattled on with an obnoxious nasal twang, one foreign to the Coast, and waited until everyone had filled their mouths and an intense quiet had settled over the table.

She said, 'I sure hope we finish early today. Me and Cal are headed to Miami for the weekend. There are some fabulous new shops down there.' All heads were bowed because no one could stomach the sight of half a dinner roll packed tightly in a jaw and clearly visible. Each syllable came forth with added sounds of food sticking to teeth.

Loreen left before taking the first bite. She was followed by Rikki Coleman, who offered the feeble excuse that she had to sit by the window. Lonnie Shaver suddenly needed to work during lunch. He excused himself and huddled with his computer while munching on a chicken club.

'Dr. Kilvan certainly is an impressive witness, isn't he?' Nicholas asked the remaining jurors at the table. A few glanced at Herman, who was eating his usual turkey sandwich on white bread with no mayonnaise or mustard or any condiment capable of sticking to his mouth or lips. A sliced turkey sandwich and a nice little pile of ridged potato chips could be easily handled and

139

consumed without the benefit of sight. Herman's jaws slowed for a second, but he said nothing.

'Those statistics are hard to ignore,' Nicholas said while smiling at Jerry Fernandez. It was a deliberate attempt to provoke the foreman.

'That's enough,' Herman said.

'Enough of what, Herm?'

'Enough talk about the trial. You know the Judge's rules.'

'Yeah, but the Judge isn't in here, is he, Herm? And he has no way of knowing what we discuss, does he? Unless, of course, you tell him.'

'I might just do that.'

'Fine, Herm. What would you like to discuss?'

'Anything but the trial.'

'Pick a topic. Football, the weather . . .'

'I don't watch football.'

'Ha, ha.'

There was a heavy pause, a stillness broken only by the slapping of food around the mouth of Stella Hulic. Evidently the quick exchange between the two men had rattled nerves, and Stella chewed even faster.

But Jerry Fernandez had had enough. 'Could you please stop smacking your food like that!' he snapped viciously.

He caught her in mid-bite, mouth open, food perceptible. He glared at her as if he might slap her, then he said, after a deep breath, 'I'm sorry, okay. It's just that you have these terrible table manners.'

She was stunned for a second, then embarrassed. Then she attacked. Her cheeks turned red and she managed to swallow the large portion already in her mouth. 'Maybe I don't like yours either,' she said, bristling as the other heads lowered. Everyone wanted the moment to pass.

'At least I eat quietly and keep my food in my

mouth,' Jerry said, very aware of how childish he sounded.

'So do I,' Stella said.

'No you don't,' said Napoleon, who had the misfortune of sitting next to Loreen Duke and across from Stella. 'You make more racket than a three-year-old.'

Herman cleared his throat loudly, said, 'Let's all take a deep breath now. And let's finish our lunch in peace.'

Not another word was spoken as they strained to quietly finish the remains of their lunch. Jerry and Poodle left first for the smoke room, followed by Nicholas Easter, who didn't smoke but needed a change of scenery. A light rain was falling, and the daily walk around the town would have to be canceled.

They met in the small, square room with folding chairs and a window that opened. Angel Weese, the quietest of all jurors, soon joined them. Stella, the fourth smoker, was wounded and had decided to wait behind.

Poodle didn't mind talking about the trial. Neither did Angel. What else did they have in common? They seemed to agree with Jerry that everybody knows cigarettes cause cancer. So if you smoke, you do so at your own risk.

Why give millions to the heirs of a dead man who smoked for thirty-five years? One should know better.

TWELVE

Though the Hulics longed for a jet, a small cute one with leather seats and two pilots, they were temporarily stuck with an old twin-engine Cessna, which Cal could fly if the sun was up and the clouds were gone. He wouldn't dare fly it at night, especially to a crowded place like Miami, so they boarded a commuter flight at the Gulfport Municipal Airport and flew to Atlanta. From there they flew to Miami International, first class, with Stella knocking down two martinis and a glass of wine in less than an hour. It had been a long week. Her nerves were ragged from the stress of civic service.

They poured their luggage into a cab and headed for Miami Beach, where they checked into a new Sheraton.

Marlee followed them. She'd sat behind them on the commuter, and she'd flown coach from Atlanta. Her cab waited as she loitered about the lobby to make sure they were checked in. She then found a room a mile down the beach at a resort hotel. She waited until almost eleven, Friday night, before she called.

Stella had been tired and simply wanted a drink and dinner in the room. Several drinks. She'd shop tomorrow, but for now she needed liquids. When the phone rang, she was flat on the bed, barely conscious. Cal, clad only in drooping boxers, grabbed the phone. 'Hello.'

'Yes, Mr. Hulic,' came the very crisp, professional voice of a young lady. 'You need to be careful.'

'Say what?'

'You're being followed.'

Cal rubbed his red eyes. 'Who is this?'

'Listen carefully please. Some men are watching your wife. They're here in Miami. They know you took flight 4476 from Biloxi to Atlanta, flight 533 on Delta to Miami, and they know exactly which room you're in now. They're watching every move.'

Cal looked at the phone and slapped himself lightly on the forehead. 'Wait a minute. I –'

'And they'll probably wire your phones tomorrow,' she added helpfully. 'So, please be very careful.'

'Who are these guys?' he asked loudly, and Stella perked up slightly. She managed to swing her bare feet onto the floor and focus on her husband through foggy eyes.

'They're agents hired by the tobacco companies,' was the reply. 'And they're vicious.'

The young lady hung up. Cal again looked at the receiver, then looked at his wife, a pathetic sight. She was reaching for the cigarettes. 'What is it?' she demanded with a thick tongue, and Cal repeated every word.

'Oh my god!' she shrieked and walked to the table by the TV where she clutched a wine bottle and poured another glass. 'Why are they after me?' she asked, falling into a chair and spilling cheap cabernet on her hotel bathrobe. 'Why me?'

'She didn't say they were gonna kill you,' he explained, with a slight trace of regret.

'Why are they following me?' She was near tears.

'I don't know, dammit,' Cal growled as he took another beer from the mini-bar. They drank in silence for a few minutes, neither wanting to look at the other, both bewildered.

Then, the phone rang again and she let out a yelp. Cal took the receiver, slowly said, 'Hello.'

143

'Hi, it's me again,' came the same voice, this time quite merry. 'Something I forgot to mention. Don't call the cops or anything. These guys are doing nothing illegal. It's best just to pretend as if nothing is wrong, okay?'

'Who are you?' he asked.

'Bye.' And she was gone.

Listing Foods owned not one but three jets, one of which was dispatched early Saturday morning to collect Mr. Lonnie Shaver and fly him to Charlotte, alone. His wife had been unable to find a baby-sitter for the three kids. The pilots greeted him warmly and offered him coffee and fruit before takeoff.

Ken met him at the airport in a company van with a company driver, and fifteen minutes later they arrived at the SuperHouse headquarters in suburban Charlotte. Lonnie was greeted by Ben, the other pal from the first meeting in Biloxi, and together Ben and Ken gave Lonnie a quick tour of their corporate center. The building was new, a one-story brick with lots of glass and completely indistinguishable from a dozen others they'd passed on the drive from the airport. The hallways were wide and tiled and spotless; the offices were sterile and filled with technology. Lonnie could almost hear the sound of money being printed.

They shared coffee with George Teaker, CEO, in his large office with a view of a small courtyard filled with plastic greenery. Teaker was youthful, energetic, clad in denim (his usual Saturday office dress, he explained). On Sundays he wore a jogging suit. He fed Lonnie the party line – the company was growing like crazy and they wanted him on board. Then Teaker was off to a meeting.

In a small, white boardroom with no windows, Lonnie was placed at a table with coffee and doughnuts before him. Ben disappeared, but Ken stuck close as the

144

lights dimmed and an image appeared on the wall. It was a thirty-minute video about SuperHouse – its brief history, its current position in the market, its ambitious growth plans. And its people, the 'real assets.'

According to the script, SuperHouse planned to increase both gross sales and number of stores by fifteen percent a year for the next six years. Profits would be stunning.

The lights came on, and an earnest young man with a name that was quickly forgotten appeared and took a position across the table. He was a benefits specialist, and had all the answers to all the questions about health care, pension plans, vacations, holidays, sick leave, employee stock options. Everything was covered in one of the packages on the table before Lonnie, so he could mull over it later.

After a long lunch with Ben and Ken in a swanky suburban restaurant, Lonnie went back to the boardroom for a few more meetings. One covered the training program they were contemplating for him. The next, presented by video, outlined the structure of the company in relation to its parent and to its competitors. Boredom hit hard. For a man who'd spent the entire week sitting on his rear listening to lawyers haggle with experts, this was no way to spend a Saturday afternoon. Excited though he was about his visit and its prospects, he suddenly needed fresh air.

Ken, of course, knew this, and the moment the video ended he suggested they go play golf, a sport Lonnie had yet to try. Ken, of course, knew this too, so he suggested they get some sunshine anyway. Ken's BMW was blue and spotless, and he drove it with great care into the countryside, past manicured farms and estates and tree-lined roads until they reached the country club.

For a black guy from a lower-middle-class family in Gulfport, the thought of stepping foot in a country club was intimidating. Lonnie at first resented the idea, and vowed to leave if he saw no other black faces. On second thought, however, he was somewhat flattered that his new employers would think so highly of him. They were really nice guys, genuine and seemingly anxious for him to adjust to their corporate culture. There'd been no mention of money yet, but how could it be less than he was earning now?

They stepped into the Club Lounge, a sprawling room of leather chairs, stuffed game on the walls, and a cloud of blue cigar smoke hanging near the pitched ceiling. A serious boy room. At a large table near the window, with the eighteenth green just below, they found George Teaker, now in golf attire, having a drink with two black gentlemen, also nicely dressed and apparently not long off the links. All three stood and warmly greeted Lonnie, who was relieved to see kindred spirits. In fact, a huge weight left his chest, and he was suddenly ready for a drink, though he was careful with alcohol. The burly black man was Morris Peel, a loud and hearty soul who smiled constantly and introduced the other, a Percy Kellum from Atlanta. Both men were in their mid-forties, and as the first round of drinks was ordered, by Peel, he explained that he was a vice president with Listing Foods, the parent company in New York, and that Kellum was a regional something or other for Listing.

No pecking order was established; none was needed. It was obvious that Peel, from the parent in New York, ranked higher than Teaker, who carried the title of CEO but only ran a division. Kellum was positioned somewhere farther down the pole. Ken, even lower. And Lonnie was just happy to be there. Over the second drink, with the formalities and polite chitchat out of the way, Peel, with great relish and humor, offered his biography. Sixteen years earlier, he had been the first black mid-level manager to enter the world of Listing

146

Foods, and he had been a pain in the ass. He'd been hired as a token, not as a talent, and he'd been forced to claw his way upward. Twice he'd sued the company, and twice he'd won. And once the boys upstairs realized he was determined to join them, and that he had the brains to do so, they accepted him as a person. It still wasn't easy, but he had their respect. Teaker, now on his third scotch, leaned in and offered, confidentially of course, that Peel was being groomed for the big job. 'You could be talking to a future CEO,' he said to Lonnie. 'One of the first black CEOs of a Fortune 500 company.'

Because of Peel, Listing Foods had implemented an aggressive program of recruiting and promoting black managers. This is where Lonnie would fit in. Hadley Brothers was a decent company, but quite old-fashioned and quite Southern, and Listing was not surprised to find but a few blacks with more authority than floor sweepers.

For two hours, as darkness fell across the eighteenth green and a piano player sang in the lounge, they drank and talked and planned the future. Dinner was just down the hall, in a private dining room with a fireplace and a moosehead above the mantel. They ate thick steaks flavored with sauce and mushrooms. Lonnie slept that night in a suite on the third floor of the country club, and awoke to a splendid fairway view, and a slight hangover.

Only two brief meetings were planned for late Sunday morning. The first, again with Ken present, was a planning session with George Teaker, in a jogging suit, and fresh from a five-miler. 'Best thing in the world for a hangover,' he said. He wanted Lonnie to run the store in Biloxi under a new contract for a period of ninety days, after which they would evaluate his performance. Assuming everyone was pleased, and they certainly expected to be, then he would be transferred to a larger store, probably in the Atlanta area. A larger store meant more responsibility, and more compensation. After a year there, he would be reevaluated, and probably moved again. During this fifteen-month period, he would be required to spend at least one weekend each month in Charlotte in a management trainee program, one that was outlined in excruciating detail in a packet on the table.

Teaker finally finished, and ordered more black coffee.

The last guest was a wiry young black man with a bald head and a meticulous suit and tie. His name was Taunton, and he was a lawyer from New York, from Wall Street, actually. His firm represented Listing Foods, he explained gravely, and in fact, he worked on nothing but Listing's business. He was there to present a proposed contract of employment, a rather routine matter but nonetheless an important one. He handed Lonnie a document, only three or four pages, but it seemed much heavier after having traveled from Wall Street. Lonnie was impressed beyond words.

'Look it over,' Taunton said, tapping his chin with a designer pen. 'And we'll talk next week. It's fairly standard. The compensation paragraph has several blanks. We'll fill them in later.'

Lonnie glanced at the first page, then placed it with the other papers and packets and memos in a pile that was growing by the moment. Taunton whipped out a legal pad and seemed to prepare himself for a nasty cross-examination. 'Just a few questions,' he said.

Lonnie had a painful flashback to the courtroom in Biloxi where the lawyers always had 'just a few more questions.'

'Sure,' Lonnie said, glancing at his watch. He couldn't help it.

'No criminal record of any sort?'

'No. Just a few speeding tickets.'

'No lawsuits pending against you personally?'

'No.'

'Any against your wife?'

'No.'

'Have you ever filed for bankruptcy?'

'No.'

'Ever been arrested?'

'No.'

'Indicted?'

'No.'

Taunton flipped a page. 'Have you, in your capacity as a store manager, ever been involved in litigation?'

'Yeah, lemme see. About four years ago, an old man slipped and fell on a wet floor. He sued. I gave a deposition.'

'Did it go to trial?' Taunton asked with great interest. He had reviewed the court file, had a copy of it in his thick briefcase, and knew every detail of the old man's claim.

'No. The insurance company settled out of court. I think they paid him twenty thousand or so.'

If was twenty-five thousand, and Taunton wrote this figure on his legal pad. The script called for Teaker to speak at this point. 'Damned trial lawyers. They're a blight on society.'

Taunton looked at Lonnie, then at Teaker, then said defensively, 'I'm not a trial lawyer.'

'Oh, I know that,' Teaker said. 'You're one of the good guys. It's those greedy ambulance chasers I hate.'

'Do you know what we paid last year for liability insurance coverage?' Taunton asked Lonnie, as if he might be able to provide an intelligent guess. He just shook his head.

'Listing paid over twenty million.'

'Just to keep the sharks away,' Teaker added.

There was a dramatic pause in the conversation, or at least a pause aimed at drama as Taunton and Teaker bit their lips and showed their disgust and seemed to appear to contemplate the money wasted for protection against lawsuits. Then Taunton looked at something on his legal pad, glanced at Teaker, and asked, 'I don't suppose you've discussed the trial, have you?'

Teaker looked surprised. 'I don't think it's necessary. Lonnie's on board. He's one of us.'

Taunton appeared to ignore this. 'This tobacco trial in Biloxi has serious implications throughout the economy, especially for companies like ours,' he said to Lonnie, who nodded gently and tried to understand how the trial might affect anyone other than Pynex.

Teaker said to Taunton, 'I'm not sure you're supposed to discuss it.'

Taunton continued, 'It's okay. I know trial procedure. You don't mind, do you, Lonnie? I mean, we can trust you on this, can't we?'

'Sure. I won't say a word.'

'If the plaintiff wins this case and there's a big verdict, it will open the floodgates of tobacco litigation. Trial lawyers will go crazy. They'll bankrupt the tobacco companies.'

'We make a lot of money off tobacco sales, Lonnie,' Teaker said with perfect timing.

'Then they'll probably sue dairy companies claiming cholesterol kills people.' Taunton's voice was rising and he was leaning forward across the table. The issue had struck a nerve. 'There has to be an end to these trials. The tobacco industry has never lost one of them. I think their record is something like fifty-five wins, no losses. Folks on juries have always understood that you smoke at your own risk.'

'Lonnie understands this,' Teaker said, almost defensively.

Taunton took a deep breath. 'Sure. Sorry if I said too much. It's just that this Biloxi trial has a lot at stake.'

'No problem,' Lonnie said. And he really wasn't

bothered by the talk. Taunton was, after all, a lawyer, and he certainly knew the law, and perhaps it was okay if he spoke of the trial in broad terms without going into specifics. Lonnie was satisfied. He was on board. No problem out of him.

Taunton was suddenly all smiles as he packed away his notes and promised to give Lonnie a call midweek. The meeting was over and Lonnie was a free man. Ken drove him to the airport where the same Lear with the same pleasant pilots sat idling and ready.

The weatherman promised a chance of afternoon showers, and that was all Stella wanted to hear. Cal insisted there wasn't a cloud to be seen, but she wouldn't take a look. She pulled the shades and watched movies until noon. She ordered a grilled cheese and two bloody marys, then slept for a while with the door chained and a chair propped against it. Cal was off to the beach, specifically a topless one he'd heard about but never got the chance to visit on account of his wife. With her safely boarded up inside their room on the tenth floor, he was free to roam the sands and admire young flesh. He sipped a beer at a thatched-roof bar and thought how wonderful the trip had become. She was afraid to be seen, thus the credit cards were safe for the weekend.

They caught an early flight Sunday morning and returned to Biloxi. Stella was hungover and weary from a weekend of being watched. She was apprehensive about Monday and the courtroom.

THIRTEEN

The hellos and howdies were muffled Monday morning. The routine of gathering by the coffeepot and inspecting the doughnuts and rolls was growing tiresome, not so much from repetition but more from the burdensome mystery of not knowing how long this all might drag on. They broke into small groups, and recounted what happened during their freedom over the weekend. Most ran their errands and shopped and visited with family and went to church, and the humdrum took on new importance for people about to be confined. Herman was late so there were whispers about the trial, nothing important, just a general consensus that the plaintiff's case was sinking in a mire of charts and graphs and statistics. They all believed smoking caused lung cancer. They wanted new information.

Nicholas managed to isolate Angel Weese early in the morning. They had exchanged brief pleasantries throughout the trial, but had talked of nothing substantive. She and Loreen Duke were the only two black women on the jury, and oddly kept their distance from each other. Angel was slender and quiet, single, and worked for a beer distributor. She kept the permanent look of someone in silent pain, and she proved difficult to talk to.

Stella arrived late and looked like death; her eyes

were red and puffy, her skin pale. Her hands shook as she poured coffee, and she went straight to the smoke room down the hall, where Jerry Fernandez and Poodle were chatting and flirting as they were now prone to do.

Nicholas was anxious to hear Stella's weekend report. 'How about a smoke?' he said to Angel, the fourth official smoker on the jury.

'When did you start?' she asked with a rare smile.

'Last week. I'll quit when the trial's over.' They left the jury room under the prying gaze of Lou Dell, and joined the others – Jerry and Poodle still talking; Stella stone-faced and teetering on the brink of a breakdown.

Nicholas bummed a Camel from Jerry, and lit it with a match. 'Well, how was Miami?' he asked Stella.

She jerked her head toward him, startled, and said, 'It rained.' She bit her filter and inhaled fiercely. She didn't want to talk. The conversation lagged as they concentrated on their cigarettes. It was ten minutes before nine, time for the last hit of nicotine.

'I think I was followed this weekend,' Nicholas said after a minute of silence.

The smoking continued without interruption, but the minds were working. 'Say what?' Jerry asked.

'They followed me,' he repeated and looked at Stella, whose eyes were wide and filled with fear.

'Who?' asked Poodle.

'I don't know. It happened Saturday when I left my apartment and went to work. I saw a guy lurking near my car, and I saw him later at the mall. Probably some agent hired by the tobacco boys.'

Stella's mouth dropped open and her jaw quivered. Gray smoke leaked from her nostrils. 'Are you gonna tell the Judge?' she asked, holding her breath. It was a question she and Cal had fought over.

'No.'

'Why not?' asked Poodle, only mildly curious.

'I don't know for certain, okay. I mean, I'm sure I

153

was followed, but I don't know for sure who it was. What am I supposed to tell the Judge?'

'Tell him you were followed,' said Jerry.

'Why would they follow you?' asked Angel.

'Same reason they're following all of us.'

'I don't believe that,' Poodle said.

Stella certainly believed it, but if Nicholas, the ex-law student, planned to keep it from the Judge, then so did she.

'Why are they following us?' Angel asked again, nervously.

'Because it's just what they do. The tobacco companies spent millions selecting us, and now they're spending even more to watch us.'

'What are they looking for?'

'Ways to get to us. Friends we might talk to. Places we might go. They typically start gossip in the various communities where we live, little rumors about the deceased, bad things he did while he was alive. They're always looking for a weak spot. That's why they've never lost a jury trial.'

'How do you know it's the tobacco company?' asked Poodle, lighting another one.

'I don't. But they have more money than the plaintiff. In fact, they have unlimited funds to fight these cases with.'

Jerry Fernandez, always ready to help with a joke or assist in a gag, said, 'You know, come to think of it, I remember seeing this strange little dude peeking around a corner at me this weekend. Saw him more than once.' He glanced at Nicholas for approval, but Nicholas was watching Stella. Jerry winked at Poodle, but she didn't see.

Lou Dell knocked on the door.

No pledges or anthems Monday morning. Judge Harkin and the lawyers waited, ready to spring forward with unabashed patriotism at the slightest hint the jurors might be in the mood, but nothing happened. The jurors took their seats, already a bit tired it seemed and resigned to another long week of testimony. Harkin flashed them a warm welcoming smile, then proceeded with his patented monologue about unauthorized contact. Stella looked at the floor without a word. Cal was watching from the third row, present to give her support.

Scotty Mangrum rose and informed the court that the plaintiff would like to resume with the testimony of Dr. Hilo Kilvan, who was fetched from the rear somewhere and placed on the witness stand. He nodded politely at the jury. No one nodded back.

For Wendall Rohr and the plaintiff's team of lawyers, the weekend had brought no break in their labors. The trial itself presented enough challenges, but the distraction of the fax from MM on Friday had wrecked all pretense of order. They had traced its origin to a truck stop near Hattiesburg, and after accepting some cash, a clerk had given a weak description of a young woman, late twenties maybe early thirties, with dark hair tucked under a brown fishing cap and a face half-hidden behind large dark sunshades. She was short, but then maybe she was average. Maybe she was about five six or five seven. She was slender, that was for sure, but after all it had been before nine on a Friday morning, one of their busiest periods. She'd paid five bucks for a one-page fax to a number in Biloxi, a law office, which in itself seemed odd and thus remembered by the clerk. Most of their faxes dealt with fuel permits and special loads.

No sign of her vehicle, but then again the place was packed.

It was the collective opinion of the eight principal plaintiff's lawyers, a group with a combined total of 150 years of trial experience, that this was something new.

Not a one could recall a single trial in which a person on the outside contacted the lawyers involved with hints of what the jury might do. They were unanimous in their belief that she, MM, would be back. And though they at first denied it, through the weekend they grudgingly arrived at the belief that she would probably ask for money. A deal. Money for a verdict.

They could not, however, muster the courage to plot a strategy to deal with her when she wanted to negotiate. Maybe later, but not now.

Fitch, on the other hand, thought of little else. The Fund currently had a balance of six and a half million dollars, with two of that budgeted for the remaining trial expenses. The money was quite liquid and very movable. He'd spent the weekend monitoring jurors and meeting with lawyers and listening to summaries from his jury people, and he'd spent time on the phone with D. Martin Jankle at Pynex. He'd been pleased with the results of the Ken and Ben show in Charlotte, and had been assured by George Teaker that Lonnie Shaver was a man they could trust. He'd even watched a secret video of the last meeting in which Taunton and Teaker had all but convinced Shaver to sign a pledge.

Fitch slept four hours Saturday and five Sunday, about average for him though sleep was difficult. He dreamed of the girl Marlee and of what she might bring him. This could be the easiest verdict yet.

He watched the opening ceremonies Monday from the viewing room with a jury consultant. The hidden camera had been working so well they had decided to try a better one, one with a larger lens and clearer picture. It was locked in the same briefcase and placed under the same table, and no one in the busy courtroom had a clue.

No Pledge of Allegiance, nothing out of the ordinary, but then Fitch had expected this. Surely Marlee would've called if something special was planned.

He listened as Dr. Hilo Kilvan resumed his testimony, and almost smiled to himself as the jurors seemed to dread it. His consultants and his lawyers were unanimous in the belief that the plaintiff's witnesses had yet to capture the jury. The experts were impressive with credentials and visual aids, but the tobacco defense had seen it all before.

The defense would be simple and subtle. Their doctors would argue strenuously that smoking does not cause lung cancer. Other impressive experts would argue people make informed choices about smoking. Their lawyers would argue that if cigarettes are allegedly so dangerous, then you smoke at your own risk.

Fitch had been through it many times before. He'd memorized the testimony. He'd suffered through the arguments of the lawyers. He'd sweated while the juries deliberated. He'd quietly celebrated the verdicts, but he'd never had the chance to purchase one.

Cigarettes kill four hundred thousand Americans each year, according to Dr. Kilvan, and he had four large charts to prove it. It is the single deadliest product on the market, nothing else comes close. Except for guns, and they, of course, are not designed to be aimed and fired at people. Cigarettes are designed to be lit and puffed; thus they are used properly. They are deadly if used exactly as intended.

This point hit home with the jury, and it would not be forgotten. But by ten-thirty they were ready for the morning coffee and potty break. Judge Harkin recessed for fifteen minutes. Nicholas slipped a note to Lou Dell, who gave it to Willis, who happened to be awake for the moment. He took the note to the Judge. Easter wanted a private conference at noon, if possible. It was urgent.

Nicholas excused himself from lunch with the explanation that his stomach was queasy and he'd lost

157

his appetite. He needed to visit the boys' room, he said, and he'd be back in a moment. No one cared. Most were leaving the table anyway to avoid being near Stella Hulic.

He cut through the narrow back hallways and entered the chambers where the Judge was waiting, alone with a cold sandwich. They greeted each other tensely. Nicholas carried a small brown leather handbag. 'We need to talk,' he said, sitting.

'Do the others know you're here?' Harkin asked.

'No. But I need to be quick.'

'Go.' Harkin ate a corn chip and pushed his plate away.

'Three things. Stella Hulic, number four, front row, went to Miami this weekend, and she was followed by unknown persons believed to be working for the tobacco company.'

His Honor stopped chewing. 'How do you know?'

'I overheard a conversation this morning. She was trying to whisper this to another juror. Don't ask me how she knew she was being followed – I didn't hear all of it. But the poor woman is a wreck. Frankly, I think she had a coupla drinks before court this morning. Vodka, I'd say. Probably bloody marys.'

'Keep going.'

'Secondly, Frank Herrera, number seven, we talked about him last time, well his mind is made up and I'm afraid he's trying to influence other people.'

'I'm listening.'

'He came into this trial with a fixed opinion. I think he wanted to serve; he's retired military or something, probably bored to death, but he is very pro-defense and, well, he just worries me. I don't know what you do with jurors like that.'

'Is he discussing the case?'

'Once, with me. Herman is very proud of his title of foreman, and he won't tolerate any talk about the trial.'

'Good for him.'

'But he can't monitor everything. And as you know, well, it's just human nature to gossip. Anyway, Herrera is poison.'

'Okay. And third?'

Nicholas opened his leather bag and removed a videocassette. 'Does this thing work?' he asked, nodding to a small-screened TV/VCR on a roller stand in the corner.

'I think so. It did last week.'

'May I?'

'Please.'

Nicholas punched the ON button and inserted the tape. 'You remember the guy I saw in court last week? The one who was following me?'

'Yes.' Harkin stood and walked to within two feet of the TV screen. 'I remember.'

'Well, here he is.' In black and white, a little fuzzy but certainly clear enough to distinguish, the door opened and the man entered Easter's apartment. He looked around anxiously, and for one very long second seemed to look in the precise direction of the camera, hidden in an air vent above the refrigerator. Nicholas stopped the video in full frontal shot of the man's face, and said, 'That's him.'

Judge Harkin repeated without breathing, 'Yeah, that's him.'

The tape continued with the man (Doyle) coming and going from view, taking pictures, leaning close to the computer, then leaving in less than ten minutes. The screen went black.

'When did –' Harkin asked slowly, still staring.

'Saturday afternoon. I worked an eight-hour shift, and this guy broke in while I was on the job.' Not entirely true, but Harkin would never know the difference. Nicholas had reprogrammed the video to reflect last Saturday's time and date in the lower right corner.

159

'Why do you –'

'I was robbed and beaten five years ago when I lived in Mobile, almost died. Happened during a break-in of my apartment. I'm careful about security, that's all.'

And this made it all perfectly plausible; the existence of sophisticated surveillance equipment in a run-down apartment; the computers and cameras on a minimum wage salary. The man was terrified of violence. Everybody could understand that. 'You want to see it again?'

'No. That's him.'

Nicholas removed the tape and handed it to the Judge. 'Keep it. I have another copy.'

Fitch's roast beef sandwich was interrupted when Konrad pecked on the door and uttered the words Fitch longed to hear: 'The girl's on the phone.'

He wiped his mouth and his goatee with the back of a hand, and grabbed the phone. 'Hello.'

'Fitch baby,' she said. 'It's me, Marlee.'

'Yes dear.'

'Don't know the guy's name, but he's the goon you sent into Easter's apartment on Thursday, the nineteenth, eleven days ago, at 4:52 P.M. to be exact.' Fitch gasped for breath and coughed up specks of sandwich. He cursed silently and stood up straight. She continued, 'It was just after I gave you the note about Nicholas wearing a gray golf shirt and starched khakis, you remember?'

'Yes,' he said hoarsely.

'Anyway, you later sent the goon into the courtroom, probably to look for me. It was last Wednesday, the twenty-fifth. Pretty stupid move because Easter recognized the man and he sent a note to the Judge, who also got an eyeful. Are you listening, Fitch?'

Listening, but not breathing. 'Yes!' he snapped.

'Well, now the Judge knows the guy broke into Easter's apartment, and he's signed a warrant for the

160

guy's arrest. So, get him out of town immediately or you're about to be embarrassed. Maybe arrested yourself.'

A hundred questions raced wildly through Fitch's brain, but he knew they wouldn't be answered. If Doyle somehow got recognized and taken in, and if he said too much, then, well, it was unthinkable. Breaking and entering was a felony anywhere on the planet, and Fitch had to move fast. 'Anything else?' he said.

'No. That's all for now.'

Doyle was supposed to be eating at a window table in a dinky Vietnamese restaurant four blocks from the courthouse, but was in fact playing two-dollar blackjack at the Lucy Luck when the beeper erupted on his belt. It was Fitch, at the office. Three minutes later, Doyle was headed east on Highway 90, east because the Alabama state line was closer than Louisiana. Two hours later he was flying to Chicago.

It took Fitch an hour to dig and determine that no arrest warrant had been issued for Doyle Dunlap, nor for any unnamed person resembling him. This was of no comfort. The fact remained that Marlee knew they'd entered Easter's apartment.

But how did she know? That was the great and troubling question. Fitch yelled at Konrad and Pang behind locked doors. It would be three hours before they found the answer.

At three-thirty, Monday, Judge Harkin called a halt to Dr. Kilvan's testimony and sent him home for the day. He announced to the surprised lawyers that there were a couple of serious matters involving the jury that had to be dealt with immediately. He sent the jurors back to their room and ordered all spectators out of the courtroom. Jip and Rasco herded them away, then locked the door.

Oliver McAdoo gently slid the briefcase under the

161

table with his long left foot until the camera was aimed at the bench. Next to it were four other assorted satchels and cases, along with two large cardboard boxes filled with bulky depositions and other legal refuse. McAdoo was not sure what was about to happen, but he assumed, correctly, that Fitch would want to see it.

Judge Harkin cleared his throat and addressed the horde of lawyers watching him intently. 'Gentlemen, it has come to my attention that some if not all of our jurors feel as if they're being watched and followed. I have clear proof that at least one of our jurors has been the victim of a break-in.' He allowed this to sink in, and sink in it did. The lawyers were stunned, each side knowing full well it was innocent of any wrongdoing and immediately placing guilt where it belonged – at the other table.

'Now, I have two choices. I can declare a mistrial, or I can sequester the jury. I'm inclined to pursue the latter, as distasteful as it will be. Mr. Rohr?'

Rohr was slow to rise, and for a rare moment could think of little to say. 'Uh, gee, Judge, we'd sure hate to see a mistrial. I mean, I'm certain that we've done nothing wrong.' He glanced at the defense table as he said this. 'Someone broke in on a juror?' he asked.

'That's what I said. I'll show you the proof in a moment. Mr. Cable?'

Sir Durr stood and buttoned his jacket right properly. 'This is quite shocking, Your Honor.'

'Certainly is.'

'I'm really in no position to respond until I hear more,' he said, returning the look of utter suspicion to the lawyers who were obviously guilty, the plaintiffs.

'Very well. Bring in juror number four, Stella Hulic,' His Honor instructed Willis. Stella was stiff with fear and already pale by the time she reentered the courtroom.

162

'Please take a seat in the witness stand, Mrs. Hulic. This won't take but a minute.' The Judge smiled with great assurance and waved at the chair in the witness box. Stella shot wild looks in all directions as she sat down.

'Thank you. Now, Mrs. Hulic, I want to ask you just a few questions.'

The courtroom was still and silent as the lawyers held their pens and ignored their sacred legal pads and waited for a great secret to be revealed. After four years of pretrial warfare, they knew virtually everything that every witness would say beforehand. The prospect of unrehearsed statements coming from the witness stand was fascinating.

Surely she was about to reveal some heinous sin committed by the other side. She looked up pitifully at the Judge. Someone had smelled her breath and squealed on her.

'Did you go to Miami over the weekend?'

'Yes sir,' she answered slowly.

'With your husband?'

'Yes.' Cal had left the courtroom before lunch. He had deals to attend to.

'And what was the purpose of this visit?'

'To shop.'

'Did anything unusual happen while you were there?'

She took a deep breath and looked at the eager lawyers packed around the long tables. Then she turned to Judge Harkin and said, 'Yes sir.'

'Please tell us what happened.'

Her eyes watered, and the poor woman was about to lose control. Judge Harkin seized the moment, and said, 'It's okay, Mrs. Hulic. You've done nothing wrong. Just tell us what happened.'

She bit her lip and clenched her teeth. 'We got in Friday night, to the hotel, and after we'd been there for two maybe three hours the phone rang, and it was some woman who told us that these men from the tobacco companies were following us. She said they had followed us from Biloxi, and they knew our flight numbers and everything. Said they'd follow us all weekend, might even try to bug our phones.'

Rohr and his squad breathed in relief. One or two shot nasty looks at the other table, where Cable et al. were frozen.

'Did you see anybody following you?'

'Well, frankly, I never left the room. It upset me so. My husband Cal ventured out a few times, and he did see this one guy, some Cuban-looking man with a camera on the beach, then he saw the same guy on Sunday as we were checking out.' It suddenly hit Stella that this was her exit, her one moment to appear so overcome she just couldn't continue. With little effort, the tears began to flow.

'Anything else, Mrs. Hulic?'

'No,' she said, sobbing. 'It's just awful. I can't keep . . .' and the words were lost in anguish.

His Honor looked at the lawyers. 'I'm going to excuse Mrs. Hulic, and replace her with alternate number one.' A small wail went up from Stella, and with the poor woman in such misery it was impossible to argue that she should be kept. Sequestration was looming, and there was no way she could keep pace.

'You may return to the jury room, get your things, and go home. Thank you for your service, and I'm sorry this has happened.'

'I'm so sorry,' she managed to whisper, then rose from the witness chair and left the courtroom. Her departure was a blow for the defense. She'd been rated highly during selection, and after two weeks of nonstop observation the jury experts on both sides were of the near-unanimous opinion that she was not sympathetic to the plaintiff. She had smoked for twenty-four years, without once trying to stop.

Her replacement was a wild card, feared by both sides but especially by the defense.

'Bring in juror number two, Nicholas Easter,' Harkin said to Willis, who was standing with the door open. As Easter was being called for, Gloria Lane and an assistant rolled a large TV/VCR to the center of the courtroom. The lawyers began chewing their pens, especially the defense.

Durwood Cable pretended to be preoccupied with other matters on the table, but the only question on his mind was, What has Fitch done now? Before the trial, Fitch directed everything; the composition of the defense team, the selection of expert witnesses, the hiring of jury consultants, the actual investigation of all prospective jurors. He handled the delicate communications with the client, Pynex, and he watched the plaintiff's lawyers like a hawk. But most of what Fitch did after the trial began was quite secretive. Cable didn't want to know. He took the high road and tried the case. Let Fitch play in the gutter and try to win it.

Easter sat in the witness chair and crossed his legs. If he was scared or nervous, he didn't show it. The Judge asked him about the mysterious man who'd been following him, and Easter gave specific times and places where he'd seen the man. And he explained in perfect detail what happened last Wednesday when he glanced across the courtroom and saw the same man sitting out there, on the third row.

He then described the security measures he'd taken in his apartment, and he took the videotape from Judge Harkin. He inserted it in the VCR, and the lawyers sat on the edge of their seats. He ran the tape, all nine and a half minutes of it, and when it stopped he sat again in the witness chair and confirmed the identity of the intruder – it was the same man who'd been following him, the same guy who'd shown up in court last Wednesday.

Fitch couldn't see the damned monitor through his hidden camera because bigfoot McAdoo or some other klutz had kicked the briefcase under the table. But Fitch heard every word Easter said, and he could close his eyes and see precisely what was happening in the courtroom. A severe headache was forming at the base of his skull. He gulped aspirin and washed it down with mineral water. He'd love to ask Easter a simple question: For one concerned enough about security to install hidden cameras, why didn't you install an alarm system on your door? But the question occurred to no one but himself.

His Honor said, 'I can also verify that the man in the video was in this courtroom last Wednesday.' But the man in the video was now long gone. Doyle was safely tucked away in Chicago when the courtroom saw him enter the apartment and slink around as if he'd never get caught.

'You may return to the jury room, Mr. Easter.'

An hour passed as the lawyers made their rather feeble and unprepared arguments for and against sequestration. Once things warmed up, allegations of wrongdoing began to fly back and forth, with the defense catching the most flak. Both sides knew things they couldn't prove and thus couldn't say, so the accusations were left somewhat broad.

The jurors got a full report from Nicholas, an embellished account of everything that happened both in court and in the video. In his haste, Judge Harkin had failed to prohibit Nicholas from discussing the matter with his colleagues. It was an omission Nicholas had immediately caught, and he couldn't wait to structure the story to suit himself. He also took the liberty of explaining Stella's rapid departure. She'd left them in tears.

Fitch narrowly averted two minor strokes as he

stomped around his office, rubbing his neck and his temples and tugging at his goatee and demanding impossible answers from Konrad, Swanson, and Pang. In addition to those three, he had young Holly, and Joe Boy, a local private eye with incredibly soft feet, and Dante, a black ex-cop from D.C., and Dubaz, another Coast boy with a lengthy record. And he had four people in the office with Konrad, another dozen he could summon to Biloxi within three hours, and loads of lawyers and jury consultants. Fitch had lots of people, and they cost lots of money, but he damned sure didn't send anyone to Miami over the weekend to watch Stella and Cal shop.

A Cuban? With a camera? Fitch actually threw a phonebook against a wall as he repeated this.

'What if it's the girl?' asked Pang, raising his head slowly after lowering it to miss the phonebook.

'What girl?'

'Marlee. Hulic said the phone call came from a girl.' Pang's composure was a sharp contrast to his boss's explosiveness. Fitch froze in mid-step, then sat for a moment in his chair. He took another aspirin and drank more mineral water, and finally said, 'I think you're right.'

And he was. The Cuban was a two-bit 'security consultant' Marlee found in the yellow pages. She'd paid him two hundred dollars to look suspicious, not a difficult task, and to get caught with a camera as the Hulics left the hotel.

The eleven jurors and three alternates were reassembled in the courtroom. Sylvia's empty chair on the first row was filled by Phillip Savelle, a forty-eight-year-old misfit neither side had been able to read. He described himself as a self-employed tree surgeon, but no record of this profession had been found on the Gulf Coast for the past five years. He was also an avant-garde

167

glass-blower whose forte was brightly colored, shapeless creations to which he gave obscure aquatic and marine names and occasionally exhibited at tiny, neglected galleries in Greenwich Village. He boasted of being an expert sailor, and had in fact once built his own ketch, which he sailed to Honduras where it sank in calm waters. At times he fancied himself an archaeologist, and after the boat dropped he spent eleven months in a Honduran prison for illegal excavations.

He was single, agnostic, a graduate of Grinnell, a nonsmoker. Savelle scared the hell out of every lawyer in the courtroom.

Judge Harkin apologized for what he was about to do. Sequestration of a jury was a rare, radical event, made necessary by extraordinary circumstances, and almost always used in sensational murder cases. But he had no choice in this case. There had been unauthorized contact. There was no reason to believe it would cease, regardless of his warnings. He didn't like it one bit, and he was very sorry for the hardship it would cause, but his job at this point was to guarantee a fair trial.

He explained that months earlier he had developed a contingency plan for this very moment. The county had reserved a block of rooms at a nearby, unnamed motel. Security would be increased. He had a list of rules which he would cover with them. The trial was now entering its second full week of testimony, and he would push the lawyers hard to finish as soon as possible.

The fourteen jurors were to leave, go home, pack, get their affairs in order, and report to court the next morning prepared to spend the next two weeks sequestered.

There were no immediate reactions from the panel; they were too stunned. Only Nicholas Easter thought it was funny.

FOURTEEN

Because of Jerry's fondness for beer and gambling and football and rowdiness in general, Nicholas suggested they meet at a casino Monday night to celebrate their last few hours of freedom. Jerry thought it was a wonderful idea. As the two left the courthouse, they toyed with the idea of inviting a few of their colleagues. The idea sounded good, but it didn't work. Herman was out of the question. Lonnie Shaver left hurriedly, quite agitated and not speaking to anyone. Savelle was new and unknown, and apparently the kind of guy you'd keep at a distance. That left Herrera, Nap the Colonel, and they simply weren't up to it. They were about to spend two weeks locked up with him.

Jerry invited Sylvia Taylor-Tatum, the Poodle. The two were becoming friends of a sort. She was divorced for the second time, and Jerry was about to be divorced for the first. Since Jerry knew all the casinos along the Coast, he suggested they meet at a new one called The Diplomat. It had a sports bar with a large screen, cheap drinks, a little privacy, and cocktail waitresses with long legs and skimpy outfits.

When Nicholas arrived at eight, Poodle was already there, holding a table in the crowded bar, sipping a draft beer and smiling pleasantly, something she never did inside the courthouse. Her flowing curly hair was pulled back. She wore tight faded jeans, a bulky sweater, and red cowboy boots. Still far from pretty, she looked much better in a bar than in the jury box.

Sylvia had the dark, sad, worldly eyes of a woman beaten by life, and Nicholas was determined to dig as fast and as deep as possible before Fernandez arrived. He ordered another round, and dispensed with the chit-chat. 'Are you married?' he asked, knowing she wasn't. The first marriage had occurred when she was nineteen, had produced twin boys, now twenty. One worked offshore on an oil rig, the other was a junior in college. Very opposite. Husband One left after five years, and she raised the boys herself. 'What about you?' she asked.

'No. Technically I'm still a student, but I'm working now.'

Husband Two was an older man, and thankfully they produced no children. The marriage lasted seven years, then he traded her in for a newer model. She vowed to never marry again. The Bears kicked off to the Packers and Sylvia watched the game with interest. She loved football because her boys had been all-conference picks in high school.

Jerry arrived in a rush, casting wary glances behind him before apologizing for being late. He gulped down the first beer in a matter of seconds, and explained that he thought he was being followed. Poodle scoffed at this, and offered the opinion that right now every member of the jury was jerking at the neck, certain that shadows were not far behind.

'Forget the jury,' Jerry said. 'I think it's my wife.'

'Your wife?' said Nicholas.

'Yeah. I think she's got some private snoop trailing me.'

'You should look forward to being sequestered,' Nicholas said.

'Oh I am,' Jerry said, winking at Poodle.

He had five hundred dollars on the Packers, plus six

points, but the bet was only for the combined score in the first half. He'd place another bet at halftime. Any pro or college game offered an amazing array of bets, he explained to the two novices seated with him, virtually none of which had anything to do with the ultimate winner. Jerry sometimes bet on who'd fumble first, who'd make the first field goal, who'd throw the most interceptions. He watched the game with the edginess of a man wagering money he could ill afford to lose. He drank four draft beers in the first quarter. Nicholas and Sylvia fell quickly behind.

In the gaps of Jerry's incessant chatter about football and the art of successful betting, Nicholas made a few awkward forays into the subject of the trial, without success. Sequestration was a sore subject, and since they had not yet experienced it there was little to say. The day's testimony had been painful enough to sit through, and the thought of rehashing Dr. Kilvan's opinions during leisure seemed cruel. Nor was there interest in the bigger picture. Sylvia in particular was disgusted by a simple inquiry into the general concept of liability.

Mrs. Grimes had been ushered from the courtroom and was in the atrium when Judge Harkin announced his rules for sequestration. As she drove Herman home he explained that he'd be spending the next two weeks in a motel room, on strange turf, without her around. Shortly after they reached their house, she had Judge Harkin on the phone, and gave him an earful of her thoughts on these most recent developments. Her husband was blind, she reminded him more than once, and he needed special assistance. Herman sat on the sofa, drinking his one beer of the day and fuming at his wife's intrusion.

Judge Harkin quickly found middle ground. He would allow Mrs. Grimes to stay with Herman in his

171

room at the motel. She could eat breakfast and dinner with Herman, and care for him, but she had to avoid contact with the other jurors. Also, she could no longer watch the trial because it was imperative that she not be able to discuss it with Herman. This didn't sit well with Mrs. Grimes, one of the few spectators who'd heard every word so far. And, though she didn't reveal this to His Honor, or to Herman, she had already developed some rather strong opinions about the case. The Judge was firm. Herman was furious. But Mrs. Grimes prevailed, and set off to the bedroom to begin packing.

Lonnie Shaver did a week's work Monday night at the office. After numerous attempts, he found George Teaker at home in Charlotte, and explained that the jury was about to be locked away for the duration of the trial. He was scheduled to talk to Taunton later in the week, and he was worried about being inaccessible. He explained that the Judge was prohibiting any direct phone calls to and from the motel room, and it would be impossible to correspond again until after the trial. Teaker was sympathetic, and as the conversation progressed he expressed somber concerns about the outcome of the trial.

'Our people in New York think an adverse verdict could send shock waves through the retail economy, especially in our business. God knows where insurance rates will go.'

'I'll do what I can,' Lonnie promised.

'Surely the jury isn't serious about a big verdict, is it?'

'Hard to tell right now. We're halfway through the plaintiff's case, it's just too early.'

'You've gotta protect us on this, Lonnie. I know it puts you in the bull's-eye, but, damn, you just happen to be there, know what I mean?'

'Yeah, I understand. I'll do what I can.'

'We're counting on you up here. Hang in there.'

172

*

The confrontation with Fitch was brief and went nowhere. Durwood Cable waited until almost nine, Monday night, when the offices were still busy with trial preparation and a late, catered dinner was being completed in the conference room. He asked Fitch to step into his office. Fitch obliged, though he wanted to leave and return to the dime store.

'I'd like to discuss a matter,' Durr said stiffly, standing on his side of his desk.

'What is it?' Fitch barked, choosing also to stand with hands on hips. He knew exactly what Cable had in mind.

'We were embarrassed in court this afternoon.'

'You were not embarrassed. As I recall, the jury was not present. So whatever happened was of no consequence to the final verdict.'

'You got caught, and we got embarrassed.'

'I did not get caught.'

'Then what do you call it?'

'I call it a lie. We did not send people to follow Stella Hulic. Why would we do that?'

'Then who called her?'

'I don't know, but it certainly wasn't any of our people. Any more questions?'

'Yeah, who was the guy in the apartment?'

'He was not one of my men. I didn't get to see the video, you understand. So I didn't see his face, but we have reason to believe he was a goon employed by Rohr and his boys.'

'Can you prove this?'

'I don't have to prove a damned thing. And I don't have to answer any more questions. Your job is to try this lawsuit, and you let me worry about security.'

'Don't embarrass me, Fitch.'

'And don't you embarrass me by losing this trial.'

'I rarely lose.'

173

Fitch turned and headed for the door. 'I know. And you're doing a fine job, Cable. You just need a little help from the outside.'

Nicholas arrived first with two gym bags stuffed with clothes and toiletries. Lou Dell and Willis and another deputy, a new one, were waiting in the hallway outside the jury room to collect the bags and store them for a while in an empty witness room. It was eight-twenty, Tuesday.

'How do the bags get from here to the motel?' Nicholas asked, still holding his and quite suspicious.

'We'll haul them over sometime during the day,' Willis said. 'But we have to inspect them first.'

'I'll be damned.'

'I beg your pardon.'

'No one is inspecting these bags,' Nicholas pronounced and stepped into the empty jury room.

'Judge's orders,' said Lou Dell, following.

'I don't care what the Judge has ordered. No one is inspecting my bags.' He placed them in a corner, walked to the coffeepot, and said to Willis and Lou Dell in the doorway, 'Leave, okay. This is the jury room.'

They shuffled backward and Lou Dell closed the door. A minute passed before there were words in the hallway. Nicholas opened the door and saw Millie Dupree, sweat lining her forehead, confronting Lou Dell and Willis with two huge Samsonite suitcases. 'They think they're gonna inspect our bags, but they're not,' Nicholas explained. 'Let's put them in here.' He grabbed the nearest, and with great effort lifted it and hauled it to the same corner in the jury room.

'Judge's orders,' Lou Dell was heard to mumble.

'We're not terrorists,' Nicholas snapped, heaving. 'What's he think we're gonna do, smuggle in some guns or drugs or something?' Millie grabbed a doughnut and expressed her gratitude to Nicholas for protecting her privacy. There were things in there that, well, she just wouldn't want men such as Willis or anybody for that matter to touch or feel.

'Leave,' Nicholas yelled, pointing at Lou Dell and Willis, who again retreated into the hallway.

By eight forty-five, all twelve jurors were present and the room was cramped with baggage Nicholas had rescued and stored. He'd ranted and raved and grown angrier with each new load, and had done a fine job of whipping the jury into a nasty bunch ready for a show-down. At nine, Lou Dell knocked on the door, then turned the knob to enter.

The door was locked from the inside.

She knocked again.

In the jury room, no one moved but Nicholas. He walked to the door, said, 'Who is it?'

'Lou Dell. It's time to go. The Judge is ready for you.'

'Tell the Judge to go to hell.'

Lou Dell turned to Willis, who was bug-eyed and reaching for his rusty revolver. The harshness of his reply startled even some of the angrier jurors, but there was no break in their unity.

'What did you say?' Lou Dell asked.

There was a loud click, then the doorknob turned. Nicholas walked into the hallway and closed the door behind him. 'Tell the Judge we're not coming out,' he said, glaring down at Lou Dell and her dirty gray bangs.

'You can't do that,' Willis said as aggressively as possible, which was not aggressive at all but rather feeble.

'Shut up, Willis.'

The excitement of jury trouble lured people back to the courtroom Tuesday morning. Word had spread quickly that one juror had been bounced and that another had had his apartment broken into, and that the Judge was angry and had ordered the entire panel locked up.

Rumors ran wild, the most popular of which was the one about a tobacco snoop actually getting caught in a juror's apartment and a warrant being issued for his arrest. Cops and FBI were looking everywhere for the man.

The morning papers from Biloxi, New Orleans, Mobile, and Jackson ran large stories either on the front page or front page Metro.

The courthouse regulars were back in droves. Most of the local bar suddenly had pressing business in the courtroom and loitered about. A half-dozen reporters from various papers held the front row, plaintiff's side. The boys from Wall Street, a group that had been dwindling as its members discovered casinos and deep sea fishing and long nights in New Orleans, were back in full force.

And so there were many witnesses to the sight of Lou Dell nervously tiptoeing through the jury door, across the front of the courtroom to the bench, where she leaned up and Harkin leaned down, and they conferred. Harkin's head cocked sideways as if he didn't catch it at first, then he looked blankly at the jury door where Willis was standing with his shoulders up in a frozen shrug.

Lou Dell finished delivering her message and walked quickly back to where Willis was waiting. Judge Harkin studied the inquiring faces of the lawyers, then looked at all the spectators out there. He scribbled something he couldn't read himself. He pondered about what to do next.

His jury was on strike!

And what exactly did his judge's handbook say about that?

He pulled his microphone closer and said, 'Gentlemen, there is a small problem with the jury. I need to go speak with them. I'll ask Mr. Rohr and Mr. Cable to assist me. Everyone else is to remain in place.'

176

The door was locked again. The Judge knocked politely, three light raps followed by a twist of the doorknob. It wouldn't open. 'Who is it?' came a male voice from inside.

'It's Judge Harkin,' he said loudly. Nicholas was standing at the door. He turned and smiled at his colleagues. Millie Dupree and Mrs. Gladys Card were hovering in a corner near a pile of luggage, fidgeting nervously, afraid of jail or whatever the Judge might throw at them. But the other jurors were still indignant.

Nicholas unlocked the door and opened it. He smiled pleasantly as if nothing were wrong, as if strikes were a routine part of trials. 'Come in,' he said.

Harkin, in a gray suit, no robe, entered with Rohr and Cable in tow. 'What's the problem here?' he asked while surveying the room. Most of the jurors were seated at the table with coffee cups and empty plates and newspapers scattered everywhere. Phillip Savelle stood alone at one window. Lonnie Shaver sat in a corner with a laptop on his knees. Easter was no doubt the spokesman, and probably the instigator.

'We don't think it's fair for the deputies to search our bags.'

'And why not?'

'It should be obvious. These are our personal effects. We're not terrorists or drug smugglers, and you're not a customs agent.' Easter's tone was authoritative, and the fact that he spoke so boldly to a distinguished judge made most of the jurors very proud. He was one of them, undoubtedly their leader regardless of what Herman thought, and he had told them more than once that they – not the Judge, not the lawyers, not the parties – but they the jurors were the most important people in this trial.

'It's routine in all sequestration cases,' His Honor said, taking a step closer to Easter, who was four inches taller and not about to be cowered.

'But it's not in black and white, is it? In fact, I'll bet it's a simple matter of discretion with the presiding judge. True?'

'There are some good reasons for it.'

'Not good enough. We're not coming out, Your Honor, until you promise our bags will be left alone.' Easter said this with a tight jaw and semi-snarl, and it was evident to the Judge and the lawyers that he meant it. He was also speaking for the group. No one else had moved.

Harkin made the mistake of glancing over his shoulder at Rohr, who couldn't wait to add a few thoughts. 'Oh hell, Judge, what's the big deal?' he blurted. 'These folks aren't carrying plastic explosives.'

'That's enough,' Harkin said, but Rohr had managed to curry a slight favor with the jury. Cable, of course, felt the same, and wanted to convey his heartfelt trust in whatever the jurors had packed in their American Touristers, but Harkin didn't give him the chance.

'Very well,' His Honor said. 'The bags will not be searched. But if it comes to my attention that any juror possesses any item prohibited by the list I handed out yesterday, then that juror will be in contempt of court and subject to being jailed. Do we understand?'

Easter looked around the room, took the measure of each of his fellow jurors, most of whom appeared relieved and a few of whom were actually nodding. 'That's fine, Judge,' he said.

'Good. Now can we get on with the trial?'

'Well, there's one other problem.'

'What is it?'

Nicholas lifted a sheet of paper from the table, read something, then said, 'According to your rules here, we're allowed one conjugal visit per week. We think we should get more.'

'How many?'

'As many as possible.'

178

This was news to most of the jurors. There had been some grumbling among some of the men, Easter and Fernandez and Lonnie Shaver in particular, about the number of conjugal visits, but the women had not discussed it. Particularly, Mrs. Gladys Card and Millie Dupree were downright embarrassed to have His Honor think they were insisting on having as much sex as they could get. Mr. Card had had prostate trouble years earlier, and, well, Mrs. Gladys Card thought about divulging this to clear her good name when Herman Grimes said, 'Two'll do me.'

The image of old Herm feeling his way around under the covers with Mrs. Grimes could not be denied, and provoked laughter that broke the tension.

'I don't think we should take a survey,' Judge Harkin said. 'Can we agree on two? We're just talking about a couple of weeks, folks.'

'Two, with a possible third,' Nicholas counter-offered.

'That's fine. Does that suit everyone?' His Honor looked around the room. Loreen Duke was giggling to herself at the table. Mrs. Gladys Card and Millie were trying their best to disappear into the walls and would not under any circumstances look the Judge in the eyes.

'Yes, that's fine,' said Jerry Fernandez, red-eyed and hung over. If Jerry went a day without sex he developed headaches, but he knew two things: his wife was delighted to have him out of the house for the next two weeks, and he and Poodle would work out an arrangement.

'I object to the wording of this,' Phillip Savelle said from the window, his first words of the trial. He was holding the sheet of rules. 'Your definition of the persons eligible to participate in conjugal visits leaves something to be desired.'

In clear English, the offending section read: 'During each conjugal visit, each juror may spend two hours,

179

alone and in his or her room, with his or her spouse, girlfriend, or boyfriend.'

Judge Harkin, along with the two lawyers looking over his shoulder, and every juror in the room read the language carefully and wondered what in the world this weirdo had in mind. But Harkin was not about to find out. 'I assure you, Mr. Savelle and members of the jury, I have no plans to restrict any of you in any way with respect to your conjugal visits. I don't care what you do, or whom you do it with, frankly.'

This seemed to satisfy Savelle as much as it humiliated Mrs. Gladys Card.

'Now, anything else?'

'That's all, Your Honor, and thank you,' Herman said loudly, reasserting himself as the leader.

'Thanks,' Nicholas said.

Scotty Mangrum announced to the court, as soon as the jury was settled and happy, that he was finished with Dr. Kilvan. Durr Cable began a cross-examination so delicate that he seemed thoroughly intimidated by the great expert. They agreed on a few statistics that were undoubtedly meaningless. Dr. Kilvan stated that, through his plethora of numbers, he believed that about ten percent of all smokers actually get lung cancer.

Cable reinforced the point, something he'd done from the beginning and something he would do to the very end. 'So Dr. Kilvan, if smoking causes lung cancer, then why do so few smokers get lung cancer?'

'Smoking greatly increases the risk of lung cancer.'

'But it doesn't cause it every time, does it?'

'No. Not every smoker gets lung cancer.'

'Thank you.'

'But for those who smoke, the risk of lung cancer is much greater.'

Cable warmed to the task and began to press. He asked Dr. Kilvan if he was familiar with a twenty-year-old study from the University of Chicago in which researchers found a greater incidence of lung cancer for smokers who lived in metropolitan areas than for smokers who lived in rural areas. Kilvan was very familiar with the study, though he had nothing to do with it.

'Can you explain it?' Cable asked.

'No.'

'Can you venture a guess?'

'Yes. It was a controversial study when it came out because it indicated factors other than tobacco smoke might cause lung cancer.'

'Such as air pollution?'

'Yes.'

'Do you believe this?'

'It's possible.'

'So you admit that air pollution causes lung cancer.'

'It might. But I stand by my research. Rural smokers get lung cancer more than rural nonsmokers, and urban smokers get cancer more than urban nonsmokers.'

Cable lifted another thick report and made an event of flipping pages. He asked Dr. Kilvan if he was familiar with a 1989 study at the University of Stockholm in which researchers determined that there was a link between heredity and smoking and lung cancer.

'I read that report,' Dr. Kilvan said.

'Do you have an opinion on it?'

'No. Heredity is not my specialty.'

'So you can't say yes or no on the issue of whether heredity might be related to smoking and lung cancer.'

'I cannot.'

'But you don't contest this report, do you?'

'I don't have a position on the report.'

'Do you know the experts who conducted the research?'

'No.'

'So you can't tell us if they're qualified or not?'

181

'No. I'm sure you've talked to them.'

Cable walked to his table, swapped reports, and walked back to the lectern.

After two weeks of severe scrutiny but little movement, Pynex stock suddenly had a reason to stir. Other than the impromptu Pledge of Allegiance, a phenomenon that so baffled the courtroom no one could decipher its meaning, the trial had produced virtually no high drama until late Monday afternoon when the jury was shaken. One of the many defense lawyers let it slip to one of the many financial analysts that Stella Hulic was generally deemed to be a decent defense juror. This got repeated a few times, and with each telling Stella's significance to the tobacco industry rose to new heights. By the time the calls were made to New York, the defense had lost its most prized possession – Stella Hulic, who was by then home on the sofa in a martini-induced coma.

Added to the rumor mill was the delicious bit about the break-in of juror Easter's apartment. It was easy to assume the intruder was paid by the tobacco industry, and since they'd been caught or at least were highly suspected, things looked bad all around for the defense. They'd lost a juror. They'd got caught cheating. The sky was falling.

Pynex opened Tuesday morning at seventy-nine and a half, quickly fell to seventy-eight in trading that became heavier as the morning progressed and the rumors mushroomed. It was at seventy-six and a quarter by mid-morning when a fresh report was received from Biloxi. An analyst who was *actually in the courtroom* down there called his office with the news that the jury had refused to come out this morning, had in fact gone on strike because it was sick and tired of the boring testimony being offered by the plaintiff's experts.

In seconds, the report was repeated a hundred times,

and it became a simple fact on the Street that the jury down there was revolting against the plaintiff. The price jumped to seventy-seven, flew past seventy-eight, hit seventy-nine, and was nearing eighty by lunch.

FIFTEEN

Of the six women remaining on the jury, the one Fitch wanted most to nail was Rikki Coleman, the wholesome, pretty, thirty-year-old mother of two. She earned twenty-one thousand dollars a year as a records administrator in a local hospital. Her husband earned thirty-six thousand dollars as a private pilot. They lived in a nice suburb with a manicured lawn and a ninety-thousand-dollar mortgage, and they each drove Japanese cars, both of which were paid for. They saved frugally and invested conservatively – eight thousand dollars last year alone in mutual funds. They were very active in a neighborhood church – she taught small kids in Sunday School and he sang in the choir.

Apparently the Colemans had acquired no bad habits. Neither smoked, and there was no evidence they drank. He liked to jog and play tennis, she spent an hour a day at a health club. Because of the clean life and because of her background in health care, Fitch feared her as a juror.

The medical records obtained from her ob-gyn revealed nothing remarkable. Two pregnancies, with perfect deliveries and recoveries. The annual checkups were done on time. A mammography two years ago showed nothing unusual. She was five feet five inches, 116 pounds.

Fitch had medical records for seven of the twelve

jurors. Easter's couldn't be found for obvious reasons. Herman Grimes was blind and had nothing to hide. Savelle was new and Fitch was digging. Lonnie Shaver hadn't been to the doctor in at least twenty years. Sylvia Taylor-Tatum's doctor had been killed months earlier in a boating accident, and his successor was a rookie who didn't know how the game was played.

The game was serious hardball, and Fitch had written most of the rules. Each year, The Fund contributed a million dollars to an organization known as the Judicial Reform Alliance, a noisy presence in Washington funded primarily by insurance companies, medical associations, and manufacturing groups. And tobacco companies. The Big Four reported annual contributions of a hundred thousand each, with Fitch and The Fund sliding another million under the door. The purpose of JRA was to lobby for laws to restrict the size of awards in damage suits. Specifically, to eliminate the nuisance of punitive damages.

Luther Vandemeer, CEO of Trellco, was a vocal member of the JRA board, and with Fitch quietly calling the shots, Vandemeer often ran roughshod over the members of the organization. Fitch wasn't seen, but he got what he wanted. Through Vandemeer and JRA, Fitch put enormous pressure on the insurance companies, which in turn put pressure on various local doctors, who in turn leaked sensitive and thoroughly confidential records of selected patients. So when Fitch wanted Dr. Dow in Biloxi to accidentally send the medical records for Mrs. Gladys Card to a nondescript post office box in Baltimore, he told Vandemeer to lean on contacts at St. Louis Mutual, Dr. Dow's malpractice carrier. Dr. Dow was told by St. Louis Mutual that his liability coverage might be dropped if he didn't play the game, and he became altogether happy to comply.

Fitch had quite a collection of medical records, but

nothing so far that might turn a verdict. His luck changed during lunch on Tuesday.

When Rikki Coleman was still Rikki Weld, she attended a small Bible college in Montgomery, Alabama, where she was very popular. Some of the prettier girls at the school were known to date boys from Auburn. As the routine investigation into her background progressed, Fitch's investigator in Montgomery got a hunch that Rikki probably had plenty of dates. Fitch pursued the hunch with serious arm-twisting through JRA, and after two weeks of dead-end probing they finally found the right clinic.

It was a small, private women's hospital in downtown Montgomery, one of only three places abortions were performed in the city at that time. During her junior year, a week after her twentieth birthday, Rikki Weld had an abortion.

And Fitch had the records. A phone call told him they were coming, and he laughed to himself as he picked the sheets off his fax machine. No name for the father, but that was fine. Rikki had met Rhea, her husband, a year after she finished college. At the time of the abortion, Rhea was a senior at Texas A & M, and it was doubtful the two had ever met.

Fitch was willing to bet a ton of money the abortion was a dark secret, all but forgotten by Rikki and definitely never revealed to her husband.

The motel was a Siesta Inn in Pass Christian, thirty minutes west along the Coast. The trip was made by charter bus with Lou Dell and Willis riding up front with the driver and the fourteen jurors scattered throughout the seats. No two sat together. Conversation was nonexistent. They were tired and disheartened, already isolated and imprisoned, though they had yet to see their new temporary home. For the first two weeks of the trial, adjournment at five meant escape; they left

186

hurriedly and raced back to reality, back to homes and kids and hot meals, back to errands and maybe the office. Adjournment now meant a chartered ride to another cell where they were to be watched and monitored and protected from evil shadows out there somewhere.

Only Nicholas Easter was delighted with sequestration, but he managed to look as dispirited as the rest.

Harrison County had rented for them the entire first floor of one wing, twenty rooms in all, though only nineteen would be needed. Lou Dell and Willis had separate rooms by the door leading to the main building where the reception and restaurant were located. A large young deputy named Chuck had a room at the other end of the hallway, ostensibly to guard the door leading to a parking lot.

The rooms were assigned by Judge Harkin himself. The bags had already been transported and placed, unopened and definitely uninspected. Keys were passed out like candy by Lou Dell, whose self-importance grew by the hour. Beds were kicked and inspected – doubles in every room for some reason. TV's were turned on, to no avail. No programs, no news during sequestration. Only movies from the motel's station. Bathrooms were scrutinized, faucets checked, toilets flushed. Two weeks here would seem like a year.

The bus was of course followed by Fitch's boys. It left the courthouse with a police escort, cops in front and back on motorcycles. It was easy to track the cops. Two detectives working for Rohr also followed along. No one expected the location of the motel to remain a secret.

Nicholas had Savelle on one side and Colonel Herrera on the other. The men's rooms were next to each other; the women were across the hall as if segregation was necessary to prevent unauthorized frolicking. Five minutes after unlocking the door the

187

walls began to close in, and ten minutes later Willis knocked loudly and inquired as to whether everything was okay. 'Just beautiful,' Nicholas said without opening the door.

The telephones had been removed, as had the mini-bars. A room at the end of the hall had been stripped of the beds and furnished with two round tables, phones, comfortable chairs, a large-screen TV, and a bar fully equipped with every possible nonalcoholic beverage. Someone dubbed it the Party Room, and it stuck. Each phone call had to be approved by one of their guardians, and no incoming calls were permitted. Emergencies would be handled through the front desk. In Room 40, directly across the hall from the Party Room, the beds had also been removed and a makeshift dining table had been set up.

No juror could leave the wing without prior approval from Judge Harkin, or on-the-spot approval from Lou Dell or one of the deputies. There was no curfew because there was no place to go, but the Party Room closed at ten.

Dinner was from six to seven, breakfast from six to eight-thirty, and they were not expected to eat en masse. They could come and go. They could fix a plate and go back to their rooms. Judge Harkin was deeply concerned about the quality of the food, and wanted to be told each morning if there were complaints.

Tuesday's smorgasbord was either fried chicken or broiled snapper, with salads and plenty of vegetables. They were amazed at their appetites. For people who'd done nothing all day but remain seated and listen, most were weak with starvation by the time the food arrived at six. Nicholas fixed the first plate and sat at the end of the table where he engaged everyone in conversation and insisted they eat as a group. He was hyper and chipper and acted as if sequestration were nothing but an adventure. His enthusiasm was slightly contagious.

Only Herman Grimes ate in his room. Mrs. Grimes prepared two plates and left in a rush. Judge Harkin had strict written instructions prohibiting her from eating with the jury. Same for Lou Dell and Willis and Chuck. So when Lou Dell entered the room with dinner in mind and found Nicholas in the middle of a tale, the conversation suddenly ceased. She flung a few green beans alongside a chicken breast and a dinner roll, and left.

They were a group now, isolated and exiled, cut off from reality and banished against their wishes to a Siesta Inn. They had no one but themselves. Easter was determined to keep them happy. They would be a fraternity, if not a family. He would work to avoid divisions and cliques.

They watched two movies in the Party Room. By ten, they were all asleep.

'I'm ready for my conjugal visit,' Jerry Fernandez announced over breakfast, in the general direction of Mrs. Gladys Card, who blushed.

'Really,' she said, rolling her eyes toward the ceiling. Jerry smiled at her as if she might be the object of his longing. Breakfast was a veritable feast of everything from fried ham to cornflakes.

Nicholas arrived mid-meal with a soft hello to the group and a troubled countenance. 'I don't understand why we can't have telephones,' were the first words from his mouth, and the pleasant morning mood suddenly turned sour. He sat across from Jerry, who read his face and caught on immediately.

'Why can't we have a cold beer?' Jerry asked. 'I have a cold beer every night when I'm home, maybe two. Who has the right to dictate what we can drink here?'

'Judge Harkin,' said Millie Dupree, a woman who avoided alcohol.

'I'll be damned.'

189

'And what about television?' Nicholas asked. 'Why can't we watch television? I've been watching television since the trial started, and I don't recall much excitement.' He turned to Loreen Duke, a large woman with a plate full of scrambled eggs. 'Have you seen any sudden newsbreaks with the latest from the trial?'

'Nope.'

He looked at Rikki Coleman, who was sitting behind a tiny bowl of harmless flakes. 'And what about a gym, someplace to go sweat after eight hours in the court-room? Surely they could've found a motel with a gym.' Rikki nodded her complete agreement.

Loreen swallowed her eggs and said, 'What I don't understand is, why can't we be trusted with a telephone? My kids might need to call me. It's not like some goon's gonna call my room and threaten me.'

'I'd just like a cold beer, or two,' Jerry said. 'Any maybe a few more conjugal visits,' he added, again looking at Mrs. Gladys Card.

The grumbling gathered speed around the table, and within ten minutes of Easter's arrival, the jurors were on the verge of revolt. The random irritations were now a full-fledged list of abuses. Even Herrera, the Retired Colonel who'd camped in jungles, was not pleased with the selection of beverages offered in the Party Room. Millie Dupree objected to the absence of newspapers. Lonnie Shaver had pressing business, and deeply resented the notion of sequestration in the first place. 'I can think for myself,' he said. 'No one can influence me.' At the least, he needed an unrestricted telephone. Phillip Savelle did yoga in the woods each morning at dawn, alone, just himself communing with nature, and there wasn't a tree within two hundred yards of the motel. And what about church? Mrs. Card was a devout Baptist who never missed prayer meeting on Wednesday nights and visitation on Tuesdays and WMU on Fridays and of course the Sabbath was crammed full of meetings.

'We'd better get things straight now,' Nicholas said solemnly. 'We're gonna be here for two weeks, maybe three. I say we get Judge Harkin's attention.'

Judge Harkin had nine lawyers packed into his chambers haggling over the daily issues to be kept away from the jury. He required the lawyers to appear each morning at eight for the warm-up bouts, and he often made them stay an hour or two after the jury left. A heavy knock interrupted a heated debate between Rohr and Cable. Gloria Lane pushed the door open until it hit a chair occupied by Oliver McAdoo.

'We have a problem with the jury,' she said gravely.

Harkin jumped to his feet. 'What!'

'They want to talk to you. That's all I know.'

Harkin looked at his watch. 'Where are they?'

'At the motel.'

'Can't we get them over here?'

'No. We've tried. They're not coming until they talk to you.'

His shoulders sagged and his mouth hung open. 'This is getting ridiculous,' Wendall Rohr offered to no one in particular. The lawyers watched the Judge, who looked absently at the pile of papers on his desk and collected his thoughts. Then he rubbed his hands together and gave them all a huge phony smile. 'Let's go see them.'

Konrad took the first call at 8:02. She didn't want to talk to Fitch, just wanted to give him the message that the jury was once again perturbed and not coming out until Harkin hauled himself over to the Siesta Inn and unruffled their feathers. Konrad ran to Fitch's room and delivered the message.

At 8:09, she called again and gave Konrad the information that Easter would be wearing a dark denim shirt over a tan T-shirt, with red socks and the usual starched khakis. Red socks, she repeated.

At 8:12, she called for the third time and asked to speak to Fitch, who was pacing around his desk and pulling on his goatee. He clenched the receiver. 'Hello.'

'Good morning, Fitch,' she said.

'Good morning, Marlee.'

'You ever been to the St. Regis Hotel in New Orleans?'

'No.'

'It's on Canal Street in the French Quarter. There's an open-air bar on the roof. It's called the Terrace Grill. Get a table overlooking the Quarter. Be there at seven tonight. I'll be there later. Are you with me?'

'Yes.'

'And come by yourself, Fitch. I'll watch you enter the hotel, and if you bring friends the meeting's off. Okay?'

'Okay.'

'And if you attempt to trail me, then I disappear.'

'You have my word.'

'Why am I not comforted by your word, Fitch?' She hung up.

Cable, Rohr, and Judge Harkin were met at the front desk by Lou Dell, who was flustered and scared and rattling on about how this had never happened to her; she'd always kept her juries under control. She led them to the Party Room where thirteen of the fourteen jurors were holed up. Herman Grimes was the lone dissenter. He had argued with the group about their tactics, and had angered Jerry Fernandez to the point of getting himself insulted. Jerry had pointed out that Herman had his wife with him, that he had no use for either televisions or newspapers, didn't drink anymore, and probably didn't need a gym. Jerry apologized after Millie Dupree asked him to.

If His Honor had a chip on his shoulder, it didn't last long. After a few uncertain hellos and good mornings, he said, starting badly, 'I'm a little bit disturbed by this.'

To which Nicholas Easter responded, 'We're not in the mood to take any abuse.'

Rohr and Cable had been expressly forbidden from speaking, and they hung near the door and watched with great amusement. Both knew this was a scene unlikely to be repeated in their litigating careers.

Nicholas had written down their list of complaints. Judge Harkin removed his coat, took a seat, and was soon hammered from all directions. He was pitifully outnumbered and virtually defenseless.

Beer was no problem. Newspapers could be censored by the front desk. Unrestricted phone calls made perfect sense. Same for televisions, but only if they promised not to watch the local news. The gym might be a problem, but he'd look into it. Visits to church could be arranged.

In fact, everything was flexible.

'Can you explain why we're here?' Lonnie Shaver demanded.

He tried. He cleared his throat and reluctantly attempted to justify his reasons for locking them away. He rambled for a bit about unauthorized contact, about what had happened so far with this jury, and he made some vague references to events that had occurred in other tobacco trials.

The misconduct was well documented, and both sides had been guilty in the past. Fitch had left a wide trail across the landscape of tobacco litigation. Operatives for some of the plaintiff's' lawyers in other cases had done dirty deeds. But Judge Harkin couldn't talk about them in front of his jury. He had to be careful and not prejudice either side.

The meeting lasted an hour. Harkin asked for a no-strike guarantee in the future, but Easter wouldn't commit.

★

Pynex opened down two points on news of a second strike, which according to an analyst waiting in the courtroom was caused by an ill-defined negative reaction by the jurors to certain tactics employed the day before by the defense team. The tactics were also ill-defined. A second rumor by another analyst in Biloxi cleared things up a little by speculating that no one in the courtroom knew for certain exactly why the jury was on strike. The stock moved half a point lower before correcting itself and inching upward in the early morning trading.

The tar in cigarettes causes cancer, at least in laboratory rodents. Dr. James Ueuker from Palo Alto had worked with mice and rats for the past fifteen years. He'd conducted many studies himself and he'd studied extensively the work of researchers around the world. At least six major studies had, in his opinion, conclusively linked cigarette smoking with lung cancer. In great detail, he explained to the jury exactly how he and his team had taken tobacco smoke condensates, usually referred to simply as 'tars,' and rubbed them directly onto the skin of what looked like a million white mice. The pictures were large and in color. The lucky mice got just a touch of tar, the others got fairly painted. To no one's surprise, the heavier the tar, the quicker skin cancer developed.

It's a long way from surface tumors on rodents to lung cancer in humans, and Dr. Ueuker, with Rohr leading the way, couldn't wait to link the two. Medical history is filled with studies in which laboratory findings have ultimately been proven to apply to humans. Exceptions have been rare. Though mice and humans live in vastly different environments, the results in some animal tests are fully consistent with the epidemiologic findings in humans.

Every available jury consultant was in the courtroom

during Ueuker's testimony. Disgusting little rodents were one thing, but rabbits and beagles could be cuddly pets. Ueuker's next study involved a similar plastering of tar on rabbits, with virtually the same results. His last test involved thirty beagles which he taught to smoke through tubes in their tracheas. The heavy smokers worked their way up to nine cigarettes a day; the equivalent of about forty cigarettes for a 150-pound man. In these dogs, serious lung damage in the form of invasive tumors was detected after 875 consecutive days of smoking. Ueuker used dogs because they exhibit the same reaction to cigarette smoking as do humans.

He would not, however, get to tell this jury about his rabbits and his beagles. An untrained amateur could look at Millie Dupree's face and tell she felt very sorry for the mice, and held a grudge against Ueuker for killing them. Sylvia Taylor-Tatum and Angel Weese also expressed overt signs of displeasure. Mrs. Gladys Card and Phillip Savelle emitted subtle evidence of disapproval. The other men were unmoved.

Rohr and company made the decision during lunch to forgo more testimony from James Ueuker.

SIXTEEN

Jumper, the courtroom deputy who took the note from Marlee thirteen days earlier and handed it to Fitch, was approached during lunch and offered five thousand dollars cash to call in sick with stomach cramps or diarrhea or some such affliction, and travel in plain clothes with Pang to New Orleans for a night of food, fun, perhaps a call girl if Jumper was so inclined. Pang needed only a few hours of light work from him. Jumper needed the money.

They left Biloxi around twelve-thirty in a rented van. By the time they arrived in New Orleans two hours later, Jumper had been convinced to temporarily retire his uniform and work for Arlington West Associates for a while. Pang offered him twenty-five thousand dollars for six months' work, nine thousand more than he was presently earning for an entire year.

They checked into their rooms at the St. Regis, two single rooms on each side of Fitch, who'd been able to extort only four from the hotel. Holly's room was down the hall. Dubaz, Joe Boy, and Dante were four blocks away in the Royal Sonesta. Jumper was first parked on a bar stool in the lounge, where he had a view of the front entrance of the hotel.

The waiting began. There was no sign of her as the afternoon dragged toward dark, and no one was surprised. Jumper was moved four times, and swiftly tired of shadow work.

Fitch left his room a few minutes before seven and rode the elevator to the roof. His table was in a corner with a nice view of the Quarter. Holly and Dubaz were at a table ten feet away, both well dressed and seemingly oblivious to everyone. Dante and a hired escort in a black mini-skirt had another table. Joe Boy would take the pictures.

At seven-thirty, she appeared from nowhere. Neither Jumper nor Pang reported seeing her anywhere near the front lobby. She simply emerged through the open French doors on the roof and was at Fitch's table in an instant. He later speculated that she did what they had done – got a room at the hotel under another name and used the stairs. She was dressed in slacks and jacket, and very pretty – dark short hair, brown eyes, strong chin and cheeks, very little makeup but then little was needed. He guessed her age to be between twenty-eight and thirty-two. She sat quickly, so fast in fact that Fitch didn't get the chance to offer her a chair. She sat directly across from him with her back to the other tables.

'A pleasure to meet you,' he said softly, glancing around at the other tables to see if anyone was listening.

'Yes, a real pleasure,' she replied, leaning on her elbows.

The waiter appeared with rapid efficiency and asked if she wanted something to drink. No, she did not. The waiter had been bribed with hard cash to carefully remove anything she touched with her fingers – glasses, plates, silver, ashtrays, anything. He would not get the chance.

'Are you hungry?' Fitch asked, sipping a mineral water.

'No. I'm in a hurry.'

'Why?'

'Because the longer I sit here the more photos your goons can take.'

'I came alone.'

'Of course you did. How'd you like the red socks?' A jazz band began across the roof, but she ignored it. Her eyes never left Fitch's.

Fitch rolled his head back and offered a snort. It was still difficult to believe he was chatting with the lover of one of his jurors. He'd had indirect contact with jurors before, several times in different forms, but never this close.

And she came to him!

'Where's he from?' Fitch asked.

'What difference does it make? He's here.'

'Is he your husband?'

'No.'

'Boyfriend?'

'You ask a lot of questions.'

'You present a lot of questions, young lady. And you expect me to ask them.'

'He's an acquaintance.'

'When did he assume the name Nicholas Easter?'

'What difference does it make? That's his legal name. He's a legal resident of Mississippi, a registered voter. He can change his name once a month if he wants.'

She kept her hands tucked together under her chin. He knew she would not make the mistake of leaving prints. 'What about you?' Fitch asked.

'Me?'

'Yeah, you're not registered to vote in Mississippi.'

'How do you know?'

'Because we checked. Assuming, of course, your real name is Marlee, and that it's spelled properly.'

'You're assuming too much.'

'It's my job. Are you from the Coast?'

'No.'

198

Joe Boy leaned down low between two plastic box-woods just long enough to take six shots of the side of her face. A decent view would require a tightrope act on top of the brick banister, eighteen floors above Canal. He'd stay in the greenery and hope for something better when she left.

Fitch rattled the ice in his glass. 'So why are we here?' he asked.

'One meeting leads to another.'

'And where do all the meetings lead us?'

'To the verdict.'

'For a fee, I'm sure.'

'Fee has an awfully small ring to it. Are you recording this?' She knew perfectly well Fitch was recording every sound.

'Of course not.'

He could play the tape in his sleep for all she cared. He had nothing to gain by sharing it with anyone. He carried too much baggage to run to the cops or to the Judge, and that didn't fit into his modus operandi anyway. The thought of blackmailing her with the authorities never occurred to Fitch, and she knew this too.

He could take all the photos he wanted, and he and his thugs scattered around the hotel could follow and watch and listen. She'd play along for a while, dodging and darting and making them work for their money. They'd find nothing.

'Let's not talk about money now, okay, Fitch?'

'We'll talk about whatever you want to talk about. This is your show.'

'Why'd you break into his apartment?'

'That's just what we do.'

'How do you read Herman Grimes?' she asked.

'Why do you ask me? You know exactly what's happening in the jury room.'

'I want to see how smart you are. I'm interested in

199

knowing if you're getting your money's worth from all those jury experts and lawyers.'

'I've never lost, so I always get my money's worth.'

'So what about Herman?'

Fitch thought for a second and motioned for another glass of water. 'He'll have a lot to do with the verdict because he is a man of strong opinions. Right now, he's open-minded. He absorbs every word in court and probably knows more than every other juror, with the exception, of course, of your friend. Am I right?'

'You're pretty close.'

'That's good to hear. How often do you chat with your friend?'

'Occasionally. Herman objected to the strike this morning, did you know that?'

'No.'

'He was the only one of the fourteen.'

'Why'd they strike?'

'Conditions. Phones, TV, beer, sex, church, the usual yearnings of mankind.'

'Who led the strike?'

'Same one who's been leading from day one.'

'I see.'

'That's why I'm here, Fitch. If my friend was not in control, I'd have nothing to offer.'

'And what are you offering?'

'I said we wouldn't talk about money now.'

The waiter set the fresh glass in front of Fitch and again asked Marlee if she wanted something to drink. 'Yes, a diet cola in a plastic cup, please.'

'We, uh, well, we don't have any plastic cups,' the waiter said with a puzzled look at Fitch.

'Then forget it,' she said, grinning at Fitch.

Fitch decided to press on. 'What's the mood of the jury right now?'

'Getting bored. Herrera's a big fan. Thinks trial

200

lawyers are dirt and severe restrictions should be placed on frivolous lawsuits.'

'My hero. Can he convince his pals?'

'No. He has no pals. He is despised by all, definitely the most disliked member of the panel.'

'Who's the friendliest girl?'

'Millie is everybody's mother, but she won't be a factor. Rikki is cute and popular, and very health conscious. She's trouble for you.'

'That's no surprise.'

'Do you want a surprise, Fitch?'

'Yeah, surprise me.'

'Which juror has actually started smoking cigarettes since the trial started?'

Fitch squinted and cocked his head a little to the left. Did he hear her correctly? 'Started smoking?'

'Yep.'

'I give up.'

'Easter. Surprised?'

'Your friend.'

'Yeah. Look, Fitch, gotta run. I'll call you tomorrow.' She was on her feet and gone, disappearing as quickly as she'd come.

Dante with the hired woman reacted before Fitch, who was stunned for a second with the speed of her departure. Dante radioed Pang in the lobby, who saw her exit the elevator and leave the hotel. Jumper tracked her on foot for two blocks before losing her in a crowded alley.

For an hour they watched the streets and parking garages and hotel lobbies and bars but did not see her. Fitch was in his room at the St. Regis when the call came from Dubaz, who'd been dispatched to the airport. She was waiting for a commuter flight that left in an hour and a half and landed in Mobile at ten-fifty. Don't follow her, Fitch instructed him, then called two standbys in Biloxi, who raced to the airport in Mobile.

Marlee lived in a rented condo facing the Back Bay of Biloxi. When she was twenty minutes from home, she called the Biloxi police by dialing 911 on her cellphone and explained to the dispatcher that a Ford Taurus with two thugs in it was following her, had been in fact since she left Mobile, that they were stalkers of some odious variety and she was fearful for her life. With the dispatcher coordinating movements, Marlee did a series of turns through a quiet subdivision and abruptly stopped at an all-night gas station. As she filled her tank, a police car pulled behind the Taurus, which was trying to hide around the corner of a closed dry cleaner. The two thugs were ordered out, then marched across the parking lot to face the woman they'd been stalking.

Marlee performed superbly as the terrified victim. The cops got angrier the more she cried. Fitch's goons were hauled away to jail.

At ten, Chuck, the large deputy with a sullen attitude, unfolded a chair at the end of the hallway near his room, and set up watch for the night. It was Wednesday, the second night of sequestration, and time to breach security. As planned, Nicholas phoned Chuck's room at eleven-fifteen. The instant he left his post to answer it, Jerry and Nicholas slipped from their rooms and walked casually through the exit door near Lou Dell's room. Lou Dell was in bed sound asleep. And though Willis had slept most of the day in court, he too was under the covers, snoring furiously.

Avoiding the front lobby, they eased through the shadows and found the taxi waiting precisely as instructed. Fifteen minutes later they entered the Nugget Casino on Biloxi Beach. They drank three beers in the sports bar as Jerry lost a hundred dollars on a hockey game. They flirted with two married women whose husbands were either winning or losing a fortune at the crap tables. The flirting took a turn toward serious, and at 1 A.M. Nicholas left the bar to play five-dollar blackjack and drink decaf coffee. He played and waited and watched as the crowd dwindled.

Marlee slipped into the chair next to him and said nothing. Nicholas pushed a short stack of chips in front of her. A drunk college boy was the only other player. 'Upstairs,' she whispered between hands as the dealer turned to talk to the pit boss.

They met on an outdoor mezzanine with a view of the parking lot and the ocean in the distance. November had arrived and the air was light and cool. There was no one else around. They kissed and huddled together on a bench. She replayed her trip to New Orleans; every detail, every word. They laughed at the two boys from Mobile who were now in the county jail. She'd call Fitch after daybreak and get his men released.

They talked business briefly because Nicholas wanted to return to the bar and collect Jerry before he drank too much and lost all his money or got caught with somebody's wife.

They each had slim pocket cellphones which could not be completely secured. New codes and passwords were exchanged.

Nicholas kissed her good-bye and left her alone on the mezzanine.

Wendall Rohr had a hunch the jury was tired of listening to researchers tout their findings and lecture from their charts and graphs. His consultants were telling him the jurors had heard enough about lung cancer and smoking, that they had probably been convinced before the trial started that cigarettes were addictive and dangerous. He was confident he had established a strong causal relationship between the Bristols and the tumors that killed Jacob Wood, and it was now time to ice the case. Thursday morning he announced that the plaintiff would like to call Lawrence Krigler as its next witness. A noticeable tension seized the defense table for the moment it took to call Mr. Krigler from somewhere in the rear. Another plaintiff's lawyer, John Riley Milton from Denver, rose and smiled sweetly at the jury.

Lawrence Krigler was in his late sixties, tanned and fit, well dressed and quick in step. He was the first witness without Doctor stuck to the front of his name since the video of Jacob Wood. He lived now in Florida, where he'd retired after he left Pynex. John Riley Milton rushed him through the preliminaries because the juicy stuff was just around the corner.

An engineering graduate of North Carolina State, he'd worked for Pynex for thirty years before leaving in the midst of a lawsuit thirteen years earlier. He'd sued Pynex. The company'd countersued him. They settled out of court with terms being nondisclosed.

When he was first hired, the company, then called Union Tobacco, or simply U-Tab, had shipped him to Cuba to study tobacco production down there. He'd worked in production ever since, or at least until the day he left. He'd studied the tobacco leaf and a thousand ways to grow it more efficiently. He considered himself an expert in this field, though he was not testifying as an expert and would not offer opinions. Only facts.

In 1969, he completed a three-year, in-house study on the feasibility of growing an experimental tobacco leaf known only as Raleigh 4. It had one third the nicotine of regular tobacco. Krigler concluded, with a wealth of research to support him, that Raleigh 4 could be grown and produced as efficiently as all other tobaccos then grown and produced by U-Tab.

It was a monumental work, one he was quite proud of, and he was devastated when his study was at first ignored by higher-ups within his company. He slogged his way through the entrenched bureaucracy above him, with disheartening results. No one seemed to care about this new strain of tobacco with much less nicotine.

Then he learned that he was very wrong. His bosses cared a great deal about nicotine levels. In the summer of 1971 he got his hands on an intercompany memo instructing upper management to quietly do whatever possible to discredit Krigler's work with Raleigh 4. His own people were silently knifing him in the back. He kept his cool, told no one he had the memo, and began a clandestine project to learn the reasons for the conspiracy against him.

At this point in his testimony, John Riley Milton introduced into evidence two exhibits – the thick study Krigler completed in 1969, and the 1971 memo.

The answer became crystal clear, and it was something he'd come to suspect. U-Tab could not afford to produce a leaf with markedly lower nicotine, because nicotine meant profits. The industry had known since the late thirties that nicotine was physically addictive.

'How do you know the industry knew?' Milton asked, very deliberately. With the exception of the defense lawyers, who were doing their best to appear bored and indifferent, the entire court-room was listening with rapt attention.

'It's common knowledge within the industry,' Krigler answered. 'There was a secret study in the late 1930s, paid for by a tobacco company, and the result was clear proof that the nicotine in cigarettes is addictive.'

'Have you seen this report?'

'No. As you might guess, it has been well concealed.' Krigler paused and looked at the defense table. The bombshell was coming, and he was thoroughly enjoying the moment. 'But I saw a memo –'

205

'Objection!' Cable shouted as he rose. 'This witness cannot state what he may or may not have seen in a written document. The reasons are plentiful and are set out more fully in the brief we filed on this point.'

The brief was eighty pages long and had been argued over for a month now. Judge Harkin had already ruled, in writing. 'Your objection is noted, Mr. Cable. Mr. Krigler, you may continue.'

'In the winter of 1973, I saw a one-page memo summarizing the nicotine study from the 1930s. The memo had been copied many times, was very old, and had been slightly altered.'

'Altered in what way?'

'The date had been deleted, as had the name of the person sending it.'

'To whom was it sent?'

'It was addressed to Sander S. Fraley, who at that time was the president of Allegheny Growers, the predecessor of a company now called ConPack.'

'A tobacco company.'

'Yes, basically. It calls itself a consumer products company, but the bulk of its business is manufacturing cigarettes.'

'When did he serve as president?'

'From 1931 to 1942.'

'Is it then safe to assume the memo was sent prior to 1942?'

'Yes. Mr. Fraley died in 1942.'

'Where were you when you saw this memo?'

'At a Pynex facility in Richmond. When Pynex was still Union Tobacco, its corporate headquarters were in Richmond. In 1979, it changed its name and moved to New Jersey. But the buildings are still in use in Richmond, and that's where I worked until I left. Most of the company's old records are there, and a person I know showed me the memo.'

'Who was this person?'

'He was a friend, and he's now dead. I promised him I'd never reveal his identity.'

'Did you actually hold the memo?'

'Yes. In fact, I made a copy of it.'

'And where is your copy?'

'It didn't last long. The day after I locked it in my desk drawer, I was called out of town on business. While I was out, someone went through my desk and removed a number of things, including my copy of the memo.'

'Do you recall what the memo said?'

'I remember very well. Keep in mind, for a long time I'd been digging for some confirmation of what I suspected. Seeing the memo was an unforgettable moment.'

'What did it say?'

'Three paragraphs, maybe four, brief and to the point. The writer explained that he had just read the nicotine report that was secretly shown to him by the head of research at Allegheny Growers, a person who went unnamed in the memo. In his opinion, the study proved conclusively and beyond any doubt that nicotine is addictive. As I recall, this was the gist of the first two paragraphs.'

'And the next paragraph?'

'The writer suggested to Fraley that the company take a serious look at increasing the nicotine levels in its cigarettes. More nicotine meant more smokers, which meant more sales and more profits.'

Krigler delivered his lines with a fine flair for the dramatic, and every ear soaked up his words. The jurors, for the first time in days, watched every move the witness made. The word 'profits' floated over the court-room and hung like a dirty fog.

John Riley Milton paused for a bit, then said, 'Now, let's keep this straight. The memo was prepared by someone at another company, and sent to the president of that company, right?'

'That's correct.'

'A company that was then and is now a competitor of Pynex?'

'That's correct.'

'How did the memo find its way to Pynex in 1973?'

'I never found out. But Pynex certainly knew about the study. In fact, the entire tobacco industry knew about the study by the early 1970s, if not sooner.'

'How do you know this?'

'I worked in the industry for thirty years, remember. And I spent my career in production. I talked to a lot of people, especially my counterparts at other companies. Let's just say that the tobacco companies at times can stick together.'

'Did you ever attempt to obtain another copy of the memo from your friend?'

'I tried. It didn't work. Let's leave it at that.'

Except for the usual fifteen-minute coffee break at ten-thirty, Krigler testified nonstop for the three-hour morning session. His testimony passed by as if it were only a matter of minutes, and was a crucial moment in the trial. The drama of an ex-employee spilling dirty secrets was played to perfection. The jurors even ignored their customary longings for lunch. The lawyers watched the jurors more closely than ever, and the Judge seemed to write down every word the witness said.

The reporters were unusually reverent; the jury consultants unusually attentive. The watchdogs from Wall Street counted the minutes until they could bolt from the room and make breathless phone calls to New York. The bored local lawyers hanging around the courtroom would talk about the testimony for years. Even Lou Dell stopped her knitting on the front row.

Fitch watched and listened from the viewing room

next to his office. Krigler had been scheduled to testify early next week, and then there'd been the chance that he wouldn't testify at all. Fitch was one of the few people still alive who'd actually seen the memo, and Krigler had described it with amazing recollection. It was clear to everyone, even Fitch, that the witness was telling the truth.

One of Fitch's first assignments nine years ago when he'd first been hired by the Big Four was to track down *every* copy of the memo, and destroy each one. He was still working on it.

Neither Cable nor any defense lawyer retained by Fitch so far had seen the memo.

The admissibility of its existence in court had caused a small war. The rules of evidence normally prevent such verbal descriptions of lost documents, for obvious reasons. The best evidence is the document itself. But, as with every area of the law, there are exceptions and exceptions to the exceptions, and Rohr et al. had done a masterful job of convincing Judge Harkin that the jury should hear Krigler's description of what was, in effect, a lost document.

Cable's cross-examination that afternoon would be brutal, but the damage was done. Fitch skipped lunch and locked himself in his office.

In the jury room, the atmosphere over lunch was remarkably different. The ordinary drivel about football and recipes was replaced by a virtual silence. As a deliberative body, the jury had been lulled into stupor with two weeks of tedious scientific testimony from experts who were being paid large sums of money to travel to Biloxi and lecture. Now the jury had been shaken back to life with Krigler's sensational inside dirt.

They ate less and stared more. Most wanted to ease into another room with their favorite friend and replay what they'd just heard. Did they hear it right? Did everyone understand what the man just said? They intentionally kept nicotine high so people got hooked!

They managed to do just that. The smokers, only three now since Stella had departed, though Easter was a semi-smoker because he preferred to spend time with Jerry and Poodle and Angel Weese, ate quickly then excused themselves. They all sat on folding chairs, staring and puffing at the open window. With the weighted nicotine, the cigarettes felt a bit heavier. But when Nicholas said so, no one laughed.

Mrs. Gladys Card and Millie Dupree managed to leave for the rest room at the same moment. They took a long pee then spent fifteen minutes washing their hands and speaking to each other in front of the mirror. They were joined in mid-conversation by Loreen Duke, who leaned by the towel dispenser and quickly threw in her amazement and disgust with tobacco companies.

After the table was cleared, Lonnie Shaver opened his laptop two chairs down from Herman, who had his braille machine plugged in and was typing away. The Colonel said to Herman, 'Don't guess you need a translator for that testimony, do you?' To which Herman replied with a grunt and said, 'Pretty amazing, I'd say.' That was the nearest Herman Grimes came to discussing any aspect of the case.

Lonnie Shaver was not amazed or impressed by anything.

Phillip Savelle had politely asked for and received permission from Judge Harkin to spend part of his lunch break doing yoga under a large oak tree behind the courthouse. He was escorted by a deputy to the oak tree, where he removed his shirt, socks, and shoes, then sat on the soft grass and creased himself into a pretzel. When he began chanting, the deputy slid away to a nearby concrete bench and lowered his face so no one would recognize him.

*

Cable said hello to Krigler as if the two were old friends. Krigler smiled and said 'Good afternoon, Mr. Cable,' with an abundance of confidence. Seven months earlier, in Rohr's office, Cable and company had spent three days taking a video deposition of Krigler. The video had been watched and studied by no fewer than two dozen lawyers and several jury experts and even two psychiatrists. Krigler was telling the truth, but the truth needed to be blurred at this point. This was a cross-examination, a crucial one, so to hell with the truth. The witness had to be discredited!

After hundreds of hours of plotting, a strategy had been developed. Cable began by asking Krigler if he was angry with his former employer.

'Yes,' he answered.

'Do you hate the company?'

'The company is an entity. How do you hate a thing?'

'Do you hate war?'

'Never been.'

'Do you hate child abuse?'

'I'm sure it's sickening, but luckily I've never had any connection with it.'

'Do you hate violence?'

'I'm sure it's awful, but, again, I've been lucky.'

'So you don't hate anything?'

'Broccoli.'

A gentle laugh came from all quarters of the courtroom, and Cable knew he had his hands full.

'You don't hate Pynex?'

'No.'

'Do you hate anyone who works there?'

'No. I dislike some of them.'

'Did you hate anyone who worked there when you worked there?'

'No. I had some enemies, but I don't remember hating anyone.'

211

'What about the people against whom you directed your lawsuit?'

'No. Again, they were enemies, but they were just doing their jobs.'

'So you love your enemies?'

'Not really. I know I'm supposed to try, but it sure is difficult. I don't recall saying I loved them.'

Cable had hoped to score a minor point by injecting the possibility of retribution or revenge on the part of Krigler. Maybe if he used the word 'hate' enough, it might stick with some of the jurors.

'What is your motive for testifying here?'

'That's a complicated question.'

'Is it money?'

'No.'

'Are you being paid by Mr. Rohr or anyone working for the plaintiff to come and testify?'

'No. They've agreed to reimburse me for my travel expenses, but that's all.'

The last thing Cable wanted was an open door for Krigler to expound upon his reasons for testifying. He had touched on them briefly during Milton's direct examination, and he'd spent five hours detailing them during the video deposition. It was crucial to keep him occupied with other matters.

'Have you ever smoked cigarettes, Mr. Krigler?'

'Yes. Unfortunately I smoked for twenty years.'

'So you wished you'd never smoked?'

'Of course.'

'When did you start?'

'When I went to work for the company, 1952. Back then they encouraged all their employees to smoke cigarettes. They still do.'

'Do you believe you damaged your health by smoking for twenty years?'

'Of course. I feel lucky I'm not dead, like Mr. Wood.'

'When did you quit?'

'In 1973. After I learned the truth about nicotine.'

'Do you feel your present health has been diminished in some way because you smoked for twenty years?'

'Of course.'

'In your opinion, was the company responsible in any way for your decision to smoke cigarettes?'

'Yes. As I said, it was encouraged. Everybody else smoked. We could purchase cigarettes at half price in the company store. Every meeting began with a bowl of cigarettes passed around. It was very much a part of the culture.'

'Were your offices ventilated?'

'No.'

'How bad was the secondhand smoke?'

'Very bad. There was always a blue fog hanging not far over your head.'

'So you blame the company today because you're not as healthy as you think you should be?'

'The company had a lot to do with it. Fortunately, I was able to kick the habit. It wasn't easy.'

'And you hold a grudge against the company for this?'

'Let's just say I wish I'd gone to work in another industry when I finished college.'

'Industry? Do you carry a grudge against the entire industry?'

'I'm not a fan of the tobacco industry.'

'Is that why you're here?'

'No.'

Cable flipped his notes and quickly changed direction. 'Now, you had a sister at one time, didn't you, Mr. Krigler?'

'I did.'

'What happened to her?'

'She died in 1970.'

'How'd she die?'

'Lung cancer. She smoked two packs a day for about

213

twenty-three years. Smoking killed her, Mr. Cable, if that's what you want.'

'Were you close to her?' Cable asked with enough compassion to deflect some of the ill will for bringing up the tragedy in the first place.

'We were very close. She was my only sibling.'

'And you took her death very hard?'

'I did. She was a very special person, and I still miss her.'

'I'm sorry to bring this up, Mr. Krigler, but it is relevant.'

'Your compassion is overwhelming, Mr. Cable, but there's nothing relevant about it.'

'How did she feel about your smoking?'

'She didn't like it. As she was dying she begged me to stop. Is that what you want to hear, Mr. Cable?'

'Only if it's the truth.'

'Oh it's true, Mr. Cable. The day before she died I promised I would quit smoking. And I did, though it took me three long years to do it. I was hooked, you see, Mr. Cable, as was my sister, because the company that manufactured the cigarettes that killed her, and could've killed me, intentionally kept the nicotine at a high level.'

'Now –'

'Don't interrupt me, Mr. Cable. Nicotine in itself is not a carcinogen, you know that, it's just a poison, a poison that gets you addicted so the carcinogens can one day take care of you. That's why cigarettes are inherently dangerous.'

Cable watched him with complete composure. 'Are you finished?'

'I'm ready for the next question. But don't interrupt me again.'

'Certainly, and I apologize. Now, when did you first become convinced that cigarettes were inherently dangerous?'

'I don't know exactly. It's been known for some time, you know. It did not then and does not now take a genius to figure it out. But I'd say at some point in the early seventies, after I finished my study, after my sister had died, and shortly before I saw the infamous memo.'

'In 1973?'

'Somewhere in there.'

'When did your employment with Pynex cease? What year?'

'In 1982.'

'So you continued working for a company which made products you considered to be inherently dangerous?'

'I did.'

'What was your salary in 1982?'

'Ninety thousand dollars a year.'

Cable paused and walked to his table where he was handed yet another yellow legal pad which he studied for a second as he bit a stem of his reading glasses, then he returned to the lectern and asked Krigler why he'd sued the company in 1982. Krigler didn't appreciate the question, and looked at Rohr and Milton for help. Cable pursued details of the events leading up to the litigation, hopelessly complicated and personal litigation, and the testimony slowed to a virtual halt. Rohr objected and Milton objected, and Cable acted as if he couldn't understand why in the world they'd object. The lawyers met at the sidebar to haggle in private in front of Judge Harkin, and Krigler grew weary of the witness stand.

Cable hammered away at Krigler's performance record during his last ten years with Pynex, and hinted strongly that other witnesses might be called to contradict him.

The ploy almost worked. Unable to shake the damaging aspects of Krigler's testimony, the defense chose instead to blow smoke at the jury. If a witness is unshakable, then beat him up with insignificant details.

The ploy was explained to the jury, however, by young Nicholas Easter, who'd had two years of law school and chose to remind his colleagues of his experiences during a late afternoon coffee break. Over Herman's objections, Nicholas voiced his resentment at Cable for throwing mud and trying to confuse the jury. 'He thinks we're stupid,' he said bitterly.

SEVENTEEN

In response to frantic calls from Biloxi, the price of Pynex shares dipped as low as seventy-five and a half by closing Thursday, down almost four points in heavy trading attributed to the dramatic events in the courtroom.

In other tobacco trials, former employees had testified about pesticides and insecticides sprayed on the crops, and experts had linked the chemicals to cancer. The juries had not been impressed. In one trial, a former employee had spilled the news that his former employer had targeted young teenagers with ads showing thin and glamorous idiots with perfect chins and perfect teeth having all manner of fun with tobacco. The same employer had targeted older teenaged males with ads depicting cowboys and stock car drivers seriously pursuing life with cigarettes stuck between their lips.

But the juries in those trials did not award the plaintiffs.

No former employee, though, did as much damage as Lawrence Krigler. The infamous memo from the 1930s had been seen by a handful of people, but never produced in litigation. Krigler's version of it for the jury was as close as any plaintiff's lawyer had come to the real thing. The fact that he'd been allowed by Judge Harkin to describe it to the jury would be hotly contested on appeal, regardless of who won at trial.

Krigler was quickly escorted out of town by Rohr's security people, and an hour after finishing his testimony he was on a private plane back to Florida. Several times since leaving Pynex he had been tempted to contact a plaintiff's lawyer in a tobacco trial, but had never mustered the courage.

Pynex had paid him three hundred thousand dollars out of court, just to get rid of him. The company had insisted he agree never to testify in trials similar to Wood, but he refused. And when he refused, he became a marked man.

They, whoever they had been, said they'd kill him. The threats had been few and scattered over the years, always from unknown voices and always dropping in when least expected. Krigler was not one to hide. He'd written a book, an exposé he said would be published in the event of his untimely death. A lawyer had it in Melbourne Beach. The lawyer was a friend who'd arranged the initial meeting with Rohr. The lawyer had also opened a dialogue with the FBI, just in case something happened to Mr. Krigler.

Millie Dupree's husband, Hoppy, owned a struggling realty agency in Biloxi. Certainly not the aggressive sort, he had few listings and few leads, but he worked diligently with what little business came his way. One wall in the front room had pictures of available OPPORTUNITIES thumbtacked to a corkboard – mainly little brick houses with neat lawns and a few run-down duplexes.

Casino fever had brought to the Coast a new herd of real estate swingers unafraid to borrow heavily and develop accordingly. Once again, Hoppy and the little guys had played it safe and got themselves squeezed even further into markets they knew all too well – darling little STARTERS for the newlyweds and hopeless FIXUPS for the desperate and MOTIVATED SELLERS

218

for those who couldn't qualify for a bank loan.

But he paid his bills and somehow provided for his family – his wife Millie and their five kids, three at the junior college and two in high school. At any given time he had attached to his office the licenses of a half a dozen part-time sales associates, for the most part a downhearted bunch of losers who shared his aversion to debt and forcefulness. Hoppy loved pinochle, and many hours were passed at his desk in the back over cards as subdivisions sprang up all around him. Realtors, regardless of their talent, love to dream of the big score. Hoppy and his motley gang were not above taking a late-afternoon nip and talking big business over cards.

Just before six on Thursday, as the pinochle was winding down and preparations were being made to end another nonproductive day, a well-dressed young businessman with a shiny black attaché entered the office and asked for Mr. Dupree. Hoppy was in the back, rinsing his mouth with Scope and hurrying to get home since Millie was locked away. Introductions were made. The young man presented a business card which declared him to be Todd Ringwald of KLX Property Group out of Las Vegas, Nevada. The card impressed Hoppy enough to shoo off the last of the lingering sales associates, and lock his office door. The mere presence of one dressed so well and having traveled such a great distance could only mean serious matters were possible.

Hoppy offered a drink, then coffee, which could be brewed in an instant. Mr. Ringwald declined, and asked if he'd come at a bad time.

'No, not at all. We work crazy hours, you know. It's a crazy business.'

Mr. Ringwald smiled and agreed because he too was once in business for himself, not too many years ago. First a bit about his company. KLX was a private outfit with holdings in a dozen states. While it did not own casinos, and had no plans to do so, it had developed a

219

related specialty, a lucrative one. KLX tracked casino development. Hoppy nodded furiously as if this type of enterprise was altogether familiar to him.

Typically, when casinos move in, the local real estate market changes dramatically. Ringwald was certain Hoppy knew all about this, and Hoppy agreed whole-heartedly as if he'd made a fortune recently. KLX moved in quietly, and Ringwald emphasized just how utterly secretive the company was, a step behind the casinos, and developed shopping areas and expensive condos and apartment complexes and upper-end subdivisions. Casinos pay well, employ many, things change in the local economy, and, well, there's just a helluva lot more money floating around and KLX wanted its share. 'Our company is a vulture,' Ringwald explained with a devious smile. 'We sit back and watch the casinos. When they move, we go in for the kill.'

'Brilliant,' Hoppy offered, unable to control himself.

However, KLX had been slow to move on the Coast, and, confidentially, this had cost a few jobs back in Vegas. There were still incredible opportunities though, to which Hoppy said, 'There certainly are.'

Ringwald opened his briefcase and removed a folded property map, which he held on his knees. He, as Vice President of Development, preferred to deal with smaller realty agents. The big firms had too many people hanging around, too many overweight house-wives reading classifieds and waiting for the slightest morsel of gossip. 'You got that right!' Hoppy said, staring at the property map. 'Plus you get better service from a small agency, like mine.'

'You have been highly recommended,' Ringwald said, and Hoppy couldn't suppress a smile. The phone rang. It was the senior in high school wanting to know what was for supper and when might Mother be coming home. Hoppy was pleasant but short. He was very busy,

220

he explained, and there might be some old lasagna in the freezer.

The property map was unfolded on Hoppy's desk. Ringwald pointed to a large red-colored plot in Hancock County, next door to Harrison and the westernmost of the three coastal counties. Both men hovered over the desk from different sides.

'MGM Grand is coming here,' Ringwald said, pointing to a large bay. 'But no one knows it yet. You certainly can't tell anyone.'

Hoppy's head was shaking Hell No! before Ringwald finished.

'They're gonna build the biggest casino on the Coast, probably middle of next year. They'll announce in three months. They'll buy a hundred acres or so of this land here.'

'That's beautiful land. Virtually untouched.' Hoppy had never been near the property with a real estate sign, but he had lived on the Coast for forty years.

'We want this,' Ringwald said, pointing again to the land marked in red. It was adjacent to the north and west of the MGM land. 'Five hundred acres, so we can do this.' He pulled the top sheet back to reveal an artist's rendering of a rather splendid Planned Unit Development. It was labeled Stillwater Bay with bold blue letters across the top. Condos, office buildings, big homes, smaller homes, playgrounds, churches, a central square, a shopping mall, a pedestrian mall, a dock, a marina, a business block, parks, jogging paths, bike trails, even a proposed high school. It was Utopia, all planned for Hancock County by some wonderfully farsighted people in Las Vegas.

'Wow,' Hoppy said. There was a bloody fortune on his desk.

'Four different phases over five years. The whole thing will cost thirty million. It's by far the biggest development ever seen in these parts.'

221

'Nothing can touch it.'

Ringwald flipped another page and revealed another drawing of the dock area, then another for a close-up of the residential section. 'These are just the preliminary drawings. I'll show you more if you can come to the home office.'

'Vegas.'

'Yes. If we can reach an agreement on your representation, then we'd like to fly you out for a few days, you know, meet our people, see the whole project from the design end.'

Hoppy's knees wobbled and he took a breath. Slow down, he told himself. 'Yes, and what type of representation did you have in mind?'

'Initially, we need a broker to handle the purchase of the land. Once we buy it, we have to convince the local authorities to approve the development. This, as you know, can take time and become controversial. We spend a lot of time before planning commissions and zoning boards. We even go to court when necessary. But it's just part of our business. You'll be involved to some extent at this point. Once it's approved, we'll need a real estate firm to handle the marketing of Stillwater Bay.'

Hoppy backed into his chair and pondered figures for a moment. 'How much will the land cost?' he asked.

'It's expensive, much too expensive for this area. Ten thousand an acre, for land worth about half that much.'

Ten thousand an acre for five hundred acres added up to five million bucks, six percent of which was three hundred thousand dollars for Hoppy's commission, assuming of course no other realtors were to be involved. Ringwald watched poker-faced as Hoppy did the mental math.

'Ten thousand's too much,' Hoppy said with authority.

'Yes, but the land is not on the market. The sellers

don't really want to sell, so we have to sneak in quickly, before the MGM story leaks, and snatch it. That's why we need a local agent. If word hits the street that a big company from Vegas is looking at the land, it'll go to twenty thousand an acre. Happens all the time.'

The fact that the land was not on the market caused Hoppy's heart to stutter. No other realtors were involved! Just him. Just little Hoppy and his full six percent commission. His ship had finally come in. He, Hoppy Dupree, after decades of selling duplexes to pensioners, was about to make a killing.

Not to mention the 'marketing of Stillwater Bay.' All those houses and condos and commercial properties, hell thirty million dollars' worth of red-hot property with Dupree Realty signs hanging all over it. Hoppy could be a millionaire in five years, he decided on the spot.

Ringwald moved in. 'I'm assuming your commission is eight percent. That's what we normally pay.'

'Of course,' Hoppy said, the words rushing forward over a very dry tongue. From three hundred thousand to four hundred thousand, just like that. 'Who are the sellers?' he asked, quickly changing the subject now that they'd agreed on eight percent.

Ringwald allowed a noticeable sigh and his shoulders sagged, but only for an instant. 'This is where it gets complicated.' Hoppy's heart sank.

'The property is in the sixth district of Hancock County,' Ringwald said slowly. 'And the sixth district is the domain of a county supervisor by the name of –'

'Jimmy Hull Moke,' Hoppy interrupted, with no small measure of sadness.

'You know him?'

'Everybody knows Jimmy Hull. He's been in office for thirty years. Slickest crook on the Coast.'

'Do you know him personally?'

'No. Only by reputation.'

223

'Which we've heard is rather shady.'

'Shady is a compliment to Jimmy Hull. On a local level, the man controls everything in his end of the county.'

Ringwald offered a puzzled look as if he and his company had no clue about how to proceed. Hoppy rubbed his sad eyes and plotted to keep his fortune. They made no eye contact for a full minute, then Ringwald said, It's not wise to buy the land unless we can get some assurances from Mr. Moke and the local people. As you know, there will be a maze of regulatory approvals for the project.'

'Planning, zoning, architectural review, soil erosion, you name it,' Hoppy said, as if he fought these wars every day.

'We've been told that Mr. Moke controls all of this.'

'With an iron fist.'

Another pause.

'Perhaps we should arrange a meeting with Mr. Moke,' Ringwald said.

'I don't think so.'

'Why not?'

'Meetings don't work.'

'I'm not following you.'

'Cash. Pure and simple. Jimmy Hull likes it under the table, large sacks of it in unmarked bills.'

Ringwald nodded with a solemn grin as if this was unfortunate but not unexpected. 'So we've heard,' he said, almost to himself. 'Actually, this is not unusual, especially in areas where casinos have appeared. There's lots of fresh foreign money and people get greedy.'

'Jimmy Hull was born greedy. He was stealing thirty years before casinos appeared here.'

'He doesn't get caught?'

'No. For a local supervisor, he's pretty bright. Everything's in cash, no trail, he covers himself carefully.

Then again, it doesn't take a rocket scientist.' Hoppy tapped his forehead lightly with a handkerchief. He bent forward and removed two tumblers from a lower drawer, then a bottle of vodka. He poured two stiff drinks and placed one across the desk in front of Ringwald. 'Cheers,' he said before Ringwald touched his glass.

'So what do we do?' Ringwald asked.

'What do you normally do in situations like this?'

'We normally find a way to work with the local authorities. There's too much money involved to pack up and go home.'

'How do you work with local authorities?'

'We have ways. We have contributed money to re-election campaigns. We have honored our friends with expensive vacations. We've paid consulting fees to spouses and children.'

'You ever paid bribes in hard cash?'

'Well, I'd rather not say.'

'That's what it'll take. Jimmy Hull is a simple man. Just cash.' Hoppy took a long sip and smacked his lips.

'How much?'

'Who knows. But it'd better be enough. You low-ball him up front, he'll kill your project later. And he'll keep the cash. Jimmy Hull doesn't do refunds.'

'You sound like you know him rather well.'

'Those of us who wheel and deal along the Coast know how he plays the game. He's sort of a local legend.'

Ringwald shook his head in disbelief. 'Welcome to Mississippi,' Hoppy said, then took another sip. Ringwald had not touched his drink.

For twenty-five years Hoppy had played it straight, and he had no plans to compromise himself now. The money wasn't worth the risk. He had kids, a family, a reputation, standing in the community. Church occasionally. The Rotary Club. And just exactly who was this stranger sitting across his desk in the fancy suit and designer loafers, offering the world if only one minor agreement could be reached? He, Hoppy, would certainly get on the phone and check out KLX Property Group and Mr. Todd Ringwald as soon as he left the office.

'This is not unusual,' Ringwald said. 'We see it all the time.'

'Then what do you do?'

'Well, I think our first step is to approach Mr. Moke and determine the likelihood of a deal.'

'He'll be ready to deal.'

'Then we determine the terms of the deal. As you put it, we'll decide how much cash.' Ringwald paused and took a tiny sip of his drink. 'Are you willing to be involved?'

'I don't know. In what way?'

'We don't know anyone in Hancock County. We try to keep a low profile. We're from Vegas. If we start asking questions, then the entire project gets blown.'

'You want me to talk to Jimmy Hull?'

'Only if you want to be involved. If not, then we'll be forced to find someone else.'

'I have a clean reputation,' Hoppy said, with astounding firmness, then swallowed hard at the thought of a competitor raking in his four hundred thousand.

'We don't expect you to get dirty.' Ringwald paused and groped for the right words. Hoppy was pulling for him. 'Let's just say that we have ways of delivering what Mr. Moke wants. You won't have to touch it. In fact, you won't know when it happens.'

Hoppy sat straighter as a burden lifted itself from his shoulders. Perhaps there was some middle ground here. Ringwald and his company did this all the time. They'd probably dealt with crooks much more sophisticated than Jimmy Hull Moke. 'I'm listening,' he said.

'Your fingers are on the pulse here. We're obviously outsiders, so we'll rely on you. Let me give you a scenario. You tell me if it'll work. What if you meet with Mr. Moke, just the two of you, and you tell him in broad strokes about the development? Our names are not mentioned, you simply have this client who wants to work with him. He'll name his price. If it's within our range, then you tell him it's a deal. We'll take care of the delivery, and you never know for certain if the cash actually changes hands. You've done nothing wrong. He's happy. We're happy because we're about to make a pot full of money, along with you, I might add.'

Hoppy liked it! None of the mud could stick to his hands. Let his client and Jimmy Hull do their dirty work. He'd stay out of the gutter and simply turn his head. Still, he was overcome by caution. He said he'd like to think about it.

They chatted some more, looked at the plans once again, and said good-bye at eight. Ringwald was to call early Friday morning.

Before heading home, Hoppy dialed the number on Ringwald's business card. An efficient receptionist in Las Vegas said, 'Good afternoon, KLX Property Group.' Hoppy smiled, then asked to speak to Todd Ringwald. The call was routed, with soft rock in the background, to Mr. Ringwald's office where Hoppy spoke to Madeline, an assistant of some variety who explained that Mr. Ringwald was out of town and not expected back until Monday. She asked who was calling, and Hoppy quickly hung up.

There now. KLX was indeed legitimate.

Incoming phone calls were stopped at the front desk where they were recorded on yellow message slips and forwarded to Lou Dell, who then distributed them like the Easter Bunny passing out chocolate eggs. The one from George Teaker arrived at seven-forty Thursday

227

night, and was delivered to Lonnie Shaver, who was skipping the movie and working with his computer. He called Teaker at once, and for the first ten minutes answered nothing but questions about the trial. Lonnie confessed that it had been a bad day for the defense. Lawrence Krigler had made a noticeable impact on the jurors, all except for Lonnie, of course. Lonnie had not been impressed, he assured Teaker. The folks in New York were certainly worried, Teaker said more than once. They're awfully relieved that Lonnie was on the jury and could be counted on no matter what, but things looked dim. Or did they?

Lonnie said it was too early to tell.

Teaker said they needed to tie up the loose ends of the employment contract. Lonnie could think of only one loose end, and that was how much his new salary would be. He currently made forty thousand dollars. Teaker said SuperHouse would raise him to fifty thousand with some stock options, and a performance-based bonus that might hit twenty thousand.

They wanted him to start a management training course in Charlotte as soon as the trial was over. Mention of the trial brought on another round of questions about the mood of the jury.

An hour later, Lonnie stood at his window, watched the parking lot, and tried to convince himself he was about to earn seventy thousand dollars a year. Three years ago, he made twenty-five thousand.

Not bad for a kid whose father drove a milk truck for three bucks an hour.

EIGHTEEN

On Friday morning, *The Wall Street Journal* ran a frontpage story about Lawrence Krigler and his testimony of the day before. Written by Agner Layson, who'd so far not missed a word of the trial, the story did a fair job of describing what the jury heard. Then Layson speculated about Krigler's impact on the jury. The remaining half of the article tried to peel skin off Krigler with quotes from the good old boys at ConPack, formerly Allegheny Growers. Not surprisingly, there were vehement denials of almost everything Krigler said. The company had not conducted a study of nicotine in the 1930s, or at least no one around now knew about any such study. It was a long time ago. No one at ConPack had ever seen the infamous memo. Probably just a figment of Krigler's imagination. It was not common knowledge in the tobacco industry that nicotine was addictive. Levels of the poison were not kept artificially high by ConPack, or any other manufacturer for that matter. The company would not admit, in fact denied again in print, that nicotine was addictive in the first place.

Pynex also delivered a few potshots, all from unnamed sources. Krigler was a corporate misfit. He fancied himself a serious scientific researcher when in fact he was just an engineer. His work with Raleigh 4 was seriously flawed. Production of that leaf was totally impractical. The death of his sister seriously affected his work and conduct. He was quick to threaten litigation. There was a strong hint that the out-of-court settlement thirteen years earlier had been heavily weighted in Pynex' favor.

A short, related story tracked the movement of Pynex common, which had closed at seventy-five and a half, down three points in heavy trading after a late rally.

Judge Harkin read the story an hour before the jury arrived. He called Lou Dell at the Siesta Inn to make sure there was no way any of the jurors could see it. She assured him they would get only the local dailies, all censored as per his instructions. She rather enjoyed cutting out the stories about the trial. Occasionally she would scissor out an unrelated story, just for the fun of it, just to make them wonder what they were missing. How could they ever know?

Hoppy Dupree slept little. After washing the dishes and vacuuming the den, he talked to Millie on the phone for almost an hour. She was in good spirits.

He left his bed at midnight to sit on the porch and ponder KLX and Jimmy Hull Moke and the fortune that was out there, almost within reach. The money would be used for the kids, he had determined before he left the office. No more junior colleges. No more part-time jobs. They'd have the best schools. A larger house would be nice, but only because the kids were cramped. He and Millie could live anywhere; such simple tastes.

No debt whatsoever. After taxes, he'd put the money in two places – mutual funds and real estate. He'd buy small commercial properties with solid leases. He could think of a half-dozen already.

The agreement with Jimmy Hull Moke worried him to no end. He'd simply never been involved with graft, never, to his knowledge, gotten near it. He had a cousin

230

who sold used cars and got himself sent away for three years for double and triple mortgaging his inventory. Wrecked his marriage. Ruined his children.

At some point before dawn, he became oddly comforted by the reputation of Jimmy Hull Moke. The man had fine-tuned the practice of corruption and made it an art form. He had become quite wealthy on a meager public servant's salary. And everybody knew it!

Surely Moke would know precisely how to handle the agreement without getting caught. Hoppy wouldn't get near the cash, wouldn't even know for sure if and when it was delivered.

He ate a Pop-Tart for breakfast and determined the risk to be minimal. He'd have a safe chat with Jimmy Hull, let the conversation run whatever course Jimmy Hull wanted because they'd soon enough get to the issue of cash, and then he'd report to Ringwald. He thawed frozen cinnamon swirls for the kids, left their lunch money on the kitchen counter, and went to the office at eight.

For the day after Krigler the defense adopted a gentler style. It was imperative to seem relaxed, unbothered by the severe blow the plaintiff had delivered yesterday. The pack of them wore suits of lighter shades, soft grays and blues and even a khaki. Gone were the harsh blacks and navys. Gone too were the serious frowns of men overburdened with their own importance. The instant the door opened and the first juror appeared, wide toothy smiles appeared from behind the defense table. Even a couple of chuckles. What a laid-back bunch.

Judge Harkin said hello, but there were few smiles inside the jury box. It was Friday, which meant the weekend started soon, a weekend to be spent incarcerated at the Siesta Inn. It had been decided over breakfast that Nicholas would pass a note to the Judge and ask him to explore the possibility of working

Saturday. The jurors would rather be in court trying to finish this ordeal than sitting around their rooms doing nothing but thinking about it.

Most of them noticed the stupid grins from Cable and company. They noticed the summer suits, the jovial air, the humorous whispers. 'Why are they so damned happy?' Loreen Duke whispered under her breath as Harkin read his list of questions.

'They want us to think everything's under control,' Nicholas whispered back. 'Just glare at them.'

Wendall Rohr stood and called the next witness. 'Dr. Roger Bunch,' he said with an air of greatness. He watched the jury for reactions to the name.

It was Friday. There would be no reactions from the jury.

Bunch had gained fame a decade earlier when, as Surgeon General of the United States, he had been a relentless critic of the tobacco industry. For the six years he'd served, he had instigated countless studies, directed frontal assaults, given a thousand anti-smoking speeches, written three books on the subject, and pushed agencies for tougher regulatory controls. His victories had been few and far between. Since leaving office, he had continued his crusade with a talent for publicity.

He was a man of many opinions and he was anxious to share them with the jury. The evidence was conclusive – cigarettes caused lung cancer. Every professional medical organization in the world that had addressed the issue had determined that smoking cigarettes caused lung cancer. The only organizations with contrary opinions were the manufacturers themselves and their hired mouthpieces – lobbying groups and the like.

Cigarettes are addictive. Ask any smoker who's tried to quit. The industry claims smoking is a matter of free choice. 'Typical hogwash from the tobacco companies,'

232

he said with disgust. In fact, during his six years as Surgeon General he released three separate studies, each of which proved conclusively that cigarettes are addictive.

Tobacco companies spend billions misleading the public. They conduct studies which claim to prove smoking is virtually harmless. They spend 2 billion a year on advertising alone, then claim people make informed choices about whether or not to smoke. It's simply not true. People, especially teenagers, receive confusing signals. Smoking appears to be fun, sophisticated, even healthy.

They spend tons of money on all sorts of screwball studies which they claim will prove whatever they're asserting. The industry as a whole is notorious for lying and covering up. The companies refuse to stand behind their products. They advertise and promote like mad, but when one of their customers dies from lung cancer they claim the person should have known better.

Bunch did a study proving cigarettes contain insecticide and pesticide residue, asbestos fibers, unidentified junk and trash swept from floors. While sparing no expense on advertising, the companies do not go to the trouble and expense of properly cleaning poisonous residues from their tobacco.

He directed a project which showed how tobacco companies elusively target the young; how they target the poor; how they develop and advertise certain brands for the different sexes and classes.

Because he was once the Surgeon General, Dr. Bunch was permitted to share his opinions on a wide range of subjects. At times throughout the morning he was unable to conceal his loathing for the tobacco industry, and when the bitterness leaked through his credibility suffered. But he connected with the jury. There were no yawns or blank stares.

*

233

Todd Ringwald was of the firm opinion that the meeting should take place in Hoppy's office, on his turf where Jimmy Hull Moke would be caught off guard. Hoppy presumed this made sense. He was really at a loss for the proper customs in these matters. He got lucky and found Moke at home, puttering with his bush-hog and heading on over to Biloxi later in the day anyway. Moke claimed he knew of Hoppy, had heard of him at some point. Hoppy said it was a very important matter involving a potentially big development in Hancock County. They agreed on lunch, a quick sandwich in Hoppy's office. Moke said he knew exactly where Hoppy was located.

For some reason, three part-time sales associates loitered in the front of the office as noon approached. One chatted with a boyfriend on the phone. One scanned the classifieds. One was apparently waiting for the pinochle. With great difficulty, Hoppy dispatched them to the streets where the real estate was to be found. He didn't want anyone around when Moke appeared.

The offices were deserted when Jimmy Hull walked through the door in jeans and cowboy boots. Hoppy greeted him with a nervous handshake and a jittery voice and showed him to his office in the back where his desk was set with two deli sandwiches and iced teas. They talked about local politics, casinos, and fishing as they ate, though Hoppy's appetite was nil. His stomach flipped with fear and his hands wouldn't stop shaking. He then cleared the desk and produced the artist's rendering of Stillwater Bay. Ringwald had delivered it earlier, and it contained no clue as to who was behind the project. Hoppy gave a quick ten-minute summary of the proposed development, and found himself getting stronger. He made a very nice presentation, if he said so himself.

Jimmy Hull stared at the drawing, rubbed his chin, and said, 'Thirty million dollars huh?'

'At least,' Hoppy answered. His bowels were suddenly loose.

'And who's doing it?'

Hoppy had practiced his answer, and he delivered it with convincing authority. He simply couldn't divulge the name, not at this point. Jimmy Hull liked the secrecy. He asked questions, all of which had to do with money and financing. Hoppy answered most of them.

'Zoning could be a real problem,' Jimmy Hull said with a frown.

'Certainly.'

'And the planning commission will put up a nasty fight.'

'We expect this.'

'Of course, the supervisors make the final decision. As you know, the recommendations from zoning and planning are merely advisory. Bottom line is the six of us do whatever we want.' He snickered and Hoppy laughed along. In Mississippi, the six county supervisors ruled supreme.

'My client understands how things work. And my client is anxious to work with you.'

Jimmy Hull removed his elbows from the desk and sat back in his chair. His eyelids narrowed. His forehead wrinkled. He stroked his chin and his beady black eyes shot lasers across the desk and hit poor Hoppy like hot bullets deep in the chest. Hoppy pressed all ten fingers onto the desk so his hands wouldn't tremble.

How many times had Jimmy Hull been at this particular moment, sizing up the prey before going in for the kill?

'You know I control everything in my district,' he said, his lips barely moving.

'I know exactly how things work,' Hoppy replied as coolly as possible.

'If I want this to be approved, it'll slide right through. If I don't like it, it's dead right now.'

235

Hoppy only nodded.

Jimmy Hull was curious about what other locals were involved at this point, who knew what, just how secret was the project right then. 'No one but me,' Hoppy assured him.

'Is your client in gambling?'

'No. But they're from Vegas. They know how to get things done at the local level. And they're anxious to move fast.'

Vegas was the operative word here, and Jimmy Hull savored it. He looked around the shabby little office. It was spare and spartan and conveyed a certain innocence, as if not much happened here and not much was expected. He had called two friends in Biloxi, both of whom reported that Mr. Dupree was a harmless sort who sold fruitcakes at Christmas for the Rotary Club. He had a large family and managed to avoid controversy, and commerce generally, for that matter. The obvious question was, why would the boys behind Stillwater Bay associate themselves with a mom-and-pop outfit like Dupree Realty?

He decided not to ask the question. He said, 'You know, my son is a very fine consultant for projects like this?'

'Didn't know that. My client would love to work with your son.'

'He's over in Bay St. Louis.'

'Shall I give him a call?'

'No. I'll handle it.'

Randy Moke owned two gravel trucks and spent most of his time tinkering with a fishing boat he advertised for saltwater charters. He had dropped out of high school two months before his first drug conviction.

Hoppy pressed on. Ringwald had insisted he try and pin down Moke as soon as possible. If a deal wasn't reached initially, then Moke might race back to Hancock County and start talking about the develop-

236

ment. 'My client is anxious to determine the preliminary fees before purchasing the land. How much might your son charge for his services?'

'A hundred thousand.'

Hoppy didn't flinch a muscle and was quite proud of his coolness. Ringwald had predicted a shakedown in the neighborhood of one to two hundred thousand. KLX would gladly pay it. Frankly, it was cheap compared to New Jersey. 'I see. Payable –'

'In cash.'

'My client is willing to discuss this.'

'No discussion. Cash up front, or no deal.'

'And the deal being?'

'A hundred thousand cash now, and the project sails through. My guarantee. A penny less, and I'll kill it with one phone call.'

Remarkably, there was not the slightest trace of menace in his voice or face. Hoppy told Ringwald later that Jimmy Hull simply laid out the terms of the deal as if he were selling used tires at a flea market.

'I need to make a phone call,' Hoppy said. 'Just sit tight.' He walked to the front room, which was thankfully still deserted, and called Ringwald, who was sitting by the phone in his hotel. The terms were relayed, discussed only for a few seconds, and Hoppy returned to his office. 'It's a deal. My client will pay it.' He said this slowly, and frankly it felt good to finally broker a deal that would lead to millions. KLX on one end, Moke on the other, and Hoppy in the middle of it all, in the fire and totally immune from the dirty work.

Jimmy Hull's face relaxed and he managed a smile. 'When?'

'I'll call you Monday.'

237

NINETEEN

Fitch ignored the trial Friday afternoon. There were urgent matters at hand with one of his jurors. He, along with Pang and Carl Nussman, locked themselves in a conference room at Cable's office and stared at the wall for an hour.

The idea had been Fitch's and his alone. It was a shot in the dark, one of his wildest hunches yet, but he got paid to dig under rocks no one else could find. Money gave him the luxury of dreaming the improbable.

Four days earlier he had ordered Nussman to ship overnight to Biloxi the entire jury file from the Cimmino trial a year before in Allentown, Pennsylvania. The Cimmino jury had listened to four weeks of testimony, then handed the tobacco company another verdict. Three hundred potential jurors had been summoned for duty in Allentown. One of them was a young man named David Lancaster.

The file on Lancaster was thin. He worked in a video store and claimed to be a student. He lived in an apartment over a struggling Korean deli, and apparently traveled by bicycle. There was no evidence of another vehicle, and the county rolls reflected no taxes levied on any car or truck titled in his name. His jury information card stated he was born in Philadelphia on May 8,1967, though this had not been verified at the time of the trial. There had been no reason to suspect he was lying.

Nussman's people had just determined that the birth-date was in fact fictitious. The card also stated he was not a convicted felon, had not served on jury duty in the county in the past year, had no medical reasons not to serve, and was a duly qualified elector. He had registered to vote five months before the trial started.

There was nothing strange in the file except a handwritten memo from a consultant which said that when Lancaster appeared for jury duty on the first day, the clerk had no record of his being summoned. He then produced what appeared to be a valid summons, and he was seated with the pool. One of Nussman's consultants noted that Lancaster seemed quite anxious to serve.

The only photo of the young man was one taken from a distance as he rode his mountain bike to work. He wore a cap, dark sunglasses, long hair, and a heavy beard. One of Nussman's operatives chatted with Lancaster as she rented videos, and reported him to be dressed in faded jeans, Birkenstocks, wool socks, and a flannel shirt. The hair was pulled back severely in a ponytail and tucked under his collar. He was polite but not talkative.

Lancaster got a bad draw when the numbers were pulled, but made the first two cuts and was four rows away when the jury was chosen.

His file was closed immediately.

Now it was open again. In the past twenty-four hours, it had been determined that David Lancaster had simply vanished from Allentown a month after the trial was over. His Korean landlord knew nothing. His boss at the video store said he failed to show up for work one day and was never heard from again. Not another person in town could be found who would admit to knowing Lancaster ever existed. Fitch's people were checking, but no one expected to find anything. He was still registered to vote, but the rolls wouldn't be purged for another five years, according to the county registrar.

By Wednesday night, Fitch was all but certain David Lancaster was Nicholas Easter.

Early Thursday morning, Nussman had received from his office in Chicago two large boxes which contained the jury file from the Glavine trial in Broken Arrow, Oklahoma. Glavine had been a vicious court-room brawl two years earlier against Trellco, with Fitch securing his verdict long before the lawyers stopped arguing. Nussman had not slept Thursday as he plowed through the Glavine jury research.

There had been a young white male in Broken Arrow named Perry Hirsch, age twenty-five at the time, allegedly born in St. Louis on a date which was ultimately determined to be false. He said he worked in a lamp factory and delivered pizzas on the weekend. Single, Catholic, college dropout, no prior jury service, all according to his own words recorded on a brief questionnaire which was given to the lawyers before the trial. He had registered to vote four months before the trial, and supposedly lived with an aunt in a trailer park. He was one of two hundred people who answered the call for jury service.

There were two photos of Hirsch. In one he was hauling a stack of pizzas to his car, a battered Pinto, in a colorful blue-and-red Rizzo's shirt and matching cap. He wore wire-rimmed glasses and a beard. The other was a shot of him standing beside the trailer where he lived, but his face could hardly be seen.

Hirsch almost made the Glavine jury, but was cut by the plaintiff for reasons that were unclear at the time. Evidently he left town at some point after the trial. The factory where he worked employed a man named Terry Hurtz, but no Perry Hirsch.

Fitch was paying a local investigator to dig furiously. The unnamed aunt had not been found; there were no

240

records from the trailer park. No one at Rizzo's remembered a Perry Hirsch.

Fitch and Pang and Nussman sat in the dark and stared at the wall Friday afternoon. The photos of Hirsch, Lancaster, and Easter were blown up and focused as clearly as possible. Easter of course was now clean-shaven. His photo was taken as he worked, so there were no sunglasses, no cap.

The three faces were of the same person.

Nussman's handwriting expert arrived after lunch Friday. He was flown in on a Pynex jet from D.C. He took fewer than thirty minutes to form a few opinions. The only handwriting samples available were the jury information cards from Cimmino and Wood, and the short questionnaire from Glavine. It was more than enough. The expert had no doubt that Perry Hirsch and David Lancaster were the same person. Easter's handwriting was quite dissimilar from Lancaster's, but he'd made a mistake in running from Hirsch. The carefully printed, block-style hand Easter had used was obviously designed to distinguish itself from earlier trails. He had worked hard to create an entirely new style of writing, one that could not be linked to the past. His mistake came at the bottom of the card when Easter signed his name. The 't' was crossed low and angled down from left to right, very distinguishable. Hirsch had used a sloppy cursive style, no doubt designed to portray a lack of education. The 't' in St. Louis, his alleged place of birth, was identical to the 't' in Easter, though to the untrained eye nothing about the two appeared remotely similar.

He announced without the slightest doubt, 'Hirsch and Lancaster are the same people. Hirsch and Easter are the same people. Therefore, Lancaster and Easter must be the same.'

'All three are the same,' Fitch said slowly as it sunk in.

'That's correct. And he's very, very bright.'

The handwriting expert left Cable's. Fitch returned to his office where he met with Pang and Konrad for the rest of Friday afternoon and into the night. He had people on the ground in both Allentown and Broken Arrow digging and bribing and hoping to pry loose employment records and tax withholding forms on Hirsch and Lancaster.

'Have you ever known a person to stalk a trial?' Konrad asked.

'Never,' Fitch growled.

The rules for conjugal visits were simple. Between 7 P.M. and 9 P.M. Friday night, each juror could entertain spouses or mates or whomever in their rooms. The guests could come and go at any time, but they first had to be registered by Lou Dell, who sized them up and down as if she and she alone possessed the power to approve what they were about to do.

The first to arrive, promptly at seven, was Derrick Maples, the handsome boyfriend of young Angel Weese. Lou Dell took his name, pointed down the hall, said, 'Room 55.' He was not seen again until nine, when he came up for air.

Nicholas would not have a guest Friday night. Neither would Jerry Fernandez. His wife had moved into a separate bedroom a month ago, and she wasn't about to waste her time visiting a man she despised. Besides, Jerry and the Poodle were exercising conjugal rights every night. Colonel Herrera's wife was out of town. Lonnie Shaver's wife couldn't find a baby-sitter. So the four men watched John Wayne in the Party Room and lamented the sorry states of their romances. Blind old Herman was getting some, but they weren't.

Phillip Savelle had a guest, but Lou Dell refused to divulge to the rest of the boys the sex, race, age, or anything else about his visitor. It happened to be a very nice young lady who appeared to be Indian or Pakistani.

Mrs. Gladys Card watched TV in her room with Mr. Nelson Card. Loreen Duke, who was divorced, visited with her two young teenaged daughters. Rikki Coleman exercised conjugal relations with her husband Rhea, then talked about their kids for the remaining one hour and forty-five minutes.

And Hoppy Dupree brought Millie some flowers and a box of chocolates, which she ate most of while he jumped around the room in a fit of excitement, the likes of which she'd rarely seen. The kids were fine, all out on dates, and business was going full speed. In fact, business had never been better. He had a secret, a large wonderful rich secret about a deal he'd stepped into, but he couldn't tell her just yet. Maybe Monday. Maybe later. But he just couldn't now. He stayed an hour and rushed back to the office for more work.

Mr. Nelson Card left at nine, and Gladys made the mistake of stepping into the Party Room where the boys were drinking beer and eating popcorn and watching boxing matches now. She found a soft drink and sat at the table. Jerry eyed her suspiciously. 'You little devil,' he said. 'Come on, tell us about it.'

Her mouth fell open and her cheeks flushed. She couldn't speak.

'Come on, Gladys. We didn't get any.'

She grabbed her Coke and jumped to her feet. 'Maybe there's a good reason you didn't,' she snapped angrily, then marched from the room. Jerry managed a laugh. The other men were too tired and despondent to care.

Marlee's car was a Lexus leased from a dealer in Biloxi, a three-year lease at six hundred a month with the lessee being Rochelle Group, a brand-spanking-new corporation Fitch had been able to learn nothing about.

243

A transmitter weighing almost a pound had been attached by a magnet under the rear left tire well, so Marlee could now be tracked by Konrad sitting at his desk. Joe Boy had stuck it under there a few hours after they'd followed her from Mobile and seen her license plates.

Her large new condo was leased by the same corporation. Almost two thousand dollars a month. Marlee had some serious overhead, but Fitch and company couldn't find a trace of a job.

She called late Friday night, just minutes after Fitch had stripped to his XX-Large boxers and black socks and sprawled on his bed like a beached whale. For now he owned the Presidential Suite on the top floor of the Colonial Hotel in Biloxi, on Highway 90, the Gulf a hundred yards away. When he bothered to look, he had a nice view of the beach. No one outside his little circle knew where he was.

The call went to the front desk, an urgent message for Mr. Fitch, and it posed a dilemma for the night clerk. The hotel was being paid large sums of money to protect the privacy and identity of Mr. Fitch. The clerk could not admit he was a guest. The young lady had it all figured out.

When Marlee called back ten minutes later, she was put straight through, pursuant to Mr. Fitch's orders. Fitch was now standing with his boxers pulled almost to his chest but still sagging down past his fleshy thighs, scratching his forehead and wondering how she'd found him. 'Good evening,' he said.

'Hi, Fitch. Sorry to call so late.' She wasn't sorry about a damned thing. The 'i' in 'Hi' was deliberately flat, something that happened occasionally with Marlee. It was an effort to sound a little Southern. The recordings of all eight phone conversations, however brief, along with the recording of their chat in New Orleans, had been scrutinized by voice and dialect experts in New York. Marlee was a Midwesterner, from eastern Kansas or western Missouri, probably from somewhere within a hundred miles of Kansas City.

'No problem,' he said, checking the recorder on a narrow folding table near his bed. 'How's your friend?'

'Lonely. Tonight was conjugal night, you know?'

'So I heard. Did everybody get conjugated?'

'Not exactly. It's pretty sad, really. The men watched John Wayne movies while the women knitted.'

'Nobody got laid?'

'Very few. Angel Weese, but she's in the middle of a hot romance. Rikki Coleman. Millie Dupree's husband showed up but didn't stay long. The Cards were together. Can't tell about Herman. And Savelle had a guest.'

'What manner of humanity did Savelle attract?'

'Don't know. It was never seen.'

Fitch lowered his wide rear to the edge of the bed and pinched the bridge of his nose. 'Why didn't you visit your friend?' he asked.

'Who said we're lovers?'

'What are you?'

'Friends. Guess which two jurors are sleeping together?'

'Now how would I know that?'

'Guess.'

Fitch smiled at himself in the mirror and marveled at his wonderful luck. 'Jerry Fernandez and somebody.'

'Good guess. Jerry's about to get a divorce, and Sylvia is lonely too. Their rooms are just across the hall, and, well, there's little else to do at the Siesta Inn.'

'Ain't love grand?'

'I gotta tell you, Fitch, Krigler worked for the plaintiff.'

'They listened to him, huh?'

'Every word. They listened and they believed. He turned them around, Fitch.'

'Tell me some good news.'

'Rohr's worried.'

His spine stiffened noticeably. 'What's bugging Rohr?' he asked, studying his puzzled face in the mirror. He shouldn't be surprised that she was talking to Rohr, so why the hell was he shocked to hear it? He felt betrayed.

'You. He knows you're loose on the streets scheming up all sorts of ways to get to the jury. Wouldn't you be worried, Fitch, if some guy like you was hard at work for the plaintiff?'

'I'd be terrified.'

'Rohr isn't terrified. He's just worried.'

'How often do you talk to him?'

'A lot. He's sweeter than you, Fitch. He's a very pleasant man to talk to, plus he doesn't record my calls, doesn't send in goons to follow my car. None of that sort of stuff.'

'Really knows how to charm a girl, huh?'

'Yeah. But he's weak where it counts.'

'Where's that?'

'In the wallet. He can't match your resources.'

'How much of my resources do you want?'

'Later, Fitch. Gotta run. There's a suspicious-looking car sitting across the street. Must be some of your clowns.' She hung up.

Fitch showered and tried to sleep. At 2 A.M., he drove himself to the Lucy Luck, where he played blackjack at five hundred dollars a hand, sipped Sprite until dawn, when he left with close to twenty thousand dollars in fresh winnings.

TWENTY

The first Saturday in November arrived with temperatures in the low sixties, unseasonably cool for the Coast and its near-tropical climate. A gentle breeze from the north rattled trees and scattered leaves on the streets and sidewalks. Fall usually arrived late and lasted until the first of the year, when it yielded to spring. The Coast did not experience winter.

A few joggers were on the street just after dawn. No one noticed the plain black Chrysler as it pulled into the driveway of a modest brick split-level. It was too early for the neighbors to see the two young men in matching dark suits exit the car, walk to the front door, ring the buzzer, and wait patiently. It was too early, but in less than an hour the lawns would be busy with leaf rakers and the sidewalks busy with children.

Hoppy had just poured the water into the Mr. Coffee when he heard the buzzer. He tightened the belt of his ragged terry-cloth bathrobe and tried to straighten his unkempt hair with his fingers. Must be the Boy Scouts selling doughnuts at this ungodly hour. Surely it wasn't the Jehovah's Witnesses again. He'd let them have it this time. Nothing but a cult! He moved quickly because the upstairs was filled with comatose teenagers. Six at last count. Five of his and a guest someone had dragged home from junior college. A typical Friday night at the Dupree home.

247

He opened the front door and met two serious young men, both of whom instantly reached into their pockets and whipped out gold medallions stuck to black leather. In the quick rush of syllables, Hoppy caught 'FBI' at least twice, and nearly fainted.

'Are you Mr. Dupree?' Agent Nitchman asked.

Hoppy gasped. 'Yes, but –'

'We'd like to ask you some questions,' said Agent Napier as he somehow managed to take a step even closer.

'About what?' Hoppy asked, his voice dry. He tried to look between them, at the street, across it where Mildred Yancy was no doubt watching all of this.

Nitchman and Napier exchanged a harsh, conspiratorial look. Then Napier said to Hoppy, 'We can do it here, or perhaps somewhere else.'

'Questions about Stillwater Bay, Jimmy Hull Moke, things like that,' Nitchman said for clarification, and Hoppy clutched the door frame.

'Oh my god,' he said as the air was sucked from his lungs and most vital organs froze.

'May we come in?' Napier said.

Hoppy lowered his head and rubbed his eyes as if to weep. 'No, please, not here.' The children! Normally they'd sleep till nine or ten, or even noon for that matter if Millie let them, but with voices downstairs they'd be up in a minute. 'My office,' he managed to say.

'We'll wait,' Napier said.

'Make it quick,' Nitchman said.

'Thank you,' Hoppy said, then quickly closed the door, and locked it. He fell onto a sofa in the den, and stared at the ceiling, which was spinning clockwise. No sounds from upstairs. The kids were still sleeping. His heart pounded fiercely and for a full minute he thought he might just lie there and die. Death would be welcome now. He could close his eyes and float away, and in a couple of hours the first kid down would see him and call 911. He was fifty-three, and bad hearts ran in his family, on his mother's side. Millie would get a hundred thousand in life insurance.

When he realized his heart was determined to continue, he slowly swung to his feet. Still dizzy, he groped his way to the kitchen and poured a cup of coffee. It was five minutes after seven, according to the digital on the oven. Fourth day of November. Undoubtedly one of the worst days of his life. How could he have been so stupid!

He thought about calling Todd Ringwald, and he thought about calling Millard Putt, his lawyer. He decided to wait. He was suddenly in a hurry. He wanted to leave the house before the kids got up, and he wanted those two agents out of his driveway before the neighbors noticed. Besides, Millard Putt did nothing but real estate law, and was not very good at that. This was a criminal matter.

A criminal matter! He skipped a shower and dressed in seconds. He was halfway through the brushing of his teeth when he finally looked at himself in the mirror. Betrayal was written all over his face, stamped in his eyes for all to see. He couldn't lie. Deceit was not in him. He was just Hoppy Dupree, an honest man with a fine family, good reputation, and all. He'd never cheated on his tax returns!

So why, Hoppy, were there two FBI agents waiting outside for a trip downtown, not to jail yet, though that would surely come, but to a private place where they could eat him for breakfast and lay bare his fraud? He decided not to shave. Perhaps he should call his minister. He brushed his swirling hair and thought of Millie, and the public disgrace, and the kids, and what would everybody think.

Before leaving the bathroom, Hoppy vomited.

Outside, Napier insisted that he ride with Hoppy.

249

Nitchman in the black Chrysler followed. Not a word was spoken.

Dupree Realty was not the sort of commercial enterprise that attracted early risers. This was true on Saturday, as it was for the rest of the week. Hoppy knew the place would be deserted until at least nine, maybe ten. He unlocked doors, turned on lights, said nothing until it was time to ask if they wanted coffee. Both declined and seemed quite anxious to proceed to the slaughter. Hoppy sat on his side of the desk. They huddled together like twins across from him. He was unable to hold their gaze.

Nitchman got it started by saying, 'Are you familiar with Stillwater Bay?'

'Yes.'

'Have you met a man by the name of Todd Ringwald?'

'Yes.'

'Have you signed any type of contract with him?'

'No.'

Napier and Nitchman looked at each other as if they knew this to be false. Napier said, smugly, 'Look, Mr. Dupree, this will go a lot smoother for you if you tell the truth.'

'I swear I'm telling the truth.'

'When did you first meet Todd Ringwald?' Nitchman asked as he pulled a narrow notepad from his pocket and began scribbling.

'Thursday.'

'Do you know Jimmy Hull Moke?'

'Yes.'

'When did you first meet him?'

'Yesterday.'

'Where?'

'Right here.'

'What was the purpose of the meeting?'

250

'To discuss the development of Stillwater Bay. I'm supposed to represent a company called KLX Properties. KLX wants to develop Stillwater Bay, which is in Mr. Moke's supervisor's district in Hancock County.'

Napier and Nitchman stared at Hoppy and pondered this for what seemed like an hour. Hoppy silently repeated his words to himself. Had he said something? Something that would speed along his journey to prison? Perhaps he should stop this right now and seek legal counsel.

Napier cleared his throat. 'We've been investigating Mr. Moke for the past six months, and two weeks ago he agreed to enter into a plea bargain arrangement whereby he will receive a light sentence in exchange for his assistance.'

This legal crap-speak meant little to Hoppy. He heard it, but things weren't registering clearly right now.

'Did you offer money to Mr. Moke?' Napier asked.

'No,' Hoppy said because there was no way he could say yes. He said it quickly, without force or conviction, it just came out. 'No,' he said again. He hadn't actually offered money. He had cleared the way for his client to offer money. At least, that was his interpretation of what he'd done.

Nitchman slowly reached into his coat pocket, slowly felt around until his fingers were just right, slowly removed a slender pocket something or other which he slowly placed in the center of the desk. 'Are you sure?' he asked, almost taunting.

'Sure I'm sure,' Hoppy said, staring slack-jawed at the sleek hideous device.

Nitchman gently pressed a button. Hoppy held his breath and clenched his fists. Then, there was his voice, chirping along nervously about local politics and casinos and fishing with an occasional entry by Moke.

'He was wired!' Hoppy exclaimed, breathless and totally defeated.

'Yes,' one of them said gravely.

Hoppy could only stare at the recorder. 'Oh no,' he mumbled.

The words had been uttered and recorded less than twenty-four hours earlier, right there at that very desk over chicken clubs and iced tea. Jimmy Hull had sat where Nitchman was and arranged a bribe for a hundred grand, and he did so with an FBI wire stuck somewhere to his body.

The tape dragged painfully on until the damage was done and Hoppy and Jimmy Hull were offering their hurried good-byes. 'Shall we listen to it again?' Nitchman asked as he touched a button.

'No, please,' Hoppy said, pinching the bridge of his nose. 'Should I talk to a lawyer?' he asked without looking up.

'Not a bad idea,' Napier said sympathetically.

When he finally looked at them his eyes were red and wet. His lip quivered but he thrust his chin outward and tried to be bold. 'So what am I looking at?' he asked.

Napier and Nitchman relaxed in unison. Napier stood and walked to a bookcase. 'It's hard to say,' Nitchman said, as if the issue would be determined by someone else. 'We've busted a dozen supervisors in the past year. The judges are sick of it. The sentences are getting longer.'

'I'm not a supervisor,' Hoppy said.

'Good point. I'd say three to five years, federal, not state.'

'Conspiracy to bribe a government official,' Napier added helpfully. Napier then returned to his seat next to Nitchman. Both men sat on the edges of their chairs as if ready to leap across the desk and flog Hoppy for his sins.

The mike was the cap of a blue Bic disposable

ballpoint sitting harmlessly with a dozen other pencils and cheap pens in a dusty fruit jar on Hoppy's desk. Ringwald had left it there Friday morning when Hoppy had gone to the rest room. The pens and pencils gave the appearance of never being used, the type of collection which would sit untouched for months before being rearranged. In the event Hoppy or someone else decided to use the blue Bic, it was out of ink and would find itself immediately in the wastebasket. Only a technician could disassemble it and discover the bug.

From the desk, the words were relayed to a small, powerful transmitter hidden behind the Lysol and air freshener under a rest room vanity, next to Hoppy's office. From the transmitter, the words were sent to an unmarked van across the street in a shopping center. In the van, the words were recorded on tape and delivered to Fitch's office.

Jimmy Hull had not been wired, was not working with the feds, had in fact been doing what he did best — hustling bribes.

Ringwald, Napier, and Nitchman were all ex-cops who were now private agents employed by an international security firm in Bethesda. It was a firm Fitch used often. The Hoppy sting would cost The Fund eighty thousand dollars.

Chicken feed.

Hoppy mentioned the possibility of legal counsel again. Napier stonewalled it with a lengthy recitation of the FBI's efforts to stop rampant corruption on the Coast. He blamed all ills on the gambling industry.

It was imperative to keep Hoppy away from a lawyer. A lawyer would want names and phone numbers, records and paperwork. Napier and Nitchman had enough fake credentials and quick lies to bluff poor Hoppy, but a good lawyer would force them to disappear.

253

What had begun as a routine probe of Jimmy Hull and graft of the local garden variety had turned into a much broader investigation into gaming and, the magic words, 'organized crime,' according to Napier's lengthy narrative. Hoppy listened when he could. It was difficult though. His mind raced away with concerns for Millie and the kids and how they would survive for the three to five years he was gone.

'So we didn't target you,' Napier said, wrapping things up.

'And, frankly, we'd never heard of KLX Properties,' added Nitchman. 'We sort of just stumbled into this.'

'Can't you just stumble out?' Hoppy asked, and actually managed a soft, helpless smile.

'Maybe,' Napier said deliberately, then glanced at Nitchman as if they had something even more dramatic to lay on Hoppy.

'Maybe what?' he asked.

They withdrew from the edge of the desk in unison, their timing perfect as if they'd either rehearsed for hours or done this a hundred times. They both stared hard at Hoppy, who wilted and looked at the desktop.

'We know you're not a crook, Mr. Dupree,' Nitchman said softly.

'You just made a mistake,' added Napier.

'You got that right,' Hoppy mumbled.

'You're being used by some awfully sophisticated crooks. They roll in here with big plans and big bucks, and well, we see it all the time in drug cases.'

Drugs! Hoppy was shocked but said nothing. Another pause as the stares continued.

'Can we offer you a twenty-four-hour deal?' Napier asked.

'How can I say no?'

'Let's keep this quiet for twenty-four hours. You don't tell a soul, we don't tell a soul. You keep it from your lawyer, we don't pursue you. Not for twenty-four hours.'

'I don't understand.'

'We can't explain everything right now. We need some time to evaluate your situation.'

Nitchman leaned forward again, elbows on desk. 'There might be a way out for you, Mr. Dupree.'

Hoppy was rallying, however faintly. 'I'm listening.'

'You're a small, insignificant fish caught in a large net,' Napier explained. 'You might be expendable.'

Sounded good to Hoppy. 'What happens in twenty-four hours?'

'We meet again right here. Nine o'clock in the morning.'

'It's a deal.'

'One word to Ringwald, one word to anyone, even your wife, and your future is in serious jeopardy.'

'You have my word.'

The chartered bus left the Siesta Inn at ten with all fourteen jurors, Mrs. Grimes, Lou Dell and her husband Benton, Willis and his wife Ruby, five part-time deputies in plain clothes, Earl Hutto, the Sheriff of Harrison County, and his wife Claudelle, and two assistant clerks from Gloria Lane's office. Twenty-eight in all, plus the driver. All approved by Judge Harkin. Two hours later they rolled along Canal Street in New Orleans, then exited the bus at the corner of Magazine. Lunch was in a reserved room in the back of an old oyster bar on Decatur in the French Quarter, and paid for by the taxpayers of Harrison County.

They were allowed to scatter throughout the Quarter. They shopped at outdoor markets; strolled with the tourists through Jackson Square; gawked at naked bodies in cheap dives on Bourbon; bought T-shirts and other souvenirs. Some rested on benches along the Riverwalk. Some ducked into bars and watched football. At four, they gathered at the river and boarded a paddle wheeler for a sight-seeing trip. At six they ate dinner at a pizza and po-boy deli on Canal.

By ten they were locked in their rooms in Pass Christian, tired and ready for sleep. Busy jurors are happy jurors.

TWENTY-ONE

With the Hoppy show proceeding flawlessly, Fitch made the decision late Saturday to launch the next assault against the jury. It was a strike made without the advantage of meticulous planning, and it would be as severe as the Hoppy sting was slick.

Early Sunday morning, Pang and Dubaz, both dressed in tan shirts with a plumber's logo above the pockets, picked the lock on the door of Easter's apartment. No alarm sounded. Dubaz went straight to the vent above the refrigerator, removed the screen, and yanked out the hidden camera that had caught Doyle earlier. He placed it in a large toolbox he'd brought to remove the goods.

Pang went to the computer. He had studied the hurried photos taken by Doyle during the first visit, and he had practiced on an identical unit which had been installed in an office next to Fitch's. He twisted screws and removed the back cover panel of the computer. The hard drive was precisely where he'd been told. In less than a minute it was out. Pang found two stacks of 3.5-inch discs, sixteen in all, in a rack by the monitor.

While Pang performed the delicate removal of the hard drive, Dubaz opened drawers and quietly turned over the cheap furniture in the search for more discs. The apartment was so small and had so few places to

257

hide anything, his task was easy. He searched the kitchen drawers and cabinets, the closets, the cardboard boxes Easter used to store his socks and underwear. He found nothing. All computer-related paraphernalia were apparently stored near the computer.

'Let's go,' Pang said, ripping cords from the computer, monitor, and printer.

They practically threw the system on the ragged sofa, where Dubaz piled on cushions and clothing, then poured charcoal lighter fluid from a plastic jug. When the sofa, chair, computer, cheap rugs, and assorted clothing were sufficiently doused, the two men walked to the door and Dubaz threw a match. The ignition was rapid and virtually silent, at least to anyone who might have been listening outside. They waited until the flames were lapping the ceiling and black smoke was boiling throughout the apartment, then made a hasty departure, locking the door behind them. Down the stairs, on the first level, they pulled a fire alarm. Dubaz ran back upstairs where the smoke was seeping from the apartment, and began yelling and beating on doors. Pang did the same on the first level. Screams followed quickly as the hallways filled with panicked people in bathrobes and sweatsuits. The shrill clanging of ancient firebells added to the hysteria.

'Make damned sure you don't kill anyone,' Fitch had warned them. Dubaz pounded on doors as the smoke thickened. He made certain every apartment near Easter's was empty. He pulled people by the arms; asked if everyone was out; pointed to the exits.

As the crowd spilled into the parking lot, Pang and Dubaz separated and slowly retreated. Sirens could be heard. Smoke appeared in the windows of two upstairs apartments – Easter's and one next door. More people scrambled out, some wrapped in blankets and clutching babies and toddlers. They joined the crowd and waited impatiently for the fire trucks.

258

When the firemen arrived, Pang and Dubaz dropped farther back, then vanished.

No one died. No one was injured. Four apartments were completely destroyed, eleven severely damaged, nearly thirty families homeless until cleanup and restoration.

Easter's hard drive proved impenetrable. He had added so many passwords, secret codes, antitampering and antiviral barriers that Fitch's computer experts were stumped. He'd flown them in Saturday from Washington. They were honest people with no idea where the hard drive and the discs came from. He simply locked them in a room with a system identical to Easter's and told them what he wanted. Most of the discs had similar protections. About halfway through the stack, though, the tension was broken when they were able to evade passwords on an older disc Easter had neglected to adequately secure. The files list showed sixteen entries with document names which revealed nothing. Fitch was notified as the first document was being printed. It was a six-page summary of current news items about the tobacco industry, dated October 11, 1994. Stories from *Time*, *The Wall Street Journal*, and *Forbes* were mentioned. The second document was a rambling two-page narrative describing a documentary Easter had just seen about breast implant litigation. The third was a gawky poem he'd written about rivers. The fourth was another compilation of recent news articles about lung cancer trials.

Fitch and Konrad read each page carefully. The writing was clear and straightforward, obviously hurriedly done because the typos were almost cumbersome. He wrote like an unbiased reporter. It was impossible to determine whether Easter was sympathetic to smokers or just keenly interested in mass tort litigation.

There were more dreadful poems. An aborted short story. And finally, pay dirt. Document number fifteen was a two-page letter to his mother, a Mrs. Pamela Blanchard in Gardner, Texas. Dated April 20,1995, it began: 'Dear Mom: I'm now living in Biloxi, Mississippi, on the Gulf Coast,' and proceeded to explain how much he loved salt water and beaches and could never again live in farm country. He apologized at length for not writing sooner, apologized for two long paragraphs about his tendency to drift, and promised to do better with his letter writing. He asked about Alex, said he hadn't talked to him in three months and couldn't believe he'd finally made it to Alaska and found a job as a fishing guide. Alex appeared to be a brother. There was no mention of a father. No mention of a girl, certainly not anyone named Marlee.

He said he'd found a job working in a casino, and it was fun for the moment but not much of a future. He still thought about being a lawyer, and was sorry about law school, but he doubted he'd ever go back. He confessed to being happy, living simply with little money and even fewer responsibilities. Oh well, gotta run now. Lots of love. Say hello to Aunt Sammie and he'd call soon.

He signed off simply as 'Jeff.' 'Love Jeff.' No last name appeared anywhere in the letter.

Dante and Joe Boy left on a private jet an hour after the letter was first read. Fitch instructed them to go to Gardner and hire every private snoop in town.

The computer people cracked one more disc, the next to the last of the bunch. Again, they were able to sidestep the antitampering barriers with a complicated series of password clues. They were very impressed by Easter's hacking ability.

The disc was filled with part of one document – the voter registration rolls of Harrison County. Starting with A and running through K, they printed over sixteen thousand names with addresses. Fitch checked on them periodically throughout the printing. He too had a complete printout of all registered voters in the county. It was not a secret list, in fact it could be purchased from Gloria Lane for thirty-five dollars. Most political candidates made the purchase during election years.

But two things were odd about Easter's list. First, it was on a computer disc, which meant he had somehow managed to enter Gloria Lane's computer and steal the information. Second, what did a part-time computer hack/part-time student need with such a list?

If Easter accessed the clerk's computer, then he certainly could tamper with it enough to have his own name entered as a prospective juror in the *Wood* case.

The more Fitch thought about it, the more it made perfect sense.

Hoppy's eyes were red and puffy as he drank thick coffee at his desk early Sunday and waited for 9 A.M. He hadn't eaten a bite since a banana Saturday morning while the Folger's brewed in his kitchen just minutes before the doorbell rang and Napier and Nitchman entered his life. His gastrointestinal system was shot. His nerves were ragged. He'd sneaked too much vodka Saturday night, and he'd done it at the house, something Millie prohibited.

The kids had slept through it all Saturday. He hadn't told a soul, hadn't been tempted to, really. The humiliation helped keep the loathsome secret safe.

At precisely nine, Napier and Nitchman entered with a third man, an older man who also wore a severe dark suit and severe facial expressions as if he'd come to personally whip and flay poor Hoppy. Nitchman introduced him as George Cristano. From Washington! Department of Justice!

261

Cristano's handshake was cold. He didn't make small talk.

'Say, Hoppy, would you mind if we had this little chat somewhere else?' Napier asked as he looked scornfully around the office.

'It's just safer,' Nitchman added for clarification.

'You never know where bugs might show up,' Cristano said.

'Tell me about it,' Hoppy said, but no one caught the humor. Was he in a position to say no to anything? 'Sure,' he said.

They left in a spotless black Lincoln Town Car, Nitchman and Napier in the front, Hoppy in the back with Cristano, who matter-of-factly began to explain that he was some type of high-ranking Assistant Attorney General from deep inside Justice. The closer they got to the Gulf the more odious his position became. Then he was silent.

'Are you a Democrat or a Republican, Hoppy?' Cristano asked softly during one particularly long lull in the conversation. Napier turned at the shore and headed west along the Coast.

Hoppy surely didn't want to offend anyone. 'Oh, I don't know. Always vote for the man, you know. I don't get hung up on parties, know what I mean?'

Cristano looked away, out the window, as if this wasn't what he wanted. 'I was hoping you were a good Republican,' he said, still looking through the window at the sea.

Hoppy could be any damned thing these boys wanted. Absolutely anything. A card-carrying, wild-eyed, fanatical Communist, if it would please Mr. Cristano.

'Voted for Reagan and Bush,' he said proudly. 'And Nixon. Even Goldwater.'

Cristano nodded ever so slightly, and Hoppy managed to exhale.

262

The car became silent again. Napier parked it at a dock near Bay St. Louis, forty minutes from Biloxi. Hoppy followed Cristano down a pier and onto a deserted sixty-foot charter boat named *Afternoon Delight*. Nitchman and Napier waited by the car, out of sight.

'Sit down, Hoppy,' Cristano said, pointing to a foam-padded bench on the deck. Hoppy sat. The boat rocked ever so slightly. The water was still. Cristano sat across from him and leaned forward so that their heads were three feet apart.

'Nice boat,' Hoppy said, rubbing the imitation leather seat.

'It's not ours. Listen, Hoppy, you're not wired, are you?'

Instinctively, he bolted upright, shocked by the suggestion. 'Of course not!'

'Sorry, but these things do happen. I guess I should frisk you.' Cristano looked him up and down quickly. Hoppy was horrified at the thought of being fondled by this stranger, alone on a boat.

'I swear I am not wired, okay,' Hoppy said, so firmly that he was proud of himself. Cristano's face relaxed. 'You wanna frisk me?' he asked. Hoppy glanced around to see if anyone was within view. Look sorta odd, wouldn't it? Two grown men rubbing each other in broad daylight on an anchored boat?

'Are you wired?' Hoppy asked.

'No.'

'Swear?'

'I swear.'

'Good.' Hoppy was relieved and quite anxious to believe the man. The alternative was simply unthinkable.

Cristano smiled then abruptly frowned. He leaned in. The small talk was over. 'I'll be brief, Hoppy. We have a deal for you, a deal which will enable you to walk away from this without a scratch. Nothing. No arrest, no indictment, no trial, no prison. No face in the newspaper. In fact, Hoppy, no one will ever know.'

He paused to catch his breath, and Hoppy charged in. 'So far so good. I'm listening.'

'It's a bizarre deal, one we've never attempted. Has nothing to do with law and justice and punishment, nothing like that. It's a political deal, Hoppy. Purely political. There'll be no record of it in Washington. No one will ever know, except for me, you, those two guys waiting by the car, and less than ten people deep inside Justice. We cut the deal, you do your part, and everything is forgotten.'

'You got it. Just point me in the right direction.'

'Are you concerned about crime, drugs, law and order, Hoppy?'

'Of course.'

'Are you sick of graft and corruption?'

Odd question. At this very moment, Hoppy felt like the poster child for the campaign against corruption. 'Yes!'

'There are good guys and bad guys in Washington, Hoppy. There are those of us at Justice who've devoted our lives to fighting crime. I mean serious crime, Hoppy. I mean drug payoffs to judges and congressmen who take money from foreign enemies, criminal activity that could threaten our democracy. Know what I mean?'

If Hoppy didn't know for sure, then he certainly was sympathetic to Cristano and his fine friends in Washington. 'Yes, yes,' he said, hanging on every word.

'But everything's political these days, Hoppy. We're constantly fighting with Congress and we're fighting with the President. Do you know what we need in Washington, Hoppy?'

Whatever it was, Hoppy wanted them to have it.

Cristano didn't give him the chance to answer. 'We

need more Republicans, more good, conservative Republicans who'll give us money and get out of our way. The Democrats are always meddling, always threatening budget cuts, restructuring, always concerned about the rights of these poor criminals we're picking on. There's a war raging up there, Hoppy. We fight it every day.'

He looked at Hoppy as if he should say something, but Hoppy was momentarily trying to adjust to the war. He nodded gravely, then looked at his feet.

'We have to protect our friends, Hoppy, and this is where you come in.'

'Okay.'

'Again, this is a strange deal. Take it, and our tape of you bribing Mr. Moke will be destroyed.'

'I'll take the deal. Just tell me what it is.'

Cristano paused and looked up and down the pier. Some fishermen were making noises far away. He leaned closer and actually touched Hoppy on the knee. 'It's about your wife,' he said, almost under his breath, then reared back to let it sink in.

'My wife?'

'Yes. Your wife.'

'Millie?'

'That's her.'

'What the hell —'

'I'll explain.'

'Millie?' Hoppy was flabbergasted. What could sweet Millie have to do with a mess like this?

'It's the trial, Hoppy,' Cristano said, and the first piece of the puzzle plunged roughly into place.

'Guess who contributes the most money to Republican congressional candidates?'

Hoppy was too stunned and confused to offer an intelligent guess.

'That's right. The tobacco companies. They pour millions into races because they're afraid of the FDA

265

and they're fed up with government regulations. They're free-enterprise people, Hoppy, same as you. They believe people smoke because they choose to smoke, and they're sick of the government and the trial lawyers trying to run them out of business.'

'It is political,' Hoppy said, staring at the Gulf in disbelief.

'Nothing but politics. If Big Tobacco loses this trial, then there will be an avalanche of litigation the likes of which this country has never seen. The companies will lose billions, and we'll lose millions in Washington. Can you help us, Hoppy?'

Jolted back to reality, Hoppy could only manage, 'Say what?'

'Can you help us?'

'Sure, I guess, but how?'

'Millie. You talk to your wife, make sure she understands how senseless and how dangerous this case is. She needs to take charge in that jury room, Hoppy. She needs to stand her ground against those liberals on the jury who might want to bring back a big verdict. Can you do it?'

'Of course I can.'

'But will you, Hoppy? We don't want to use the tape, okay. You help us, and the tape goes down the toilet.'

Hoppy suddenly remembered the tape. 'Yeah, you gotta deal. I'll see her tonight, as a matter of fact.'

'Go to work on her. It's terribly important – important for us at Justice, for the good of the country, and, of course, it'll keep you outta prison for five years.' Cristano delivered the last line with a horselaugh and a slap on the knee. Hoppy laughed too.

They talked about strategy for half an hour. The longer they sat on the boat, the more questions Hoppy had. What if Millie voted with the tobacco company but the rest of the jury disagreed and delivered a big verdict? What would happen to Hoppy then?

Cristano promised to hold his end of the deal regardless of the verdict, as long as Millie voted right.

Hoppy virtually skipped along the pier as they returned to the car. He was a new man when he saw Napier and Nitchman.

After deliberating on his decision for three days, Judge Harkin reversed himself late Saturday and decided the jurors would not be permitted to attend their churches Sunday. He was convinced all fourteen would suddenly possess an amazing desire to commune with the Holy Spirit, and the idea of them fanning out to all parts of the county was simply unworkable. He called his minister, who in turn made more calls, and a young divinity student was located. A chapel service was planned for eleven o'clock Sunday morning, in the Party Room at the Siesta Inn.

Judge Harkin sent a personal note to each juror. The notes were slid under their doors before they returned from New Orleans Saturday night.

Six people attended the service, a rather dull affair. Mrs. Gladys Card was there, in a surprisingly nasty mood for the Sabbath. She hadn't missed Sunday School at the Calvary Baptist Church in sixteen years, the last absence caused by the death of her sister in Baton Rouge. Sixteen straight years without a miss. She had the Perfect Attendance Pins lined up on her dresser. Esther Knoblach in the Women's Mission Union had twenty-two years, the current record at Calvary, but she was seventy-nine and was afflicted with high blood pressure. Gladys was sixty-three, in fine health, and thus considered Esther catchable. She couldn't admit this to anyone, but everyone at Calvary suspected it.

But now she'd blown it, thanks to Judge Harkin, a man she didn't like from the start and now despised. And she didn't like the divinity student either.

Rikki Coleman came in a jogging suit. Millie Dupree brought her Bible. Loreen Duke was a devout churchgoer, but was appalled at the brevity of the service. On at eleven and over by eleven-thirty, typical hurried style of white folks. She'd heard of such foolishness, but had never worshiped in such a manner. Her pastor never got to the pulpit before one, and often didn't leave it until three, when they broke for lunch, which they ate on the grounds if the weather was nice, then trooped back inside for another dose. She nibbled on a sweet roll and suffered in silence.

Mr. and Mrs. Herman Grimes attended, not through any calling of faith but because the walls in Room 58 were closing in. Herman in particular had not voluntarily gone to church since childhood.

Throughout the course of the morning, it had come to be known that Phillip Savelle was angered at the notion of worship. He told someone he was an atheist, and this news had spread in a flash. To protest, he positioned himself on his bed, apparently nude or certainly close to it, folded and tucked his wiry legs and arms into some type of yoga drill, and hollered chants at full volume. He did this with the door open.

He could be heard faintly in the Party Room, during the service, and this no doubt was a factor in the young divinity student's rather hastened wrap-up and benediction.

Lou Dell marched down the first time to tell Savelle to shut up, but backed away quickly when she noticed Savelle's nakedness. Willis tried next, but Savelle kept his eyes closed and his mouth open and simply ignored the deputy. Willis kept his distance.

The nonworshiping jurors hunkered down behind locked doors and watched loud televisions.

At two, the first relatives began to arrive with fresh clothing and supplies for the week. Nicholas Easter was the only juror with no close contact on the outside. It

268

was determined by Judge Harkin that Willis would drive Easter in a squad car to his apartment.

The fire had been out for several hours. The trucks and firemen were long gone. The narrow front lawn and sidewalk in front of the building were strewn with charred debris and piles of soggy clothing. Neighbors milled about, stunned, but busily going about the cleanup.

'Which one's yours?' Willis asked as he stopped the car and gaped at the burnt crater in the center of the building.

'Up there,' Nicholas said, trying to point and nod at the same time. His knees were weak as he left the car and walked to the first cluster of people, a family of Vietnamese who were mutely studying a melted plastic table lamp.

'When did this happen?' he asked. The air was thick with the acrid smell of freshly burnt wood and paint and carpet.

They said nothing.

'This morning, about eight,' answered a woman as she walked by with a heavy cardboard box. Nicholas looked at the people and realized he didn't know a single name. In the small foyer, a busy lady with a clipboard was scribbling notes while talking on a cellphone. The main staircase to the second level was guarded by a private security guard who at the moment was helping an elderly woman drag a wet throw rug down the steps.

'Do you live here?' the woman asked when she finished her conversation.

'Yes. Easter, in 312.'

'Wow. Totally destroyed. That's probably where it started.'

'I'd like to see it.'

The security guard led Nicholas and the woman up the steps to the second floor, where the damage was quite apparent. They stopped at a yellow caution tape at the edge of the crater. The fire had gone upward, through the plaster ceilings and cheap rafters, and had managed to burn two large holes in the roof, directly over the spot where his bedroom used to be, as far as he could tell. And it had burned downward, severely damaging the apartment directly under him. Nothing was left of number 312, except for the kitchen wall, where the sink hung by one end and seemed ready to fall. Nothing. No sign of the cheap furniture in the den, no sign of the den itself. Nothing from the bedroom except blackened walls.

And, to his horror, no computer.

Virtually all the floors, ceilings, and walls of the apartment had vanished, leaving nothing but a gaping hole.

'Anybody hurt?' Nicholas asked softly.

'No. Were you home?' she asked.

'No. Who are you?'

'I'm with the management company. I have some forms for you to fill out.'

They returned to the foyer where Nicholas hurriedly did the paperwork and left with Willis.

270

TWENTY-TWO

It was pointed out to Judge Harkin by Phillip Savelle, in a tersely worded, hardly legible message, that the word 'conjugal' as defined by Webster covered husband and wife only, and he objected to the term. He did not have a wife, and had little regard for the institution of marriage. He suggested 'Communal Interludes,' and he went on to bitch about the worship service held that morning. He faxed the letter to Harkin, who received it at home during the fourth quarter of the Saints game. Lou Dell arranged the fax through the front desk. Twenty minutes later she received a return fax from His Honor changing the word 'conjugal' to 'personal,' and relabeling the whole thing 'Personal Visits.' He directed her to make copies for all jurors. Because it was Sunday, he threw in another hour, from 6 P.M. to 10, instead of 9. He then called her to ask what else Mr. Savelle might want, and inquired as to the general mood of his jury.

Lou Dell just couldn't tell him about seeing Mr. Savelle all nude and perched on his bed like that. She figured the Judge had enough things to worry about. Everything was fine, she assured him.

Hoppy was the first guest to arrive and Lou Dell whisked him away quickly to Millie's room, where he once again delivered chocolates and a small bouquet of flowers. They kissed briefly on the cheeks, never considered anything conjugal, and lounged on the beds

271

during '60 Minutes.' Hoppy slowly brought the conversation around to the trial, where he struggled to keep it for a while. 'Just doesn't make sense, you know, for people to sue like this. I mean, it's silly, really. Everybody knows cigarettes are addictive and dangerous, so why smoke? Remember Boyd Dogan, smoked Salems for twenty-five years, quit just like that,' he said, snapping his fingers.

'Yeah, he quit five minutes after the doctor found that tumor on his tongue,' Millie reminded him, then added a mocking snap of her own.

'Yeah, but lots of people quit smoking. It's mind over matter. Not right to keep smoking then sue for millions when the damned things kill you.'

'Hoppy, your language.'

'Sorry.' Hoppy asked about the other jurors and their reactions so far to the plaintiff's case. Mr. Cristano thought it would be best to try and win Millie over with the merits, instead of terrorizing her with the truth. They'd talked about this over lunch. Hoppy felt treacherous plotting against his own wife, but each time the guilt hit him so did the thought of five years in prison.

Nicholas left his room during halftime of the Sunday-night game. The hall was empty of jurors and guards. Voices were heard in the Party Room, generally male voices it seemed. Once again the men drank beer and watched football while the women made the most of their personal visits and communal interludes.

He slid silently through the double glass doors at the end of the hallway, ducked around the corner, past the soft-drink machines, then bounded up the stairs to the second floor. Marlee was waiting in a room she'd paid cash for and registered under the name of Elsa Broome, one of her many aliases.

They went straight to bed, with a minimum of words and preliminaries. Both had agreed that eight

272

consecutive nights apart was not only a record for them, but also unhealthy.

Marlee met Nicholas when both had other names. The point of contact was a bar in Lawrence, Kansas, where she worked as a waitress and he spent late nights with pals from law school. She had collected two degrees by the time she settled in Lawrence, and because she wasn't eager to initiate a career, she was pondering the option of law school, that great American baby-sitter for directionless postgrads. She was in no hurry. Her mother had died a few years before she met Nicholas, and Marlee had inherited almost two hundred thousand dollars. She served drinks because the hangout was cool and she would've been bored otherwise. It kept her in shape. She drove an old Jaguar, watched her money closely, and dated only law students.

They noticed each other long before they spoke. He'd come in late with a small group, the usual faces, sit in a booth in a corner, and debate abstract and incredibly boring legal theories. She'd deliver draft beer in pitchers, and try to flirt, with varying degrees of success. During his first year, he was enamored with the law and paid little attention to girls. She asked around and learned he was a good student, top third in his class, but nothing outstanding. He survived the first year and returned for the second. She cut her hair and lost ten pounds, though it wasn't necessary.

He had finished college and applied to thirty law schools. Eleven said yes, though none were top ten. He flipped a coin and drove to Lawrence, a place he'd never seen. He found a two-room apartment stuck to the rear of a spinster's crumbling house. He studied hard and had little time for a social life, at least during the first two semesters.

The summer after his first year he clerked for a large firm in Kansas City where he pushed interoffice mail from floor to floor with a cart. The firm had three hundred lawyers under one roof, and at times it seemed as though all were working on one trial – the defense of Smith Greer in a tobacco/lung cancer case down in Joplin. The trial lasted five weeks and ended with a defense verdict. Afterward, the firm threw a party and a thousand people showed up. Rumor was that the catered celebration cost Smith Greer eighty grand. Who cared? The summer was a miserable experience.

He hated the big firm, and midway through his second year he was fed up with the law in general. No way he would spend five years locked in a cubbyhole writing and rewriting the same briefs so rich corporate clients could be milked.

Their first date was to a law school keg party after a football game. The music was loud, the beer plentiful, the pot passed around like candy. They left early because he didn't like noise and she didn't like the smell of cannabis. They rented videos and cooked spaghetti in her apartment, a rather spacious and well-furnished layout. He slept on the sofa.

A month later he moved in and first broached the subject of dropping out of law school. She was thinking about applying. As the romance blossomed, his interest in things academic diminished to the point of barely completing his fall exams. They were madly in love, and nothing else mattered. Plus, she had the benefit of a little cash, so the pressure was off. They spent Christmas in Jamaica between semesters of his second, and final, year.

By the time he quit, she'd been in Lawrence for three years, and was ready to move on. He would follow her anywhere.

Marlee had been able to learn little about the fire Sunday afternoon. They suspected Fitch, but couldn't pinpoint a reason. The only asset of value was the

274

computer, and Nicholas was certain no one could breach its security system. The important discs were locked away in a vault in Marlee's condo. What could Fitch gain by burning a run-down apartment? Intimidation maybe, but it didn't fit. Fire officials were conducting a routine investigation. Arson seemed unlikely.

They'd slept in finer places than the Siesta Inn, and they'd slept in worse. In four years they'd lived in four towns, traveled to a half-dozen countries, seen most of North America, backpacked in Alaska and Mexico, rafted the Colorado twice, and floated the Amazon once. They had also tracked tobacco litigation, and that journey had forced them to set up housekeeping in places such as Broken Arrow, Allentown, and now Biloxi. Together, they knew more about nicotine levels, carcinogens, statistical probabilities of lung cancer, jury selection, trial tactics, and Rankin Fitch than any group of high-powered experts.

After an hour under the covers, a light came on beside the bed and Nicholas emerged, hair ruffled, reaching for clothing. Marlee got dressed and peeked through the shades at the parking lot.

Directly below them, Hoppy was trying his best to discount the scandalous revelations of Lawrence Krigler, testimony Millie seemed quite impressed with. She dished it out to Hoppy in heavy doses, and was puzzled by his desire to argue so much.

Just for the fun of it, Marlee had left her car parked on the street a half a block from the offices of Wendall Rohr. She and Nicholas were operating under the assumption that Fitch was following every move she made. It was amusing to imagine Fitch squirming with the idea that she was in there, in Rohr's office, actually meeting with him face-to-face and agreeing to who knew what. For the personal visit, she had arrived in a rental car, one of several she'd used in the past month.

275

Nicholas was suddenly weary of the room, an exact replica of the one he was confined to. They went for a long drive along the Coast; she drove, he sipped beer. They walked down a pier above the Gulf, and kissed as the water rocked gently below them. They talked little of the trial.

At ten-thirty, Marlee emerged from the car at a point two blocks from Rohr's office. As she walked hurriedly along the sidewalk, Nicholas followed nearby. Her car was parked alone. Joe Boy saw her get into it and radioed Konrad. After she drove away, Nicholas hurried back to the motel in the rental car.

Rohr was in the midst of a heated council meeting, the daily gathering of the eight trial lawyers who'd put up a million each. The issue Sunday night was the number of witnesses left to be called by the plaintiff, and as usual, there were eight separate opinions about what to do next. Two schools of thought, but eight very firm and very different inclinations about precisely what would be effective.

Including the three days spent selecting the jury, the trial was now three weeks old. Tomorrow would start week four, and the plaintiff had enough experts and other witnesses to go on for at least two more weeks. Cable had his own army of experts, though typically the defense in these cases used less than half the time of the plaintiff. Six weeks was a reasonable prediction, which meant the jury would be sequestered for almost four weeks, a scenario that troubled everyone. At some point the jury would rebel, and since the plaintiff used the bulk of the court time, the plaintiff had the most to lose. But on the other hand, since the defense went last, and the jury would tire at the end, then perhaps the jury's venom would be aimed at Cable and Pynex. This argument raged for an hour.

Wood v. Pynex was unique because it was the first tobacco trial featuring a sequestered jury. It was, in fact, the first sequestered civil jury in the history of the state. Rohr was of the opinion that the jury had heard enough. He wanted to call only two more witnesses, finish their case by noon Tuesday, then rest and wait for Cable. He was joined by Scotty Mangrum of Dallas and André Durond of New Orleans. Jonathan Kotlack of San Diego wanted three more witnesses.

The opposing view was vigorously pushed by John Riley Milton of Denver and Rayner Lovelady of Savannah. Since they'd spent so damned much money on the world's greatest collection of experts, why be in a hurry, they argued. There remained some crucial testimony from outstanding witnesses. The jury wasn't going anywhere. Sure they'd get tired, but didn't every jury? It was far safer to stick to the game plan and try the case thoroughly than to jump ship in midstream because a few jurors were getting bored.

Carney Morrison of Boston harped repeatedly on the weekly summaries from the jury consultants. This jury was not convinced! Under Mississippi law, it would take nine of the twelve to get a verdict. Morrison was certain they didn't have nine. Rohr especially paid little attention to the current analyses of how Jerry Fernandez rubbed his eyes and how Loreen Duke shifted her weight and how poor old Herman twisted at the neck when Dr. So-and-So was testifying. Frankly, Rohr was sick of the jury experts and especially sick of the obscene sums of money they were getting. It was one thing to have their assistance while investigating potential jurors. It was a far different matter to have them lurking everywhere during the trial, always anxious to prepare a daily report to tell the lawyers how the case was trying. Rohr could read a jury far better than any consultant.

Arnold Levine of Miami said little because the group knew his feelings. He'd once taken on General Motors in a trial that lasted eleven months, so six weeks was a warm-up for him.

There was no coin toss when the vote was even. It had been agreed long before jury selection that this was Wendall Rohr's trial, filed in his hometown, fought in his courtroom before his judge and his jurors. The plaintiff's trial council was a democratic body to a point, but Rohr had veto power which could not be overridden.

He made his decision late Sunday, and the serious egos left bruised but not permanently damaged. There was too much at stake for bickering and second-guessing.

TWENTY-THREE

The first order of business Monday morning was a private meeting between Judge Harkin and Nicholas, the topic being the fire and his well-being. They met alone in chambers. Nicholas assured him he was fine and had enough clothing at the motel to wash and rewash. He was just a student with little to lose, with the exception of a fine computer and some expensive surveillance equipment, all of which was, of course, uninsured along with everything else.

The fire was dispensed with quickly, and since they were alone Harkin asked, 'So how are the rest of our friends doing?' Chatting off the record like this with a juror was not improper, but was certainly in the gray area of trial procedure. The better practice was to have the lawyers present and to record every word with a court reporter. But Harkin wanted just a few minutes of gossip. He could trust this kid.

'Everything's fine,' Nicholas said.

'Nothing unusual?'

'Not that I can think of.'

'Is the case being discussed?'

'No. In fact, when we're together, we try to avoid it.'

'Good. Any spats or squabbles?'

'Not yet.'

'Food's okay?'

'Food's fine.'

'Enough personal visits?'

'I think so. I haven't heard any complaints.'

Harkin would have loved to know if there was any hanky-panky among the jurors, not that it would carry any legal significance. He just had a dirty mind. 'Good. Let me know if there's a problem. And let's keep this quiet.'

'Sure,' Nicholas said. They shook hands and he left.

Harkin greeted the jurors warmly and welcomed them back for another week. They seemed eager to get to work and finish this ordeal.

Rohr rose and called Leon Robilio as the next witness, and the players settled down to business. Leon was led from a side door into the courtroom. He shuffled gingerly in front of the bench to the witness stand, where the deputy assisted him in having a seat. He was old and pale, dressed in a dark suit, white shirt, no tie. He had a hole in his throat, an opening covered by a thin white dressing and camouflaged with a white linen neckerchief. When he swore to tell the truth, he did so by holding a pencil-like mike to his neck. The words were the flat, pitchless monotone of a throat cancer victim without a larynx.

But the words were audible and understandable. Mr. Robilio held the microphone close to his throat and his voice rattled around the courtroom. This was how he talked, dammit, and he did so every day of his life. He meant to be understood.

Rohr got quickly to the point. Mr. Robilio was sixty-four years old, a cancer survivor who'd lost his voice box eight years earlier and had learned to talk through his esophagus. He had smoked heavily for nearly forty years, and his habits had almost killed him. Now, in addition to the aftereffects of the cancer, he suffered from heart disease and emphysema. All because of the cigarettes.

His listeners quickly adjusted to his amplified, robot-like voice. He grabbed their attention for good when he told them he'd made his living for two decades as a lobbyist for the tobacco industry. He quit the job when he got cancer and realized that even with the disease he couldn't stop smoking. He was addicted, physically and psychologically addicted to the nicotine in cigarettes. For two years after his larynx was removed and the chemotherapy ravaged his body, he continued to smoke. He finally quit after a near-fatal heart attack.

Though obviously in bad health, he still worked full-time in Washington, but now he was on the other side of the fence. He had the reputation of a fiercely committed antismoking activist. A guerrilla, some called him.

In a prior life, he had been employed at the Tobacco Focus Council. 'Which was nothing more than a slick lobbying outfit funded entirely by the industry,' he said with disdain. 'Our mission was to advise the tobacco companies on current legislation and attempts to regulate them. We had a fat budget with unlimited resources to wine and dine influential politicians. We played hardball, and we taught other tobacco apologists the ins and outs of political fistfighting.'

At the Council, Robilio had access to countless studies of cigarettes and the tobacco industry. In fact, part of the mission of the Council was the meticulous assimilation of all known studies, projects, experiments. Yes, Robilio had seen the infamous nicotine memo Krigler had described. He'd seen it many times, though he did not keep a copy. It was well known at the Council that all tobacco companies kept nicotine at high levels to ensure addiction.

Addiction was a word Robilio used over and over. He'd seen studies paid for by the companies in which all sorts of animals had been quickly addicted to cigarettes through nicotine. He'd seen and helped hide studies proving beyond any doubt that once young

281

teenagers were hooked on cigarettes the rates of kicking the habit were much lower. They became customers for life.

Rohr produced a box of thick reports for Robilio to identify. The studies were admitted into evidence, as if the jurors would find the time to plow through ten thousand pages of documents before making their decision.

Robilio regretted many things he'd done as a lobbyist, but his greatest sin, one he struggled with daily, had been the artfully worded denials he'd issued claiming the industry did not target teenagers through advertising. 'Nicotine is addictive. Addiction means profits. The survival of tobacco depends upon each new generation picking up the habit. Kids receive mixed messages through advertising. The industry spends billions portraying cigarettes as cool and glamorous, even harmless. Kids get hooked easier, and stay hooked longer. So it's imperative to seduce the young.' Robilio managed to convey bitterness through his manmade voice box. And he managed to sneer at the defense table while looking warmly at the jurors.

'We spent millions studying kids. We knew that they could name the three most heavily advertised brands of cigarettes. We knew that almost ninety percent of the kids under eighteen who smoked preferred the top three advertised brands. So what did the companies do? They increased the advertising.'

'Did you know how much money the tobacco companies were making off cigarette sales to children?' Rohr asked, certain of the answer.

'About two hundred million a year. And that's in sales to kids eighteen or under. Of course we knew. We studied it annually, kept our computers filled with the data. We knew everything.' He paused and waved his right hand at the defense table, sneering as if it were surrounded by lepers. 'They still know. They know that three thousand kids start smoking every day, and they can give you an accurate breakdown of the brands they're buying. They know that virtually all adult smokers began as teenagers. Again, they have to hook the next generation. They know that one third of the three thousand kids who start smoking today will eventually die from their addiction.'

The jury was captivated with Robilio. Rohr flipped pages for a second so the drama wouldn't be rushed. He took a few steps back and forth behind the lectern as if his legs needed limbering. He scratched his chin, looked at the ceiling, then asked, 'When you were with the Tobacco Focus Council, how did you counter the arguments that nicotine is addictive?'

'The tobacco companies have a party line; I helped formulate it. It goes something like this: Smokers choose the habit. So it's a matter of choice. Cigarettes are not addictive, but, hey, even if they are, no one forces anybody to smoke. It's all a matter of choice.

'I could make this sound real good, back in those days. And they make it sound good today. Trouble is, it's not true.'

'Why isn't it true?'

'Because the issue is addiction, and the addict cannot make choices. And kids become addicted much quicker than adults.'

Rohr for once avoided the natural lawyerly compulsion of overkill. Robilio was efficient with words, and the strain of being clear and being heard tired him after an hour and a half. Rohr tendered him to Cable for cross-examination, and Judge Harkin, who needed coffee, called a recess.

Hoppy Dupree made his first visit to the trial Monday morning, slipping into the courtroom midway through Robilio's testimony. Millie caught his eye during a lull, and was thrilled he would stop by. His sudden interest in the trial was odd, though. He'd talked of nothing else for four hours last night.

283

After a twenty-minute coffee break, Cable stepped to the lectern and tore into Robilio. His tone was strident, almost mean, as if he viewed the witness as a traitor to the cause, a turncoat. Cable scored immediately with the revelation that Robilio was being paid to testify, and that he had sought out the plaintiff's lawyers. He was also on retainer in two other tobacco cases.

'Yes, I'm being paid to be here, Mr. Cable, same as you,' Robilio said, delivering the typical expert's response. But the stain of money slightly tainted his character.

Cable got him to confess that he started smoking when he was almost twenty-five, married, with two children, hardly a teenager who could've been seduced by slick work from Madison Avenue. Robilio had a temper, a fact proven to all the lawyers during a two-day marathon deposition five months earlier, and Cable was determined to exploit it. His questions were sharp, rapid, and designed to provoke.

'How many children do you have?' Cable asked.

'Three.'

'Did any of them ever smoke cigarettes regularly?'

'Yes.'

'How many?'

'Three.'

'How old were they when they started?'

'It varies.'

'On the average?'

'Late teens.'

'Which ads do you blame for getting them hooked on cigarettes?'

'I don't recall exactly.'

'You can't tell the jury which ads were responsible for getting your own kids hooked on cigarettes?'

'There were so many ads. Still are. It would be impossible to pinpoint one or two or five that worked.'

'So it was the ads?'

284

'I'm sure the ads were effective. Still are.'

'So it was somebody else's fault?'

'I didn't encourage their smoking.'

'Are you sure? You're telling this jury that your own children, the children of a man whose job for twenty years was to encourage the world to smoke, began smoking because of slick advertising?'

'I'm sure the ads helped. They were designed to.'

'Did you smoke in the home, in front of your children?'

'Yes.'

'Did your wife?'

'Yes.'

'Did you ever tell a guest he couldn't smoke in your home?'

'No. Not then.'

'Safe to say, then, that the environment of your home was smoker friendly?'

'Yes. Then.'

'But your children started smoking because of devious advertising? Is that what you're telling this jury?'

Robilio took a deep breath, counted slowly to five, then said, 'I wish I'd done a lot of things differently, Mr. Cable. I wish I'd never picked up the first cigarette.'

'Did your children stop smoking?'

'Two of them did. With great difficulty. The third has been trying to quit for ten years now.'

Cable had asked the last question on an impulse, and wished for a second he hadn't. Time to move on. He shifted gears. 'Mr. Robilio, are you aware of efforts by the tobacco industry to curb teenage smoking?'

Robilio chuckled, which sounded like a gargle when amplified through his little mike. 'No serious efforts,' he said.

'Forty million dollars last year to Smoke Free Kids?'

'Sounds like something they'd do. Makes 'em seem warm and fuzzy, doesn't it?'

'Are you aware that the industry is on record supporting legislation to restrict vending machines in areas where kids congregate?'

'I think I've heard of that. Sounds lovely, doesn't it?'

'Are you aware that the industry last year gave ten million dollars to California for a statewide kindergarten program designed to warn youngsters about underage smoking?'

'No. What about overage smoking? Did they tell the little fellas that it was okay to smoke after their eighteenth birthdays? Probably did.'

Cable had a checklist, and seemed content to fire off the questions while ignoring the answers.

'Are you aware that the industry supports a bill in Texas to ban smoking in all fast-food establishments, places frequented by teenagers?'

'Yeah, and do you know why they do things like that? I'll tell you why. So they can hire people like you to tell jurors like these about it. That's the only reason – it sounds good in court.'

'Are you aware that the industry is on record supporting legislation which imposes criminal penalties against convenience stores which sell tobacco products to minors?'

'Yeah, I think I heard that one too. It's window dressing. They'll drop a few bucks here and there to preen and posture and buy respectability. They'll do this because they know the truth, and the truth is that two billion dollars a year in advertising will guarantee addiction by the next generation. And you're a fool if you don't believe this.'

Judge Harkin leaned forward. 'Mr. Robilio, that is uncalled-for. Don't do it again. I want it stricken from the record.'

'Sorry, Your Honor. And sorry to you, Mr. Cable.

You're just doing your job. It's your client I can't stand.'

Cable was thrown off track. He offered up a lame 'Why?' and wished immediately he'd kept his mouth shut.

'Because they're so devious. These tobacco people are bright, intelligent, educated, ruthless, and they'll look you in the face and tell you with all sincerity that cigarettes are not addictive. And they know it's a lie.'

'No further questions,' Cable said, halfway to his table.

Gardner was a town of eighteen thousand an hour from Lubbock. Pamela Blanchard lived in the old section of town, two blocks off Main Street in a house built at the turn of the century and nicely renovated. Brilliant red and gold maple trees covered the front lawn. Children roamed the street on bikes and skateboards.

By ten Monday, Fitch knew the following: She was married to the president of a local bank, a man who'd been married once before and whose wife had died ten years ago. He was not the father of Nicholas Easter or Jeff or whoever the hell he was. The bank had almost collapsed during the oil bust of the early eighties, and many locals were still afraid to use it. Pamela's husband was a native of the town. She was not. She may have come from Lubbock, or maybe it was Amarillo. They got married in Mexico eight years ago, and the local weekly barely recorded it. No wedding picture. Just an announcement next to the obituaries that N. Forrest Blanchard, Jr., had married Pamela Kerr. After a brief honeymoon in Cozumel, they would reside in Gardner.

The best source in town was a private investigator named Rafe who'd been a cop for twenty years and claimed to know everyone. Rafe, after being paid a sizable retainer in cash, worked without sleep Sunday night. No sleep, but plenty of bourbon, and by dawn he reeked of sour mash. Dante and Joe Boy worked beside him, in his grungy office on Main, and repeatedly declined the whiskey.

Rafe talked to every cop in Gardner, and finally found one who could talk to a lady who lived across the street from the Blanchards. Bingo. Pamela had two sons by a previous marriage; it ended in divorce. She didn't talk much about them, but one was in Alaska and one was a lawyer, or was studying to be a lawyer. Something like that.

Since neither son grew up in Gardner, the trail soon ran cold. No one knew them. In fact, Rafe couldn't find anyone who'd ever seen Pamela's sons. Then Rafe called his lawyer, a sleazy divorce specialist who routinely used Rafe's primitive surveillance services, and the lawyer knew a secretary at Mr. Blanchard's bank. The secretary talked to Mr. Blanchard's personal secretary, and it was discovered that Pamela was from neither Lubbock nor Amarillo, but Austin. She'd worked there for a bankers' association, and that's how she'd met Mr. Blanchard. The secretary knew of the prior marriage, and was of the opinion that it had ended many years ago. No, she had never seen Pamela's sons. Mr. Blanchard never discussed them. The couple lived quietly and almost never entertained.

Fitch received reports every hour from Dante and Joe Boy. Late Monday morning, he called an acquaintance in Austin, a man he'd worked with six years earlier in a tobacco trial in Marshall, Texas. It was an emergency, Fitch explained. Within minutes, a dozen investigators were scouring phone books and making calls. It wasn't long before the bloodhounds picked up the trail.

Pamela Kerr had been an executive secretary for the Texas Bankers' Association, in Austin. One phone call led to another, and a former co-worker was located working as a private school guidance counselor. Using the ruse that Pamela was a prospective juror in a capital murder case in Lubbock, the investigator described himself as an assistant district attorney who was trying to gather legitimate information about the jurors. The co-worker felt obligated to answer a few questions, though she hadn't seen or talked to Pamela in years.

Pamela had two sons, Jeff and Alex. Alex was two years older than Jeff, and had graduated from high school in Austin, then drifted to Oregon. Jeff had also finished high school in Austin, with honors, then gone to college at Rice. The boys' father had abandoned the family when they were toddlers, and Pamela had done an outstanding job as a single mother.

Dante, fresh off the private jet, accompanied an investigator to the high school, where they were allowed to rummage through old yearbooks in the library. Jeff Kerr's 1985 senior picture was in color – a blue tux, large blue bow tie, short hair, earnest face looking directly at the camera, the same face Dante had studied for hours in Biloxi. Without hesitation he said, 'This is our man,' then quietly ripped the page from the yearbook. He immediately called Fitch on a cellphone from between the stacked tiers of books.

Three phone calls to Rice revealed that Jeff Kerr graduated there in 1989 with a degree in psychology. Posing as a representative from a prospective employer, the caller found a Rice professor of political science who'd taught and who remembered Kerr. He said the young man went to law school at Kansas.

With the guarantee of serious cash, Fitch found by phone a security firm willing to drop everything and began scouring Lawrence, Kansas, for any trace of Jeff Kerr.

For one normally so chipper, Nicholas was quite reserved during lunch. He didn't say a word as he ate a heavily stuffed baked potato from O'Reilly's. He avoided glances and looked downright sad.

The mood was shared. Leon Robilio's voice stayed with them, a robotic voice substituted for a real one lost to the ravages of tobacco, a robotic voice which delivered the sickening dirt he once helped hide. It still rang in their ears. Three thousand kids a day, one third of whom die from their addiction. Gotta hook the next generation!

Loreen Duke tired of picking at her chicken salad. She looked across the table at Jerry Fernandez, and said, 'Can I ask you something?' Her voice broke a weary silence.

'Sure,' he said.

'How old were you when you started smoking?'

'Fourteen.'

'Why did you start?'

'The Marlboro Man. Every kid I hung around with smoked Marlboros. We were country kids, liked horses and rodeos. The Marlboro Man was too cool to resist.'

At that moment, every juror could see the billboards – the rugged face, the chin, the hat, the horse, the worn leather, maybe the mountains and some snow, the independence of lighting up a Marlboro while the world left him alone. Why wouldn't a young boy of fourteen want to be the Marlboro Man?

'Are you addicted?' asked Rikki Coleman, playing with her usual fat-free plate of lettuce and boiled turkey. The 'addicted' rolled off her tongue as if they were discussing heroin.

Jerry thought for a moment and realized his friends were listening. They wanted to know what powerful urges kept a person hooked.

'I don't know,' he said. 'I guess I could quit. I've tried a few times. Sure would be nice to stop. Such a nasty habit.'

'You don't enjoy it?' Rikki asked.

'Oh, there are times when a cigarette hits the spot, but I'm doing two packs a day now and that's too much.'

290

'What about you, Angel?' Loreen asked Angel Weese, who sat next to her and generally said as little as possible. 'How old were you when you started?'

'Thirteen,' Angel said, ashamed.

'I was sixteen,' Sylvia Taylor-Tatum admitted before anyone could ask.

'I started when I was fourteen,' Herman offered from the end in an effort at conversation. 'Quit when I was forty.'

'Anybody else?' Rikki asked, finishing the confessional.

'I started at seventeen,' the Colonel said. 'When I joined the Army. But I kicked the habit thirty years ago.' As usual, he was proud of his self-discipline.

'Anybody else?' Rikki asked again, after a long, silent pause.

'Me. I started when I was seventeen and quit two years later,' Nicholas said, though it was not true.

'Did anybody here start smoking after the age of eighteen?' Loreen asked.

Not a word.

Nitchman, in plain clothes, met Hoppy for a quick sandwich. Hoppy was nervous about being seen in public with an FBI agent, and was quite relieved when Nitchman appeared in jeans and a plaid shirt. Wasn't like Hoppy's pals and acquaintances around town could instantly spot the local feds, but he was still nervous nevertheless. Besides, Nitchman and Napier were from a special unit in Atlanta, they'd told Hoppy.

He replayed what he'd heard in court that morning, said the voiceless Robilio made quite an impression and seemed to have the jury in his pocket. Nitchman, not for the first time, professed little interest in the trial and explained again he was just doing what his bosses in Washington told him to do. He handed Hoppy a folded sheet of paper, plain white with tiny numbers and words scattered on the top and bottom, and said this had just come from Cristano at Justice. They wanted Hoppy to see it.

It was really a creation of Fitch's document people, two retired CIA boys who puttered around D.C. enjoying the mischief.

It was a faxed copy of a sinister-looking report on Leon Robilio. No source, no date, just four paragraphs under the ominous headline of CONFIDENTIAL MEMO. Hoppy read it quickly while chomping on french fries. Robilio was being paid half a million dollars to testify. Robilio had been fired from the Tobacco Focus Council for embezzling funds; had even been indicted, though charges were later dropped. Robilio had a history of psychiatric problems. Robilio had sexually harassed two secretaries at the Council. Robilio's throat cancer had probably been caused by his alcoholism, and not by tobacco. Robilio was a notorious liar who hated the Council and was on a crusade of revenge.

'Wow,' Hoppy said, showing a mouthful of potatoes.

'Mr. Cristano thought you should sneak this to your wife,' Nitchman said. 'She should show it only to those she can trust on the jury.'

'Right about that,' Hoppy said, quickly folding and stuffing it into a pocket. He looked around the crowded dining room as if he was completely guilty of something.

Working from law school yearbooks and the limited records the registrar would release, it was learned that Jeff Kerr enrolled as a first-year law student at Kansas in the fall of 1989. His unsmiling face appeared with the second-year class in 1991, but there was no trace of him after that. He did not receive a law degree.

He played rugby for the law school team his second year. A team photo showed him arm in arm with two pals – Michael Dale and Tom Ratliff – both of whom had finished law school the following year. Dale was working for Legal Services in Des Moines. Ratliff was an associate for a firm in Wichita. Investigators were sent to both places.

Dante arrived in Lawrence and was taken to the law school, where he confirmed the identity of Kerr in the yearbooks. He spent an hour looking at faces from 1985 through 1994, and saw no female resembling the girl known as Marlee. It was a shot in the dark. Many law students skipped the picture taking. Yearbooks were sophomoric. These were serious young adults. Dante's work was nothing but a series of shots in the dark.

Late Monday, the investigator named Small found Tom Ratliff hard at work in his tiny windowless office at Wise & Watkins, a large firm in downtown Wichita. They agreed to meet in a bar in an hour.

Small talked to Fitch and gathered as much background as he could, or as much as Fitch would give him. Small was an ex-cop with two ex-wives. His title was security specialist, which in Lawrence meant he did everything from motel watching to polygraph exams. He was not bright, and Fitch realized this immediately.

Ratliff arrived late and they ordered drinks. Small did his best to bluff and act knowledgeable. Ratliff was suspicious. He said little at first, which was what could be expected from a person unexpectedly asked by a stranger to talk about an old acquaintance.

'I haven't seen him in four years,' Ratliff said.

'Have you talked to him?'

'No. Not a word. He dropped out of school after our second year.'

'Were you close to him?'

'I knew him well our first year, but we were not the best of friends. He withdrew after that. Is he in trouble?'

'No. Not at all.'

'Perhaps you should tell me why you're so interested.'

Small recited in general terms what Fitch had told

him to say, got most of it right and it was close to the truth. Jeff Kerr was a prospective juror in a large trial somewhere, and he, Small, had been hired by one of the parties to dig through his background.

'Where's the trial?' Ratliff asked.

'I can't say. But I assure you, none of this is illegal. You're a lawyer. You understand.'

Indeed he did. Ratliff had spent most of his brief career slaving under a litigation partner. Jury research was a chore he'd already learned to hate. 'How can I verify this?' he asked, like a real lawyer.

'I don't have the authority to divulge specifics about the trial. Let's do it like this. If I ask something which you think might be harmful to Kerr, then don't answer. Fair enough?'

We'll give it a shot, okay? But if I get nervous, then I'm outta here.'

'Fair enough. Why did he quit law school?'

Ratliff took a sip of his beer and tried to remember. 'He was a good student, very bright. But after the first year, he suddenly hated the idea of being a lawyer. He clerked in a firm that summer, a big firm in Kansas City, and it soured him. Plus, he fell in love.'

Fitch desperately wanted to know if there was a girl. 'Who was the woman?' Small asked.

'Claire.'

'Claire who?'

Another sip. 'I can't remember right now.'

'You knew her?'

'I knew who she was. Claire worked at a bar in downtown Lawrence, a college hangout favored by law students. I think that's where she met Jeff.'

'Could you describe her?'

'Why? I thought this was about Jeff.'

'I was asked to get a description of his girlfriend in law school. That's all I know.' Small shrugged as if he couldn't help it.

294

They studied each other for a bit. What the hell, thought Ratliff. He'd never see these people again. Jeff and Claire were distant memories anyway.

'Average height, about five six. Slender. Dark hair, brown eyes, pretty girl, all the bells and whistles.'

'Was she a student?'

'I'm not sure. I think maybe she had been. Maybe a grad student.'

'At KU?'

'I don't know.'

'What was the name of the hangout?'

'Mulligan's, downtown.'

Small knew it well. At times he went there himself to drown his worries and admire the college girls. 'I've knocked back a few at Mulligan's,' he said.

'Yeah. I miss it,' Ratliff said wistfully.

'What did he do after he dropped out?'

'I'm not sure. I heard that he and Claire left town, but I never heard from him again.'

Small thanked him and asked if he could call him at the office if he had more questions. Ratliff said he was awfully busy, but give it a try.

Small's boss in Lawrence had a friend who knew the guy who'd owned Mulligan's for fifteen years. The advantages of a small town. Employment records weren't exactly confidential, especially for the owner of a bar who reported fewer than half of his cash sales. Her name was Claire Clement.

Fitch rubbed his stubby hands together with glee as he took the news. He loved the chase. Marlee was now Claire, a woman with a past who'd worked hard to cover it up.

'Know thine enemy,' he said aloud to his walls. The first rule of warfare.

TWENTY-FOUR

The numbers returned with a vengeance Monday afternoon. The messenger was an economist, a man trained to look at the life of Jacob Wood and put a concise dollar figure on it. His name was Dr. Art Kallison, a retired professor from a private school in Oregon no one had heard of. The math was not complicated, and Dr. Kallison had obviously seen a courtroom before. He knew how to testify, how to keep the figures simple. He placed them on a chalkboard with a neat hand.

When he died at fifty-one, Jacob Wood's base salary was $40,000 a year, plus a retirement plan funded by his employer, plus other benefits. Assuming he would live and work until the age of sixty-five, Kallison placed his lost future earnings at $720,000. The law also allowed the factoring of inflation into this projection, and this upped the total to $1,180,000. Then the law required that this total be reduced to its present value, a concept that muddied the water a bit. Here, Kallison delivered a quick, friendly lecture to the jury on present value. The money might be worth $1,180,000 if paid out over fifteen years, but for purposes of the lawsuit he had to determine what it was worth at the moment. Thus, it had to be discounted. His new figure was $835,000.

He did a superb job of assuring the jury that this figure dealt only with lost salary. He was an economist, quite untrained to place a value on the noneconomic value of one's life. His job had nothing to do with the pain and suffering Mr. Wood endured as he died; had nothing to do with the loss his family had endured.

A young defense lawyer named Felix Mason uttered his first word of the trial. He was one of Cable's partners, a specialist in economic forecasts, and, unfortunately for him, his only appearance would be brief. He began his cross-examination of Dr. Kallison by asking him how many times a year he testified. 'That's all I do these days. I've retired from teaching,' Kallison answered. He took the question in every trial.

'Are you being paid to testify?' Mason asked. The question was as tired as the answer.

'Yes. I'm paid to be here. Same as you.'

'How much?'

'Five thousand dollars for consultation and testimony.' No doubt among the lawyers that Kallison was by far the cheapest expert of the trial.

Mason had a problem with the rate of inflation Kallison used in his calculations, and they haggled over the historical rise of the consumer price index for thirty minutes. If Mason scored a point, no one noticed. He wanted Kallison to agree that a more reasonable figure for Mr. Wood's lost wages would be $680,000.

It really didn't matter. Rohr and his blue-ribbon pack of trial lawyers would take either number. Lost wages were merely the starting point. Rohr would add to it pain and suffering, loss of enjoyment of life, loss of companionship, and a few incidentals such as the cost of Mr. Wood's medical care and the price of his funeral. Then Rohr would go for the gold. He would show the jury how much cash Pynex owned and would ask them for a large chunk of it as punitive damages.

With an hour to go, Rohr proudly announced to the court that 'The plaintiff will call its last witness. Mrs. Celeste Wood.'

The jury had been given no warning that the plaintiff was almost finished. A burden was suddenly lifted. The sluggish air of the late afternoon was immediately lighter. Several jurors couldn't conceal smiles. Several more lost their frowns. Their chairs rocked as they came to life.

Tonight would be their seventh in sequestration. According to Nicholas' latest theory, the defense would take no more than three days. They did the math. They could be home by the weekend!

In the three weeks she'd been sitting silently at the table, with hordes of lawyers around her, Celeste Wood had barely uttered a whisper. She'd shown an amazing ability to ignore the lawyers, ignore the faces of the jurors, and stare straight ahead with a blank face at the witnesses. She'd worn every shade of black and gray dress, always with black hose and black shoes.

Jerry had dubbed her Widow Wood during the first week.

She was now fifty-five, the same age her husband would have been but for the lung cancer. She was very thin, diminutive, with short gray hair. She worked for a regional library and had raised three children. Family portraits were passed to the jury.

Celeste had given her deposition a year earlier, and she had been rehearsed by the professional handlers Rohr had brought in. She was under control, nervous but not fidgety, and determined to show no emotion. After all, her husband had been dead for four years.

She and Rohr walked through their script without a flaw. She talked of her life with Jacob, how happy they'd been, the early years, the kids, then the grandchildren, their dreams of retirement. A few bumps in the road but nothing serious, nothing until he got sick. He had wanted to quit smoking so badly, had tried many times with little success. The addiction was just too powerful.

Celeste was sympathetic without working too hard

for it. Her voice never waivered. Rohr had guessed, correctly, that false tears might not be well received by the jury. She didn't cry easily anyway.

Cable passed on any cross-examination. What could he ask her? He rose and with a sad countenance and humble air, said simply, 'Your Honor, we have no questions for this witness.'

Fitch had a bunch of questions for the witness, but he couldn't get them asked in open court. After a proper grieving period, in fact it was over a year after the funeral, Celeste had started seeing a divorced man who was seven years younger. According to good sources, they were planning a quiet wedding as soon as the trial was over. Fitch knew that Rohr himself had ordered her not to get married until after the trial.

The jury wouldn't hear this in the courtroom, but Fitch was working on a plan to sneak it through the back door.

'The plaintiff rests,' Rohr announced after he'd seated Celeste at the table. The lawyers on both sides clutched one another and huddled into small groups of serious whispering.

Judge Harkin studied some of the clutter on his bench, then he looked at his weary jury. 'Ladies and gentlemen, I have good news and bad. The good news is obvious. The plaintiff has rested, and we're more than halfway finished. The defense is expected to call fewer witnesses than the plaintiff. The bad news is that we're required at this point in the trial to argue a bunch of motions. We'll do that tomorrow, probably all day. I'm sorry, but we have no choice.'

Nicholas raised his hand. Harkin looked at him for a few seconds, then managed to say, 'Yes, Mr. Easter?'

'You mean we have to sit around the motel all day tomorrow?'

'I'm afraid so.'

'I don't understand why.'

The lawyers unclutched and stopped their tiny conferences and gawked at Easter. It was rare for a juror to speak in open court.

'Because we have a list of things to do outside the presence of the jury.'

'Oh, I understand that. But why do we have to sit around?'

'What do you want to do?'

'I can think of a lot of things. We could charter a big boat, go for a ride in the Gulf, fish if we want to.'

'I can't ask the taxpayers of this county to pay for that, Mr. Easter.'

'I thought we were taxpayers.'

'The answer is no. I'm sorry.'

'Forget the taxpayers. I'm sure these lawyers here wouldn't mind passing the plate. Look, ask each side to put up a thousand dollars. We can charter a huge boat and have a wonderful time.'

Though Cable and Rohr both reacted at the same instant, Rohr managed to speak first as he jumped to his feet. 'We'd be more than happy to pay half, Your Honor.'

'It's a great idea, Judge!' Cable added quickly, and loudly.

Harkin raised both hands, palms out. 'Hold it,' he said. Then he rubbed his temples and searched his brain for a precedent. Of course there was none. No rule or law prohibiting it. No conflicts of interest.

Loreen Duke tapped Nicholas on the arm and whispered something in his ear.

His Honor said, 'Well, I've certainly never heard of this. It seems to fall into the discretionary category. Mr. Rohr?'

'It's harmless, Your Honor. Each side pays half. No problem.'

'Mr. Cable?'

'I can think of no statute or rule of procedure which

300

would prevent it. I agree with Mr. Rohr. If both sides split the cost, what's the harm?'

Nicholas raised his hand again. 'Excuse me, Your Honor. It's come to my attention that perhaps some of the jurors would rather shop in New Orleans than take a boat ride in the Gulf.'

Again, Rohr was a beat quicker. 'We'll be happy to split the cost of a bus, Your Honor. And lunch.'

'Same here,' Cable said. 'Dinner too.'

Gloria Lane hustled to the jury box with a clipboard. Nicholas, Jerry Fernandez, Lonnie Shaver, Rikki Coleman, Angel Weese, and Colonel Herrera opted for the boat. The rest chose the French Quarter.

Including the video of Jacob Wood, Rohr and company presented ten witnesses to the jury and took thirteen days to do it. A solid case was built; now it was up to the jury to determine not if cigarettes were dangerous but if it was time to punish their makers.

Had the jury not been sequestered, Rohr would have called at least three more experts: one to discuss the psychology of advertising; one an expert on addiction; one ready to describe in detail the application of insecticides and pesticides to tobacco leaves.

But the jury was very sequestered, and Rohr knew it was time to stop. It was obvious this was no ordinary jury. A blind man. A misfit who did yoga at lunch. At least two strikes so far. Lists of demands at every turn. China and silver for lunch. Beer after work, paid for by the taxpayers. Communal interludes and personal visits. Judge Harkin was finding sleep difficult.

It was certainly not ordinary for Fitch, a man who'd sabotaged more juries than any person in the history of American jurisprudence. He'd laid the usual traps and gathered the usual dirt. His scams were proceeding flawlessly. Only one fire, so far. No broken bones. But the girl Marlee had changed everything. Through her

301

he'd be able to purchase a verdict, a slam-dunk defense judgment that would humiliate Rohr and frighten away the legion of hungry trial lawyers circling like vultures, waiting for the carcass.

In this, the biggest tobacco trial yet, with the biggest plaintiff's lawyers lined up with millions, his beloved little Marlee would hand him a verdict. Fitch believed this, and it consumed him. He thought of her every minute and he saw her in his dreams.

If not for Marlee, Fitch wouldn't be sleeping at all. The time was right for a plaintiff's verdict; right courtroom, right judge, right mood. The experts were by far the best Fitch had encountered in his nine years of directing the defense. Nine years, eight trials, eight defense verdicts. As much as he hated Rohr, he could admit, only to himself, that he was the right lawyer to nail the industry.

A victory over Rohr in Biloxi would be a huge barricade to future tobacco litigation. It might very well save the industry.

When Fitch tallied the jury's vote, he always started with Rikki Coleman, because of the abortion. He had her vote in his pocket, she just didn't know it yet. Then he added Lonnie Shaver. Then Colonel Herrera. Millie Dupree would be easy. His jury people were convinced that Sylvia Taylor-Tatum was virtually incapable of sympathy, and besides she smoked. But his jury people didn't know she was sleeping with Jerry Fernandez. Jerry and Easter were buddies. Fitch was predicting the three of them – Sylvia, Jerry, and Nicholas – would vote the same. Loreen Duke sat next to Nicholas, and the two were often seen whispering during the trial. Fitch thought she would follow Easter. And if Loreen did, then so would Angel Weese, the only other black female. Weese was impossible to read.

No one doubted that Easter would dominate the deliberations. Now that Fitch knew Easter had two years of law school, he was willing to bet that this information had been shared with the entire jury.

It was impossible to predict how Herman Grimes might vote. But Fitch wasn't counting on him. Likewise with Phillip Savelle. Fitch felt good about Mrs. Gladys Card. She was old and conservative and likely to be turned off when Rohr asked them for twenty million or so.

So Fitch had four in the bag, with Mrs. Gladys Card being a possible fifth. Flip a coin on Herman Grimes. Concede Savelle on the grounds that anyone so in tune with nature had to dislike tobacco companies. That left Easter and his gang of five. Nine votes were needed by either side for a verdict. Anything less would hang the jury and force Harkin to declare a mistrial. Mistrials become retrials, something Fitch did not want in this case.

The horde of legal analysts and scholars closely watching the trial agreed on little, but they were unified in their prediction that a unanimous, twelve-vote verdict in favor of Pynex would chill, if not completely freeze, tobacco litigation for a decade.

Fitch was determined to deliver one, whatever the cost.

The mood in Rohr's office was much lighter Monday night. With no more witnesses to call, the pressure was momentarily off. Some fine scotch was poured in the conference room. Rohr sipped his mineral water and nibbled on cheese and crackers.

The ball was now in Cable's court. Let him and his crew spend a few days prepping witnesses and labeling documents. Rohr had only to react, to cross-examine, and he had watched every video-taped deposition of every defense witness a dozen times.

Jonathan Kotlack, the lawyer in charge of jury research, likewise drank only water and speculated with

303

Rohr about Herman Grimes. Both felt they had him. And they felt good about Millie Dupree and Savelle, the strange one. Herrera worried them. All three of the blacks – Lonnie, Angel, and Loreen – were solidly on board. It was, after all, a case of a little person against a large powerful corporation. Surely the blacks would come through. They always did.

Easter was the key because he was the leader, everybody knew that. Rikki would follow him. Jerry was his pal. Sylvia Taylor-Tatum was passive and she'd follow the crowd. As would Mrs. Gladys Card.

They only needed nine, and Rohr was convinced he had them.

TWENTY-FIVE

Back in Lawrence, Small, the investigator, worked his list of leads diligently and got nowhere. He loafed around Mulligan's Monday night, drinking against orders, chatting occasionally with the waitresses and law students and succeeding at nothing but arousing suspicion among the youth.

Early Tuesday morning, he made one visit too many. The woman's name was Rebecca, and a few years back, while still a grad student at KU, she had worked at Mulligan's with Claire Clement. They had been friends, according to a source dug up by Small's boss. Small found her in a downtown bank, where she worked as manager. He introduced himself awkwardly, and she was immediately suspicious.

'Didn't you work with Claire Clement a few years back?' he asked, looking at a notepad, standing on one side of her desk because she was standing on the other. He had not been invited in, and she was busy.

'Maybe. Who wants to know?' Rebecca asked, arms crossed, head cocked, phone buzzing somewhere behind her. In marked contrast to Small, she was sharply dressed and missed nothing.

'Do you know where she is now?'

'No. Why are you asking?'

Small repeated the narrative he'd memorized. It was all he had. 'Well, see, she's a potential juror in a big trial, and my firm has been hired to conduct a thorough investigation into her background.'

'Where's the trial?'

'Can't tell you that. You guys worked together at Mulligan's, right?'

'Yes. That was a long time ago.'

'Where was she from?'

'Why is that important?'

'Well, to be honest, it's on my list of questions. We're just checking her out, okay? Do you know where she came from?'

'No.'

This was an important question because Claire's trail had started and stopped in Lawrence. 'Are you sure?'

She cocked her head the other way and glared at this klutz. 'I don't know where she came from. When I met her, she was working at Mulligan's. The last time I saw her, she was working at Mulligan's.'

'Have you talked to her recently?'

'Not in the last four years.'

'Did you know Jeff Kerr?'

'No.'

'Who were her friends here in Lawrence?'

'I don't know. Look, I'm very busy, and you're wasting your time. I didn't know Claire that well. Nice girl and all, but we were not close. Now, please, I have things to do.' She was pointing to the door by the time she finished, and Small reluctantly left her office.

With Small out of the bank, Rebecca closed her office door and dialed the number to an apartment in St. Louis. The recorded voice on the other end belonged to her friend Claire. They chatted at least once a month, though they hadn't seen each other in a year. Claire and Jeff lived an odd life, drifting and never staying long in one place, never anxious to reveal their whereabouts. Only the apartment in St. Louis remained the same. Claire had warned her that people

306

might come poking around with curious questions. She had hinted more than once that she and Jeff were working for the government in some mysterious capacity.

At the sound of the tone, Rebecca left a brief message about Small's visit.

Marlee checked her voice mail each morning, and the message from Lawrence made her blood run cold. She wiped her face with a moist cloth, and tried to calm herself.

She called Rebecca and managed to sound perfectly normal, though her mouth was dry and her heart was pounding. Yes, the man named Small had specifically asked about Claire Clement. And he had mentioned Jeff Kerr. With Marlee's prompting, Rebecca managed to replay the entire conversation.

Rebecca knew not to ask too many questions. 'Are you okay?' was about the extent of her inquiry.

'Oh we're fine,' Marlee assured her. 'Living on the beach for a while.'

Which beach would be nice, but Rebecca let it pass. No one dug too deep with Claire. They said their goodbyes with the usual promises to keep in touch.

Neither she nor Nicholas had believed they would ever be tracked to Lawrence. Now that they had, the questions fell like hard rain around her. Who had found them? Which side, Fitch or Rohr? Most likely Fitch, simply because he had more money and more cunning. What had been their mistake? How did the trail ever leave Biloxi? How much did they know?

And how far would they go? She needed to speak to Nicholas, but he was, at the moment, on a boat somewhere in the Gulf trolling for mackerel and bonding with his fellow jurors.

Fitch, of course, was not fishing. In fact he hadn't taken a day of rest or pleasure in three months. He was at his desk, neatly arranging piles of paperwork, when the call came. 'Hello, Marlee,' he said into the receiver, to the girl of his dreams.

'Hey, Fitch. You've lost another one.'

'Another what?' he asked, biting his tongue to keep from calling her Claire.

'Another juror. Loreen Duke was enthralled by Mr. Robilio, and now she's leading the parade to reward the plaintiff.'

'But she hasn't heard our case yet.'

'True. You have four smokers now – Weese, Fernandez, Taylor-Tatum, and Easter. Guess how many started smoking after the age of eighteen.'

'Don't know.'

'None. They all started as kids. Herman and Herrera used to smoke. Guess how old they were when they started.'

'Don't know.'

'Fourteen and seventeen. That's half of your jury, Fitch, and all started smoking as minors.'

'What am I supposed to do about it?'

'Keep lying, I guess. Look, Fitch, what are the chances of us getting together for a little chat, private you know, without all your goons ducking behind bushes?'

'The chances are excellent.'

'Another lie. Let's do it this way. Let's meet and talk, and if my people see your people anywhere near us, then it will be our last conversation.'

'Your people?'

'Anybody can hire goons, Fitch. You should know this.'

'It's a deal.'

'You know Casella's, the little seafood joint with outdoor tables at the end of the Biloxi pier.'

'I can find it.'

'That's where I am now. So when you walk down the

pier, I'll be watching. And if I see any character who looks the least bit suspicious, deal's off.'

'When?'

'Right now. I'm waiting.'

José slowed for a second in the parking lot near the small-craft harbor, and Fitch practically jumped from the Suburban. It drove away, and Fitch, very much alone and unwired, strolled down the wooden pier with the heavy wooden planks shifting gently in the tide. Marlee sat at a wooden table with an umbrella above it, with her back to the Gulf, her face to the pier. Lunch was an hour away and the place was deserted.

'Hello, Marlee,' Fitch said as he approached, stopped, then sat across from her. She wore jeans and a denim shirt, a fishing cap, and sunglasses. 'A pleasure, Fitch,' she said.

'Are you always so surly?' he asked, settling his squatty frame into a narrow chair, trying his best to smile and be chummy.

'Are you wired, Fitch?'

'No. Of course not.'

Slowly, she removed from her bulky purse a thin black device resembling a small Dictaphone. She pushed a button and placed it on the table, aimed at Fitch's ample gut. 'Pardon me, Fitch, just checking to see if you had time to stick a bug here or there.'

'I said I wasn't wired, okay,' Fitch said, very relieved. Konrad had suggested a small body mike with a tech van parked nearby, but Fitch, in a hurry, had said no.

She glanced at the tiny digital monitor on the end of the sensor-scan, then placed it back in her purse. Fitch smiled, but only for a second.

'I got a call from Lawrence this morning,' she said, and Fitch swallowed hard. 'Evidently you've got some real meatheads up there banging on doors and kicking over trash cans.'

309

'I don't know what you're talking about,' Fitch said, somewhat unsteadily and without sufficient conviction.

It was Fitch! His eyes betrayed him; they fluttered and dropped and darted away quickly before returning to see her, then dropped again, all in an instant but with plenty of proof that she'd caught him. His breath was short for a second, and his shoulders jerked ever so slightly. He'd been nailed.

'Right. One more phone call from old friends and you'll never hear my voice again.'

He rallied adequately though. 'What's in Lawrence?' he demanded as if his integrity had been questioned.

'Give it up, Fitch. And call off the dogs.'

He exhaled heavily while shrugging in utter bewilderment. 'Fine. Whatever. I just wish I knew what you were talking about.'

'You do. One more phone call and it's over, okay?'

'Okay. Whatever you say.'

Though Fitch couldn't see her eyes, he could feel them beaming at him from behind the thick glasses. She said nothing for a minute. A waiter busied himself at a nearby table, but made no effort to serve them.

Finally, Fitch leaned forward and said, 'When do we stop playing games?'

'Now.'

'Wonderful. What do you want?'

'Money.'

'I figured. How much?'

'I'll name a price later. I take it you're ready to deal.'

'I'm always ready to deal. But I gotta know what I get in return.'

'It's very simple, Fitch. It depends on what you want. As far as you're concerned this jury can do one of four things. It can deliver a verdict for the plaintiff. It can split and hang and go home, and you'll be back down here in a year or so doing this again. Rohr isn't going away. It can come back nine to three for you, and you get a huge victory. And it can come back twelve to zero, and your clients can relax for several years.'

'I know all this.'

'Of course you do. If we rule out a plaintiff's verdict, then we have three choices.'

'What can you deliver?'

'Anything I want. Including a plaintiff's verdict.'

'So the other side is willing to pay.'

'We're talking. Let's just leave it at that.'

'Is this an auction? Your verdict to the highest bidder?'

'It's whatever I want it to be.'

'I'd feel better if you'd stay away from Rohr.'

'I'm not too concerned with your feelings.'

Another waiter appeared and noticed them. He reluctantly asked if they'd like something to drink. Fitch wanted iced tea. Marlee asked for a Diet Coke in a can.

'Tell me how the deal works,' he said when the waiter left.

'It's very simple. We agree on the verdict you want, just look at the menu and place your order. Then we agree on the price. You get your money ready. We wait until the very end, until the lawyers finish their closing arguments and the jury retires to deliberate. At that point, I furnish you with wiring instructions and the money is immediately sent to a bank in, say, Switzerland. Once I get confirmation the money has been received, then the jury returns with your verdict.'

Fitch had spent hours predicting a scenario remarkably similar to this, but to hear it come from Marlee's lips with such a cool precision made his heart pound and his head spin. This could be the easiest one yet!

'Won't work,' he said smugly, like a man who'd negotiated many such verdict deals.

'Oh really. Rohr thinks it will.'

311

Damn, she was quick! She knew just exactly where to stick the knife.

'But there's no guarantee,' he protested.

She adjusted her sunglasses and leaned forward on her elbows. 'So you doubt me, Fitch?'

'That's not the issue. You're asking me to wire what I'm sure will be a large sum of money on the hope and prayer that your friend will control the deliberations. Juries are so unpredictable.'

'Fitch, my friend is controlling the deliberations even as we speak. He'll have his votes long before the lawyers stop talking.'

Fitch would pay. He'd made the decision a week earlier to pay whatever she wanted, and he knew that when the money left The Fund there were no guarantees. He didn't care. He trusted his Marlee. She and her friend Easter or whatever the hell his name was had patiently stalked Big Tobacco to reach this point, and they would happily hand over a verdict for the right price. They had lived for this moment.

Oh, the questions he wanted to ask. He'd love to start with the two of them and ask whose idea this was, such an ingenious, devious plan to study litigation, then follow it across the country, then plant oneself on the jury so a deal could be cut for a verdict. It was nothing short of brilliant. He could grill her for hours, maybe days, about the specifics, but he knew there would be no answers.

He also knew she'd deliver. She had worked too hard and had come too far with their plot to fail.

'I'm not totally helpless in this matter, you know,' he said, still holding his ground.

'Of course not, Fitch. I'm sure you've laid enough traps to snag at least four jurors. Shall I name them?'

The drinks arrived and Fitch gulped his tea. No, he did not want her to name them. He would not play a guessing game with someone who had the hard facts.

312

Talking with Marlee was like talking to the leader of the jury, and though Fitch cherished the moment it made the conversation quite one-sided. How was he to know if she was bluffing or telling the truth? It simply wasn't fair.

'I sense you doubt whether I'm in control,' she said.

'I doubt everything.'

'What if I get a juror bumped?'

'You've already bumped Stella Hulic,' Fitch said, and drew the first and only very small smile from her.

'I can do it again. What if, say, I decided to send home Lonnie Shaver? Would you be impressed?'

Fitch almost choked on his tea. He wiped his mouth with the back of a hand, said, 'I'm sure Lonnie would be happy. He's probably the most bored of the twelve.'

'Shall I bump him?'

'No. He's harmless. Plus, since we'll be working together, I think we should keep Lonnie.'

'He and Nicholas talk a lot, you know?'

'Is Nicholas talking to everyone?'

'Yes, at various levels. Give him time.'

'You seem confident.'

'I'm not confident in the ability of your lawyers. But I am confident in Nicholas, and that's all that matters.'

They sat quietly and waited for two waiters to set the table next to them. Lunch began at eleven-thirty, and the café was coming to life.

When the waiters finished and left, Fitch said, 'I can't cut a deal if I don't know the terms.'

Without the slightest hesitation, she said, 'And I'm not cutting a deal as long as you're digging through my past.'

'Got something to hide?'

'No. But I have friends, and I don't like getting phone calls from them. Stop it now, and this meeting will lead to the next. One more phone call, and I'll never speak to you again.'

313

'Don't say that.'

'I mean it, Fitch. Call off the dogs.'

'They're not my dogs, I swear.'

'Call them off anyway, or I'll spend more time with Rohr. He might want to cut a deal, and a verdict for him means you're out of work and your clients lose billions. You can't afford it, Fitch.'

She was certainly right about that. Whatever she planned to ask for would be a tiny sum compared to the ultimate cost of a plaintiff's verdict.

'We'd better move fast,' he said. 'This trial won't last much longer.'

'How long?' she asked.

'Three or four days for the defense.'

'Fitch, I'm hungry. Why don't you leave and retrace your steps? I'll call you in a couple of days.'

'What a coincidence. I'm hungry too.'

'No thanks. I'll eat alone. Plus, I want you away from here.'

He rose, said, 'Sure, Marlee. Whatever you want. Good day.'

She watched him saunter back down the pier to the parking lot next to the beach. He stopped there and called someone from a cellphone.

After repeated attempts to reach Hoppy by phone, Jimmy Hull Moke dropped in unannounced on Dupree Realty Tuesday afternoon and was told by a sleepy-eyed receptionist that Mr. Dupree was somewhere in the back. She left to fetch him, and returned fifteen minutes later with the apology that she had been wrong, that Mr. Dupree was not in his office and had in fact left for an important meeting.

'I see his car out there,' Jimmy Hull said, agitated, pointing to the small parking lot just outside the door. Sure enough, there was Hoppy's old station wagon.

314

'He rode with someone else,' she said, obviously lying.

'Where'd he go?' Jimmy Hull asked as if he might go after him.

'Somewhere near Pass Christian. That's all I know.'

'Why won't he return my phone calls?'

'I have no idea. Mr. Dupree is a very busy man.'

Jimmy Hull shoved both hands deep in the pockets of his jeans and glared down at the woman. 'You tell him I stopped by, that I'm very irritated, and that he'd better call me. You got that?'

'Yes sir.'

He left the office, got in his Ford pickup, and drove away. She watched to be safe, then raced to the back to free Hoppy from the broom closet.

The sixty-footer with Captain Theo at the helm traveled fifty miles into the Gulf, where under a cloudless sky and amid gentle sea breezes, half the jury fished for mackerel, snapper, and redfish. Angel Weese had never been on a boat, couldn't swim, and got sick two hundred yards from shore, but with the help of a seasoned deckhand and a bottle of Dramamine she recovered and actually caught the first fish of any size. Rikki looked splendidly cute with shorts, Reeboks, tanned legs. The Colonel and the Captain were inevitably kindred spirits, and it wasn't long before Nap was on the bridge talking naval strategy and exchanging war stories.

Two deckhands prepared a fine lunch of boiled shrimp, fried oyster sandwiches, crab claws, and chowder. The first round of beer was served with lunch. Only Rikki abstained and drank water.

The beer continued throughout the afternoon as the fishing alternated between frenzy and boredom, and as the sun grew warmer on the deck. The boat was large enough to find privacy. Nicholas and Jerry made certain

315

that Lonnie Shaver kept a cold beer in hand. They were determined to chat him up for the first time.

Lonnie had an uncle who'd worked on a shrimp boat for many years, before it sank in a storm and the entire crew was never found. When he was a kid, he'd fished these waters with his uncle, and, frankly, he'd had his share of fishing. Despised it, really, and hadn't been in years. Still, the boat trip sounded a bit more tolerable than the bus ride to New Orleans.

It took four beers to knock the edge off and loosen the tongue. They lounged in a small upper-deck cabin, open on all sides. On the main deck below them Rikki and Angel were watching the deckhands clean their catch.

'I wonder how many experts the defense will call,' Nicholas said, changing the subject from fishing with near total exasperation. Jerry was lying on a plastic cot, his socks and shoes off, his eyes closed, cold beer in hand.

'They don't have to call any as far as I'm concerned,' Lonnie said, gazing at the sea.

'You've had enough, huh?' Nicholas said.

'Pretty damned ridiculous. Man smokes for thirty-five years, then wants millions for his estate after he kills himself.'

'See what I told you,' Jerry said without opening his eyes.

'What?' Lonnie asked.

'Jerry and I had you pegged as a defense juror,' Nicholas explained. 'It was difficult though, because you've had so little to say.'

'And what are you?' Lonnie asked.

'Me, I'm still open-minded. Jerry's leaning toward the defense, right, Jerry?'

'I have not discussed the case with anyone. I have had no unauthorized contact. I have not taken any bribes. I am a juror Judge Harkin can be proud of.'

'He's leaning toward the defense,' Nicholas said to Lonnie. 'Because he's addicted to nicotine, can't kick the habit, but he's convinced himself he can throw them away whenever he wants. He can't, because he's a wimp. But he wants to be a real man like Colonel Herrera.'

'Who doesn't?' Lonnie said.

'Jerry thinks that because he can quit, if he really wanted to, then anyone should be able to quit, which he can't do himself, and therefore Jacob Wood should've stopped long before he got cancer.'

'That's about right,' Jerry said. 'But I object to the part about the wimp.'

'Makes good sense to me,' Lonnie said. 'How can you be open-minded?'

'Gee, I don't know. Maybe it's because I haven't heard all the testimony yet. Yeah, that's it. The law says that we must refrain from reaching verdicts until all the evidence is in. Forgive me.'

'You're forgiven,' Jerry said. 'Now it's your turn to fetch another round.' Nicholas drained his can and walked down the narrow stairway to the cooler on the main deck.

'Don't worry about him,' Jerry said. 'He'll be with us when it counts.'

TWENTY-SIX

The boat returned a few minutes after five. The hearty band of fishermen staggered from the deck onto the pier, where they posed for photos with Captain Theo and their trophies, the largest of which was a ninety-pound shark hooked by Rikki and landed by a deckhand. They were gathered by two deputies and led down the pier, leaving behind their catch because there was certainly no use for it at the motel.

The bus with the shoppers would be another hour. Its arrival, as was the arrival of the boat, was duly watched, recorded, and relayed to Fitch, but for whatever purpose no one was sure. Fitch just wanted to know. They had to watch something. It was a slow day, not much to do but sit and wait for the jury to return.

Fitch was locked in his office with Swanson, who'd spent most of the afternoon on the phone. The 'meat-heads,' as Marlee had described them, had been called off. In their place, Fitch was sending in the pro-fessionals, the same Bethesda firm he was using for the Hoppy sting. Swanson had once worked there, and many of the agents were either ex-FBI or ex-CIA.

Results were guaranteed. It was hardly a job to get them excited – the uncovering of a young woman's past. Swanson was to leave in an hour and fly to Kansas City, where he would monitor things.

There was also a guarantee not to get caught. Fitch

was in a quandary – he had to hold Marlee, yet he also had to know who she was. Two factors pushed him to keep digging. First, it was terribly important to her that he stop. There was something hidden back there that was crucial. And second, she had gone to such lengths to leave no trail.

Marlee had left Lawrence, Kansas, four years ago, after living there for three years. She was not Claire Clement until she arrived, and she certainly was not when she left. In the meantime, she met and recruited Jeff Kerr, who was now Nicholas Easter and was now doing hell knows what to the jury.

Angel Weese was in love with and planned to marry Derrick Maples, a strapping young man of twenty-four who was between jobs and between wives. He'd lost his job selling car phones when the company merged, and he was now in the process of dispensing with his first wife, the result of a teenage romance gone bad. They had two young children. His wife and her lawyer wanted six hundred dollars a month in child support. Derrick and his lawyer waved his unemployment like a burning flag. The negotiations had turned bitter and a final divorce was months away.

Angel was two months' pregnant, though she'd told no one but Derrick.

Derrick's brother Marvis had once been a deputy sheriff and was now a part-time minister and community activist. Marvis was approached by a man named Cleve, who said he'd like to meet Derrick. Introductions were made.

For lack of a better job description, Cleve was known as a runner. He ran cases for Wendall Rohr. Cleve's task was to find good, solid death and injury claims and make sure they found their way to Rohr's office. Good running was an art form, and of course Cleve was a fine runner because Rohr would have nothing but the best.

Like all good runners, Cleve moved in shadowy circles because the soliciting of clients was still technically an unethical practice, though any decent car wreck would attract more runners than emergency personnel. In fact, Cleve's business card pronounced him to be an 'Investigator.'

Cleve also delivered papers for Rohr, served summonses, checked on witnesses and potential jurors, and spied on other lawyers, the usual functions of a runner when he wasn't running. He received a salary for his investigating, and Rohr paid him cash bonuses when he landed a particularly good case.

Over a beer in a tavern, he talked with Derrick and realized quickly the guy had financial problems. He then steered the conversation toward Angel, and asked if anyone had beaten him to the punch. No, said Derrick, no one had come around asking about the trial. But then, Derrick had been living with a brother, sort of laying low and trying to avoid his wife's greedy lawyer.

Good, said Cleve, because he'd been hired as a consultant by some of the lawyers, and, well, the trial was awfully important. Cleve ordered a second round and talked awhile about just how damned important the trial was.

Derrick was bright, had a year of junior college and a desire to make a buck, and he picked it up quickly. 'Why don't you get to the point?' he asked.

Cleve was ready to do just that. 'My client is willing to purchase influence. For cash. No trail whatsoever.'

'Influence,' Derrick repeated, then took a long sip. The smile on his face encouraged Cleve to press the deal.

'Five thousand cash,' Cleve said, glancing around. 'Half now, half when the trial is over.'

The smile widened with another sip. 'And I do what?'

'You talk with Angel when you see her during the personal visits, and make sure she understands how important this case is to the plaintiff. Just don't tell her about the money, or about me or any of this. Not now. Maybe later.'

'Why not?'

'Because this is illegal as hell, okay? If the Judge somehow found out that I was talking to you, offering you money to talk to Angel, then both of us would go to jail. Understand?'

'Yeah.'

'It's important for you to realize that this is dangerous. If you don't wanna pursue it, then say so now.'

'Ten thousand.'

'What?'

'Ten. Five now, five when the trial is over.'

Cleve grunted as if slightly disgusted. If only Derrick knew the stakes. 'Okay. Ten.'

'When can I get it?'

'Tomorrow.' They ordered sandwiches and talked for another hour about the trial, and the verdict, and how best to persuade Angel.

The chore of keeping D. Martin Jankle away from his cherished vodka fell to Durwood Cable. Fitch and Jankle had fought bitterly over the question of whether or not Jankle could drink Tuesday night, the night before he testified. Fitch, the former drunk, accused Jankle of having a problem. Jankle cursed Fitch viciously for trying to tell him, the CEO of Pynex, a Fortune 500 company, if and when and how much he could drink.

Cable was dragged into the brawl by Fitch. Cable insisted that Jankle hang around his office throughout the night to prepare for his testimony. A mock direct exam was followed by a lengthy cross, and Jankle performed adequately. Nothing spectacular. Cable made him watch the video of it with a panel of jury experts.

When he was finally taken to his hotel room after ten, he found that Fitch had removed all liquor from the mini-bar and replaced it with soft drinks and fruit juices. Jankle cursed and went to his overnight bag, where he kept a flask hidden in a leather pouch. But there was no flask. Fitch had removed it too.

At 1 A.M., Nicholas silently opened his door and looked up and down the hall. The guard was gone, no doubt asleep in his room.

Marlee was waiting in a room on the second floor. They embraced and kissed but never got around to anything else. She had hinted on the phone that there was trouble, and she hurriedly spilled the story, beginning with her early morning chat with Rebecca in Lawrence. Nicholas took it well.

Other than the natural passion of two young lovers, their relationship rarely saw emotion. And when it surfaced, it was almost always from Nicholas, who had a slight temper, which, regardless of how slight, was certainly more than she possessed. He might raise his voice when angry, but that almost never occurred. Marlee wasn't cold, just calculating. He'd never seen her cry, the one exception being at the end of a movie he'd hated. They had never been through a difficult fight, and the usual squabbles were snuffed out quickly because Marlee had taught him to bite his tongue. She didn't tolerate wasted sentiment, didn't pout or carry petty grudges, and didn't put up with him when he tried to.

She replayed her conversation with Rebecca, and she tried to recall every word from her meeting with Fitch.

The realization that they'd been partially discovered hit hard. They were sure it was Fitch, and they wondered how much he knew. They were convinced, and always had been, that Jeff Kerr would have to be discovered in order to find Claire Clement. Jeff's background was harmless. Claire's had to be protected or they might as well flee now.

There was little to do but wait.

Derrick entered Angel's room by wedging himself through the fold-out window. He hadn't seen her since Sunday, a gap of almost forty-eight hours, and he simply couldn't wait until tomorrow night because he loved her madly and missed her and had to hold her. She immediately noticed he had been drinking. They fell into bed, where they quietly consummated an unauthorized personal visit.

Derrick rolled over and fell fast asleep.

They awoke at dawn, and Angel panicked because she had a man in her room and this was, of course, against the Judge's orders. Derrick was unconcerned. He said he'd simply wait until they left for court, then sneak out of the room. This did little to calm her nerves. Angel took a long shower.

Derrick had taken Cleve's plan and improved on it immensely. After leaving the tavern, he bought a six-pack and drove along the Gulf for hours. Slowly, up and down Highway 90, past the hotels and casinos and boat docks, from Pass Christian to Pascagoula he had driven, sipping beer and expanding the scheme. Cleve, after a few drinks, had let it slip that the lawyers for the plaintiff were seeking millions. It took only nine of the twelve for a verdict, so Derrick figured Angel's vote was worth a helluva lot more than ten thousand dollars.

Ten thousand sounded great at the tavern, but if they would pay that much, and agree to do it so quickly, then they would pay more with pressure. The more he drove, the more her vote was worth. It was now at fifty, and rising almost by the hour.

Derrick was intrigued by the notion of percentages. What if the verdict was ten million, for example? One percent, one lousy little percent, would be a hundred thousand dollars. A twenty-million-dollar verdict? Two hundred thousand dollars. What if Derrick proposed to Cleve a deal whereby they paid him cash up front and a percentage of the verdict? That would motivate Derrick, and of course his girlfriend, to press hard during deliberations for a large verdict. They'd become players. It was a chance they'd never see again.

Angel returned in her bathrobe and lit a cigarette.

TWENTY-SEVEN

Pynex' defense of its good corporate name got off to a miserable start Wednesday morning, through no fault of its own. An analyst named Walter Barker, writing in *Mogul*, a popular weekly financial, laid two-to-one odds that the jury down in Biloxi would find against Pynex, and return a large verdict. Barker was no lightweight. Trained as a lawyer, he had developed a formidable reputation on Wall Street as the man to watch when litigation affected commerce. His specialty was monitoring trials and appeals and settlements, and predicting their outcomes before they were final. He was usually right, and had made a fortune with his research. He was widely read, and the fact that he was betting against Pynex shocked Wall Street. The stock opened at seventy-six, dropped to seventy-three, and by mid-morning was at seventy-one and a half.

The courtroom crowd was larger Wednesday. The Wall Street boys were back in force, each reading a copy of *Mogul* and all suddenly agreeing with Barker, though over breakfast an hour earlier the consensus had been that Pynex had weathered the plaintiff's witnesses and should close strongly. Now they read with worried faces and revised their reports to their offices. Barker had actually been in the courtroom last week. He'd sat alone on the back row. What had he seen that they'd missed?

The jurors filed in promptly at nine, with Lou Dell

proudly holding the door as if she'd collected her brood after they'd scattered yesterday and was now delivering them back to where they belonged. Harkin welcomed them as if they'd been gone for a month, made some flat crack about fishing, then raced through his standard 'Have you been molested?' questions. He promised the jurors a speedy end to the trial.

Jankle was called as a witness, and the defense began. Free of the effects of alcohol, Jankle was primed and sharp. He smiled easily and seemed to welcome the chance to defend his tobacco company. Cable waltzed him through the preliminaries without a hitch.

Seated on the second row was D. Y. Taunton, the black lawyer from the Wall Street firm who'd met with Lonnie in Charlotte. He listened to Jankle while cutting his eyes at Lonnie, and it didn't take long to connect. Lonnie glanced once, couldn't help it as he glanced again, and on the third look managed to nod and smile because it seemed like the proper thing to do. The message was clear – Taunton was an important person who'd traveled all the way down to Biloxi because this was an important day. The defense was now speaking, and it was critical for Lonnie to understand that he should listen and believe every word now being said from the witness stand. No problem with Lonnie.

Jankle's first defensive thrust was on the issue of choice. He conceded that a lot of people think cigarettes are addictive, but only because he and Cable realized he would sound foolish otherwise. But, then, maybe they're not addictive. No one really knows, and the folks in research are just as confused as anyone. One study leans this way, the next one leans another, but he'd never seen positive proof that smoking was addictive. Personally, he just did not believe it. Jankle had smoked for twenty years, but only because he enjoyed it. He smoked twenty cigarettes a day, by choice, and he'd chosen a lower-tar brand. No, he most certainly was not addicted. He could quit whenever he wanted. He smoked because he liked to. He played tennis four times a week and his annual physical revealed nothing to worry about.

Seated one row behind Taunton was Derrick Maples, making his first appearance at the trial. He'd left the motel just minutes after the bus, and had planned to spend the day looking for work. Now, he was dreaming of an easy payday. Angel saw him, but kept her eyes on Jankle. Derrick's sudden interest in the trial was baffling. He'd done nothing but complain since they'd been sequestered.

Jankle described the various brands his company made. He stepped down and stood before a colorful chart with each of the eight brands, each with its tar and nicotine levels labeled beside it. He explained why some cigarettes have filters, some don't, some have more tar and nicotine than others. It all boiled down to choice. He was proud of his product line.

A crucial point was made here, and Jankle conveyed it well. By offering such a wide selection of brands, Pynex allowed each consumer to decide how much tar and nicotine he or she wanted. Choice. Choice. Choice. Choose the level of tar and nicotine. Choose the number of cigarettes you smoke each day. Choose whether or not to inhale. Make the intelligent choice of what you do to your body with cigarettes.

Jankle pointed to a bright drawing of a red pack of Bristols, the brand with the second-highest level of tar and nicotine. He conceded that if Bristols were 'abused' then the results could be damaging.

Cigarettes were responsible products, if used with restraint, like many other products – alcohol, butter, sugar, and handguns, just to name a few – they could become dangerous if abused.

Seated across the aisle from Derrick was Hoppy, who had stopped by for a quick update on what was happening. Plus he wanted to see and smile at Millie, who was delighted to see him but also curious about his sudden obsession with the trial. Tonight the jurors were allowed personal visits, and Hoppy couldn't wait to spend three hours in Millie's room with sex the last thing on his mind.

When Judge Harkin stopped for lunch, Jankle was completing his thoughts about advertising. Sure his company spent tons of money, but not as much as beer companies or car companies or Coca-Cola. Advertising was crucial to survival in a fiercely competitive world, regardless of the product. Of course children saw his company's ads. How do you design a billboard ad so that it won't be seen by children? How do you keep kids from looking at the magazines their parents subscribe to? Impossible. Jankle readily admitted he'd seen the statistics showing eighty-five percent of the kids who smoke buy the three most heavily advertised brands. But so do adults! Again, you can't design an ad campaign that targets adults without affecting kids.

Fitch watched all of Jankle's testimony from a seat near the back. To his right was Luther Vandemeer, CEO of Trellco, the largest tobacco company in the world. Vandemeer was the unofficial head of the Big Four, and the only one Fitch could tolerate. He, in return, had the perplexing gift of being able to tolerate Fitch.

They ate lunch at Mary Mahoney's, alone at a table in a corner. They were relieved by Jankle's success so far, but knew the worst was yet to come. Barker's column in *Mogul* had ruined their appetites.

'How much influence do you have with the jury?' Vandemeer asked, picking at his food.

Fitch wasn't about to answer truthfully. He wasn't expected to. His dirty deeds were kept from everyone except his own agents.

'The usual,' Fitch said.

'Maybe the usual is not enough.'

'What are you suggesting?'

Vandemeer didn't answer, but instead studied the legs of a young waitress taking an order at the next table.

'We're doing everything possible,' Fitch said, with uncharacteristic warmth. But Vandemeer was scared, and rightly so. Fitch knew the pressure was enormous. A large plaintiff's verdict wouldn't bankrupt Pynex or Trellco, but the results would be messy and far-reaching. An in-house study predicted an immediate twenty percent loss in shareholder value for all four companies, and that was just for starters. In the same study, a worst-case scenario predicted one million lung cancer lawsuits filed during the five years after such a verdict, with the average lawsuit costing a million dollars in legal fees alone. The study didn't dare predict the cost of a million verdicts. The doomsday scenario called for the certification of a class-action suit, the class being any person who had ever smoked and felt injured because of it. Bankruptcy would be a possibility at that point. And it would be probable that serious efforts would be made in Congress to outlaw the production of cigarettes.

'Do you have enough money?' Vandemeer asked.

'I think so,' Fitch said, asking himself for the hundredth time just how much his dear Marlee might have in mind.

'The Fund should be in good shape.'

'It is.'

Vandemeer chewed on a tiny piece of grilled chicken. 'Why don't you just pick out nine jurors and give them a million bucks apiece?' he said, with a quiet laugh as if he were only joking.

'Believe me, I've thought about it. It's just too risky. People would go to jail.'

'Just kidding.'

'We have ways.'

Vandemeer stopped smiling. 'We have to win, Rankin, you understand? We have to win. Spend whatever it takes.'

A week earlier, Judge Harkin, pursuant to another written request from Nicholas Easter, had changed the lunch routine a bit and declared that the two alternate jurors could eat with the twelve. Nicholas had argued that since all fourteen now lived together, watched movies together, ate breakfast and dinner together, then it was almost ludicrous to separate them at lunch. The two alternates were both men, Henry Vu and Shine Royce.

Henry Vu had been a South Vietnamese fighter pilot who ditched his plane in the China Sea the day after Saigon fell. He was picked up by an American rescue vessel and treated at a hospital in San Francisco. It took a year to smuggle his wife and kids through Laos and Cambodia and into Thailand, and finally to San Francisco, where the family lived for two years. They settled in Biloxi in 1978. Vu bought a shrimp boat and joined a growing number of Vietnamese fishermen who were squeezing out the natives. Last year his youngest daughter was the valedictorian of her senior class. She accepted a full scholarship to Harvard. Henry bought his fourth shrimp boat.

He made no effort to avoid jury service. He was as patriotic as anyone, even the Colonel.

Nicholas, of course, had befriended him immediately. He was determined that Henry Vu would sit with the chosen twelve, and be present when the deliberations began.

With a jury blindsided by sequestration, the last thing Durwood Cable wanted was to prolong the case. He had pared his list of witnesses to five, and he had planned for their testimony to run no more than four days.

It was the worst time of the day for a direct examination – the first hour after lunch – when Jankle took his seat on the witness stand and resumed his testimony.

'What is your company doing to combat underage smoking?' Cable asked him, and Jankle rambled for an hour. A million here for this do-gooder cause, and a million there for that ad campaign. Eleven million last year alone.

At times, Jankle sounded as if he almost despised tobacco.

After a very long coffee break at three, Wendall Rohr was given his first crack at Jankle. He started with a vicious question, and matters went from bad to worse.

'Isn't it true, Mr. Jankle, that your company spends hundreds of millions trying to convince people to smoke, yet when they get sick from your cigarettes your company won't pay a dime to help them?'

'Is that a question?'

'Of course it is. Now answer it!'

'No. That's not true.'

'Good. When was the last time Pynex paid a penny of one of your smoker's medical bills?'

Jankle shrugged and mumbled something.

'I'm sorry, Mr. Jankle. I didn't catch that. The question is, when was the last time –'

'I heard the question.'

'Then answer it. Just give us one example where Pynex offered to help with the medical bills of someone who smoked your products.'

'I can't recall one.'

'So your company refuses to stand behind its products?'

'We certainly do not.'

'Good. Give the jury just one example of Pynex standing behind its cigarettes.'

331

'Our products are not defective.'

'They don't cause sickness and death?' Rohr asked incredulously, arms flopping wildly at the air.

'No. They don't.'

'Now lemme get this straight. You're telling this jury that your cigarettes do not cause sickness and death?'

'Only if they are abused.'

Rohr laughed as he spat out the word 'abused' in thorough disgust. 'Are your cigarettes supposed to be lit with some type of lighter?'

'Of course.'

'And is the smoke produced by the tobacco and the paper supposed to be sucked through the end opposite the end that is lit?'

'Yes.'

'And is this smoke supposed to enter the mouth?'

'Yes.'

'And is it supposed to be inhaled into the respiratory tract?'

'Depends on the choice of the smoker.'

'Do you inhale, Mr. Jankle?'

'Yes.'

'Are you familiar with studies showing ninety-eight percent of all cigarette smokers inhale?'

'Yes.'

'So it's accurate to say that you know the smoke from your cigarettes will be inhaled?'

'I suppose so.'

'Is it your opinion that people who inhale the smoke are actually abusing the product?'

'No.'

'So tell us, please, Mr. Jankle, how does one abuse a cigarette?'

'By smoking too much.'

'And how much is too much?'

'I guess it depends on each individual.'

332

'I'm not talking to each individual smoker, Mr. Jankle. I'm talking to you, the CEO of Pynex, one of the largest cigarette producers in the world. And I'm asking you, in your opinion, how much is too much?'

'I'd say more than two packs a day.'

'More than forty cigarettes a day?'

'Yes.'

'I see. And what study do you base this on?'

'None. It's just my opinion.'

'Below forty, and smoking is not unhealthy. Above forty, and the product is being abused. Is this your testimony?'

'It's my opinion.' Jankle was starting to squirm and cast his eyes at Cable, who was angry and looking away. The abuse theory was a new one, a creation of Jankle's. He insisted on using it.

Rohr lowered his voice and studied his notes. He took his time for the setup because he didn't want to spoil the kill. 'Would you describe for the jury the steps you've taken as CEO to warn the public that smoking more than forty cigarettes a day is dangerous?'

Jankle had a quick retort, but he thought the better of it. His mouth opened, then he hung in mid-thought for a long, painful pause. After the damage was done, he gathered himself and said, 'I think you misunderstand me.'

Rohr wasn't about to let him explain. 'I'm sure I do. I don't believe I've ever seen a warning on any of your products to the effect that more than two packs a day is abusive and dangerous. Why not?'

'We're not required to.'

'Required by whom?'

'The government.'

'So if the government doesn't make you warn folks that your products can be abused, then you're certainly not going to do it voluntarily, are you?'

'We follow the law.'

'Did the law require Pynex to spend four hundred million dollars last year in advertising?'

'No.'

'But you did, didn't you?'

'Something like that.'

'And if you wanted to warn smokers of potential dangers you could certainly do it, couldn't you?'

'I suppose.'

Rohr switched quickly to butter and sugar, two products Jankle had mentioned as being potentially dangerous. Rohr took great delight in pointing out the differences between them and cigarettes, and made Jankle look silly.

He saved the best for last. During a short recess, the video monitors were once again rolled into place. When the jury returned, the lights were dimmed and there was Jankle on-screen, right hand raised while being asked to tell the truth and nothing but the truth. The occasion was a hearing before a congressional subcommittee. Standing next to Jankle were Vandemeer and the other two CEO's of the Big Four, all summoned against their will to give testimony to a bunch of politicians. They looked like four Mafia dons about to tell Congress there was no such thing as organized crime. The questioning was brutal.

The tape was heavily edited. One by one, they were asked point-blank if nicotine was addictive, and each emphatically said no. Jankle went last, and by the time he made his angry denial, the jury, just like the subcommittee, knew he was lying.

TWENTY-EIGHT

During a tense forty-minute meeting with Cable in his office, Fitch unloaded most of what had been bothering him about the way the case was being defended. He started with Jankle and his brilliant new tobacco defense, the abused-cigarette strategy, a harebrained approach that just might doom them. Cable, in no mood to be scolded, especially by a nonlawyer he loathed anyway, repeatedly explained that they had begged Jankle not to raise the issue of abuse. But Jankle had been a lawyer in another life and fancied himself as an original thinker who'd been given the golden chance to save Big Tobacco. Jankle was now on a Pynex jet en route to New York.

And Fitch thought the jury might be tired of Cable. Rohr had spread the courtroom work among his gang of thieves. Why couldn't Cable allow another defense lawyer besides Felix Mason to handle a few witnesses? God knew there were enough of them. Was it ego? They yelled at each other from across the desk.

The article in *Mogul* had unraveled nerves and added another, much heavier layer of pressure.

Cable reminded Fitch that he was the lawyer, and he had thirty rather outstanding years in the courtroom. He could better read the mood and texture of the trial.

And Fitch reminded Cable that this was the ninth tobacco trial he'd directed, not to mention the two mistrials he'd engineered, and he'd certainly seen more effective courtroom advocacy than what was being offered by Cable.

When the yelling and cursing died down, and after both men made efforts to pull themselves together, they did agree that the defense should be brief. Cable projected three more days, and that included whatever cross-examination Rohr would offer. Three days and no more, Fitch said.

He slammed the door as he left the office, and gathered José in the hallway. Together they stormed through the offices, offices still very much alive with lawyers in shirtsleeves and paralegals eating pizza and harried secretaries darting about trying to finish and get home to the kids. The mere sight of Fitch swaggering at full speed and the beefy José stomping after him made grown men cower and duck into doorways.

In the Suburban, José handed Fitch a stack of faxes, which he scanned as they sped away to headquarters. The first was a list of Marlee's movements since the meeting on the pier yesterday. Nothing unusual.

Next was the recap of what was happening in Kansas. A Claire Clement had been found in Topeka, but she was a resident of a nursing home. The one in Des Moines actually answered the phone at her husband's used-car lot. Swanson said they were pursuing many leads, but the report was rather scant on details. One of Kerr's law school chums had been found in Kansas City, and they were trying to arrange a meeting.

They drove past a convenience store, and in the front window a neon beer sign caught Fitch's attention. The smell and taste of a cold beer filled his senses, and Fitch ached for a drink. Just one. Just a sweet, frosty beer in a tall mug. How long had it been?

The urge to stop hit hard. Fitch closed his eyes and tried to think of something else. He could send José in to buy just one, one cold bottle and that would be it.

Wouldn't it? Surely, after nine years of sobriety he could handle a single drink. Why couldn't he have just one?

Because he'd had a million. And if José stopped here then he'd stop again two blocks away. And by the time they eventually reached the office the Suburban would be filled with empty bottles and Fitch would be throwing them at passing cars. He was not a pretty drunk.

But just one to settle his nerves, to help forget this miserable day.

'You okay, boss?' José asked.

Fitch grunted something, and stopped thinking about beer. Where was Marlee, and why hadn't she called today? The trial was winding down. A deal would take time to negotiate and execute.

He thought of the column in *Mogul,* and he longed for Marlee. He heard Jankle's idiotic voice expounding a brand-new defense theory, and he longed for Marlee. He closed his eyes and saw the faces of the jurors, and he longed for Marlee.

Since Derrick now considered himself to be a major player, he chose a new meeting place for Wednesday night. It was a rough bar in the black section of Biloxi, a place Cleve had actually been before. Derrick figured he'd have the upper hand if the rendezvous occurred on his turf. Cleve insisted they meet in the parking lot first.

The lot was almost filled. Cleve was late. Derrick spotted him when he parked, and walked to the driver's side.

'I don't think this is a good idea,' Cleve said, peeking through the crack in his window and looking at the dark, cinder-block building with steel rods across the windows.

'It's okay,' said Derrick, himself a bit worried but unwilling to show it. 'It's safe.'

'Safe? They've had three stabbings here in the last month. I've got the only white face here, and you expect me to walk in there with five thousand bucks in cash and hand it over to you. Reckon who'd get cut first? Me or you?'

Derrick saw his point, but was unwilling to concede so quickly. He leaned closer to the window, glanced around the parking lot, suddenly more fearful.

'I say we go in,' he said, in his best tough-guy routine.

'Forget it,' Cleve said. 'If you want the money, meet me at the Waffle House on 90.' Cleve started his engine and raised the window. Derrick watched him drive away, with the five thousand dollars in cash somewhere within his reach, then ran to his car.

They ate pancakes and drank coffee at the counter. Conversation was low because the cook was flipping eggs and sausage on a grill less than ten feet away and seemed to be straining to hear every word.

Derrick was nervous and his hands were jittery. Runners handled cash payoffs daily. The affair was of little significance to Cleve.

'So I'm thinking that maybe ten grand ain't enough, know what I mean?' Derrick said finally, repeating a line he'd rehearsed most of the afternoon.

'Thought we had a deal,' Cleve said, unmoved, chomping on pancakes.

'I think you're trying to screw me, though.'

'Is this your way of negotiating?'

'You ain't offering enough, man. I've been thinking about it. I even went by the courtroom this morning and watched some of the trial. I know what's going on now. I got it figured out.'

'You do?'

'Yeah. And you guys ain't playing fair.'

'There were no complaints last night when we agreed on ten.'

'Things are different now. You caught me off guard last night.'

Cleve wiped his mouth with a paper napkin and waited for the cook to serve someone at the far end of the counter. 'Then what do you want?' he asked.

'A lot more.'

'We don't have time to play games. Tell me what you want.'

Derrick swallowed hard and glanced over his shoulder. Under his breath he said, 'Fifty thousand, plus a percentage of the verdict.'

'What percentage?'

'I figure ten percent would be fair.'

'Oh you do.' Cleve tossed his napkin onto his plate. 'You're outta your mind,' he said, then put a five-dollar bill beside his plate. He stood and said, 'We cut a deal for ten. That's it. Anything larger and we'll get caught.'

Cleve left in a hurry. Derrick searched both pockets and found nothing but coins. The cook was suddenly hovering nearby watching the desperate search for money. 'I thought he was gonna pay,' Derrick said, checking his shirt pocket.

'How much you got?' the cook asked, picking the five-dollar bill from beside Cleve's plate.

'Eighty cents.'

'That's enough.'

Derrick raced into the parking lot where he caught Cleve waiting with his engine running and his window down. 'I'll bet the other side'll pay more,' he said, leaning over.

'Then go try. Walk up to them tomorrow and tell them you want fifty thousand bucks for one vote.'

'And ten percent.'

'You're clueless, son.' Cleve slowly switched off the ignition and got out of the car. He lit a cigarette. 'You don't understand. A defense verdict means no money changes hands. Zero for the plaintiff means zero for the

339

defense. It means no percentages for anybody. The plaintiff's lawyers get forty percent of zero. Does that make sense?'

'Yeah,' Derrick said slowly, though obviously still confused.

'Look, what I'm offering you is something that's illegal as hell. Don't get greedy. If you do, then you'll get caught.'

'Ten thousand seems cheap for something this big.'

'No, don't look at it that way. Think of it like this. She's entitled to nothing, okay. Zero. She's doing her civic duty, getting fifteen bucks a day from the county for being a good citizen. The ten thousand is a bribe, a dirty little gift that has to be forgotten as soon as it's received.'

'But if you offer a percentage, then she'll be motivated to work harder in the jury room.'

Cleve drew a long puff and exhaled slowly, shaking his head. 'You just don't understand. If there's a plaintiff's verdict, it will be years before the money changes hands. Look, Derrick, you're making this too complicated. Take the money. Talk to Angel. Help us out.'

'Twenty-five thousand.'

Another long puff, then the cigarette fell to the asphalt, where Cleve ground it with his boot. 'I'll have to talk to my boss.'

'Twenty-five thousand, per vote.'

'Per vote?'

'Yeah. Angel can deliver more than one.'

'Who?'

'I ain't saying.'

'Lemme talk to my boss.'

In room 54, Henry Vu read letters from his daughter at Harvard while his wife Qui studied new insurance policies for their fleet of fishing boats. Because Nicholas was watching movies down the hall, 48 was

340

empty. In 44, Lonnie and his wife cuddled under the covers for the first time in almost a month, but they had to hurry since her sister had the kids. In 58, Mrs. Grimes watched sitcoms while Herman loaded trial narratives into his computer. Room 50 was empty because the Colonel was in the Party Room, alone again because Mrs. Herrera was off in Texas visiting a cousin. And 52 was also empty because Jerry was drinking beer with the Colonel and Nicholas and waiting until later to sneak across the hall to Poodle's room. In 56, Shine Royce, alternate number two, worked on a large bag of rolls and butter he'd taken from the dining room, watched TV, and once again thanked God for his good fortune. Royce was fifty-two, unemployed, lived in a rented trailer with a younger woman and her six kids, and hadn't earned fifteen dollars a day doing anything in years. Now, he simply had to sit and listen to a trial and the county would not only pay him but feed him too. In 46, Phillip Savelle and his Pakistani mate drank herbal tea and smoked pot with the windows open.

Across the hall in Room 49, Sylvia Taylor-Tatum talked on the phone with her son. In 45, Mrs. Gladys Card played gin rummy with Mr. Nelson Card, he of the prostate history. In 51, Rikki Coleman waited for Rhea, who was running late and might not make it because the baby-sitter hadn't called. In 53, Loreen Duke sat on her bed, eating a brownie and listening with wretched envy as Angel Weese and her boyfriend rattled the walls next door in 55.

And in 47, Hoppy and Millie Dupree made love like never before. Hoppy had arrived early with a large sack of Chinese food and a bottle of cheap champagne, something he hadn't tried in years. Under normal circumstances, Millie would've fussed about the alcohol, but these days were far from normal. She sipped a little of the beverage from a plastic motel cup, and ate a

341

generous portion of sweet and sour pork. Then Hoppy attacked her.

When they finished, they lay in the darkness and talked softly about the kids and school and the home in general. She was quite weary of this ordeal, and anxious to get back to her family. Hoppy spoke forlornly of her absence. The kids were testy. The house was a wreck. Everybody missed Millie.

He dressed and turned on the television. Millie found her bathrobe and poured another tiny bit of champagne.

'You're not gonna believe this,' Hoppy said, fishing through a coat pocket and retrieving a folded piece of paper.

'What is it?' she asked, taking the paper and unfolding it. It was a copy of Fitch's bogus memo listing the many sins of Leon Robilio. She read it slowly, then looked suspiciously at her husband. 'Where did you get this?' she demanded.

'It came across the fax yesterday,' Hoppy said sincerely. He'd practiced his answer because he couldn't stand the thought of lying to Millie. He felt like a wretch, but then Napier and Nitchman were out there somewhere, just waiting.

'Who sent it?' she asked.

'Don't know. It looks like it came from Washington.'

'Why didn't you throw it away?'

'I don't know. I –'

'You know it's wrong to show me stuff like this, Hoppy.' Millie flung the paper on the bed and walked closer to her husband, hands on hips. 'What are you trying to do?'

'Nothing. It just got faxed to my office, that's all.'

'What a coincidence! Somebody in Washington just happened to know your fax number, just happened to know your wife was on the jury, just happened to know Leon Robilio testified, and just happened to suspect

342

that if they sent you this you'd be stupid enough to bring it over here and try to influence me. I want to know what's going on!'

'Nothing. I swear,' Hoppy said, on his heels.

'Why have you taken such a sudden interest in this trial?'

'It's fascinating.'

'It was fascinating for three weeks and you hardly mentioned it. What's going on, Hoppy?'

'Nothing. Relax.'

'I can tell when something's bothering you.'

'Get a grip, Millie. Look, you're edgy. I'm edgy. This thing has all of us somewhat out of whack. I'm sorry for bringing it.'

Millie finished off her champagne and sat on the edge of the bed. Hoppy sat next to her. Mr. Cristano at Justice had suggested in rather strong terms that Hoppy get Millie to show the memo to all of her friends on the jury. He dreaded telling Mr. Cristano that this probably wouldn't happen. But then, how would Mr. Cristano know for sure what happened to the damned thing?

As Hoppy pondered this Millie started crying. 'I just want to go home,' she said, eyes red, lip quivering. Hoppy put his arm around her and squeezed tightly.

'I'm sorry,' he said. She cried even harder.

Hoppy felt like crying too. This meeting had proved worthless, the sex notwithstanding. According to Mr. Cristano, the trial would end in a few short days. It was imperative that Millie soon be convinced that the only verdict was one for the defense. Since their time together was scarce, Hoppy would be forced to tell her the awful truth. Not now, not tonight, but surely during the next personal visit.

TWENTY-NINE

The Colonel's routine never varied. Like a good soldier, he rose at precisely five-thirty every morning for fifty pushups and situps before a quick, cold shower. At six, he went to the dining room, where there'd damned well better be some fresh coffee and plenty of newspapers. He ate toast with jam and no butter, and greeted each of his colleagues with a hale and hearty good morning as they drifted in and out. They were sleepy-eyed and anxious to return to their rooms where they could sip coffee and watch the news in private. It was a helluva way to start the day, being forced to greet the Colonel and return his verbal barrage. The longer they were sequestered, the more hyper he became before sunrise. Several of the jurors waited until eight, when he was known to promptly leave and return to his room.

At six-fifteen Thursday morning, Nicholas said hello to the Colonel as he poured a cup of coffee, then endured a brief discussion about the weather. He left the makeshift dining room and eased quietly down the empty, darkened hall. Several TV's could already be heard. Someone was talking on the phone. He unlocked his door and quickly set the coffee on the dresser, removed a stack of newspapers from a drawer, then left the room.

Using a key he'd stolen from the rack under the front desk, Nicholas entered Room 50, the Colonel's. The smell of cheap aftershave lingered heavily. Shoes were assembled in a perfect row against one wall. The clothes in the closet were neatly hung and precisely starched. Nicholas fell to his knees, lifted the edge of the bedspread, and deposited the newspapers and magazines under the bed. One was a copy of yesterday's *Mogul*.

He silently left the room and returned to his. An hour later he called Marlee. Assuming Fitch was listening to all of her calls, he simply said, 'Darlene, please.' To which she said, 'Wrong number.' Both hung up. He waited five minutes and dialed the number to a cellphone Marlee kept hidden in a closet. They expected Fitch to tap her phones and wire her apartment.

'Delivery's complete,' he said.

Thirty minutes later Marlee left her apartment and found a pay phone at a biscuit drive-through. She called Fitch, and waited for her call to be routed.

'Good morning, Marlee,' he said.

'Hey, Fitch. Look, I'd love to talk on the phone, but I know all this is getting recorded.'

'No it's not. I swear.'

'Right. There's a Kroger at the corner of Fourteenth and Beach Boulevard, five minutes from your office. There are three pay phones near the front entrance, right side. Go to the one in the middle. I'll call in seven minutes. Hurry, Fitch.' She hung up.

'Sonofabitch!' Fitch screamed as he threw down the receiver and bolted for the door. He yelled at José and together they raced out the back door and jumped into the Suburban.

As expected, the pay phone was ringing when Fitch got there.

'Hey, Fitch. Look, Herrera, number seven, is really getting on Nick's nerves. I think we'll lose him today.'

'What!'

'You heard me.'

'Don't do it, Marlee!'

345

'Guy's a real pain. Everybody's sick of him.'

'But he's on our side!'

'Oh, Fitch. They'll all be on our side when it's over. Anyway, be there at nine for the suspense.'

'No, listen, Herrera is vital to –' Fitch got himself cut off in mid-sentence when he heard the click on her end. Then the line was dead. He gripped the receiver and began pulling on it, as if he'd slowly rip it from the phone and hurl it across the parking lot. Then he released it, and without cursing or yelling he calmly walked back to the Suburban and told José to go to the office.

Whatever she wanted. It didn't matter.

Judge Harkin lived in Gulfport, fifteen minutes from the courthouse. For obvious reasons, his phone number was not listed in the local directory. Who needed convicts from the jail calling at all hours of the night?

As he was in the process of kissing his wife and gathering his cup of coffee for the road, the phone in the kitchen rang and Mrs. Harkin took it. 'It's for you, dear,' she said, handing it to His Honor, who set down his coffee and briefcase and glanced at his watch.

'Hello,' he said.

'Judge, I'm sorry to bother you at home like this,' said a nervous voice, one almost in a whisper. 'This is Nicholas Easter, and if you want me to hang up right now, I'll do it.'

'Not yet. What's the matter?'

'We're still at the motel, getting ready to leave, and, well, I think I need to talk to you first thing this morning.'

'What is it, Nicholas?'

'I hate to call you, but I'm afraid some of the other jurors might be getting suspicious of our notes and chats in chambers.'

'Maybe you're right.'

346

'So I thought I'd call you. This way they'll never know we've talked.'

'Let's try it. If I think we should stop the conversation, then I'll do so.' Harkin wanted to ask how a sequestered juror obtained his phone number, but decided to wait.

'It's about Herrera. I think maybe he's reading some stuff that isn't on the approved list.'

'Like what?'

'Like *Mogul*. I walked into the dining room early this morning. He was there all alone, and he tried to hide a copy of *Mogul* from me. Isn't that some kind of business magazine?'

'Yes, it is.' Harkin had read yesterday's column by Barker. If Easter was telling the truth, and why should he doubt him, then Herrera would be sent home immediately. The reading of any unauthorized material was grounds for dismissal, maybe even contempt. The reading of yesterday's *Mogul* by any juror bordered on grounds for a mistrial. 'Do you think he's discussed it with anyone else?'

'I doubt it. Like I said, he was trying to hide it from me. That's why I got suspicious. I don't think he'd discuss it with anyone. But I'll listen carefully.'

'You do that. I'll call Mr. Herrera in first thing this morning and interrogate him. We'll probably search his room.'

'Please don't tell him I'm the snitch. I feel rotten doing this.'

'It's okay.'

'If the other jurors get word we're talking, then my credibility is gone.'

'Don't worry.'

'I'm just nervous, Judge. We're all tired and ready to go home.'

'It's almost over, Nicholas. I'm pushing the lawyers as hard as I can.'

347

'I know. Sorry, Judge. Just make sure no one knows I'm playing the mole here. I can't believe I'm doing this.'

'You're doing the right thing, Nicholas. And I thank you for it. I'll see you in a few minutes.'

Harkin kissed his wife much quicker the second time, and left the house. By car phone, he called the Sheriff and asked him to go to the motel and wait. He called Lou Dell, something he did most mornings while driving to court, and asked her if *Mogul* was sold at the motel. No, it wasn't. He called his law clerk and asked her to locate both Rohr and Cable and have them waiting in chambers when he arrived. He listened to a country station and wondered how in the world a sequestered juror got a copy of a business magazine not readily available on the streets of Biloxi.

Cable and Rohr were waiting with the law clerk when Judge Harkin entered his chambers and closed his door. He removed his jacket, took his seat, and summarized the allegations against Herrera without divulging his source. Cable was annoyed because Herrera was deemed by all to be a solid defense juror. Rohr was irritated because they were losing another juror and a mistrial couldn't be far away.

With both lawyers unhappy, Judge Harkin felt much better. He sent his law clerk to the jury room to fetch Mr. Herrera, who was sipping his umpteenth cup of decaf and chatting with Herman over his braille computer. Frank glanced around quizzically after Lou Dell called his name, and left the room. He followed Willis the deputy through the back corridors behind the courtroom. They stopped at a side door, where Willis knocked politely before entering.

The Colonel was greeted warmly by the Judge and the lawyers, and he was shown a chair in the cramped room, a chair sitting snugly next to one occupied by the court reporter, who sat ready with her stenographic machine.

Judge Harkin explained that he had a few questions which would require responses under oath, and the lawyers suddenly produced yellow legal pads and started their scribbling. Herrera immediately felt like a criminal.

'Have you been reading any materials not expressly authorized by me?' Judge Harkin asked.

A pause as the lawyers looked at him. The law clerk and the court reporter and the Judge himself were poised to pounce on his response. Even Willis by the door was awake and paying remarkable attention.

'No. Not to my knowledge,' the Colonel said, truthfully.

'Specifically, have you been reading a business weekly called *Mogul*?'

'Not since I've been sequestered.'

'Do you normally read *Mogul*?'

'Once, maybe twice a month.'

'In your room at the motel, do you possess any reading materials not authorized by me?'

'Not to my knowledge.'

'Will you consent to a search of your room?'

Frank's cheeks went red and his shoulders jerked. 'What're you talking about?' he demanded.

'I have reason to believe you've been reading unauthorized materials, and that this has occurred at the motel. I think a quick search of your room might settle the matter.'

'You're questioning my integrity,' Herrera said, wounded and angry. His integrity was vital to him. A glance at the other faces revealed that they all thought he was guilty of some heinous transgression.

'No, Mr. Herrera. I simply believe a search will allow us to proceed with this trial.'

It was just a motel room, not like a home where all sorts of private things are hidden. And, besides, Frank knew damned well there was nothing in his room that

349

could incriminate him. 'Then search it,' he said with clenched teeth.

'Thank you.'

Willis led Frank into the hallway outside chambers, and Judge Harkin called the Sheriff at the motel. The manager opened the door to Room 50. The Sheriff and two deputies conducted a delicate search of the closet and drawers and bathroom. Under the bed, they found a stack of *Wall Street Journals* and *Forbes* magazines, and also a copy of yesterday's *Mogul*. The Sheriff called Judge Harkin, relayed what they'd found, and was instructed to bring the unauthorized items to chambers at once.

Nine-fifteen, no jury. Fitch sat rigid on a back pew, eyes peering just barely over the top of a newspaper and staring hard at the door near the jury box, knowing full and damned well that when they finally emerged, juror number seven would not be Herrera but rather Henry Vu. Vu was mildly tolerable from a defense view because he was Asian, and Asians typically weren't the big spenders of other people's moneys in tort cases. But Vu was no Herrera, and Fitch's jury people had been telling him for weeks now that the Colonel was with them and would be a force during deliberations.

If Marlee and Nicholas could bounce Herrera on a whim, who might be next? If they were doing this solely to get Fitch's attention, then they were surely successful.

The Judge and the lawyers stared in disbelief at the newspapers and magazines now lined neatly across Harkin's desk. The Sheriff dictated into the record a brief narrative of how and where the items were found, then left.

'Gentlemen, I have no choice but to excuse Mr. Herrera,' His Honor said, and the lawyers said nothing.

Herrera was brought back into the room and directed to the same chair.

'On the record,' Judge Harkin said to the court reporter. 'Mr. Herrera, what is your room number at the Siesta Inn?'

'50.'

'These items were found under the bed in Room 50 just minutes ago.' Harkin waved at the periodicals. 'All are recent, most are dated after the date of sequestration.'

Herrera was dumbfounded.

'All, of course, are unauthorized, some are highly prejudicial.'

'They're not mine,' Herrera said slowly, his anger building.

'I see.'

'Somebody put them there.'

'Who might have done this?'

'I don't know. Maybe the same person who gave you the tip.'

A very good point, thought Harkin, but not one to be pursued right now. Both Cable and Rohr looked at the Judge as if to ask, Okay, who gave you the tip?

'We can't escape the fact that these were found in your room, Mr. Herrera. For this reason, I have no choice but to excuse you from further jury service.'

Frank's mind was focusing now, and there were many questions he wanted to ask. He wanted to raise his voice and get in Harkin's face when he suddenly realized he was about to be set free. After four weeks of trial and nine nights at the Siesta Inn, he was about to walk out of this courthouse and go home. He'd be on the golf course by lunchtime.

'I don't think this is right,' he said halfheartedly, trying not to push too hard.

'I'm very sorry. I'll deal with the contempt of court issue at a later date. As for now, we need to get on with the trial.'

351

'Whatever you say, Judge,' Frank said. Dinner tonight at Vrazel's, fresh seafood and a wine list. He could see his grandson tomorrow.

'I'll have a deputy take you back to the motel so you can pack. I am instructing you not to repeat any of this to anyone, especially members of the press. You are under a gag order until further notice. Do you understand this?'

'Yes sir.'

The Colonel was escorted down the rear stairway and out the back door of the courthouse, where the Sheriff was waiting for Herrera's quick and final trip to the Siesta Inn.

'I hereby move for a mistrial,' Cable said, in the direction of the court reporter. 'On the grounds that this jury may have been improperly influenced by the story appearing in *Mogul* yesterday.'

'Motion denied,' Judge Harkin said. 'Anything else?'

The lawyers shook their heads and stood.

The eleven jurors and two alternates took their seats at a few minutes after ten, as the courtroom watched silently. Frank's seat on the second row, far left, was empty, and this was immediately noticed by everyone. Judge Harkin greeted them with a solemn face and got quickly to the point. He held a copy of yesterday's *Mogul* and asked if anyone had seen or read it, or if anyone had heard anything about what was in it. No volunteers.

He then said, 'For reasons that have been made clear in chambers, and placed in the record, juror number seven, Frank Herrera, has been dismissed and will now be replaced by the next alternate, Mr. Henry Vu.' At this point, Willis said something to Henry, who left his padded folding chair and took four steps to seat number seven, where he became an official member of the panel and left Shine Royce as the sole remaining alternate.

Desperate to move things along and divert attention away from his jury, Judge Harkin said, 'Mr. Cable, call your next witness.'

Fitch's newspaper dropped six inches, down to his chest, and his mouth dropped too as he stared at the new composition with bewilderment. He was scared because Herrera was gone, and he was thrilled because his girl Marlee had waved her wand and delivered exactly what she'd promised. Fitch couldn't help but look at Easter, who must have felt it because he turned slightly and caught Fitch's eyes with his own. For five or six seconds, an eternity for Fitch, they stared at each other from ninety feet. Easter's face was smirking and proud, as if to say, 'Look what I can do. Are you impressed?' Fitch's face said, 'Yes. Now, what do you want?'

In the pretrial order, Cable had listed twenty-two possible witnesses, virtually all with the word Doctor somewhere in their names, and all with solid credentials. His stable included battle-tested veterans of other cigarette trials, and prickly researchers funded by Big Tobacco, and myriad other mouthpieces assembled to counterattack what the jury had already heard.

During the past two years, all twenty-two had been deposed by Rohr and his gang. There would be no surprises.

The consensus was that the plaintiff's heaviest blows had been landed by Leon Robilio and his claims that kids were targeted by the industry. Cable thought it best to attack there first. 'The defense calls Dr. Denise McQuade,' he announced.

She presented herself through a side door, and the courtroom, heavily dominated by middle-aged men, seemed to stiffen a bit as she strolled in front of the bench, smiled up at His Honor, who was most definitely smiling down, and took her seat in the witness chair. Dr. McQuade was a beautiful woman, tall and thin with a short red dress just inches above her knees, and blond hair pulled severely back and tucked away behind her head. She took her oath with a comely smile, and when she crossed her legs she had an audience. She seemed much too young and much too pretty to be involved in a nasty brawl like this.

The six men on the jury, especially Jerry Fernandez, along with Shine Royce, the alternate, paid very close attention as she gently pulled the microphone close to her mouth. Red lipstick. Long red fingernails.

If they were expecting a bimbo they were quickly disappointed. Her husky voice detailed her education, background, training, field of expertise. She was a behavioral psychologist with her own firm in Tacoma. She'd written four books, published over three dozen articles, and Wendall Rohr had no objection when Cable moved to have Dr. McQuade declared as an expert.

She got right to the point. Advertising permeates our culture. Ads directed at one age group or one class of people quite naturally are heard and seen by those not in the target group. This cannot be prevented. Kids see tobacco ads because kids see newspapers and magazines and billboards and flashing neon lights in convenience store windows, but this doesn't mean the kids are targeted. Kids also see beer commercials on TV, commercials often made by their favorite sports heroes. Does this mean beer companies are subliminally trying to hook the next generation? Of course not. They're simply trying to sell more beer to their market. The kids just get in the way, but there's nothing that can be done about it short of banning all advertising for all offensive products. Cigarettes, beer, wine, liquor, what about coffee and tea and condoms, and butter? Do ads by credit card companies encourage people to spend more and save less? Dr. McQuade made the point repeatedly that in a society where free speech is a valued right, restrictions on advertising are carefully scrutinized.

Cigarette ads are no different from others. Their purpose is to reinforce a person's desire to buy and use the product. Good ads stimulate the natural response to rush out and purchase what's being advertised. Ineffective ads do not, and normally are quickly pulled. She used the example of McDonald's, a company she had studied, and she just happened to have a report handy in the event the jury wanted to peruse it. By the time a child is three, the child can hum, whistle, or sing whatever the current McDonald's jingle happens to be. The child's first trip to McDonald's is a momentous occasion. This is no accident. The corporation spends billions to hook children before its competitors do. American children consume more fat and cholesterol than the last generation. They eat more cheeseburgers, fries, and pizza, and drink more sodas and sugared fruit drinks. Do we charge McDonald's and Pizza Hut with devious advertising practices for targeting the young? Do we sue them because our kids are fatter?

No. We as consumers make informed choices about the foods we feed our children. No one can argue that we make the best choices.

And we as consumers make informed choices about smoking. We are bombarded with ads for thousands of products, and we respond to those ads which reinforce our needs and desires.

She crossed and recrossed her legs every twenty minutes or so, and each crossing was duly noted by the packs of lawyers around both tables and by the six male jurors and most of the females as well.

Dr. McQuade was pleasant to look at and easy to believe. Her testimony made perfect sense, and she connected with most of the jurors.

Rohr sparred with her politely for an hour on cross but didn't land a serious punch.

355

THIRTY

According to Napier and Nitchman, Mr. Cristano at Justice desperately wanted a full report on what had happened last night when Hoppy met Millie for their latest personal visit. 'Everything?' Hoppy asked. The three were huddled over a rickety table in a smoky diner, sipping boiled coffee from paper cups and waiting for greasy grilled cheese sandwiches.

'Skip the personal stuff,' Napier said, doubtful if there was much personal stuff to skip.

If they only knew, Hoppy thought, still quite proud of himself. 'Well, I showed Millie the memo on Robilio,' he said, not knowing how much of the truth he should tell.

'And?'

'And, well, she read it.'

'Of course she read it. Then what did she do?' Napier asked.

'What was her response?' Nitchman asked.

Sure, he could lie and tell them she was stunned by the memo, believed every word of it, and couldn't wait to show it to her pals on the jury. That's what they wanted to hear. But Hoppy didn't know what to do. Lying could only make matters worse. 'She didn't respond too well,' he said, then told them the truth.

When the sandwiches arrived, Nitchman left to call

Mr. Cristano. Hoppy and Napier ate without looking at each other. Hoppy felt like such a failure. Surely he was one step closer to prison.

'When do you see her again?' asked Napier.

'Not sure. The Judge hasn't said yet. There's a chance the trial could be over this weekend.'

Nitchman returned and took his seat. 'Mr. Cristano is on his way,' he said gravely, and Hoppy's stomach began to churn. 'He'll be here late tonight and wants to meet with you first thing in the morning.'

'Sure.'

'He is not a happy man.'

'Neither am I.'

Rohr spent his lunch hour locked in his office with Cleve, doing the dirty work that had to be kept to themselves. Most of the other lawyers used runners like Cleve to spread cash and chase cases and perform dark little deeds not taught in law school, but none of them would ever admit to such unethical activity. Trial lawyers keep their runners to themselves.

Rohr had several choices. He could tell Cleve to tell Derrick Maples to get lost. He could pay Derrick Maples $25,000 in cash, and he could promise another $25,000 for each plaintiff's vote in the final verdict, assuming there would be at least nine. This would cost $225,000 at most, a sum Rohr was perfectly willing to pay. But he was extremely doubtful Angel Weese could deliver more than two votes – her own and maybe Loreen Duke's. She was not a leader. He could manipulate Derrick into approaching the lawyers for the defense, then try to catch them in bed together. This would probably result in Angel's getting removed, an event Rohr did not want.

Rohr could wire Cleve, capture incriminating statements from Derrick, then threaten the kid with criminal prosecution if he didn't lean on his girlfriend. This was risky, because the bribery plot had been hatched in Rohr's own office.

They covered each scenario with the seasoned judgment of men who'd done it before. A hybrid was developed.

'Here's what we'll do,' Rohr said. 'We'll give him fifteen grand now, promise the other ten after the verdict, and we'll also get him on tape now. We'll mark some of the bills, set him up for later. We'll promise him twenty-five for the other votes, and if we get our verdict, then we'll screw him when he demands the rest. We'll have him on tape, and when he makes noise we'll threaten to call the FBI.'

'I like it,' Cleve said. 'He gets his money, we get our verdict, he gets screwed. Sounds like justice to me.'

'Get yourself wired and get the cash. This needs to be done this afternoon.'

But Derrick had other plans. They met in a lounge at the Resort Casino, a dark bar sadly filled with losers massaging their losses with cheap drinks while outside the sun was shining brightly and the temperature was inching toward seventy.

Derrick wasn't about to get a postverdict screwing. He wanted Angel's twenty-five thousand in cash, now, up front, and he also wanted a 'deposit,' as he called it, for each of the other jurors. A preverdict deposit. In cash too, of course, something reasonable and fair, say, five thousand per juror. Cleve did the quick math, and got it wrong. Derrick was figuring on a unanimous verdict, so the deposit of five grand times eleven other jurors worked out nicely to fifty-five thousand dollars. Add Angel's, and all Derrick wanted was eighty thousand cash now.

He knew a girl in the clerk's office, and this friend had looked at the file. 'You guys are suing the tobacco company for millions,' he said, every word getting captured by a body mike in Cleve's shirt pocket. 'Eighty thousand is a drop in the bucket.'

'You're crazy,' Cleve said.

'And you're crooked.'

'There's no way we can pay eighty thousand cash. Like I said before, when the money gets too big, then we run the risk of getting caught.'

'Fine. I'll go talk to the tobacco company.'

'You do that. I'll read about it in the newspapers.'

They didn't finish their drinks. Cleve again left early, but this time Derrick did not chase him.

The parade of beauties continued Thursday afternoon as Cable put on the stand Dr. Myra Sprawling-Goode, a black professor and researcher at Rutgers who turned every head in the depraved courtroom as she presented herself for testimony. She was almost six feet tall, as striking and slender and well dressed as the last witness. Her creamy light brown skin creased perfectly as she smiled at the jurors, a smile that lingered on Lonnie Shaver, who actually smiled back.

Cable had an unlimited budget when he began his search for experts, so he was not compelled to use people who weren't sharp and glib and able to connect with average folk. He had video-taped Dr. Sprawling-Goode twice before he hired her, then once during her deposition in Rohr's office. Like all his witnesses, she had spent two days getting grilled in a mock courtroom setting a month before the trial began. She crossed her legs and the courtroom took a collective deep breath.

She was a professor of marketing with two doctorates and impressive credentials, no surprise. She'd spent eight years in advertising on Madison Avenue after she had completed her education, then returned to academia, where she belonged. Her field of expertise was consumer advertising, a subject she taught at the graduate level and one she researched continually. Her

359

purpose at the trial soon became clear. A cynic might have claimed she was there to look pretty, to connect with Lonnie Shaver and Loreen Duke and Angel Weese, to make them proud that a fellow African-American was perfectly capable of projecting expert opinions in this crucial trial.

She was actually there because of Fitch. Six years earlier, after a scare in New Jersey in which a jury stayed out three days before returning with a defense verdict, Fitch had hatched the plan to find an attractive female researcher, preferably at a reputable university, to take a chunk of grant money and study cigarette advertising and its effects on teenagers. The parameters of the project would be vaguely defined by the source of the money, and Fitch was hoping the study would one day be useful in a trial.

Dr. Sprawling-Goode had never heard of Rankin Fitch. She had received an eight-hundred-thousand-dollar grant from the Consumer Product Institute, an obscure and previously unheard of think tank in Ottawa which existed, it claimed, to study the marketing trends of thousands of consumer products. She knew little about the Consumer Product Institute. Neither did Rohr. He and his investigators had been digging for two years. It was very private, protected to some degree by Canadian law, and apparently funded by large consumer product companies, none of which appeared to be cigarette manufacturers.

Her findings were contained in a handsome, bound, two-inch-thick report, which Cable got admitted into evidence. It joined a stack of other exhibits as an official piece of the record. Exhibit number eighty-four, to be exact, adding to the twenty thousand or so pages already in evidence and expected to be reviewed by the jury during deliberations.

After the thorough and efficient setup, her findings were succinct and unsurprising. With certain clearly defined and obvious exceptions, all advertising for consumer products is aimed at young adults. Cars, toothpaste, soap, cereal, beer, soft drinks, apparel, cologne – all of the most heavily advertised products have young adults as their target audience. The same is true for cigarettes. Sure, they are portrayed as the products of choice of the thin and beautiful, the active and carefree, the rich and glamorous. But so are countless other products.

She then ticked off a list of specifics, starting with automobiles. When was the last time you saw a TV ad for a sports car with a fat fifty-year-old man behind the wheel? Or a mini-van driven by an obese housewife with six kids and a dirty dog hanging out the windows? Never happens. Beer? You got ten guys sitting in a den watching the Super Bowl. Most have hair, strong chins, perfect jeans, and flat stomachs. This is not reality, but it's successful advertising.

Her testimony became quite humorous as she went through her list. Toothpaste? Ever see an ugly person with ugly teeth grinning at you through the TV? Of course not. They all have perfect teeth. Even in the acne commercials the troubled teens have only a pimple or two.

She smiled easily and even giggled at times at her own comments. The jury smiled along with her. Her point found its mark repeatedly. If successful advertising depends on targeting young adults, why shouldn't tobacco companies be allowed to do it?

She stopped smiling when Cable moved her to the issue of targeting kids. She and her research team had found no evidence of this, and they had studied thousands of tobacco ads over the past forty years. They had watched, studied, and cataloged every cigarette ad used during the TV days. And she noted, almost in an aside, that smoking had increased since such ads were banned from TV. She had spent almost two years

361

searching for evidence that tobacco companies target teens, because she had started the project with this unfounded bias. But it simply wasn't true.

In her opinion, the only way to prevent kids from being influenced by cigarette ads was to ban all of them – billboards, buses, newspapers, magazines, coupons. And, in her opinion, this would do nothing to slow tobacco sales. It would have no impact whatsoever on underage smoking.

Cable thanked her as if she were a volunteer. She'd already been paid sixty thousand dollars to testify, and would send a bill for another fifteen. Rohr, who was anything but a gentleman, knew the pitfalls of attacking such a pretty lady in the Deep South. He delicately probed instead. He had lots of questions about the Consumer Product Institute, and the eight hundred thousand dollars it had paid for this study. She told him everything she knew. It was an academic body established to study trends and formulate policy. It was funded by private industry.

'Any tobacco companies?'

'Not that I'm aware of.'

'Any subsidiaries of tobacco companies?'

'I'm not sure.'

He asked her about companies related to tobacco companies, parent companies, sister companies, and divisions and conglomerates, and she knew nothing.

She knew nothing because that was the way Fitch had planned it.

Claire's trail took an unexpected turn Thursday morning. The ex-boyfriend of a friend of Claire's took a thousand dollars in cash and said his ex-girlfriend was now in Greenwich Village working as a waitress while aspiring to do serious work in soap operas. His ex-girlfriend and Claire had worked together at Mulligan's and allegedly had been close friends. Swanson flew to

362

New York, arrived late Thursday afternoon, and took a cab to a small hotel in SoHo where he paid cash for one night and started making calls. He found Beverly at work in a pizzeria. She answered the phone in a hurry.

'Is this Beverly Monk?' Swanson asked, in his best imitation of Nicholas Easter. He'd listened to his recorded voice many times.

'It is. Who is this?'

'The Beverly Monk who once worked at Mulligan's in Lawrence?'

A pause, then, 'Yes. Who is this?'

'This is Jeff Kerr, Beverly. It's been a long time.' Swanson and Fitch were gambling that after Claire and Jeff left Lawrence they had not kept in touch with Beverly.

'Who?' she asked, and Swanson was relieved.

'Jeff Kerr. You know, I went with Claire. I was a law student.'

'Oh yeah,' she said as if maybe she remembered him and maybe she didn't.

'Look, I'm in the city, and I was wondering if you've heard from Claire recently.'

'I don't understand,' she said slowly, obviously trying to place the name with the face and figure out who was who and why was he here.

'Yeah, it's a long story, but Claire and I split six months ago. I'm sorta looking for her.'

'I haven't talked to Claire in four years.'

'Oh, I see.'

'Look, I'm real busy. Maybe some other time.'

'Sure.' Swanson hung up and called Fitch. They decided it was worth the risk to approach Beverly Monk, with cash, and ask about Claire. If she hadn't talked to her in four years, it would be impossible for her to quickly find Marlee and report the contact. Swanson would follow her, and wait until tomorrow.

Each jury consultant was required by Fitch to

prepare a one-page report at the close of trial each day. One page, double-spaced, straightforward, with no words beyond four syllables and setting forth in clear language that expert's impressions of the day's witnesses and how their testimony was received by the jury. Fitch demanded honest opinions, and had berated his experts before when the language was too sugary. He insisted on pessimism. The reports were due on his desk precisely one hour after Judge Harkin recessed for the day.

Wednesday's reports on Jankle were mixed to bad, but Thursday's summaries of Dr. Denise McQuade and Dr. Myra Sprawling-Goode were nothing short of magnificent. Aside from brightening up a drab courtroom packed with boring men in dull suits, both women had performed well on the stand. The jurors paid attention, and seemed to believe what they heard. Especially the men.

Still, Fitch was not consoled. He had never felt worse at this point in a trial. The defense had lost one of its most sympathetic jurors with the exit of Herrera. The New York financial press had suddenly declared the defense to be on the ropes and was openly concerned about a plaintiff's verdict. Barker's column in *Mogul* was the week's hottest topic. Jankle had been a disaster. Luther Vandemeer of Trellco, the smartest and most influential of the Big Four CEO's, had called with harsh words during lunch. The jury was sequestered, and the longer the trial dragged on, the more blame the jurors would heap upon the party now calling the witnesses.

The tenth night of sequestration passed without incident. No wayward lovers. No unauthorized trips to casinos. No spontaneous yoga at full volume. Herrera was missed by no one. He had packed in minutes and left, telling the Sheriff repeatedly he was being framed and vowing to get to the bottom of it.

An impromptu checkers tournament began in the dining room after dinner. Herman had a braille board with numbered spaces, and the night before he'd whipped Jerry eleven straight games. Challenges were issued, and Herman's wife brought his board to the room and a crowd gathered. In less than an hour, he took three straight from Nicholas, three more from Jerry, three from Henry Vu, who'd never played the game, three straight from Willis, and was about to play Jerry again, this time for a small wager, when Loreen Duke entered the room in search of another dessert. She'd played the game as a child with her father. When she beat Herman in the first game, there was not the slightest trace of sympathy for the blind man. They played until curfew.

Phillip Savelle stayed in his room, as usual. He spoke occasionally during meals at the motel and during coffee breaks in the jury room, but he was perfectly content to keep his nose in a book and ignore everyone.

Nicholas had tried twice to reach him, to no avail. He would not suffer small talk, and wanted no one to know anything about him.

THIRTY-ONE

After almost twenty years of shrimping, Henry Vu seldom slept past four-thirty. He got his hot tea early on Friday, and with the Colonel gone he sat alone at the table and scanned a newspaper. Nicholas soon joined him. As he often did, Nicholas hurried through the pleasantries and asked about Vu's daughter at Harvard. She was the source of immense pride, and Henry's eyes danced when he told of her last letter.

Others came and went. The conversation turned to Vietnam and the war. Nicholas confided in Henry for the first time that his father had been killed there in 1972. It wasn't true, but Henry was deeply touched by the story. Then, when they were alone, Nicholas asked, 'So what do you think about this trial?'

Henry took a long drink of heavily creamed tea, and licked his lips. 'Is it okay to talk about it?'

'Sure. It's just me and you. Everybody's talking, Henry. That's the nature of a jury. Everybody but Herman.'

'What does everybody else think?'

'I think most of us have an open mind. The most important thing is that we stick together. It's crucial that this jury reach a verdict, preferably unanimous, but at least a vote of nine to three one way or the other. A hung jury would be disastrous.'

Henry took another drink and pondered this. He understood English perfectly, could speak it well though with an accent, but like most laymen, natives and immigrants alike, had little grasp of the law. 'Why?' he asked. He trusted Nicholas, as did virtually all the jurors, because Nicholas had studied the law and seemed incredibly adept at comprehending facts and issues the rest of them missed.

'Very simple. This is the mother of all tobacco trials – Gettysburg, Iwo Jima, Armageddon. This is where the two sides have met to unload their heaviest ammo. There's gotta be a winner, and there's gotta be a loser. Clear and decisive. The issue of whether tobacco companies are to be held liable for cigarettes has to be settled right here. By us. We've been chosen, and it's up to us to reach a verdict.'

'I see,' Henry said, nodding, still confused.

'The worst thing we can do is hang ourselves, split down the middle and have a mistrial declared.'

'Why would that be so bad?'

'Because it's a cop-out. We'd simply be passing the buck to the next jury. If we get hung up and go home, it'll cost each side millions of dollars because they'll have to come back in two years and replay the whole thing. Same judge, same lawyers, same witnesses, everything will be the same but the jury. We will, in effect, be saying that we didn't have enough sense to reach a decision, but the next jury from Harrison County will be smarter.'

Henry leaned to his right a bit, in the direction of Nicholas. 'What're you gonna do?' he asked, just as Millie Dupree and Mrs. Gladys Card entered giggling and went for the coffee. They chatted with the guys for a moment, then left to watch Katie on the 'Today Show.' They just loved Katie.

'What're you gonna do?' Henry whispered again, eyes on the door.

367

'I don't know right now, and it's not important. The important thing is for us to stick together. All of us.'

'You're right,' Henry said.

During the course of the trial, Fitch had developed the habit of keeping himself busy at his desk during the hours before court while staring at the phone. His eyes seldom left it. He knew she would call Friday morning, though he had no idea what scheme or ploy or heart-stopping prank she'd be up to.

At eight sharp, Konrad interrupted on the intercom with the simple words 'It's her.'

Fitch lunged for the phone. 'Hello,' he said pleasantly.

'Hey, Fitch. Look, guess who's bothering Nicholas now?'

He stifled a groan and closed his eyes hard. 'I don't know,' he said.

'I mean, this guy is really giving Nicholas a hard time. We might have to bump him.'

'Who?' Fitch pleaded.

'Lonnie Shaver.'

'Oh! Damn! No! You can't do that!'

'Gee, Fitch.'

'Don't do it, Marlee! Dammit!'

She paused to let him despair for a second. 'You must be fond of Lonnie.'

'You gotta stop this, Marlee, okay? This is getting us nowhere.' Fitch was very aware of how desperate he sounded, but he was no longer in control.

'Nicholas has to have harmony on his jury. That's all. Lonnie has become a thorn.'

'Don't do it, please. Let's talk about this.'

'We're talking, Fitch, but not for long.'

Fitch took a deep breath, then another. 'The game is almost over, Marlee. You've had your fun, now what do you want?'

'Got a pen?'

'Sure.'

'There's a building on Fulton Street, Number 120. White brick, two stories, an old building chopped into tiny offices. Upstairs, Number 16, belongs to me, for at least another month. It's not pretty, but that's where we'll meet.'

'When?'

'In an hour. Just the two of us. I'll watch you come and go, and if I see any of your goons then I'll never speak to you again.'

'Sure. Whatever.'

'And I'll check you for bugs and mikes.'

'There won't be any.'

Every lawyer on Cable's defense team held the opinion that Rohr had spent too much time with his scientists; nine full days in all. But with the first seven, the jury had at least been free to go home at night. The mood was vastly different now. The decision was made to pick their two best researchers, get them on the stand, and get them off as quickly as possible.

They had also made the decision to ignore the issue of nicotine addiction, a radical departure from the normal defense in cigarette cases. Cable and his crew had studied each of the sixteen previous trials. They had talked to many of the jurors who had decided those cases, and they were repeatedly told that the weakest part of the defense came when the experts put forth all sorts of fancy theories to prove that nicotine was in fact not addictive. Everyone knew the opposite to be true. It was that simple.

Don't try to convince jurors otherwise.

The decision required Fitch's approval, which he grudgingly gave.

The first witness Friday morning was a shaggy-headed nerd with a thin red beard and heavy bifocals.

369

The beauty show was apparently over. His name was Dr. Gunther, and it was his opinion that cigarette smoking really didn't cause cancer after all. Only ten percent of smokers get cancer, so what about the other ninety percent? Not surprisingly, Gunther had a stack of relevant studies and reports, and couldn't wait to stand before the jury with a tripod and a pointer and explain in breathless detail his latest findings.

Gunther was not there to prove anything. His job was to contradict Dr. Hilo Kilvan and Dr. Robert Bronsky, experts for the plaintiff, and to muddy the waters so there would be considerable doubt in the minds of the jurors about just how deadly smoking really was. He couldn't prove smoking didn't cause lung cancer, and he argued that no amount of research had proved that smoking absolutely does cause it. 'More research is needed,' he said every ten minutes.

On the chance that she might be watching, Fitch walked the last block to 120 Fulton Street, a pleasant stroll along the shaded sidewalk with leaves dropping gently from above. The building was in the old part of town, four blocks from the Gulf, in a neat line of carefully painted two-stories, most of which seemed to be offices. José was told to wait three streets over.

No chance of a body mike or a wire. She'd broken him of that habit at their last meeting, on the pier. Fitch was alone, wireless, mikeless, bugless, without a camera or an agent nearby. He felt liberated. He would have to survive by brains and wit, and he welcomed the challenge.

He climbed the sagging wooden stairs, stood before her unmarked office door, took notice of the other unmarked doors in the cramped hallway, and gently knocked. 'Who is it?' came her voice.

'Rankin Fitch,' he answered just loud enough to be heard.

A dead bolt rattled from the inside, then Marlee appeared in a gray sweatshirt and blue jeans, no smile at all, no greeting of any sort. She closed the door behind Fitch, locked it, and walked to one side of a rented folding table. Fitch took the measure of the room, a cubbyhole with no window, one door, peeling paint, three chairs, and a table. 'Nice place,' he said, looking at the brown water spots on the ceiling.

'It's clean, Fitch. No phones for you to tap, no vents for cameras, no wires in the walls. I'll check it every morning, and if I find your trail, then I'll simply walk out the door and never come back.'

'You have a low impression of me.'

'It's one you deserve.'

Fitch looked again at the ceiling, then the floor. 'I like the place.'

'It'll serve its purpose.'

'Its purpose being?'

Her purse was the only item on the table. She removed the same sensor-scan from it, and aimed it at Fitch from head to toe.

'Come on, Marlee,' he protested. 'I promised.'

'Yeah right. You're clean. Have a seat,' she said, nodding at one of two chairs on his side of the table. Fitch shook the folding chair, a rather thin job that might not meet his challenge. He lowered himself onto it, then leaned forward with his elbows on the table, which was also not too stable, so he was perched precariously at both ends. 'Are we ready to talk money?' he asked with a nasty grin.

'Yes. It's a simple deal, really, Fitch. You wire me a bunch of money, and I promise to deliver you a verdict.'

'I think we should wait until after the verdict.'

'You know I'm not that stupid.'

The folding table was three feet wide. Both were leaning on it, their faces not far apart. Fitch often used his bulk and his nasty eyes and his sinister goatee to

371

physically intimidate those around him, especially the younger lawyers in the firms he hired. If Marlee was intimidated, she certainly didn't show it. Fitch admired her poise. She stared straight into his eyes, never blinking, a most difficult task.

'Then there are no guarantees,' he said. 'Juries are unpredictable. We could give you the money –'

'Drop it, Fitch. You and I both know the money will be paid before the verdict.'

'How much money?'

'Ten million.'

He managed a guttural discharge, as if choking on a golf ball, then he coughed loudly as his elbows flew up and his eyes rolled and his fat jowls shook in utter, sheer disbelief. 'You must be kidding,' he managed to say in a raspy voice, glancing around for a cup of water or a bottle of pills or anything to help him through this horrible shock.

She watched the show calmly, never blinking, never taking her eyes off him. 'Ten million, Fitch. It's a bargain. And it's nonnegotiable.'

He coughed again, his face slightly redder. Then he gathered his composure and thought of a response. He'd guessed in the millions, and he knew he'd sound foolish trying to negotiate down as if his client couldn't afford it. She probably had the latest quarterly reports for each of the Big Four.

'How much is in The Fund?' she asked, and Fitch's eyes instinctively narrowed. As far as he could tell, she hadn't blinked yet.

'The what?' he asked. No one knew about The Fund!

'The Fund, Fitch. Don't play games with me. I know all about your little slush fund. I want the ten million wired from The Fund account to a bank in Singapore.'

'I don't think I can do that.'

'You can do anything you want, Fitch. Stop playing

games. Let's cut the deal now and get on with our business.'

'What if we wire five now and five after the verdict?'

'Forget it, Fitch. It's ten million now. I don't like the idea of tracking you down and trying to collect the last installment after the trial. For some reason, I think I'd waste a lot of time.'

'When do we wire it?'

'I don't care. Just make sure it's received before the jury gets the case. Otherwise the deal is off.'

'What happens if the deal is off?'

'One of two things. Either Nicholas will hang the jury, or he'll send it nine to three for the plaintiff.'

The veneer cracked above the eyebrows, two long wrinkles pinched together as he absorbed these predictions, delivered so matter-of-factly. Fitch had no doubts about what Nicholas could do because Marlee had no doubts. He slowly rubbed his eyes. The game was over. No more exaggerated reactions to anything she said. No more feigned disbelief at her demands. She was in control.

'It's a deal,' he said. 'We'll wire the money, pursuant to your instructions. I must warn you, though, that wires can take time.'

'I know more about wiring money than you do, Fitch. I'll explain precisely how I want it done. Later.'

'Yes ma'am.'

'So we have a deal?'

'Yes,' he said, extending his hand across the table. She shook it limply. Both smiled at the absurdity. Two crooks shaking hands over an agreement no court of law could enforce because no court of law would ever know about it.

Beverly Monk's apartment was a fifth-floor loft in a dingy Village warehouse. She shared it with four other starving actresses. Swanson followed her to a corner

373

coffee shop and waited until she had settled at a window table with an espresso, a bagel, and a newspaper with want ads. With his back to the other tables, he approached her and asked, 'Excuse me. Are you Beverly Monk?'

She looked up, startled, and said, 'Yes. Who are you?'

'A friend of Claire Clement's,' he said as he quickly slid into the chair across from her.

'Have a seat,' she said. 'What do you want?' She was nervous but the shop was crowded. She was safe, she thought. He looked nice enough.

'Information.'

'You called me yesterday, didn't you?'

'Yes, I did. I lied, said I was Jeff Kerr. I'm not.'

'Then who are you?'

'Jack Swanson. I work for some lawyers in Washington.'

'Is Claire in trouble?'

'None whatsoever.'

'Then what's all the fuss?'

Swanson gave a quick version of Claire's summons for jury service in a huge trial and his duty to track down the backgrounds of certain prospective jurors. This time it was a contaminated landfill case in Houston where billions were at stake, thus the expense of digging so deeply.

Swanson and Fitch were gambling on two things. The first was Beverly's slow recognition of Jeff Kerr's name on the phone yesterday. The second was her assertion that she hadn't talked to Claire in four years. They were assuming both to be genuine.

'We'll pay for information,' Swanson said.

'How much?'

'A thousand dollars cash to tell me everything you know about Claire Clement.' Swanson quickly removed an envelope from his coat pocket and laid it on the table.

374

'Are you sure she's in no trouble?' asked Beverly, staring at the gold mine before her.

'I'm sure. Take the money. If you haven't seen her in four or five years, why should you care?'

Good point, thought Beverly. She grabbed the envelope and stuck it in her purse. 'There's not much to tell.'

'How long did you work with her?'

'Six months.'

'How long did you know her?'

'Six months. I was working as a waitress at Mulligan's when she started. We got to be friends. Then I left town and drifted east. I called her once or twice when I lived in New Jersey, then we sorta just forgot about each other.'

'Did you know Jeff Kerr?'

'No. She wasn't dating him at the time. She told me about him later, after I'd left town.'

'Did she have other friends, male and female?'

'Yeah, sure. Don't ask me to name them. I left Lawrence five, maybe six years ago. I really don't remember when I left.'

'You can't name any of her friends?'

Beverly drank some espresso and thought for a minute. Then she rattled off the names of three people who'd worked with Claire. One had been checked out with no results. One was being tracked at the moment. One had not been found.

'Where did Claire go to college?'

'Somewhere in the Midwest.'

'You don't know the name of the school?'

'I don't think so. Claire was very quiet about her past. You got the impression something bad happened back there, and she didn't talk about it. I never knew. I thought maybe it was a bad romance, maybe even a marriage, or maybe a bad family, rotten childhood, or something. But I never knew.'

375

'Did she discuss it with anybody?'

'Not to my knowledge.'

'Do you know her hometown?'

'She said she moved around a lot. Again, I didn't ask a lot of questions.'

'Was she from the Kansas City area?'

'I don't know.'

'Are you sure her real name was Claire Clement?'

Beverly withdrew and frowned. 'You think maybe it wasn't?'

'We have reason to believe she was someone else before she arrived in Lawrence, Kansas. Do you remember anything about another name?'

'Wow. I just assumed she was Claire. Why would she change her name?'

'We'd love to know.' Swanson removed a small notepad from a pocket and studied a checklist. Beverly was another dead end.

'Did you ever go to her apartment?'

'Once or twice. We'd cook and watch movies. She didn't party much, but she invited me over with friends.'

'Anything unusual about her apartment?'

'Yeah. It was very nice, a modern condo, well furnished. It was obvious she had money from sources other than Mulligan's. I mean, we got paid three bucks an hour plus tips.'

'So she had money?'

'Yeah. A lot more than we did. But, again, she was very secretive. Claire was a casual friend and a fun person to be around. You just didn't ask a lot of questions.'

Swanson pressed her on other details and came up dry. He thanked her for her help and she thanked him for the cash, and as he was leaving she offered to make a few calls. It was an obvious solicitation for more money. Swanson said fine, but then cautioned her about revealing what she was doing.

'Look, I'm an actress, okay. This is a piece of cake.'

He left her a business card with his Biloxi hotel number written on the back.

Hoppy thought Mr. Cristano was a bit too harsh. But then, the situation was deteriorating, according to the mysterious folks in Washington whom Mr. Cristano answered to. There was discussion at Justice about simply aborting the whole scheme and sending Hoppy's case on to the federal grand jury.

If Hoppy couldn't convince his own wife, how the hell was he supposed to influence an entire jury?

They sat in the back of the long black Chrysler and drove along the Gulf toward nowhere in particular but Mobile in general. Nitchman drove and Napier rode shotgun and both managed to act completely oblivious to the mauling of Hoppy in the backseat.

'When do you see her again?' Cristano asked.

'Tonight, I think.'

'The time has come, Hoppy, for you to tell her the truth. Tell her what you've done, tell her everything.'

Hoppy's eyes watered and his lip quivered as he stared at the tinted window and saw his wife's pretty eyes as he laid bare his soul. He cursed himself for his stupidity. If he had a gun he could almost shoot Todd Ringwald and Jimmy Hull Moke, but he could most definitely shoot himself. Maybe he'd take these three clowns out first, but, no doubt about it, Hoppy could blow his own brains out.

'I guess so,' he mumbled.

'Your wife must become an advocate, Hoppy. Do you realize this? Millie Dupree has to be a force in that jury room. Since you've been unable to convince her with the merits, now you have to motivate her with the fear of seeing you go off to prison for five years. You have no choice.'

At the moment, he'd rather face prison than face

Millie with the truth. But he didn't have that choice. If he didn't convince her, she'd learn the truth *and* he'd go off to prison.

Hoppy started crying. He bit his lip and covered his eyes and tried to stop the damned tears, but he couldn't help it. As they drove peacefully along the highway, the only sounds for several miles were the pitiful whimperings of a broken man.

Only Nitchman couldn't conceal a tiny grin.

THIRTY-TWO

The second meeting in Marlee's office began an hour after the first one ended. Fitch arrived again on foot with a briefcase and a large cup of coffee. Marlee scanned the briefcase for hidden devices, much to his amusement.

When she finished, he closed his briefcase and sipped his coffee. 'I have a question,' he announced.

'What?'

'Six months ago, neither you nor Easter lived in this county, probably not in this state. Did you move here to watch this trial?' He knew the answer, of course, but he wanted to see how much she would admit, now that they were business partners and supposedly working on the same side.

'You could say that,' she said. Marlee and Nicholas were assuming that Fitch had now tracked them back to Lawrence, and this was not altogether bad. Fitch had to appreciate their ability to hatch such a plot, and their commitment to carry it out. It was Marlee's pre-Lawrence days that had them losing sleep.

'You're both using aliases, aren't you?' he asked.

'No. We're using our legal names. No more questions about us, Fitch. We're not important. Time is short, and we have work to do.'

'Perhaps we should begin by your telling me how far you've gone with the other side. How much does Rohr know?'

379

'Rohr knows nothing. We danced and shadowboxed, but never connected.'

'Would you have cut a deal with him had I not been willing?'

'Yes. I'm in it for the money, Fitch. Nicholas is on that jury because we planned it that way. We have worked for this moment. It'll work because all the players are corrupt. You're corrupt. Your clients are corrupt. My partner and I are corrupt. Corrupt but smart. We pollute the system in such a way that we cannot be detected.'

'What about Rohr? He'll be suspicious when he loses. In fact, he'll suspect you've cut a deal with the tobacco company.'

'Rohr doesn't know me. We never met.'

'Come on.'

'I swear it, Fitch. I made you think I had met him, but it never happened. It would have, though, had you not been willing to negotiate.'

'You knew I'd be willing.'

'Of course. We knew you'd be more than anxious to purchase a verdict.'

Oh, he had so many questions. How did they learn of his existence? How did they get his phone numbers? How did they make certain Nicholas would be summoned for jury duty? How did they get him on the jury? And how in hell did they learn about The Fund?

He would ask them one day when this was behind them and the pressure was off. He'd love to chat with Marlee and Nicholas over a long dinner and get all his questions answered. His admiration for them grew by the moment.

'Promise me you won't bump Lonnie Shaver,' he said.

'I'll make the promise, Fitch, if you'll tell why you're so fond of Lonnie.'

'He's on our side.'

'How do you know this?'

'We have ways.'

'Look, Fitch, if we're both working for the same verdict, then why can't we be honest?'

'You know, you're right. Why'd you bump Herrera?'

'I told you. He's an ass. He didn't like Nicholas and Nicholas didn't like him. Plus, Henry Vu and Nicholas are buddies. So we didn't lose anything.'

'Why'd you bump Stella Hulic?'

'Just to get her out of the jury room. She was horribly obnoxious. Everything about her was disruptive.'

'Who's next?'

'I don't know. We have one left. Who should we get rid of?'

'Not Lonnie.'

'Then tell me why.'

'Let's just say Lonnie has been bought and paid for. His employer is someone who'll listen to us.'

'Who else have you bought and paid for?'

'No one.'

'Come on, Fitch. Do you want to win or not?'

'Of course I do.'

'Then come clean. I'm your easiest way to a quick verdict.'

'And most expensive.'

'You didn't expect me to be cheap. What do you gain by withholding information from me?'

'What do I gain by giving it to you?'

'That should be obvious. You tell me. I tell Nicholas. He has a better handle on where the votes are. He knows where to spend his time. What about Gladys Card?'

'She's a follower. We have nothing on her. What does Nicholas think?'

'The same. What about Angel Weese?'

'She smokes and she's black. Flip a coin. Another follower. What does Nicholas think?'

'She'll follow Loreen Duke.'

381

'And who will Loreen Duke follow?'

'Nicholas.'

'How many followers does he have now? How many members are in his little cult?'

'Jerry for starters. Since Jerry is sleeping with Sylvia, then count her in. Add Loreen and you get Angel.'

Fitch held his breath and counted rapidly. 'That's five. Is that all?'

'And Henry Vu makes six. Six in the bank. You do the math, Fitch. Six and counting. What do you have on Savelle?'

Fitch actually glanced at some notes as if he wasn't sure. Everything brought to the meeting in his briefcase had been read a dozen times. 'Nothing. He's too much of a weirdo,' he said sadly, as if he'd been a miserable failure in his efforts to find some way to coerce Savelle.

'Any dirt on Herman?'

'No. What does Nicholas think?'

'Herman will be listened to, but not necessarily followed. He hasn't made a lot of friends, but then he's not disliked either. His vote will probably stand alone.'

'Which way is he leaning?'

'He's the one juror who's hardest to read now because he is determined to follow the Judge's orders against discussing the case.'

'Of all the nerve.'

'Nicholas will have nine votes before the closing arguments, maybe more. He just needs a little leverage with some of his friends.'

'Like who?'

'Rikki Coleman.'

Fitch took a drink without looking at the cup. He set it down and pressed the whiskers around his mouth. She watched every move. 'We, uh, may have something there.'

'Why are you playing games, Fitch? Either you have something or you don't. Either you tell me so I can tell

Nicholas so we can nail her vote, or you sit there hiding your memos and hoping she jumps on board.'

'Let's just say it's a nasty personal secret she'd prefer to keep from her husband.'

'Why keep the secret from me, Fitch?' Marlee said angrily. 'Are we working together?'

'Yes, but I'm not sure I need to tell you at this point.'

'Great, Fitch. Something in her past, right? An affair, an abortion, a DUI?'

'I'll think about it.'

'You do that, Fitch. You keep playing games, I'll keep playing games. What about Millie?'

Fitch was reeling while appearing cool and calm. How much should he tell her? His instincts said to be cautious. They'd meet again tomorrow, and the next day, and if he chose to he could tell her about Rikki and Millie and maybe even Lonnie. Go slow, he told himself. 'Nothing on Millie,' he said, glancing at his watch and thinking that at that very moment poor Hoppy was locked inside a big black car with three FBI men and probably bawling by now.

'Are you sure, Fitch?'

Nicholas had met Hoppy in the hallway of the motel, just outside his room, a week ago as Hoppy was arriving with flowers and fudge for his wife. They had chatted for a moment. The next day Nicholas had noticed Hoppy sitting in the courtroom, a new face filled with wonder, a new face suddenly interested after almost three weeks of trial.

With Fitch in the game, Nicholas and Marlee were assuming that any juror was a potential target for outside influence. So Nicholas watched everyone. He sometimes loitered in the hallway as the guests were arriving for the personal visits, and he sometimes loitered there as they left. He eavesdropped on the gossip in the jury room. He listened to three conversations at once during the daily walks around town after

383

lunch. He took notes on every person in the courtroom, even had nicknames and code names for them all.

It was only a hunch that Fitch was working on Millie through Hoppy. They seemed like such a nice, good-hearted pair; the type Fitch could easily snare in one of his insidious plots.

'Of course I'm sure. Nothing on Millie.'

'She's been acting strange,' Marlee said, lying.

Wonderful, thought Fitch. The Hoppy sting was working.

'What does Nicholas think about Royce, the last alternate?' he asked.

'White trash. Not bright at all. Easily manipulated. The type we could slip five grand to and we'd own him. That's another reason Nicholas wants to bump Savelle. We get Royce, and he'll be easy.'

Her casualness about bribery warmed Fitch's heart. Many times, in other trials, he'd dreamed of finding angels like Marlee, little saviors with sticky hands who were anxious to fix his juries for him. This was almost unbelievable!

'Who else might take cash?' he asked eagerly.

'Jerry's broke, lots of gambling debts, plus a messy divorce around the corner. He'll need twenty thousand or so. Nicholas hasn't cut the deal with him yet, but it'll happen over the weekend.'

'This could get expensive,' Fitch said, trying to be serious.

Marlee laughed loudly, and continued to laugh until Fitch was forced to snicker at his own humor. He'd just promised her ten million, and he was in the process of spending another two million for the defense. His clients had a net worth of something close to eleven billion.

The moment passed, and they spent a while ignoring each other. Finally, Marlee looked at her watch, and said, 'Write this down, Fitch. It's now three-thirty,

Eastern Time. The money's not going to Singapore. I want the ten million wired to the Hanwa Bank in the Netherlands Antilles, and I want it done immediately.'

'Hanwa Bank?'

'Yes. It's Korean. The money is not going to my account, but to yours.'

'I don't have an account there.'

'You'll open one with the wire.' She pulled folded papers from her purse and slid them across the table. 'Here are the forms and instructions.'

'It's too late in the day to do this,' he said, taking the papers. 'And tomorrow is Saturday.'

'Shut up, Fitch. Just read the instructions. Everything'll work fine if you simply do as you're told. Hanwa is always open for preferred customers. I want the money parked there, in your account, over the weekend.'

'How will you know it's there?'

'You'll show me a confirmation of the wire. The money is diverted briefly until the jury retires, then it leaves Hanwa and goes to my account. This should happen Monday morning.'

'What if the jury gets the case sooner?'

'Fitch, I assure you, there will be no verdict until the money is in my account. That's a promise. And if for some reason you try to screw us, then I can also promise you there'll be a nice verdict for the plaintiff. A huge verdict.'

'Let's not talk about that.'

'No, let's not. This has all been carefully planned, Fitch. Don't mess it up. Just do as you're told. Start the wire now.'

Wendall Rohr yelled at Dr. Gunther for an hour and a half, and when he finished there were no calm nerves anywhere in the courtroom. Rohr himself was probably the most relaxed person because his own badgering bothered him not in the least. Everybody else was sick of it. It was almost five, Friday, another week finished. Another weekend planned at the Siesta Inn.

Judge Harkin was worried about his jury. They were obviously bored and irritated, weary of sitting captive and listening to words they no longer cared about.

The lawyers were worried about them too. They weren't responding to testimony as expected. When they weren't fidgeting they were nodding off. When they weren't gazing about with blank looks they were pinching themselves to stay awake.

But Nicholas wasn't the least bit concerned about his colleagues. He wanted them fatigued and on the verge of revolt. A mob needs a leader.

During a late afternoon recess, he had prepared a letter to Judge Harkin in which he requested the trial be continued on Saturday. The issue had been debated during lunch, a debate which lasted only a few minutes because he had planned it and had all the answers. Why sit around the motel room when they could be sitting in the jury box trying to finish this marathon?

The other twelve readily added their signatures, under his, and Harkin had no choice. Saturday court was rare but not unheard of, especially in sequestration trials.

His Honor quizzed Cable as to what they might expect tomorrow, and Cable confidently predicted the defense would finish its case. Rohr said the plaintiff would have no rebuttal. Sunday court was out of the question.

'This trial should be over Monday afternoon,' Harkin said to the jury. 'The defense will finish tomorrow, then we'll have closing arguments Monday morning. I anticipate you'll receive the case before noon Monday. That's the best I can do, folks.'

There were suddenly smiles throughout the jury box.

386

With the end in sight, they could endure one last weekend together.

Dinner would be at a notorious rib place in Gulfport, followed by four hours of personal visits tonight, tomorrow night, and Sunday. He sent them away with apologies.

After the jury left, Judge Harkin reconvened the lawyers for two hours of arguments on a dozen motions.

THIRTY-THREE

He arrived late with no flowers or chocolates, no champagne or kisses, nothing but his tortured soul, which he wore on his sleeve. He took her by the hand at the door, led her to the bed, where he sat on the edge and tried to utter something before choking up. He buried his face in his hands.

'What's the matter, Hoppy?' she asked, fully alarmed and certain she was about to hear some dreadful confession. He had not been himself lately. She sat beside him, patted his knee, and listened. He began by blurting out just how stupid he'd been. He said repeatedly she wouldn't believe what he'd done, and he rambled on about how stupid it was until she finally said, firmly, 'What have you done?'

He was suddenly angry – angry at himself for such a ridiculous stunt. He clenched his teeth, curled his upper lip, scowled, and launched into Mr. Todd Ringwald and KLX Property Group and Stillwater Bay and Jimmy Hull Moke. It was a setup! He'd been minding his own business, not out looking for trouble, just hustling with his sad little properties, just trying to help newlyweds into their first charming little starters. Then this guy walked in, from Vegas, nice suit, thick wad of architect's plans which, when unraveled on Hoppy's desk, looked like a gold mine.

Oh how could he have been so stupid! He lost his edge and began sobbing.

When he got to the part about the FBI coming to the house, Millie couldn't contain herself. 'To our house?!'

'Yes, yes.'

'Oh my god! Where were the kids?'

So Hoppy told her how it happened, how he deftly maneuvered Agents Napier and Nitchman away from the house and down to his office, where they presented him with – the tape!

It was awful. He forged ahead.

Millie began crying too, and Hoppy was relieved. Maybe she wouldn't scold him so bad. But there was more.

He got to the part where Mr. Cristano came to town and they met on the boat. Lots of folks, good folks really, in Washington were concerned about the trial. The Republicans and all that. The crime stuff. And, well, they cut a deal.

Millie wiped her cheeks with the back of a hand, and abruptly stopped the crying. 'But I'm not sure I want to vote for the tobacco company,' she said, dazed.

Hoppy dried it up quickly too. 'Oh that's just great, Millie. Send me away for five years just so you can vote your conscience. Wake up.'

'This is not fair,' she said, looking at herself in the mirror on the wall behind the dresser. She was stunned.

'Of course it's not fair. Won't be fair either when the bank forecloses on the house because I'm locked away. What about the kids, Millie? Think of the kids. We got three in junior college and two in high school. The humiliation will be bad enough, but who'll educate the kids?'

Hoppy, of course, had the benefit of many hours of rehearsal for this. Poor Millie felt as though she'd been hit by a bus. She couldn't think quickly enough to ask the right questions. Under different circumstances, Hoppy might have felt sorry for her.

'I just can't believe it,' she said.

'I'm sorry, Millie. I'm so sorry. I've done a terrible thing, and it's not fair to you.' He was leaning forward, elbows on knees, head drooping low in utter defeat.

'It's not fair to the people in this trial.'

Hoppy couldn't have cared less about the other people involved in the trial, but he bit his tongue. 'I know, honey. I know. I'm a total failure.'

She found his hand and squeezed it. Hoppy decided to go for the kill. 'I shouldn't tell you this, Millie, but when the FBI came to the house, I thought about getting the gun and ending it all right there.'

'Shooting them?'

'No, myself. Blowing my brains out.'

'Oh, Hoppy.'

'I'm serious. I've thought about it many times in the past week. I'd rather pull the trigger than humiliate my family.'

'Don't be silly,' she said, and started to weep again.

Fitch at first had considered faking the wire, but after two phone calls and two faxes with his forgers in Washington, he was not convinced it would be safe. She seemed to know everything about wire transfers, and he had no idea how much she knew about the bank in the Netherlands Antilles. With her precision, she probably had someone down there waiting for the wire. Why run the risk?

In a flurry of phone calls, he located in D.C. an ex-Treasury official who now ran his own consulting firm, a man who allegedly knew everything about the rapid movements of money. Fitch gave him the bare essentials, hired him by fax, then sent him a copy of Marlee's instructions. She definitely knew what she was doing, the man said, and assured Fitch his money would be safe, at least during its first leg. The new account would belong to Fitch; she would have no access to it. Marlee was requiring a copy of the confirmation, and the man warned Fitch not to show her the account number either from the originating bank or from Hanwa in the Caribbean.

The Fund had a balance of six and a half million when Fitch cut his deal with Marlee. Throughout Friday, Fitch had called each of the Big Four CEO's and instructed them to immediately wire another two million dollars each. And he had no time for questions. He would explain later.

At five-fifteen Friday, the money left The Fund's untitled account in a bank in New York and within seconds landed at Hanwa in the Netherlands Antilles, where it was expected. The new account, numbered only, was created upon arrival, and a confirmation was immediately faxed to the originating bank.

Marlee called at six-thirty, and, not surprisingly, knew the wire was complete. She instructed Fitch to erase the account numbers on the confirmation, something he planned to do anyway, and fax it to the front desk of the Siesta Inn at precisely 7:05.

'That's a bit risky, isn't it?' Fitch asked.

'Just do as you're told, Fitch. Nicholas will be standing by the fax machine. The clerk thinks he's cute.'

At seven-fifteen, Marlee called back to report that Nicholas had received the confirmation, and that it looked authentic. She instructed Fitch to be at her office at ten in the morning. Fitch quite happily agreed.

Though no money had changed hands, Fitch was elated with his success. He collected José and went for a silent stroll, something he rarely did. The air was crisp and invigorating. The sidewalks were deserted.

At this very moment, there was a sequestered juror holding a piece of paper with the amount '$10,000,000'

391

printed twice on it. This juror, and this jury, belonged to Fitch. This trial was over. For certain, he would skip sleep and sweat bullets until he heard the verdict, but for all practical purposes, the trial was over. Fitch had won again. He'd snatched another victory from near defeat. The cost was much greater this time, but so were the stakes. He'd be forced to listen to some pointed bitching from Jankle and the others about the price of this operation, but it would just be a formality. They had to bitch about costs. They were corporate executives.

The real costs were the ones they wouldn't mention: the price of a plaintiff's verdict, certainly with the potential to exceed ten million, and the incalculable cost of a torrent of lawsuits.

He deserved this rare moment of pleasure, but his work was far from finished. He couldn't rest until he knew the real Marlee, where she came from, what motivated her, how and why she hatched this plot. There was something back there that Fitch had to know, and the unknown scared him immensely. If and when he found the real Marlee, then he would have his answers. Until then, his precious verdict was not safe.

Four blocks into his walk, Fitch was once again his angry, pouting, tormented self.

Derrick made it to the front lobby and was poking his head through an open door when a young woman politely asked him what he wanted. She held a stack of files and looked quite busy. It was almost eight, Friday night, and the law offices were still swarming.

What he wanted was a lawyer, one of those he'd seen in court who represented the tobacco company, one he could sit down with and cut a deal behind closed doors. He'd done his homework and learned the names of Durwood Cable and a few of his partners. He'd found this place, and he'd waited outside in his car for two hours, rehearsing his lines, steadying his nerves, mustering the guts to leave the car and walk through the front door.

There wasn't another black face to be seen.

Weren't all lawyers crooks? He figured that if Rohr would offer cash, then it made sense that all lawyers involved in the trial would offer cash. He had something to sell. There were rich buyers out there. It was a golden opportunity.

But the right words failed him as the secretary lingered and looked, and then began glancing around as if she might need some help with the situation. Cleve had said more than once that this was highly illegal, that he'd get caught if he got too greedy, and the fear suddenly hit him like a brick.

'Uh, is Mr. Gable in?' he asked with great uncertainty.

'Mr. Gable?' she said, eyebrows arched.

'Yeah, that's him.'

'There is no Mr. Gable here. Who are you?'

A group of young coatless honkies walked slowly behind her, sizing him up and down, each knowing he didn't belong. Derrick had nothing else to offer. He was sure he had the right firm, but the wrong name, the wrong game, and he wasn't about to go to jail.

'I guess I have the wrong place,' he said, and she gave him an efficient little smile. Of course you have the wrong place; now please leave. He stopped at a table in the front lobby and gathered five business cards from a small bronze rack. He'd show these to Cleve as proof of his visit.

He thanked her and left in a hurry. Angel was waiting.

Millie wept and tossed and flung sheets until midnight, then she changed into her favorite outfit, a well-worn red sweat suit, size XX-Large, a Christmas gift from

393

one of the kids years ago, and quietly opened her door. Chuck, the guard at the far end, called softly to her. She was just going down for a snack, she explained, then eased down the semi-lit hall to the Party Room, where she heard a faint noise. Inside, Nicholas sat alone on a sofa, eating microwave popcorn and sipping carbonated water. He was watching rugby from Australia. Harkin's Party Room curfew had long since been forgotten.

'Why are you up so late?' he asked, muting the wide-screen TV with the remote. Millie sat nearby in a chair, her back to the door. Her eyes were red and puffy. Her short gray hair was tousled. She didn't care. Millie lived in a house which was continually filled with teenagers. They came and went, stayed, slept, ate, watched TV, cleaned out the fridge, saw her all the time in her red sweats, and she wouldn't have it any other way. Millie was everybody's mother.

'Can't sleep. You?' she said.

'It's hard to sleep here. You want some popcorn?'

'No thanks.'

'Did Hoppy stop by tonight?'

'Yes.'

'Seems like a nice man.'

She paused, then said, 'He is.'

There was a longer pause as they sat in silence and thought about what they should say next. 'You wanna watch a movie?' he finally asked.

'No. Can I ask you something?' she said, very seriously, and Nicholas punched the remote and the TV was off. The room was now lit only by a shadowy table lamp.

'Sure. You look troubled.'

'I am. It's a legal question.'

'I'll try to answer.'

'Okay.' She took a deep breath and squeezed her hands together. 'What if a juror becomes convinced she cannot be fair and impartial? What should she do?'

He looked at the wall, the ceiling, then took a sip of water. Slowly, he said, 'I think it would depend on the reasons behind her decision.'

'I don't follow you, Nicholas.' He was such a sweet boy, and so sharp. Her youngest son wanted to be a lawyer, and she'd caught herself hoping he'd turn out as smart as Nicholas.

'For the sake of simplicity, let's skip the hypotheticals,' he said. 'Let's say this juror is actually you, okay?'

'Okay.'

'So something has happened since the trial started to affect your ability to be fair and impartial?'

Slowly, she said, 'Yes.'

He pondered this for a moment, then said, 'I think it would depend on whether it was something you heard in court, or something that has happened out of court. As jurors, we're expected to become biased and partial as the trial progresses. That's how we reach our verdict. There's nothing wrong with that. It's part of the decision-making process.'

She rubbed her left eye, and slowly asked, 'What if it's not that? What if it's something out of court?'

He seemed shocked by this. 'Wow. That's a lot more serious.'

'How serious?'

For dramatic effect, Nicholas stood and walked a few steps to a chair, which he pulled close to Millie, their feet almost touching.

'What's the matter, Millie?' he asked softly.

'I need help, and there's no one to turn to. I'm locked up here in this awful place, away from my family and friends, and there's just nowhere to turn. Can you help me, Nicholas?'

'I'll try.'

Her eyes watered for the umpteenth time that night. 'You're such a nice young man. You know the law and this is a legal matter, and there's just no one else I can talk to.' She was crying now, and he handed her a cocktail napkin from the table.

She told him everything.

Lou Dell awoke for no reason at 2 A.M., and took a quick patrol of the hallway in her cotton nightgown. In the Party Room, she found Nicholas and Millie with the TV off, deep in conversation, with a large bowl of popcorn between them. Nicholas was actually polite to her as he explained they couldn't sleep, were just talking about families, everything was fine. She left, shaking her head.

Nicholas suspected a scam, but he did not indicate that to Millie. Once her tears stopped, he grilled her on the details and took a few notes. She promised to do nothing until they could talk again. They said good night.

He went to his room, dialed Marlee's number, and hung up when she answered the phone with a rather sleepy hello. He waited two minutes, then dialed the same number. It rang six times, unanswered, then he hung up. After another two minutes, he dialed the number of her hidden cellphone. She answered it in the closet.

He gave her the full Hoppy story. Her night's rest was over. There was much work to be done, and quickly.

They agreed to start with the names of Napier, Nitchman, and Cristano.

THIRTY-FOUR

The courtroom didn't change on Saturday. The same clerks wore the same clothes and busied themselves with the same paperwork. Judge Harkin's robe was just as black. The lawyers' faces all blurred, same as Monday through Friday. The deputies were just as bored, maybe more so. Minutes after the jury was seated and Harkin finished his questions, the monotony settled in, same as Monday through Friday.

After Gunther's tedious performance on Friday, Cable and crew thought it best to start the day with a bit of action. Cable called forward and got qualified as an expert a Dr. Olney, a researcher no less, who'd done some amazing things with laboratory mice. He had a video of his cute little subjects, all of them alive and seemingly filled with energy, certainly not diseased and dying. They were in several groups, boxed in glass cages, and it was Olney's task to apply various quantities of cigarette smoke each day to each cage. This he did over a period of years. Massive doses of cigarette smoke. The prolonged exposure failed to produce a single case of lung cancer. He'd tried everything short of suffocation to force death upon his little creatures, but it just wouldn't work. He had the stats and details. And he had lots of opinions about how cigarettes do not cause lung cancer, either in mice or in humans.

Hoppy was listening, from what was now his usual seat in the courtroom. He had promised to stop by, to wink at her, to give moral support, to once again let her know how awfully sorry he was. It was the least he could do. And after all it was Saturday, a busy day for realtors, but Dupree Realty seldom got cranked up until late in the morning. Since the disaster of Stillwater Bay, Hoppy had lost his drive. The thought of several years in prison sapped his will to hustle.

Taunton was back, on the front row now behind Cable, still wearing an immaculate dark suit, taking important notes and glancing at Lonnie, who did not need the reminder.

Derrick sat near the rear, watching it all and scheming. Rikki's husband Rhea sat on the rear seat with both kids. They tried to wave at their mother when the jury was seated. Mr. Nelson Card sat next to Mrs. Herman Grimes. Loreen's two teenaged daughters were present.

The families were there to be supportive, and to satisfy their curiosities. They'd heard enough to form their own opinions about the issues, the lawyers, the parties, the experts, and the Judge. They wanted to listen, so that perhaps they could later share an insight into what ought to be done.

Beverly Monk slipped out of her coma mid-morning, the remnants of gin and crack and what else she couldn't remember still lingering hard and blinding her as she covered her face and realized she was lying on a wooden floor. She wrapped herself in a dirty blanket, stepped over a snoring male she didn't recognize, and found her sunglasses on a wooden crate she used as a dresser. With the glasses on, she could see. The open loft was a mess – bodies sprawled on beds and floors, empty liquor bottles perched on every stick of cheap furniture. Who were these people? She shuffled toward a small loft window, stepping over a roommate here and a stranger there. What had she done last night?

The window was frosted; an early light snow was falling on the streets, where the flakes melted as they landed. She pulled the blanket around her emaciated body and sat on a beanbag near the window, watching the snow and wondering how much of the thousand bucks was left.

She inhaled the chilly air close to a windowpane, and her eyes began to clear. The throbbing in her temples ached but the dizziness was fading. Before she'd met Claire years ago, she'd chummed with a KU student named Phoebe, a flaky girl with a substance problem who'd spent time in recovery but was always on the brink of succumbing. Phoebe had worked briefly at Mulligan's with Claire and Beverly, then left the place under a cloud. Phoebe was from Wichita. She had once told Beverly that she knew something about Claire's past, something she'd learned from a boy who'd dated Claire. It wasn't Jeff Kerr, but some other guy, and if her head wasn't pounding she maybe could remember more of the details.

It was a long time ago.

Someone grunted under a mattress. Then there was silence again. Beverly had spent a weekend with Phoebe and her large, Catholic family in Wichita. Her father was a physician there. Should be easy to find. If that nice thug Mr. Swanson would fork over a thousand bucks for a few harmless answers, how much would he pay for some real background on Claire Clement?

She'd find Phoebe. Last she heard, she was in L.A. playing the same game Beverly was playing in New York. She'd shake down Swanson for all she could, then maybe find another place to live, a larger flat with nicer friends who'd keep the riffraff out.

Where was Swanson's card?

*

399

Fitch skipped the morning's testimony to engage in a rare briefing, an event he despised. His guest was important, though. The man's name was James Local, head of the private investigation company to which Fitch was paying a fortune. Hidden in Bethesda, Local's firm hired lots of former government intelligence agents, and in the normal course of things an excursion into the heartland to locate a lone American female with no criminal record would be a nuisance. Their specialty was monitoring illegal arms shipments, tracking terrorists, and the like.

But Fitch had plenty of money, and the work involved only the slightest risk of flying bullets. The work had also been quite fruitless, and this was the reason Local was in Biloxi.

Swanson and Fitch listened as Local, without the slightest trace of apology, detailed their efforts of the past four days. Claire Clement had not existed before she appeared in Lawrence in the summer of 1988. Her first apartment was a two-bedroom condo she rented by the month and paid for with cash. The utilities were in her name – water, electric, gas. If she'd used the courts of Kansas for a legal name change, there was no record of it. Such files are kept locked, but they had managed to access them nonetheless. She didn't register to vote, didn't purchase car tags, didn't purchase real estate, but she did possess a Social Security number, which she'd used for employment purposes at two places – Mulligan's and a clothing boutique just off campus. A Social Security card is relatively easy to get, and it makes life much easier for a person on the run. They had managed to obtain a copy of her application for it, which revealed nothing useful. She had not applied for a passport.

It was Local's opinion that she had legally changed her name in another state, just pick one of the other forty-nine, then moved to Lawrence with a fresh identity.

They had her phone records for the three years she lived in Lawrence. There were no long distance calls billed to her. He repeated this twice so it would sink in. No long distance calls in three years. At the time, the phone company did not keep records of incoming long distance calls, so the printouts revealed nothing but the local activity. They were checking numbers. She used her phone sparingly.

'How does a person live with no long distance calls? What about family, old friends?' Fitch asked incredulously.

'There are ways,' Local said. 'Lots of ways, really. Maybe she borrowed a friend's phone. Maybe she went to a motel once a week, some budget place where they let you charge calls to your room, then pay for them with the bill when you check out. There's no way to trace that.'

'Unbelievable,' Fitch mumbled.

'I gotta tell you, Mr. Fitch, this girl is good. If she made a mistake, we haven't found it yet.' The respect was obvious in Local's voice. 'A person like this plans every move from the viewpoint that someone will come looking later.'

'Sounds like Marlee,' Fitch said, as if he were admiring a daughter.

She had two credit cards in Lawrence – a Visa and a Shell gas card. Her credit history revealed nothing remarkable or helpful. Evidently, most of her expenditures were in cash. No telephone cards either. She wouldn't dare make that mistake.

Jeff Kerr was a different story. His trail to law school at KU had been easy to follow, most of the work having been done by Fitch's initial operatives. Only after he met Claire did he pick up her habits of secrecy.

They left Lawrence in the summer of 1991, after his second year of law school, and Local's men had yet to find anyone who knew exactly when they left or where

401

they were going. Claire had paid cash for the June rent that year, then vanished. They had spot-checked a dozen cities for signs of a Claire Clement after May of 1991, but so far had found nothing helpful. For obvious reasons, it was not possible to check every city.

'My guess is that she ditched Claire as soon as she left town, and became someone else,' Local said.

Fitch had figured this out long ago. 'This is Saturday. The jury gets the case on Monday. Let's forget what happened after Lawrence, and concentrate on finding out who she really is.'

'We're working on that now.'

'Work harder.'

Fitch glanced at his watch and explained that he had to go. Marlee would be expecting him in a matter of moments. Local left for a private plane and a quick trip back to Kansas City.

Marlee had been in her little office since six. She slept little after Nicholas called her around three. They talked four times before he left for the courtroom.

The Hoppy scam had Fitch stamped all over it – why else would Mr. Cristano threaten to crush Hoppy if he didn't pressure Millie to vote right? Marlee had scribbled pages of notes and flow charts, and she'd made dozens of calls on her cellphone. Information was trickling in. The only George Cristano with a listed phone number in the metropolitan D.C. area lived in Alexandria. Marlee had called him around 4 A.M., and explained she was so-and-so with Delta Airlines, a plane had gone down near Tampa, a Mrs. Cristano was on board, and was this the George Cristano who worked with the Justice Department. No, he worked at Health and Human Services, thank God. She apologized, hung up, and snickered at the thought of the poor man racing to CNN to see the story.

Dozens of similar calls had led her to believe that

402

there were no FBI agents working out of Atlanta named Napier and Nitchman. Nor were there any in Biloxi, New Orleans, Mobile, or any nearby city. At eight, she made contact with an investigator in Atlanta who was now pursuing leads on Napier and Nitchman. Marlee and Nicholas were almost positive the two were stooges, but this had to be confirmed. She called reporters, cops, FBI hotlines, government information services.

When Fitch arrived promptly at ten, the table was clear and the phone was hidden in a small closet. They barely said hello. Fitch was wondering who she was before she was Claire, and she was still analyzing the next move to uncover his Hoppy scam.

'You'd better wrap it up, Fitch. The jury is numb.'

'We'll be through by five this afternoon. That soon enough?'

'Let's hope so. You're not making it easier on Nicholas.'

'I've told Cable to hurry. That's all I can do.'

'We got problems with Rikki Coleman. Nicholas has spent time with her, and she'll be a hard sell. She's well respected on the jury, by the men and women alike, and Nicholas says she's slowly becoming a major player. He's surprised by this, actually.'

'She wants a big verdict?'

'It looks that way, though they haven't discussed specifics. Nicholas detects a real bitterness toward the industry for duping kids into addiction. She doesn't appear to have much sympathy for the Wood family, she's more inclined to punish Big Tobacco for hooking the younger generation. Anyway, you said we might have a surprise for her.'

Without comment or formality, Fitch lifted a single sheet of paper from his briefcase and slid it across the table. Marlee scanned it quickly. 'Abortion, huh?' she said, still reading, unsurprised.

'Yep.'

'You're sure this is her?'

'Positive. She was in college.'

'This should do it.'

'Does he have the guts to show it to her?'

Marlee released the paper and glared at Fitch. 'Would you, for ten million bucks?'

'Of course. And why not? She sees this, she votes right, this is forgotten, and her dirty little secret is safe. She leans the other way, then threats are made. It's an easy sell.'

'Precisely.' She folded the piece of paper and removed it from the table. 'Don't worry about Nick's courage, okay? We've been planning this for a long time.'

'How long?'

'That's not important. You have nothing on Herman Grimes?'

'Not a thing. Nicholas will have to deal with him during deliberations.'

'Gee thanks.'

'He's damned sure getting paid for it, don't you think? For ten million, you'd think he should be able to sway a few votes.'

'He's got the votes, Fitch. They're in his pocket right now. He wants it unanimous. Herman might be a problem.'

'Then bump the sonofabitch. Seems to be a game you enjoy.'

'We're thinking about it.'

Fitch shook his head in amazement. 'Do you realize how utterly corrupt this is?'

'Yes, I think so.'

'I love it.'

'Go love it somewhere else, Fitch. That's all for now. I have work to do.'

'Yes dear,' Fitch said, bouncing to his feet and closing his briefcase.

★

Early Saturday afternoon, Marlee located an FBI agent in Jackson, Mississippi, who happened to be at the office catching up with paperwork when the phone rang. She gave an alias, said she was employed by a real estate company in Biloxi, and suspected two men of posing as FBI agents when in fact they were not. The two men had been harassing her boss, making threats, flashing badges, etc. She thought they had something to do with the casinos, and for good measure she threw in the name of Jimmy Hull Moke. He gave her the home number of a young FBI agent in Biloxi named Madden.

Madden was in bed with flu, but willing to talk nonetheless, especially when Marlee informed him she might have confidential information about Jimmy Hull Moke. Madden had never heard of either Napier or Nitchman, and hadn't heard of Cristano either. He was unaware of any special crime-fighting unit from Atlanta now operating on the Coast, and the more she talked, the more excited he became. He wanted to investigate a bit, and she promised to call him back in an hour.

He sounded much stronger when she phoned later. There was no FBI agent named Nitchman. There was a Lance Napier in the San Francisco office, but he would have no business on the Coast. Cristano was likewise a bogus identity. Madden had talked to the agent in charge of the investigation into Jimmy Hull Moke, and confirmed that Nitchman, Napier, and Cristano, whoever they might be, were certainly not FBI agents. He'd love to talk to these boys, and Marlee said she'd try to arrange a meeting.

The defense rested at three Saturday afternoon. Judge Harkin announced proudly, 'Ladies and gentlemen, you've just heard the last witness.' There would be some last-minute motions and arguments for him and the lawyers to tend to, but the jurors were free to go. For their Saturday night entertainment, one bus would travel to a junior college football game, and the other would go to a local movie theater. Afterward, personal visits would be allowed until midnight. For tomorrow, each juror would be allowed to leave the motel from 9 A.M. until 1 for worship services, unsupervised as long as they promised not to say a word to anybody about the trial. For Sunday night, personal visits from seven until ten. First thing Monday they would hear closing arguments, and receive the case before lunch.

THIRTY-FIVE

Explaining football to Henry Vu was more trouble than it was worth. But then, everyone seemed to be an expert. Nicholas had played high school junior varsity, in Texas, no less, where the sport is something only slightly less than a religion. Jerry followed twenty games a week, followed in fact with his wallet and thus claimed to know the game intimately. Lonnie, sitting behind Henry, had also played in high school and was quick to lean over his shoulder and point. The Poodle, sitting next to Jerry, closely under the quilt, had learned the game thoroughly when her two sons played. Even Shine Royce didn't hesitate to throw in a few pointers. He'd never played the game but watched a lot of television.

They sat in a tiny huddled group on the visitors' side, on cold aluminum bleachers, away from the rest of the crowd, watching a Gulf Coast school play one from Jackson. It was a perfect football setting – cool weather, nice crowd on the home side, a rowdy band in the stands, cute cheerleaders, close score.

Henry asked all the wrong questions: Why are their trousers so tight? What do they say when they group together between plays and why do they hold hands? Why do they pile up like that? He claimed it was his first live football game.

Across an aisle, Chuck and another deputy watched

407

the game in plain clothes, ignoring six of the jurors in the most important civil trial in the country.

It was expressly forbidden for any juror to have contact with another juror's visitors. The prohibition had been in writing since the beginning of sequestration, and Judge Harkin had harped on it repeatedly. But an occasional hello in the hallway was unavoidable, and Nicholas had been especially determined to violate the rule whenever possible.

Millie had no interest in movies and certainly none in football. Hoppy arrived with a sack of burritos, which they ate slowly with few words. After dinner, they tried to watch a TV show but finally gave it up and began to rehash Hoppy's mess. There were more tears, more apologies, even a few of Hoppy's casual references to suicide, which Millie found a bit overly dramatic. She finally confessed she'd spilled her guts to Nicholas Easter, a fine young man who knew the law and could be trusted implicitly. Hoppy at first was shocked and angry, then his curiosity got the better of him and he longed to know what someone else thought of his situation. Especially someone who'd studied the law, as Millie said. More than once she'd mentioned her admiration for the young man.

Nicholas had promised to make a few calls, and this alarmed Hoppy. Oh how Nitchman and Napier and Cristano lectured him on the necessity of silence! Nicholas could be trusted, Millie repeated, and Hoppy eventually warmed to the idea.

The phone rang at ten-thirty; it was Nicholas, back from the game, settled in his room, and anxious to meet with the Duprees. Millie unlocked the door. Willis watched with great surprise from the end of the hall as Easter sneaked into Millie's room. Was her husband still in there? He couldn't remember. Many of the guests had yet to leave, and he'd been napping anyway. Surely

408

Easter and Millie weren't seeing each other! Willis made a mental note of it, then drifted back to sleep.

Hoppy and Millie sat on the edge of the bed facing Nicholas, who leaned on the dresser near the TV. He began by lecturing them kindly on the need for silence, as if Hoppy hadn't heard this in the past week. They were violating a Judge's orders, enough said.

He broke the news gently. Napier, Nitchman, and Cristano were minor players in a large fraud, a conspiracy orchestrated by the tobacco company to pressure Millie. They were not government agents. The names were aliases. Hoppy had been duped.

He took it well. At first he felt even more stupid, if that was possible, then the room began to spin as Hoppy got yanked this way and that. Was it good news or bad? What about the tape? What was his next move? What if Nicholas was wrong? A hundred thoughts raced through his overloaded brain as Millie squeezed his knee and started crying.

'Are you sure?' he was able to ask, his voice on the verge of cracking.

'Positive. They have no connection with either the FBI or the Department of Justice.'

'But, but they had badges and –'

Nicholas raised both hands, nodded compassionately, and said, 'I know, Hoppy. Believe me, that stuff was easy. The cover was simple to create.'

Hoppy rubbed his forehead and tried to arrange things. Nicholas went on to explain that KLX Property Group in Las Vegas was a sham. They had been unable to find a Mr. Todd Ringwald, which was almost certainly an alias too.

'How do you know all this?' Hoppy asked.

'Good question. I have a close friend on the outside who's very good at digging for information. He is completely trustworthy. Took about three hours on the phone, which is not bad considering it's Saturday.'

Three hours. On a Saturday. Why hadn't Hoppy made a few calls? He'd had a week. He sunk lower until his elbows rested on his knees. Millie wiped her cheeks with a tissue. A quiet minute passed.

'What about the tape?' Hoppy asked.

'Of you and Moke?'

'Yes. That tape.'

'I'm not worried about it,' Nicholas said confidently, as if he was now Hoppy's lawyer. 'Legally, there are lots of problems with the tape.'

Tell me about it, Hoppy thought but said nothing. Nicholas continued, 'It was obtained by false pretenses. It's a clear case of entrapment. It's in the possession of men who themselves are violating the law. It was not obtained by law enforcement officials. There was no search warrant for it, no court order allowing your words to be recorded. Forget it.'

What sweet words! Hoppy's shoulders jerked upward and he exhaled mightily. 'You're serious?'

'Yes, Hoppy. The tape will never be played again.'

Millie leaned over and clutched Hoppy, and they hugged without shame or embarrassment. Her tears were now of unbridled joy. Hoppy jumped to his feet and bounced around the room. 'So what's the game plan?' he asked, cracking his knuckles, ready for battle.

'We have to be careful.'

'Just point me in the right direction. The bastards.'

'Hoppy!'

'Sorry, dear. I'm just ready to kick some ass.'

'Your language!'

Sunday began with a birthday cake. Loreen Duke had mentioned to Mrs. Gladys Card that her thirty-sixth birthday was approaching. Mrs. Card called her sister out in the free world, and early Sunday her sister delivered a thick chocolate caramel cake. Three layers with thirty-six candles. The jurors met in the dining room at nine and ate the cake for breakfast. Most then left in a hurry for four hours of much-awaited worship. Some had not been to church in years, but felt drawn by the Spirit.

One of Poodle's boys picked her up, and Jerry tagged along. They headed in the general direction of some unnamed church, but as soon as they realized no one was watching they went to a casino instead. Nicholas left with Marlee, and they attended Mass. Mrs. Gladys Card made a grand entrance at the Calvary Baptist Church. Millie went home with good intentions of dressing for church, but she was overcome with emotion at the sight of her kids. No one was watching, so she spent her time in the kitchen, cooking and cleaning and doting on her brood. Phillip Savelle remained behind.

Hoppy went to his office at ten. He had called Napier at eight Sunday morning with the news that he had important trial developments to discuss; said he'd made much progress with his wife and she was now scoring major points with other jurors. He wanted to meet with Napier and Nitchman at his office to give a full report, and to receive further instructions.

Napier took the call in a run-down two-room apartment he and Nitchman were using as a front for the scam. Two phone lines were temporarily installed – one as the office number, the other as their residence for the duration of their hard-charging investigation into corruption along the Gulf Coast. Napier chatted with Hoppy, then called Cristano for orders. Cristano's room was at a Holiday Inn near the beach. Cristano in turn called Fitch, who was delighted with the news. Finally, Millie was off dead-center and moving their way. Fitch had begun to wonder if his investment would pay off. He green-lighted the meeting at Hoppy's office.

Wearing their standard dark suits and dark

sunshades, Napier and Nitchman arrived at the office at eleven to find Hoppy brewing coffee and in great spirits. They settled around his desk and waited for the coffee. Millie was in there fighting like hell to save her husband, Hoppy said, and she felt quite confident she had already convinced Mrs. Gladys Card and Rikki Coleman. She had shared the Robilio memo with them, and they had been shocked at the man's deceit.

He poured coffee as Napier and Nitchman dutifully took notes. Another guest quietly entered the building through the front door, which had been left unlocked by Hoppy. He eased along the hall behind the open reception area, stepping lightly on the worn carpet until he came to a wooden door with HOPPY DUPREE painted on it. He listened for a moment, then knocked loudly.

Inside, Napier jumped and Nitchman set down his coffee, and Hoppy stared at them as if startled. 'Who is it?' he growled loudly. The door opened suddenly, and Special Agent Alan Madden stepped in, said loudly, 'FBI!' while walking to the edge of Hoppy's desk and glaring at all three. Hoppy kicked his chair back and stood as if he might have to get frisked.

Napier would've fainted had he been standing. Nitchman's mouth dropped open. Both turned pale as their hearts stopped.

'Agent Alan Madden, FBI,' he said as he opened his badge for all to inspect. 'Are you Mr. Dupree?' he demanded.

'Yes. But the FBI is already here,' Hoppy said, looking at Madden, then at the other two, then back at Madden.

'Where?' he asked, scowling down at Napier and Nitchman.

'These two guys,' Hoppy said, acting brilliantly. It was his finest moment. 'This is Agent Ralph Napier, and this is Agent Dean Nitchman. You guys don't know each other?'

'I can explain,' Napier started, nodding confidently as if he could in fact make everything satisfactory.

'FBI?' Madden said. 'Show me some identification,' he demanded, shoving forward an empty palm.

They hesitated, and Hoppy pounced on them. 'Go ahead. Show him your badges. Same ones you showed me.'

'Identification please,' Madden insisted, his anger growing by the second.

Napier started to stand, but Madden returned him to his seat by pressing down on his shoulder. 'I can explain,' Nitchman said, his voice an octave higher than normal.

'Go ahead,' Madden said.

'Well, you see, we're not really FBI agents, but instead –'

'What!' Hoppy screamed from across the desk. He was wild-eyed and ready to throw something. 'You lying sonofabitch! You've been telling me for the last ten days that you're FBI agents!'

'Is that true?' Madden demanded.

'Not, not really,' Nitchman said.

'What!' Hoppy screamed again.

'Cool it!' Madden snapped at him. 'Now continue,' he said to Nitchman.

Nitchman didn't want to continue. He wanted to bolt through the door, kiss Biloxi good-bye, and never be seen again. 'We're private investigators, and, well –'

'We work for a firm in D.C.,' Napier chimed in helpfully. He was about to add something else when Hoppy lunged for a desk drawer, yanked it open, and removed two business cards – one for Ralph Napier, one for Dean Nitchman, both labeled as FBI agents, both from the Southeast Regional Unit in Atlanta. Madden studied both cards, saw the local numbers scrawled on the back.

'What's going on here?' Hoppy demanded.

413

'Who's Nitchman?' Madden asked. There was no answer.

'He's Nitchman,' Hoppy yelled, pointing at Nitchman.

'Not me,' Nitchman said.

'What!' Hoppy screamed.

Madden took two steps toward Hoppy and pointed at his chair. 'I want you to sit down and shut up, okay? Not another word until I ask for it.' Hoppy fell into his seat, his eyes glaring fiercely at Nitchman.

'Are you Ralph Napier?' Madden asked.

'Nope,' Napier said, looking down, away from Hoppy.

'Sonofabitches,' Hoppy mumbled.

'Then who are you?' Madden asked. He waited, but there was no response.

'They gave me those cards, okay?' Hoppy said, not about to keep quiet. 'I'll go to the grand jury and swear on a stack of Bibles that they gave me those cards. They've held themselves out as FBI agents, and I want them prosecuted.'

'Who are you?' Madden asked the one previously known as Nitchman. No response. Madden then removed a service revolver, an action that greatly impressed Hoppy, and made the two stand and spread their legs and lean forward on the desk. A quick frisk of each revealed nothing but pocket change, some keys, and a few dollars. No wallets. No fake FBI badges. No identification whatsoever. They were too well trained to make that mistake.

He handcuffed them and led them from the office to the front of the building, where another FBI agent was sipping coffee from a paper cup and waiting. Together, they loaded Napier and Nitchman into the back of a real FBI car. Madden said good-bye to Hoppy, promised to call him later, and drove away with the two stooges in the backseat, sitting on their hands. The other FBI agent followed in the fake FBI car Napier always drove.

Hoppy waved farewell.

Madden drove along Highway 90, in the direction of Mobile. Napier, the quicker wit of the two, concocted a fairly reasonable story, which Nitchman added to slightly. They explained to Madden that their firm had been hired by some vague and unnamed casino interests to investigate various parcels of real estate along the Coast. This is where they'd run into Hoppy, who was quite corrupt and had tried to shake 'em down for cash. One thing led to another, and their boss made them pose as FBI agents. No harm had been done, really.

Madden listened with hardly a word. They would later tell Fitch that he seemed not to have a clue about Hoppy's wife Millie and her current civic responsibilities. He was a young agent, obviously amused with his catch and not certain what to do with them.

For his part, Madden deemed it a minor offense, unworthy of prosecution, certainly not worth any more effort on his part. His caseload was staggering anyway. The last thing he needed was to waste time pursuing convictions for two small-time liars. When they crossed into Alabama, he delivered a stern lecture on the penalties for impersonating a federal officer. They were truly sorry. It would never happen again.

He stopped at a rest station, uncuffed them, gave them their car, and told them to stay out of Mississippi. They thanked him profusely, promised never to return, and sped away.

Fitch broke a lamp with his fist when he got the call from Napier. Blood dripped from a knuckle as he seethed and cursed and listened to the story, as told from a noisy truck stop somewhere in Alabama. He sent Pang to collect the two.

Three hours after they were first handcuffed, Napier and Nitchman were seated in a room next to Fitch's office in the rear of the old dime store. Cristano was present.

'Start at the beginning,' Fitch said. 'I want to hear every word.' He punched a button and a recorder started. They painstakingly collaborated on the narrative until they'd recollected virtually all of it.

Fitch dismissed them and sent them back to Washington.

Alone, he dimmed the lights in his office and sulked in the darkness. Hoppy would tell Millie tonight. Millie would be lost as a defense juror; in fact, she'd probably swing so far to the other side she'd want billions in damages for the poor widow Wood.

Marlee could salvage this disaster. Only Marlee.

THIRTY-SIX

It was the strangest thing, Phoebe said not long into the surprise call from Beverly, because the day before yesterday some guy had called her too, claimed he was Jeff Kerr looking for Claire. She knew immediately the guy was faking, but she strung him along anyway to see what he wanted. She hadn't talked to Claire in four years.

Beverly and Phoebe compared notes about their calls, though Beverly didn't mention the meeting with Swanson or the jury trial he was investigating. They reminisced about the college days in Lawrence, which seemed so long ago. They lied about their acting careers and the speed with which each was progressing. They promised to get together at the first opportunity. Then they said good-bye.

Beverly called back an hour later, as if she'd forgotten something. She'd been thinking about Claire. They'd parted on less than good terms, and this bothered her. It was a trivial matter they'd never resolved. She wanted to see Claire, to patch things up, if for no other reason than to relieve the guilt. But she didn't have a clue where to find her. Claire had disappeared so fast and so thoroughly.

At this point, Beverly decided to take a chance. Since Swanson had mentioned the possibility of a prior name, and since she remembered the mystery surrounding Claire's past, she decided to cast the bait and see if Phoebe would take it. 'Claire was not her real name, you know?' she said, acting quite effectively.

'Yeah, I know,' Phoebe said.

'She told me once, but I can't remember now.'

Phoebe hesitated. 'She had the prettiest name, not that Claire was bad.'

'What was it?'

'Gabrielle.'

'Oh yes, Gabrielle. And what was her last name?'

'Brant. Gabrielle Brant. She was from Columbia, Missouri, that's where she went to school, at the university there. Did she tell you the story?'

'Maybe, but I don't remember.'

'She had a boyfriend who was abusive and crazy. She tried to ditch him, and he began stalking her. That's why she left town and changed her name.'

'Never heard that. What's her parents' name?'

'Brant. I think her father's dead. Her mother was a professor of medieval studies at the university.'

'Is she still there?'

'I have no idea.'

'I'll try to find her through her mom. Thanks, Phoebe.'

It took an hour to get Swanson on the phone. Beverly asked him how much the information was worth. Swanson called Fitch, who needed some good news. He authorized a ceiling of five thousand dollars, and Swanson called her back with an offer of half that. She wanted more. They negotiated for ten minutes and settled on four thousand, which she wanted in cash and in hand before she'd say a word.

All four of the CEO's were in town for the closing arguments and the verdict, so Fitch had a small fleet of finely appointed corporate jets at his disposal. He sent Swanson to New York on the Pynex plane.

Swanson arrived in the city at dusk and checked into a small hotel near Washington Square. According to a roommate, Beverly was not in, was not working, but she might be at a party. He called the pizzeria where she worked, and was told she had been fired. He called the roommate again, and got himself hung up on when he asked too many questions. He slammed the phone down and stomped around his room. How the hell do you find a person on the streets of Greenwich Village? He walked a few blocks to her apartment, his feet freezing in the cold rain. He drank coffee where he'd met her before while his shoes thawed and dried. He used a pay phone for another fruitless chat with the same roommate.

Marlee wanted one last meeting before the big Monday. They met in her little office. Fitch could've kissed her feet when he saw her.

He decided to tell her everything about Hoppy and Millie and his great scam gone bad. Nicholas had to work on Millie immediately, to soothe her before she contaminated her friends. After all, Hoppy had told Napier and Nitchman early Sunday that Millie was now a fierce advocate for the defense, that she was in there showing copies of the Robilio memo to her comrades. Was this true? If so, what in the world would she do now when she learned the truth about Hoppy? She'd be furious, no doubt. She'd flip-flop immediately. She'd probably tell her friends what a heinous thing the defense had done to her husband in an effort to pressure her.

It would be a disaster, no question about it.

Marlee listened straight-faced as Fitch unraveled the story. She wasn't shocked, but quite amused to see Fitch sweat.

'I think we should bump her,' Fitch declared when he was finished.

419

'Do you have a copy of the Robilio memo?' she asked, completely unmoved.

He picked one out of his briefcase and handed it to her. 'Some of your work?' she asked after she'd read it.

'Yes. It's completely bogus.'

She folded it and placed it under her chair. 'A helluva scam, Fitch.'

'Yeah, it was beautiful until we got caught.'

'Is this something you do in every tobacco trial?'

'We certainly try.'

'Why'd you pick Mr. Dupree?'

'We studied him carefully, and decided he'd be easy. Smalltown realtor, barely paying his bills, lots of money changing hands with the casinos and all, lots of his friends making big bucks. He fell for it immediately.'

'Have you been caught before?'

'We've had to abort scams, but we've never been caught red-handed.'

'Until today.'

'Not really. Hoppy and Millie might suspect it was somebody working for the tobacco company, but they don't know who. So, in that respect, there's still some doubt.'

'What's the difference?'

'None.'

'Relax, Fitch. I think her husband may have been exaggerating her effectiveness. Nicholas and Millie are quite close, and she hasn't become an advocate for your client.'

'Our client.'

'Right. Our client. Nicholas hasn't seen the memo.'

'You think Hoppy was lying?'

'Would you blame him? Your boys had him convinced he was about to be indicted.'

Fitch breathed a little easier and almost smiled. He said, 'It's imperative Nicholas talk to Millie tonight.

Hoppy will go over in a couple of hours and tell her all about it. Can Nicholas get to her quickly?'

'Fitch, Millie will vote the way he wants. Relax.'

Fitch relaxed. He removed his elbows from the table and tried to smile again. 'Just out of curiosity, how many votes do we have right now?'

'Nine.'

'Who are the other three?'

'Herman, Rikki, and Lonnie.'

'He hasn't discussed Rikki's past with her?'

'Not yet.'

'That'll make ten,' Fitch said, his eyes dancing, his fingers suddenly twitching. 'We can get eleven if we can bump somebody and pick up Shine Royce, right?'

'Look, Fitch, you're worrying too much. You've paid your money, you've hired the best, now relax and wait on your verdict. It's in very good hands.'

'Unanimous?' Fitch asked gleefully.

'Nicholas is determined to bring it back unanimous.'

Fitch sprang down the steps of the sagging building and bounced along the short sidewalk until he hit the street. For six blocks he whistled and almost skipped in the night air. José met him on foot and tried to keep up. He'd never seen his boss in such good spirits.

On one side of the conference room sat seven lawyers who'd each paid a million dollars for the privilege of sharing this event. No one else was in the room, no one but Wendall Rohr, who stood on the other side of the conference table and paced slowly back and forth, speaking softly with measured words, to his jury. His voice was warm and rich, filled with compassion one second and harsh words for Big Tobacco the next. He lectured and he cajoled. He was comical and he was angry. He showed them photographs, and he wrote figures on a chalkboard.

He finished in fifty-one minutes, the shortest

rehearsal so far. The closing had to be an hour or less, Harkin's orders. The comments from his peers were fast and mixed, some complimentary but most probing for ways to improve. No tougher audience could be found. The seven had combined for hundreds of closing arguments, arguments which had produced close to half a billion dollars in verdicts. They knew how to extract large sums of money from juries.

They had agreed to park their egos outside the door. Rohr took another beating, something he didn't do well, and agreed to perform again.

It had to be perfect. Victory was so close.

Cable underwent similar abuse. His audience was much larger – a dozen lawyers, several jury consultants, lots of paralegals. He was videotaped so he could study himself. He was determined to do it in half an hour. The jury would be appreciative. Rohr would no doubt run longer. The contrast would be nice – Cable the technician sticking to the facts versus Rohr the flamboyant mouthpiece tugging at their emotions.

He delivered his closing, then watched the video. Again and again, throughout Sunday afternoon and deep into the night.

By the time Fitch arrived at the beach house, he had managed to work himself back into his usual state of cautious pessimism. The four CEO's were waiting, having just finished a fine meal. Jankle was drunk and kept to himself by the fireplace. Fitch took some coffee and analyzed the last-minute efforts of the defense. The questions quickly got around to the wire transfers he'd demanded on Friday; two million from each of the four.

Prior to Friday, The Fund had a balance of six and a half million, certainly more than enough to complete the trial. What was the additional eight million for? And how much was in The Fund now?

Fitch explained that the defense had had a sudden, unplanned expenditure of the grandest proportions.

'Stop the games, Fitch,' said Luther Vandemeer of Trellco. 'Have you managed to finally purchase a verdict?'

Fitch tried not to lie to these four. They were, after all, his employers. He never told them the complete truth, and they didn't expect him to. But in response to a direct question, especially one of this magnitude, he felt compelled to make some effort at honesty. 'Something like that,' he said.

'Do you have the votes, Fitch?' asked another CEO.

Fitch paused and looked carefully at each of the four, including Jankle, who was suddenly attentive. 'I believe I do,' he said.

Jankle jumped to his feet, unsteady but quite focused, and stepped into the center of the room. 'Say it again, Fitch,' he demanded.

'You heard me,' Fitch said. 'The verdict has been purchased.' His voice couldn't resist a touch of pride.

The other three stood too. All four eased toward Fitch, forming a loose semicircle. 'How?' one of them asked.

'I'll never tell,' Fitch said coolly. 'The details are not important.'

'I demand to know,' Jankle said.

'Forget it. Part of my job is to do the dirty work while protecting you and your companies. If you want to terminate me, fine. But you'll never know the details.'

They stared at him during a long pause. The circle grew tighter. They slowly sipped their drinks and admired their hero. Eight times they'd been to the brink of disaster, and eight times Rankin Fitch had worked his dirty tricks and saved them. Now he'd done it for the ninth time. He was invincible.

And he'd never promised victory before, not like this. Just the opposite. He'd always anguished before each verdict, always predicting defeat and taking pleasure in making them miserable. This was so uncharacteristic.

'How much?' Jankle demanded.

It was something Fitch couldn't hide. For obvious reasons, these four had the right to know where the money went. They had installed a primitive accounting format for The Fund. Each company contributed equal amounts when Fitch said so, and each CEO was entitled to a monthly list of all expenses.

'Ten million,' Fitch said.

The drunk barked first. 'You've paid ten million dollars to a juror!' The other three were equally shocked.

'No. Not to a juror. Let's put it this way. I've purchased the verdict for ten million dollars, okay? That's all I will say. The Fund now has a balance of four-point-five million. And I'm not going to answer any questions about how the money changed hands.'

Maybe a sack of cash under the table might make sense. Five, ten thousand bucks maybe. But it was impossible to picture any of these small-town hicks on the jury possessing brains big enough to dream of ten million dollars. Surely it wasn't all going to one person.

They hung together near Fitch in stunned silence, each having the same thoughts. Surely Fitch had worked his wizardry on ten of them. That would make sense. He'd gotten ten and offered them a million each. That made a helluva lot more sense. Ten fresh new millionaires on the Gulf Coast. But how do you hide that kind of money?

Fitch savored the moment. 'Of course, nothing is guaranteed,' he said. 'You never know until the jury comes back.'

Well, it damned sure better be guaranteed, at the rate of ten million bucks. But they said nothing. Luther Vandemeer backed away first. He poured a stiffer brandy and sat on the piano bench near the baby grand.

Fitch would tell him later. He'd wait a month or two, get Fitch up to New York on business, and pick the story out of him.

Fitch said he had things to do. He wanted each of the four in the courtroom tomorrow for closing arguments. Don't sit together, he instructed.

THIRTY-SEVEN

There was a general feeling among the jurors that
Sunday night would be their last in sequestration. They
whispered that perhaps if they got the case by noon
Monday, then certainly they could reach a verdict by
Monday night and go home. This wasn't discussed
openly because it necessarily involved speculation about
the verdict, something Herman was quick to stifle.

The mood was light, though, and many of the jurors
quietly packed and tidied up their rooms. They
wanted their last visit to the Siesta Inn to be quick – a
dash in from court to gather packed bags and grab
toothbrushes.

Sunday was the third consecutive night of personal
visits, and collectively they'd had enough of their mates.
Especially the married ones. Three straight nights of
coziness in a small room was trying for most marriages.
Even the singles needed a night off. Savelle's woman
friend stayed away. Derrick told Angel he might stop by
later, but had some important business first. Loreen
didn't have a boyfriend, but she'd had enough of her
teenaged daughters for one weekend. Jerry and Poodle
were having their first little spat.

The motel was quiet Sunday night; no football and
beer in the Party Room, no checkers tournaments.
Marlee and Nicholas ate pizza in his room. They
covered their checklists and made final plans. Both

426

were nervous and tense, and managed only slight humor at her recounting of Fitch's sad story about Hoppy.

Marlee left at nine. She drove her leased car to her rented condo, where she finished packing her own things.

Nicholas walked across the hall where Hoppy and Millie were waiting like a couple of honeymooners. They couldn't thank him enough. He had exposed this horrible fraud and set them free again. It was shocking to think of the extreme measures the tobacco industry would go to just to pressure a juror.

Millie expressed her concern about remaining on the jury. She and Hoppy had already discussed it, and she didn't feel she could be fair and impartial in light of what they'd done to her husband. Nicholas had anticipated this. It was his opinion that he needed Millie.

And there was a more compelling reason. If Millie told Judge Harkin about the Hoppy scam, then he'd probably declare a mistrial. And that would be a tragedy. A mistrial would mean that in a year or two another jury would be picked to hear the same case. Each side would spend another fortune doing what they were doing right now. 'It's up to us, Millie. We've been chosen to decide this case, and it's our responsibility to reach a verdict. The next jury will be no smarter than us.'

'I agree,' Hoppy said. 'This trial will be over tomorrow. It'd be a shame to have a mistrial declared here at the last minute.'

So Millie bit her lip and found new resolve. Her friend Nicholas made everything easier.

Cleve met Derrick in the sports bar of the Nugget Casino Sunday night. They drank a beer, watched a football game, said little because Derrick was pouting and trying to appear angry at the screwing he claimed to be receiving. The fifteen thousand in cash was in a small brown packet that Cleve slid across the table and which Derrick took and stuffed in a pocket, without saying thanks or anything. Pursuant to their latest deal, the other ten thousand would be paid after the verdict, assuming of course that Angel voted with the plaintiff.

'Why don't you leave now?' Derrick said a few minutes after the money landed near his heart.

'Great idea,' Cleve said. 'Go see your girlfriend. Explain things carefully.'

'I can handle her.'

Cleve took his longneck with him, and disappeared.

Derrick drained his beer and rushed to the men's room, where he locked himself in a stall and counted the money, a hundred and fifty fresh, new, neatly packed hundred-dollar bills. He pressed the stack together and was amazed at its size – less than an inch thick. He divided it in quarters, and placed a folded wad in each pocket of his jeans.

The casino was bustling. He'd learned to shoot craps from an older brother who'd served in the Army, and for some reason, as if drawn by a magnet, he wandered near the crap tables. He watched for a minute, then decided to resist the temptation and go see Angel. He stopped for a quick beer at a small bar overlooking the roulette pit. Everywhere below him fortunes were being won and lost. It takes money to make money. It was his lucky night.

He bought a thousand dollars' worth of chips at a crap table, and enjoyed the attention that all big spenders command. The pit boss examined the unused bills, then smiled at Derrick. A blond waitress appeared from nowhere and he ordered another beer.

Derrick bet heavily, heavier than any white person at the table. The first batch of chips disappeared in fifteen minutes, and he never hesitated before cashing in for a thousand more.

Another thousand soon followed, then the dice got hot and Derrick won eighteen hundred dollars in five minutes. He bought more chips. The beers kept coming. The blond started flirting. The pit boss asked if he wanted to become a gold member of the Nugget.

He lost track of the money. He pulled it from all four pockets, then he replaced some of it. He bought more chips. After an hour, he was down six thousand dollars and wanted desperately to quit. But his luck had to change. The dice had been hot earlier; they'd get hot again. He decided to keep betting heavily, and when his luck turned he'd get it all back. Another beer, and he switched to scotch.

After a bad run, he pulled himself away from the table and returned to the men's room, same stall. He locked it and pulled loose bills from all four pockets. Down to seven thousand dollars, and he felt like crying. But he had to get it back. He decided to go out there and reclaim his money. He'd try a different table. He'd alter his betting. And, regardless of what happened, he would throw up his hands and bolt from the floor if, God help him, his pot dwindled down to five thousand. There was no way he'd lose the last five thousand.

He walked past a roulette table with no players, and on a whim placed five hundred-dollar chips on red. The dealer spun, red played, Derrick made five hundred dollars. He left the chips on red, and won again. With no hesitation, he left the twenty hundred-dollar chips on red, and won for the third straight time. Four thousand dollars in less than five minutes. He got a beer in the sports bar and watched a boxing match. Wild shouting from the crap pit told him to stay away. He felt fortunate to have almost eleven thousand dollars in his pocket.

It was past time for visiting Angel, but he had to see her. He purposely walked through the rows of slot machines, as far away from the crap tables as he could get. He walked fast, hoping to reach the front door before changing his mind and racing toward the dice. He made it.

He'd driven for only a minute, it seemed, when he saw blue lights behind him. It was a City of Biloxi police car, fast on his bumper, headlights flickering. Derrick had no mints or gum. He stopped, got out of the car, and waited for orders from the cop, who got up close and immediately smelled alcohol.

'Been drinking?' he asked.

'Oh, you know, couple of beers at the casino.'

The cop checked Derrick's eyes with a blinding flashlight, then made him walk a straight line and touch his nose with his fingers. Derrick was obviously drunk. He was handcuffed and taken to jail. He consented to a breath test and registered .18.

There were lots of questions about the cash stuffed in his pockets. The explanation made sense – he'd had a good night at the casino. But he had no job. He lived with a brother. No criminal record. The jailer listed his cash and other pocket items and locked it all away in a vault.

Derrick sat on a top bunk in the drunk tank, with two winos moaning on the floor. A phone would not help because he couldn't call Angel direct. A five-hour stay was mandatory for drunk drivers. He had to reach Angel before she left for court.

The phone woke Swanson at three-thirty Monday morning. The voice on the other end was thick and groggy, the words slurred but obviously belonging to Beverly Monk. 'Welcome to the Big Apple,' she said loudly, then laughed crazily, bombed out of her mind.

'Where are you?' Swanson demanded. 'I've got the money.'

'Later,' she said, then he heard two angry male voices in the background. 'We'll do it later.' Someone turned up the music.

430

'I need the information fast.'

'And I need the money.'

'Great. Tell me when and where.'

'Oh, I don't know,' she said, then yelled an obscenity at someone in the room.

Swanson gripped the receiver tighter. 'Look, Beverly, listen to me. You remember that little coffee shop where we met last time?'

'Yeah, I think.'

'On Eighth, near Balducci's.'

'Oh yeah.'

'Good. Meet me there as soon as you can.'

'How soon is that?' she asked, then erupted in laughter.

Swanson was patient. 'How about seven o'clock?'

'What time is it now?'

'Three-thirty.'

'Wow.'

'Look, why don't I come get you right now? Tell me where you are, and I'll grab a cab.'

'Naw, I'm okay. Just having some fun.'

'You're drunk.'

'So.'

'So, if you want this four thousand bucks, you'd better stay sober enough to meet me.'

'I'll be there, baby. What's your name again?'

'Swanson.'

'Right, Swanson. I'll be there at seven, or close to it.' She laughed as she hung up.

Swanson didn't bother to sleep again.

At five-thirty, Marvis Maples presented himself to the jailer and asked if he could collect his brother Derrick. The five hours were up. The jailer retrieved Derrick from the drunk tank, then unlocked a metal tray and placed it on the counter. Derrick inventoried the contents of the tray – eleven thousand dollars in cash, car keys, pocketknife, lip balm – as his brother stared in disbelief.

In the parking lot, Marvis asked about the cash and Derrick explained he'd had a good night at the crap tables. He gave Marvis two hundred dollars and asked if he could borrow his car. Marvis took the money and agreed to wait at the jail until Derrick's car was brought from the city lot.

Derrick raced to Pass Christian and parked behind the Siesta Inn just as the sky was dawning in the east. He crouched low, in case anyone happened by, and sneaked through shrubbery until he came to the window of Angel's room. It was locked, of course, and he began pecking on it. There was no response, and so he picked up a small rock and tapped louder. Daylight was landing all around him, and he was beginning to panic.

'Freeze!' came a loud voice very near his back.

Derrick jerked around to see Chuck, the uniformed deputy, aiming a long shiny black pistol at his forehead. He waved the gun. 'Get away from that window! Hands up.'

Derrick raised his hands and stepped through the shrubbery. 'On the ground' was the next command, and Derrick went spread-eagle on the cold sidewalk, hands behind him. Chuck radioed for help.

Marvis was still loitering around the jail waiting for Derrick's car when his brother returned for his second arrest of the night.

Angel slept through it all.

THIRTY-EIGHT

It was a shame the juror who'd been the most diligent, listened more carefully than the others, remembered more of what had been said, and obeyed every one of Judge Harkin's rules would be the last one bumped and thus prevented from affecting the verdict.

As reliable as the clock itself, Mrs. Herman Grimes arrived in the dining room at exactly seven-fifteen, took a tray, and began gathering the same breakfast items she had been gathering for almost two weeks. Bran cereal, skim milk, and a banana for Herman. Cornflakes, two percent milk, a strip of bacon, and apple juice for herself. As he often did, Nicholas met her at the buffet and offered to help. He still prepared Herman's coffee throughout the day in the jury room, and he felt obligated to help in the morning. Two sugars and one cream for Herman. Black for Mrs. Grimes. They chatted about whether or not they were packed and ready to go. She seemed genuinely excited at the prospect of eating dinner at home Monday night.

The mood had been downright festive throughout the morning as Nicholas and Henry Vu held court at the dining table and greeted the early stragglers. They were going home!

Mrs. Grimes reached for the silverware, and Nicholas quickly dropped four small tablets into Herman's coffee while saying something about the lawyers. It wouldn't kill him. It was Methergine, an obscure prescription drug used primarily in emergency rooms to revive bodies which were all but dead. Herman would be a sick man for four hours, then recover completely.

As he often did, Nicholas followed her down the hall to their room, carrying the tray and chatting on about this and that. She thanked him generously; such a nice young man.

The commotion hit thirty minutes later, and Nicholas was in the middle of it. Mrs. Grimes stepped into the hallway and yelled at Chuck, who was sitting at his post, sipping coffee and reading the newspaper. Nicholas heard her call, and rushed from his room. Something was wrong with Herman!

Lou Dell and Willis arrived amid panicked voices, and soon most of the jurors were outside the Grimeses' room, where the door was open and people were swarming. Herman was on the bathroom floor, bent double at the waist, clutching his stomach and in terrible pain. Mrs. Grimes and Chuck crouched over him. Lou Dell ran to the phone and called 911. Nicholas said gravely to Rikki Coleman that it was chest pains, maybe a heart attack. Herman had already had one, six years earlier.

Within minutes, everyone knew Herman was suffering from cardiac arrest.

The paramedics arrived with a stretcher, and Chuck pushed the other jurors farther down the hall. Herman was stabilized and given oxygen. His blood pressure was only slightly above normal. Mrs. Grimes said repeatedly it reminded her of his first heart attack.

They rolled him out and pushed him rapidly down the hall. In the confusion, Nicholas managed to knock over Herman's coffee cup.

The sirens wailed as Herman was sped away. The jurors retreated to their rooms to try and settle their frazzled nerves. Lou Dell called Judge Harkin to tell him Herman had fallen violently ill. The consensus was he'd had another heart attack.

'They're dropping like flies,' she said, then went on to recollect how she'd never lost so many jurors in her eighteen years as the jury madam. Harkin cut her off.

He really didn't expect her to arrive promptly at seven for coffee and the cash. Just a few hours earlier she'd been smashed and gave no indication of relenting, so how could he expect her to keep this appointment. He ate a long breakfast and read the first of many news-papers. Eight o'clock came and went. He moved to a better table near the window so he could watch the people on the sidewalk hustle by.

At nine, Swanson called her apartment and managed to pick another fight with the same roommate. No, she was not there, had not been there all night, and maybe she'd moved anyway.

This is someone's daughter, he told himself, living from loft to loft, day to day, scrounging for food and enough money to stay alive and buy the next round of chemicals. Did her parents know what she was doing?

He had plenty of time to consider these matters. At ten, he ordered dry toast because the waiter was staring now, obviously irritated that Swanson had evidently camped out for the day.

Fueled by rumors that were apparently well founded, Pynex' common opened strong. After closing Friday at seventy-three, it jumped to seventy-six at the opening bell and was at seventy-eight within minutes. There was good news out of Biloxi, though no one seemed to know the source. All tobacco stocks rose quickly in early, heavy trading.

Judge Harkin didn't appear until almost nine-thirty, and when he stepped to the bench he noted, without surprise, that his courtroom was packed. He'd just finished a heated argument with Rohr and Cable, the latter of whom wanted a mistrial because another juror had been removed. There were insufficient grounds for a mistrial. Harkin had done his homework. He'd even found an old case allowing eleven jurors to decide a civil case. Nine votes had been required, but the jury's verdict had been upheld by the Supreme Court.

As expected, news of Herman's cardiac arrest spread quickly among the many watching the trial. The jury consultants hired by the defense quietly declared it a major victory for their side because Herman was obviously pro-plaintiff. The jury consultants hired by the plaintiff assured Rohr and company that Herman's removal was a major blow to the defense because Herman was obviously pro-tobacco. All jury experts claimed to welcome the addition of Shine Royce, though most had difficulty with their reasoning.

Fitch just sat in stunned amazement. How in hell do you give someone a heart attack? Was Marlee cold-blooded enough to poison a blind man? Thank God she was on his side.

The door opened. The jurors filed in. Everyone watched to make sure Herman was in fact not among them. His seat was empty.

Judge Harkin had talked to a doctor at the hospital, and he began by telling the jurors that Herman appeared to be responding well, that perhaps it was not as serious as initially thought. The jurors, especially Nicholas, were mightily relieved. Shine Royce became juror number five, and took Herman's old seat on the front row between Phillip Savelle and Angel Weese.

Shine was right proud of himself.

When all was settled and still, His Honor instructed Wendall Rohr to begin his final summation. Keep it under an hour, he warned. Rohr, wearing his favorite gaudy jacket but with a starched shirt and clean bow tie,

436

began softly by apologizing for the length of the trial, and thanking them for being such a wonderful jury. With the friendly remarks behind him, he launched into a vicious description of '. . . the deadliest consumer product ever manufactured. The cigarette. It kills four hundred thousand Americans each year, ten times more than illegal drugs. No other product comes close.'

He hit the high points of the testimony of Drs. Fricke, Bronsky, and Kilvan, and he did so without belaboring what they'd said. He reminded them of Lawrence Krigler, a man who'd worked in the industry and knew its dirty secrets. He spent ten minutes talking casually about Leon Robilio, the voiceless one who'd worked for twenty years promoting tobacco, then realized how corrupt the industry was.

Rohr hit his stride when he got around to the kids. For Big Tobacco to survive, it must hook teenagers and ensure the next generation will buy its products. As if he'd been listening in the jury room, Rohr asked the jurors to ask themselves how old they'd been when they started smoking.

Three thousand kids a day pick up the habit. A third of these will eventually die from it. What else had to be said? Wasn't it time to force these rich corporations to stand behind their products? Time to get their attention? Time to make them leave our children alone? Time to make them pay for the damages caused by their products?

He turned nasty when he dwelt on nicotine and Big Tobacco's stubborn insistence that it is not addictive. Former drug addicts had testified that it was easier to quit marijuana and cocaine than cigarettes. He got even meaner when he mentioned Jankle and his abuse theory.

Then he blinked once and was a different person. He talked about his client, Mrs. Celeste Wood, a fine wife, mother, friend, a real victim of the tobacco industry. He

437

talked about her husband, the deceased Mr. Jacob Wood, who'd gotten hooked on Bristols, the star of the Pynex product line, and tried to kick the habit for twenty years. He left behind children and grand-children. Dead at the age of fifty-one because he'd used a legally manufactured product precisely in the manner in which it was supposed to be used.

He stepped to a white marker board on a tripod and did some quick math. The monetary value of Jacob Wood's life was, say, a million dollars. He added in some other damages and the total became two million. These were the actual damages, monetary amounts the family was entitled to because of Jacob's death.

But the case wasn't about actual damages. Rohr delivered a mini-lecture on punitive damages and their role in keeping corporate America in line. How do you punish a company that has eight hundred million dollars in cash?

You get the company's attention.

Rohr was careful not to suggest a figure, though legally he could have. He simply left $800,000,000 CASH in bold print on the board as he returned to the lectern and finished his remarks. He thanked the jury again, and sat down. Forty-eight minutes.

His Honor declared a ten-minute recess.

She was four hours late, but Swanson could've hugged her nonetheless. He didn't, though, because he feared infectious diseases, and because she was escorted by a grimy young man in black leather from toe to cap, jet black hair and goatee, dyed. The word JADE was tattooed impressively in the center of his forehead, and he wore a handsome collection of earrings on both sides of his head.

Jade said nothing as he pulled a chair close and perched on guard like a Doberman.

Beverly appeared to have been beaten. Her lower lip

was cut and puffy. She'd tried to cover a bruise on her cheek with makeup. The corner of her right eye was swollen. She smelled of rancid pot smoke and cheap bourbon, and she was on something, probably speed.

With little provocation, Swanson could've slapped Jade across his tattoo and slowly ripped out the earrings.

'Have you got the money?' she asked, glancing at Jade, who stared blankly at Swanson. No doubt where the money was going.

'Yes. Tell me about Claire.'

'Lemme see the money.'

Swanson removed a small envelope, opened it slightly to reveal the bills, then tucked it under both hands on the table. 'Four thousand bucks. Now talk quickly,' he said, glaring at Jade.

Beverly looked at Jade, who nodded like a bad actor and said, 'Go ahead.'

'Her real name is Gabrielle Brant. She's from Columbia, Missouri. She went to college at the university there, where her mother taught medieval studies. That's all I know.'

'What about her father?'

'I think he's dead.'

'Anything else?'

'No. Gimme the money.'

Swanson slid it across the table, and immediately jumped to his feet. 'Thanks,' he said, and disappeared.

It took Durwood Cable slightly more than half an hour to skillfully discount the ridiculous notion of giving millions to the family of a man who'd voluntarily smoked for thirty-five years. The trial was hardly more than a naked grab for money.

What he resented most about the plaintiff's case was that they had attempted to shift the issues away from Jacob Wood and his habits, and turn the trial into an emotional debate on teenage smoking. What did Jacob Wood have to do with current cigarette advertising? There wasn't an ounce of proof that the late Mr. Wood had been influenced by an ad campaign. He had started smoking because he chose to start.

Why bring the kids into this fight? Emotion, that's why. We respond angrily when we think children are being hurt or manipulated. And before the plaintiff's lawyers can convince you, the jurors, to hand them a fortune, they must first make you angry.

Cable deftly appealed to their sense of fairness. Decide the case on its facts, not on emotions. When he finished, he had their complete attention.

As he took his seat, Judge Harkin thanked him and said to the jury, 'Ladies and gentlemen, the case now belongs to you. I suggest you select a new foreman to take the place of Mr. Grimes, who I'm told is doing much better. I talked to his wife during the last recess, and he is still quite ill but expected to recover fully. If for any reason you need to speak to me, please notify madam clerk. The rest of your instructions will be handed to you in the jury room. Good luck.'

As Harkin bid them farewell, Nicholas turned slightly to the audience and locked eyes with Rankin Fitch, just a brief acknowledgment of where matters were at the moment. Fitch nodded, and Nicholas stood with his colleagues.

It was almost noon. Court was in recess subject to the call of the bench, which meant that those who wanted to were free to loiter about until the jury reached a verdict. The horde from Wall Street sprinted out to call their offices. The Big Four CEO's mingled with underlings for a moment, then made their way out of the courtroom.

Fitch left immediately and went to his office. Konrad was hovering over a bank of phones. 'It's her,' he said anxiously. 'She's calling from a pay phone.' Fitch

440

walked even faster to his office, where he grabbed his phone. 'Hello.'

'Fitch, look. New wiring instructions. Put me on hold and go to your fax.' Fitch looked at his private fax, which was transmitting.

'It's right here,' he said. 'Why new instructions?'

'Shut up, Fitch. Just do as I say, and do it immediately.'

Fitch yanked the fax from his machine and skimmed the handwritten message. The money was now headed to Panama. Banco Atlántico, in Panama City. She had routing instructions and account numbers.

'You have twenty minutes, Fitch. The jury is eating lunch. If I don't have a confirmation by twelve-thirty, then the deal is off and Nicholas changes directions. He has a cellphone in his pocket, and he's waiting for me to call.'

'Call back at twelve-thirty,' Fitch said, hanging up. He told Konrad to hold all calls. No exceptions. He immediately faxed her message to his wiring expert in D.C., who in turn faxed the necessary authorization to Hanwa Bank in the Netherlands Antilles. Hanwa had been on standby all morning, and within ten minutes the money left Fitch's account and bounced across the Caribbean to the bank in Panama City, where it had been expected. A confirmation from Hanwa was faxed to Fitch, who, at the moment, would've loved to fax it to Marlee, but he didn't have her number.

At twelve-twenty, Marlee called her banker in Panama, who confirmed the receipt of ten million dollars.

Marlee was in a motel room five miles away, working with a portable fax. She waited five minutes, then sent instructions to the same banker to wire the money to a bank in the Cayman Islands. All of it, and once it's gone, close the account in Banco Atlántico.

Nicholas called at exactly twelve-thirty. He was

441

hiding in the men's room. Lunch was over, and it was time to start the deliberations. Marlee said the money was safe, and that she was leaving.

Fitch waited until almost one. She called from another pay phone. 'The money has arrived, Fitch,' she said.

'Great. How about lunch?'

'Maybe later.'

'So when can we expect a verdict?'

'Late afternoon. I hope you're not worried, Fitch.'

'Me. Never.'

'Just relax. It'll be your finest hour. Twelve to zip, Fitch. How does that sound?'

'Like music. Why'd you bump poor old Herman?'

'Don't know what you're talking about.'

'Yeah right. When can we celebrate?'

'I'll call you later.'

She sped away in a rented car, watching every movement behind her. Her leased car was sitting in front of her condo, abandoned for all she cared. In the backseat she had two bags stuffed with clothing, the only personal items she could pack, along with the portable fax. The furniture in the condo would belong to whoever bought it at a sidewalk sale.

She looped through a subdivision, a run she'd practiced yesterday in case anyone wanted to follow. Fitch's boys weren't behind her. She zigzagged through side streets until she came to the Gulfport Municipal Airport, where the small Lear Jet was waiting. She grabbed her two bags and locked the keys in the car.

Swanson called once, but couldn't get through. He called the supervisor in Kansas City, and three agents were immediately dispatched to Columbia, an hour away. Two more worked the phones, making rapid calls to the University of Missouri, to the medieval studies department, in a desperate attempt to locate someone

442

who knew something and was willing to talk. Six Brants were listed in the Columbia phone book. All were called more than once and none claimed to know Gabrielle Brant.

He finally got Fitch on the phone just after one. Fitch had been barricaded in his office for an hour, taking no calls. Swanson was on his way to Missouri.

THIRTY-NINE

When the lunch dishes were cleared and all the smokers had returned from the smoke room, it became apparent that they were now supposed to do what they'd been dreaming about for a month. They took their places around the table, and stared at the empty seat at the end, the one Herman had so proudly occupied.

'Guess we need a new foreman,' Jerry said.

'And I think it should be Nicholas,' Millie added quickly.

There really wasn't any doubt about who the new foreman would be. No one else wanted the job, and Nicholas seemed to know as much about the trial as the lawyers themselves. He was elected by acclamation.

He stood by Herman's old chair and summarized a list of suggestions from Judge Harkin. He said, 'He wants us to carefully consider all the evidence, including the exhibits and documents, before we start voting.' Nicholas turned to his left and stared at a table in a corner piled high with all those wonderful reports and studies they'd been collecting for the last four weeks.

'I'm not planning on staying here for three days,' Lonnie said as they all looked at the table. 'In fact, I'm ready to vote now.'

'Not so fast,' Nicholas said. 'This is a complicated, very important case, and it would be wrong to rush things without thoughtful deliberation.'

'I say we vote,' Lonnie said.

'And I say we do what the Judge says. We can call him in for a chat, if necessary.'

'We're not going to read all that stuff, are we?' asked Sylvia the Poodle. Reading was not one of her favorite pastimes.

'I have an idea,' Nicholas said. 'Why don't we each take a report, skim it, then summarize it for everyone else? We can then honestly tell Judge Harkin that we reviewed all the exhibits and documents.'

'Do you really think he'll want to know?' asked Rikki Coleman.

'Probably so. Our verdict must be based on the evidence before us – the testimony we heard and the exhibits we've been given. We at least have to make an effort to follow his orders.'

'I agree,' said Millie. 'We all want to go home, but our duty demands that we carefully consider what's before us.'

With that, the other protests were snuffed out. Millie and Henry Vu lifted the bulky reports and placed them in the center of the table, where they were slowly taken by the jurors.

'Just skim through them,' Nicholas said, coaxing them along like a flustered schoolteacher. He grabbed the thickest one, a study by Dr. Milton Fricke on the effects of cigarette smoke on the respiratory tract, and he read it as if he'd never seen such dynamic prose.

In the courtroom, a few of the curious hung around for a spell in hopes there might be a quick verdict. This often happened – get the jury back there, feed 'em lunch, let 'em vote, and you've got yourself a verdict. The jury had made up its mind before the first witness.

But not this one.

At forty-one thousand feet and at five hundred miles per hour, the Lear made the trip from Biloxi to George

Town, Grand Cayman, in ninety minutes. Marlee cleared customs with a new Canadian passport, one issued to Lane MacRoland, a pretty young lady from Toronto who was down for a week of pleasure, no business. As required by Caymanian law, she also possessed a return air ticket, which showed her booked on a Delta flight to Miami in six days. The Caymanians were delighted to have tourists, but had other thoughts about new citizens.

The passport was part of a perfect set of new papers she'd purchased from a noted forger in Montreal. Passport, driver's license, birth certificate, voter's registration card. Cost: three thousand dollars.

She took a cab into George Town and found her bank, the Royal Swiss Trust, in a stately old building a block from the seafront. She'd never been to Grand Cayman before, though it felt like a second home. She'd been studying the place for two months. Her financial affairs there had been carefully arranged by fax.

The tropical air was heavy and warm, but she hardly noticed. She wasn't there for the sun and beaches. It was three o'clock in George Town and New York. Two P.M. in Mississippi.

She was greeted by a receptionist and led to a small office where another form had to be completed, one that couldn't be faxed. Within minutes, a young man named Marcus introduced himself. They had spoken many times on the phone. He was slender, well groomed, well tailored, very European, with a slight accent to his perfect English.

The money had arrived, he informed her, and Marlee managed to take the news while suppressing any sign of a smile. It was difficult. The paperwork was in order. She followed him upstairs to his office. Marcus' title was vague, like a lot of bankers' titles in Grand Cayman, but he was a vice president of this or that, and he managed portfolios.

A secretary brought coffee and Marlee ordered a sandwich.

Pynex was at seventy-nine, up strongly all day in heavy trading, Marcus reported while pecking at his computer. Trellco was up three and a quarter to fifty-six. Smith Greer was up two to sixty-four and a half. ConPack was trading even at around thirty-three.

Working from notes which were virtually memorized, Marlee made her first trade by selling short fifty thousand shares of Pynex at seventy-nine. Hopefully, she would buy it back in the very near future at a much lower price. Short selling was a tricky maneuver normally used by only the most sophisticated investors. If the price of a stock was about to fall, trading rules allowed the stock to be sold first at the higher price, then purchased later at a lower one.

With ten million in cash, Marlee would be allowed to sell approximately twenty million dollars' worth of stocks.

Marcus confirmed the trade with a flurry of key-punching, and he excused himself for a second while he put on his headset. Her second trade was the short selling of Trellco – thirty thousand shares at fifty-six and a quarter. He confirmed it, and then came the flurry. She sold forty thousand shares of Smith Greer at sixty-four and a half; sixty thousand more of Pynex at seventy-nine and an eighth; thirty thousand more of Trellco at fifty-six and an eighth; fifty thousand of Smith Greer at sixty-four and three-eighths.

She paused and instructed Marcus to watch Pynex closely. She had just unloaded one hundred and ten thousand shares of its stock, and was very concerned about the immediate response on Wall Street. It stalled at seventy-nine, dropped to seventy-eight and three-quarters, then eased back to seventy-nine.

'I think it's safe now,' said Marcus, who'd been watching the stock closely for two weeks.

'Sell fifty thousand more,' she said without hesitation.

Marcus skipped one beat, then nodded at his monitor and completed the trade.

Pynex dipped to seventy-eight and a half, then down another quarter. She sipped her coffee and fiddled with her notes as Marcus watched and Wall Street reacted. She thought about Nicholas, and what he was doing right now, but she wasn't worried. In fact, she was remarkably calm at the moment.

Marcus removed his headset. 'That's approximately twenty-two million dollars, Ms. MacRoland. I think we should stop. More sales will require approval from my superior.'

'That's enough,' she said.

'The market closes in fifteen minutes. You're welcome to wait in our client lounge.'

'No thanks. I'll go to the hotel, maybe get some sun.'

Marcus stood and buttoned his jacket. 'One question. When do you anticipate movement on these stocks?'

'Tomorrow. Early.'

'Significant movement?'

Marlee stood and held her notes. 'Yes. If you want your other clients to think you're a genius, then short sell tobacco right now.'

He sent for a company car, a small Mercedes, and Marlee was driven to a hotel on Seven Mile Beach, not far from downtown and the bank.

If Marlee's present seemed under control, her past was rapidly catching up with her. An operative digging for Fitch at the University of Missouri found a collection of old admissions manuals in the main library. In 1986, a Dr. Evelyn Y. Brant was listed and briefly described as a professor of medieval studies, but she was absent from the 1987 handbook.

He immediately called an associate who was checking through tax rolls at the Boone County Courthouse. The associate went straight to the clerk's office and within minutes found the Wills and Estates register. Evelyn Y. Brant's will had been received for probate in April of 1987. A clerk helped him find the file.

It was pay dirt. Mrs. Brant had died on March 2, 1987, in Columbia, at the age of fifty-six. She left no husband and one child, Gabrielle, age twenty-one, who inherited everything under a will Dr. Brant signed three months before her death.

The file was an inch thick, and the agent scanned it with great speed. The inventory consisted of a house valued at $180,000 with a mortgage of half that, a car, an unimpressive list of furniture and furnishings, a certificate of deposit at a local bank in the amount of $32,000, and a stock and bond portfolio valued at $202,000. There were only two creditors' claims filed; evidently Dr. Brant had known death was imminent and obtained legal advice. With the approval of Gabrielle, the house was sold, the estate was reduced to cash, and after estate taxes, legal fees, and court costs, the sum of $191,500 was placed in a trust. Gabrielle was the only beneficiary.

The estate had been handled without the slightest hint of acrimony. The lawyer appeared to be prompt and quite competent. Thirteen months after Dr. Brant's death, the estate was closed.

He flipped through again, making notes. Two pages stuck together, and he delicately pulled them apart. The bottom one was a half sheet with an official stamp on it.

It was the death certificate. Dr. Evelyn Y. Brant had died of lung cancer.

He stepped into the hallway and called his supervisor.

By the time the call was placed to Fitch, they knew more. A careful reading of the file by another operative,

449

this one a former FBI agent with a law degree, revealed a series of donations to such groups as the American Lung Association, the Coalition for a Smoke Free World, the Tobacco Task Force, the Clean Air Campaign, and a half-dozen other antismoking causes. One of the creditors' claims was a bill for almost twenty thousand dollars for her last hospital stay. Her husband, the late Dr. Peter Brant, was listed on an old insurance policy. A quick search of the register listed the opening of his estate in 1981. His file was located on the other side of the clerk's office. He died in June of 1981 at the age of fifty-two, leaving his beloved wife and cherished daughter, Gabrielle, then age fifteen. He died at home, according to his death certificate, which was signed by the same doctor who'd signed Evelyn Brant's. An oncologist.

Peter Brant had also succumbed to the ravages of lung cancer.

Swanson made the call, but only after being repeatedly assured that the facts were correct.

Fitch took the call in his office, alone, with the door locked, and he took it calmly because he was too shocked to react. He was seated at his desk with his jacket off, tie undone, shoes unlaced. He said little.

Both of Marlee's parents had died of lung cancer.

He actually scribbled this on a yellow pad, then drew a circle around it, with lines branching off, as if he could flow-chart this news, break it down, analyze it; somehow he could make it fit with her promise to deliver a verdict.

'Are you there, Rankin?' Swanson asked after a long silence.

'Yeah,' Fitch said, then continued saying nothing for a while. The flow chart grew but went nowhere.

'Where's the girl?' Swanson asked. He was standing in the cold outside the county courthouse in Columbia

450

with an impossibly small phone pressed to his jaw.

'Don't know. We'll have to find her.' He said this with no conviction whatsoever, and Swanson knew the girl was gone.

Another long pause.

'What shall I do?' Swanson asked.

'Get back here, I guess,' Fitch said, then abruptly hung up. The numbers on his digital clock were blurred, and Fitch closed his eyes. He massaged his pounding temples, pressed his goatee hard against his chin, contemplated an eruption with the desk flying against the wall and phones ripped from sockets, but thought the better of it. A cool head was needed.

Short of burning the courthouse or tossing grenades at the jury room, there was nothing he could do to stop the deliberations. They were in there, the last twelve, with deputies by the door. Perhaps if their work was slow, and if they had to retire for another night in sequestration, then perhaps Fitch could pull a rabbit from his hat and spark a mistrial.

A bomb threat was a possibility. The jurors would be evacuated, sequestered some more, led away to some hidden place so they could continue.

The flow chart fizzled and he made lists of possibilities – outrageous acts, all of which would be dangerous, illegal, and destined for failure.

The clock was ticking.

The chosen twelve – eleven disciples and their master.

He slowly rose to his feet and took the cheap ceramic lamp with both hands. It was a lamp Konrad had earlier wanted to remove because it sat on Fitch's desk, a place of great chaos and violence.

Konrad and Pang were loitering in the hallway, waiting for instructions. They knew something had gone terribly wrong. The lamp crashed with great force against the door. Fitch screamed. The plywood walls rattled. Another object hit and splintered; maybe it was a telephone. Fitch yelled something about 'the money!' and then the desk landed loudly against a wall.

They backed away, petrified and not wanting to be near the door when it opened. Bam! Bam! Bam! It sounded like a jackhammer. Fitch was punching the plywood with his fists.

'Find the girl!' he screamed in anguish. Bam! Bam! 'Find the girl!'

FORTY

After a painful stretch of forced concentration, Nicholas sensed some debate was needed. He elected to go first, and briefly summarized Dr. Fricke's report on the condition of Jacob Wood's lungs. He passed around the autopsy photos, none of which attracted much attention. This was old territory and the audience was bored.

'Dr. Fricke's report says that prolonged cigarette smoking causes lung cancer,' Nicholas said dutifully, as if this might surprise someone.

'I have an idea,' Rikki Coleman said. 'Let's see if we can all agree that cigarettes cause lung cancer. It'll save us a lot of time.' She'd been waiting for a crack in the door, and seemed ready to quarrel.

'Great idea,' Lonnie said. He was by far the most hyper and frustrated of the bunch.

Nicholas shrugged his approval. He was the foreman, but he still had only one vote. The jury could do what it pleased. 'Fine with me,' he said. 'Does everyone believe cigarettes cause lung cancer? Raise your hands.'

Twelve hands shot up, and a giant step was taken toward a verdict.

'Let's go ahead and take care of addiction,' Rikki said, looking up and down the table. 'Who thinks nicotine is addictive?'

Another unanimous yes.

She savored the moment and appeared on the verge of venturing onto the thin ice of liability.

'Let's keep it unanimous, folks,' Nicholas said. 'It's crucial that we walk out of here united. If we split, then we fail.'

Most of them had already heard this little pep talk. The legal reasons behind his quest for a unanimous verdict were not clear, but they believed him nonetheless.

'Now, let's finish these reports. Is someone ready?'

Loreen Duke's was a glossy publication prepared by Dr. Myra Sprawling-Goode. She'd read the introduction, which declared the study to be a thorough review of advertising practices by tobacco companies, especially how said practices related to children under the age of eighteen, and she'd read the conclusion, which absolved the industry of targeting underage smokers. Most of the two hundred pages in between had gone untouched.

She summarized the summary. 'Just says here they couldn't find any evidence of tobacco companies advertising to attract kids.'

'Do you believe that?' asked Millie.

'No. I thought we'd already decided that most folks start smoking before they're eighteen. Didn't we take a poll in here one day?'

'We did,' Rikki answered. 'And all the smokers here started when they were young teenagers.'

'And most of them quit, as I recall,' Lonnie said, with no small amount of bitterness.

'Let's move along,' Nicholas said. 'Anybody else?'

Jerry offered a lame effort at describing the tedious findings of Dr. Hilo Kilvan, the statistical genius who'd proven the increased risks of lung cancer among smokers. Jerry's summation sparked no interest, no questions, no debate, and he left the room for a quick smoke.

Then there was silence as they continued to plow through the printed material. They came and went at will – to smoke, to stretch, to use the rest rooms. Lou Dell and Willis and Chuck guarded the door.

Mrs. Gladys Card had once taught biology to ninth-graders. She had a grasp of science. She did a superb job of dissecting Dr. Robert Bronsky's report on the composition of cigarette smoke – the more than four thousand compounds, the sixteen known carcinogens, the fourteen alkalis, the irritants, and all that other stuff. She used her best classroom diction and looked from face to face.

Most faces cringed as she droned on and on.

When she finished, Nicholas, still awake, thanked her warmly and stood to get more coffee.

'So what do you think about all that?' Lonnie asked. He was standing in front of the window, his back to the room, eating peanuts and holding a soft drink.

'To me, it proves cigarette smoke is pretty harmful,' she answered.

Lonnie turned around and looked at her. 'Right. I thought we'd already decided that.' He then looked at Nicholas. 'I say we get on with the voting. We've been reading now for almost three hours, and if the Judge asks me if I've looked at all that stuff, I'm gonna say, "Hell yeah. Read every word."'

'Do what you wanna do, Lonnie,' Nicholas shot back.

'All right. Let's vote.'

'Vote on what?' Nicholas asked. The two were now standing on opposite sides of the table, with the seated jurors between them.

'Let's see who's standing where. I'll go first.'

'Go. Let's hear it.'

Lonnie took a deep breath and everyone turned to watch him.

'My position is real easy. I believe cigarettes are dangerous products. They're addictive. They're deadly. That's why I leave them alone. Everybody knows this, in fact we've already decided it. I believe every person has a right to choose. Nobody can force you to smoke, but if you do, then you suffer the consequences. Don't puff like hell for thirty years, then expect me to make you rich. These crazy lawsuits need to be stopped.'

His voice was loud and every word got absorbed.

'You finished?' Nicholas asked.

'Yeah.'

'Who's next?'

'I have a question,' said Mrs. Gladys Card. 'How much money does the plaintiff expect us to award? Mr. Rohr sort of left it hanging.'

'He wants two million in actual damages. The punitive is left to our discretion,' Nicholas explained.

'Then why'd he leave eight hundred million on the board?'

'Because he'd take eight hundred million,' Lonnie replied. 'Are you gonna give it to him?'

'I don't think so,' she said. 'I didn't know there was that much money in the world. Would Celeste Wood get all of it?'

'You see all those lawyers out there?' Lonnie asked sardonically. 'She'll be lucky to get anything. This trial ain't about her or her dead husband. This trial is about a bunch of lawyers getting rich suing tobacco companies. We're stupid if we fall for it.'

'Do you know when I started smoking?' Angel Weese asked Lonnie, who was still standing.

'No. I don't.'

'I remember the exact day. I was thirteen, and I saw this big billboard on Decatur Street, not far from my house, had this big, lean black guy, really good-looking, with his jeans rolled up, splashing water on a beach, cigarette in one hand and a slinky black chick on his

456

back. All smiles. All perfect teeth. Salem menthols. What great fun. I thought to myself, Now there's the good life. I'd like to have some of that. So I went home, went to my drawer, got my money, walked down the street, and bought a pack of Salem menthols. My friends thought I was so cool, so I've been smoking them ever since.' She paused and glanced at Loreen Duke, then back to Lonnie. 'Don't try to tell me anyone can kick the habit. I'm addicted, okay. It ain't that easy. I'm twenty years old, two packs a day, and if I don't quit I won't see fifty. And don't tell me they don't target kids. They target blacks, women, kids, cowboys, rednecks, they target everybody, and you know it.'

For one who'd shown no emotion in the four weeks they'd been together, the anger in Angel's voice was a surprise. Lonnie glared down at her, but said nothing.

Loreen came to her aid. 'One of my girls, the fifteen-year-old, told me last week she'd started smoking at school because all of her friends are now smoking. These kids are too young to know about addiction, and by the time they realize, they'll be hooked. I asked her where she gets her cigarettes. You know what she told me?'

Lonnie said nothing.

'Vending machines. There's one next to the arcade at the mall where the kids hang out. And there's one in the lobby of the cinema where the kids hang out. A couple of the fast-food places have machines. And you're gonna tell me they don't target kids. It makes me sick. I can't wait to get home and straighten her out.'

'So what're you gonna do when she starts drinking beer?' Jerry asked. 'You gonna sue Budweiser for ten million because all the other kids are sneaking beer?'

'There's no proof that beer is physically addictive,' Rikki responded.

'Oh, so it doesn't kill?'

'There's a difference.'

457

'Please explain it,' Jerry said. The debate now covered two of his favorite vices. Could gambling and philandering be next?

Rikki arranged her thoughts for a second, then launched into an unpleasant defense of alcohol. 'Cigarettes are the only products that are deadly if used exactly as intended. Alcohol is supposed to be consumed, of course, but in reasonable amounts. And if it's taken in moderation, then it's not a dangerous product. Sure, people get drunk and kill themselves in all sorts of ways, but a strong argument can be made that the product is not being used properly in those instances.'

'So if a person drinks for fifty years he's not killing himself?'

'Not if he drinks in moderation.'

'Boy, that's good to hear.'

'And there's something else. Alcohol has a natural warning. You get an immediate feedback when you use the product. Not so with tobacco. It takes years of smoking before you realize the damage to your body. By then, you're hooked and can't quit.'

'Most people can quit,' Lonnie said from the window, without looking at Angel.

'And why do you think everyone's trying to quit?' Rikki asked calmly. 'Is it because they're enjoying their cigarettes? Is it because they feel young and glamorous? No, they're trying to quit to avoid lung cancer and heart disease.'

'So how are you voting?' Lonnie asked.

'I guess it's pretty obvious,' she answered. 'I started this trial with an open mind, but I've come to realize that the only way to hold the tobacco companies responsible is for us to do it.'

'What about you?' Lonnie asked Jerry, hoping to find a friend.

'I'm undecided right now. I think I'll listen to everybody else.'

'And you?' he asked Sylvia Taylor-Tatum.

'I'm having a hard time understanding why we're supposed to make this woman a multimillionaire.'

Lonnie walked around the table, looking at faces, most of which tried to avoid him. There was no doubt he was enjoying his role as a rebel leader. 'What about you, Mr. Savelle? You don't seem to say much.'

This would be interesting. No one on the panel had a clue about what Savelle was thinking.

'I believe in choice,' he said. 'Absolute choice. I deplore what these corporations do to the environment. I hate their products. But each person has the power to choose.'

'Mr. Vu?' Lonnie said.

Henry cleared his throat, pondered things for a minute, then said, 'I'm still thinking.' Henry would follow Nicholas, who for the moment was incredibly quiet.

'What about you, Mr. Foreman?' Lonnie asked.

'We can finish these reports in thirty minutes. Let's do it, then we'll start voting.'

After the first serious skirmish, they were relieved to read for a few more minutes. The shootout was clearly not far away.

At first he felt like roaming the streets in his Suburban with José at the wheel, up and down Highway 90 to no place in particular, no chance of catching her. At least he'd be out there doing something, trying to find her, hoping maybe to stumble upon her.

He knew she was gone.

So he stayed instead in his office, alone by the phone praying she'd call one more time and tell him a deal was a deal. Throughout the afternoon Konrad came and went, bearing the news that Fitch expected to hear: Her car was outside the condo, and it hadn't been moved in eight hours. No activity in or out of the condo. No sign of her whatsoever. She was gone.

459

Oddly, the longer the jury stayed out, the more hope Fitch managed to create for himself. If she planned to take the money and run, and screw Fitch with a plaintiff's verdict, then where was the verdict? Maybe it wouldn't be that easy. Nicholas could be having a hard time in there getting his votes.

Fitch had never lost one of these, and he kept reminding himself he'd been here before, sweating blood while the jury fought.

At precisely five, Judge Harkin reconvened his courtroom, and sent for the jury. The lawyers scurried to get in place. Most of the spectators returned.

The jurors took their seats. They looked tired, but then all jurors did at this point.

'Just a few quick questions,' His Honor said. 'Have you elected a new foreman?'

They nodded, and then Nicholas raised his hand. 'I have the honor,' he said softly, without the slightest trace of pride.

'Good. Just so you'll know, I talked with Herman Grimes about an hour ago, and he's doing fine. Seems to be something other than a heart attack, and he's expected to be released tomorrow. He sent his best wishes.'

Most of them managed a pleasant expression.

'Now, you've had the case for five hours, and I'd like to know if you're making progress.'

Nicholas stood awkwardly, and stuffed his hands in his khakis. 'I think so, Your Honor.'

'Good. Without indicating anything that's been discussed, do you think the jury will reach a verdict, one way or the other?'

Nicholas glanced around at his peers, then said, 'I think we will, Your Honor. Yes, I'm confident we'll have a verdict.'

'When might you have a verdict? Mind you, I'm not

rushing. You can take as much time as you wish. I just need to make plans for this courtroom if we're gonna be here into the night.'

'We want to go home, Your Honor. We're determined to wrap this up and have a verdict sometime tonight.'

'Wonderful. Thank you. Dinner is on the way. I'll be in my chambers if you need me.'

461

FORTY-ONE

Mr. O'Reilly was back for the last time, serving his final meal and saying good-bye to people he now considered friends. He and three employees fed and served them as if they were royalty.

Dinner was over at six-thirty, and the jury was ready to go home. They agreed to vote first on the issue of liability. Nicholas couched the question in layman's terms: 'Are you willing to hold Pynex liable for the death of Jacob Wood?'

Rikki Coleman, Millie Dupree, Loreen Duke, and Angel Weese said yes, unequivocally. Lonnie, Phillip Savelle, and Mrs. Gladys Card said no, without question. The rest fell somewhere in between. Poodle was uncertain, but leaning toward no. Jerry was suddenly vacillating, but probably leaning toward no. Shine Royce, the newest member of the panel, hadn't said three words all day and was simply drifting in the breeze. He'd jump on the nearest bandwagon, as soon as he could identify one. Henry Vu declared himself to be undecided, but he was really waiting for Nicholas, who was waiting until everybody had finished. He was disappointed that the jury was so divided.

'I think it's time for you to declare,' Lonnie said to Nicholas, itching for a fight.

'Yeah, let's hear it,' Rikki said, also ready to argue. All eyes were glued to the foreman.

462

'Okay,' he said, and the room went perfectly still. After years of planning, it all came down to this. He chose his words carefully, but in his mind he'd made the speech a thousand times. 'I'm convinced cigarettes are dangerous and deadly; they kill four hundred thousand people a year; they're loaded with nicotine by their makers, who've known for a long time that the stuff is addictive; they could be a lot safer if the companies wanted, but the nicotine would be reduced and thus sales would suffer. I think cigarettes killed Jacob Wood, and none of you will argue this. I'm convinced the tobacco companies lie and cheat and cover up, and do everything in their power to get kids to smoke. They're a ruthless bunch of sonofabitches, and I say we stick it to them.'

'I agree,' said Henry Vu.

Rikki and Millie felt like clapping.

'You want punitives?' Jerry asked, in disbelief.

'The verdict means nothing if it's not significant, Jerry. It has to be huge. A verdict for actual damages only means we don't have the guts to punish the tobacco industry for its corporate sins.'

'We have to make it hurt,' Shine Royce said, but only because he wanted to sound intelligent. He'd found his bandwagon.

Lonnie looked at Shine and Vu in disbelief. He counted quickly – seven votes for the plaintiff. 'You can't talk money, because you don't have your votes yet.'

'They're not my votes,' Nicholas said.

'The hell they're not,' he said bitterly. 'This is your verdict.'

They went around the table again – seven for the plaintiff, three for the defense, Jerry and Poodle straddling the fence but looking for a place to land. Then Mrs. Gladys Card upset the tally by saying, 'I don't like voting for the tobacco company, but, at the same time, I just can't understand giving Celeste Wood all this money.'

'How much money would you give her?' Nicholas asked.

She was flustered and confused. 'I just don't know. I'll vote to give something, but, well, I just don't know.'

'How much do you have in mind?' Rikki asked the foreman, and the room was still again. Very still and quiet.

'A billion,' Nicholas said with a completely straight face. It landed like a percussion bomb on the center of the table. Mouths fell open and eyes bulged.

Before anyone could speak, Nicholas explained himself. 'If we're serious about sending a message to the tobacco industry, then we have to shock them. Our verdict should be a landmark. It should be famous and known from this day forward as the moment the American public, acting through its jury system, finally stood up to the tobacco industry and said, "Enough is enough."'

'You're outta your mind,' Lonnie said, and at the moment, most felt the same way.

'So you want to be famous,' Jerry said, heavy on the sarcasm.

'Not me, but the verdict. Nobody will remember our names next week, but everyone will remember our verdict. If we're gonna do it, then let's do it right.'

'I like it,' Shine Royce chimed in. The thought of dispensing so much money made him giddy. Shine was the only juror ready to spend another night at the motel so he could eat free and collect another fifteen dollars tomorrow.

'Tell us what will happen,' Millie said, still stunned.

'It'll be appealed, and some day, probably two years from now, a bunch of old goats in black robes will reduce it. They'll lower it to something more reasonable. They'll say it was a runaway verdict from a

464

runaway jury, and they'll fix it. The system works most of the time.'

'Then why should we do it?' Loreen asked.

'For change. We'll start the long process of making the tobacco companies accountable for killing so many people. Keep in mind, they've never lost a trial such as this. They think they're invincible. We prove otherwise, and we do it in such a way that other plaintiffs are not afraid to take on the industry.'

'So you want to bankrupt them,' Lonnie said.

'Wouldn't bother me. Pynex is worth one-point-two billion, and virtually all its profits have come at the expense of people who use their products but would love to quit. Yeah, come to think of it, the world would be a better place without Pynex. Who'd cry if it folded?'

'Maybe its employees,' Lonnie said.

'Good point. But I have more sympathy for the thousands of people hooked on their products.'

'How much will the appeals court give Celeste Wood?' Mrs. Gladys Card asked. She was troubled by the idea that one of her neighbors, albeit a person she didn't know, was going to get rich. Sure, she'd lost her husband, but Mr. Card had survived prostate cancer with no thought of suing anybody.

'I have no idea,' Nicholas said. 'And that's not something we should worry about. That's another day in another courtroom, and there are guidelines to be followed when reducing large verdicts.'

'A billion dollars,' Loreen repeated to herself, but audibly enough to be heard. It was as easy to say as 'A million dollars.' Most of the jurors stared at the table and repeated the word 'billion.'

Not for the first time, Nicholas thanked himself for Herrera's absence. At a moment like this, with a billion dollars on the table, Herrera would be raising hell and probably throwing things. But the room was quiet.

465

Lonnie was the only advocate left for the defense, and he was busy counting and recounting votes.

Herman's absence was also important, probably more so than the Colonel's because people would listen to Herman. He was thoughtful and calculating, not prone to emotion and certainly not susceptible to an outrageous verdict.

But they were gone.

Nicholas had steered the talk away from liability and onto the issue of damages, a crucial shift that no one recognized but himself. The billion dollars had stunned them and forced them to think about money, not fault.

He was determined to keep their thoughts on money. 'It's just an idea,' he said. It's important to get their attention.'

Nicholas quickly winked at Jerry, who entered perfectly on cue. 'I can't go that high,' he said in his best car salesman routine, which was pretty effective. It's, well, it's outrageous. I can see some damages, but, damn, this is just plain crazy.'

'It's not outrageous,' Nicholas argued. 'The company has eight hundred million in cash. The place is like a mint. All tobacco companies print their own money.'

Jerry made eight, and Lonnie withdrew to a corner, where he began clipping his fingernails.

And Poodle made nine. 'It is outrageous, and I can't do that,' she said. 'Something lower maybe, but not a billion dollars.'

'So how much?' Rikki asked.

Only five hundred million. Only one hundred million. They could not force themselves to utter these ridiculous sums of money.

'I don't know,' Sylvia said. 'What do you think?'

'I like the idea of putting these guys on the ropes,' Rikki said. 'If we're going to send a message, then let's not be shy about it.'

'A billion?' Sylvia asked.

'Yeah, I can do that.'

'Me too,' Shine said, feeling wealthy just by being there.

There was a long pause; the only sound came from Lonnie snipping his fingernails.

Finally, Nicholas said, 'Who cannot vote to return any damages whatsoever?'

Savelle raised his hand. Lonnie ignored the question, but then he didn't need to respond.

'The vote stands at ten to two,' Nicholas reported, and wrote this down. 'This jury has hereby reached its decision on liability. Now, let's settle the issue of damages. Can the ten of us agree that the Wood estate is entitled to the two million in actual damages?'

Savelle kicked his chair back and left the room. Lonnie poured a cup of coffee and sat by the window, his back to the group, but listening to every word.

The two million sounded like pocket change in light of the previous discussion, and it was approved by the ten. Nicholas wrote this on a form approved by Judge Harkin.

'Can the ten of us agree that punitive damages should be imposed, in some amount?' He slowly went around the table and got a 'Yes' from each. Mrs. Gladys Card hesitated. She could change her mind, but it would have no impact. Only nine votes were needed for a verdict.

'All right. Now, as to the amount of punitive damages. Any ideas?'

'I have one,' Jerry said. 'Get everybody to write their amount on a piece of paper, fold it, keep it secret, then add them up and divide by ten. That way we'll see what the average is.'

'Will it be binding?' Nicholas asked.

'No. But it'll give us an idea of where we are.'

The idea of a secret ballot was very appealing, and they quickly scribbled their numbers on scraps of paper.

467

Nicholas slowly unfolded each ballot and called the amounts to Millie, who wrote them down. One billion, one million, fifty million, ten million, one billion, one million, five million, five hundred million, one billion, and two million.

Millie did the math. 'The total is three billion, five hundred sixty-nine million. Divide by ten, and the average is three hundred fifty-six million, nine hundred thousand.'

It took a moment for the zeros to settle in. Lonnie jumped to his feet and walked by the table. 'You people are crazy,' he said just loud enough to be heard, then left the room, slamming the door.

'I can't do this,' Mrs. Gladys Card said, visibly shaken. 'I'm living on a pension, okay. It's a good pension, but I cannot fathom these numbers.'

'The numbers are real,' Nicholas said. 'The company has eight hundred million in cash, equity of over a billion. Last year our country spent six billion on medical costs directly related to smoking, and the number goes up each year. The four largest tobacco companies had combined sales last year of almost sixteen billion. And their numbers are going up. You gotta think big, okay. These guys'll laugh at a five-million-dollar verdict. They won't change a thing, business as usual. Same ads directed at kids. Same lies to Congress. Same everything, unless we wake them up.'

Rikki leaned forward on her elbows, and stared across the table at Mrs. Card. 'If you can't do it, then leave with the rest of them.'

'Don't taunt me.'

'I'm not taunting. This takes guts, okay. Nicholas is right. If we don't slap them in the face and bring them to their knees, nothing will change. These are ruthless people.'

Mrs. Gladys Card was nervous and shaking and

ready for a breakdown. 'I'm sorry. I want to help, but I just can't do this.'

'It's okay, Mrs. Card,' Nicholas said, trying to soothe. The poor lady was distraught and needed a friend. Sure, things were fine as long as there were nine other votes. He could afford to be comforting; he just couldn't afford to lose another vote.

There was a silence as they waited to see if she would regroup or come unglued. She took a deep breath, jutted her chin forward, and found inner strength.

'Can I ask a question?' Angel said in the direction of Nicholas, as if he were now the sole source of wisdom.

'Sure,' he said, shrugging.

'What will happen to the tobacco industry if we bring back a big verdict, the kind we're talking about?'

'Legally, economically, or politically?'

'All.'

He thought for a second or two, but was anxious to respond. 'A lot of panic, initially. Lots of shock waves. Lots of scared executives worrying about what's next. They'll hunker down and wait to see if the trial lawyers flood them with litigation. They'll be forced to reexamine their advertising strategies. They won't go bankrupt, at least not in the near future, because they have so much money. They'll run to Congress and demand special laws, and I suspect Washington will treat them with less and less favor. In short, Angel, the industry will never be the same if we do what we should do.'

'Hopefully, one day cigarettes will be outlawed,' Rikki added.

'That, or the companies will not be financially able to manufacture them,' said Nicholas.

'What will happen to us?' Angel asked. 'I mean, will we be in any danger? You said these people have been watching us since before the trial started.'

'Naw, we'll be safe,' Nicholas said. 'They can't do

469

anything to us. Like I said earlier, next week they won't remember our names. But everyone will remember our verdict.'

Phillip Savelle returned and took his seat. 'So what have you Robin Hoods decided now?' he asked.

Nicholas ignored him. 'We need to decide on an amount, folks, if we want to go home.'

'I thought we'd made that decision,' said Rikki.

'Do we have at least nine votes?' Nicholas asked.

'For how much, may I ask?' Savelle inquired in a mocking tone.

'Three hundred and fifty million, give or take a few,' Rikki answered.

'Ah, the old distribution of wealth theory. Funny, you folks don't look like a bunch of Marxists.'

'I have an idea,' Jerry said. 'Let's round it off to four hundred, half their cash. That shouldn't bankrupt them. They can tighten their belts, load up some more nicotine, hook some more kids, and, presto, they'll have the money back in a couple of years.'

'Is this an auction?' Savelle asked, and no one answered.

'Let's do it,' Rikki said.

'Count the votes,' Nicholas said, and nine hands went up. He then polled them by asking each of the other eight if they were voting to return a verdict of two million dollars in actual damages and four hundred million in punitive. Each of them said yes. He filled in the verdict form, and made each of them sign it.

Lonnie returned after a long absence.

Nicholas addressed him. 'We've reached a verdict, Lonnie.'

'What a surprise. How much?'

'Four hundred and two million dollars,' Savelle said. 'Give or take a few million.'

Lonnie looked at Savelle, then looked at Nicholas. 'You're kidding?' he said, barely audible.

470

'Nope,' Nicholas said. 'It's true, and we have nine votes. Care to join?'

'Hell no.'

'Pretty incredible, ain't it?' Savelle said. 'And just think, we'll all be famous.'

'This is unheard of,' Lonnie said, leaning against the wall.

'Not really,' Nicholas replied. 'Texaco got hit with a ten-billion-dollar verdict a few years back.'

'Oh, so this is a bargain?' Lonnie said.

'No,' Nicholas said, standing. 'This is justice.' He walked to the door, opened it, and asked Lou Dell to inform Judge Harkin that his jury was ready.

While they waited for a minute, Lonnie cornered Nicholas, and in a whisper asked, 'Is there any way I can keep my name out of this?' He was more nervous than angry.

'Sure. Don't worry. The Judge will poll us, ask us one at a time if this is our verdict. When he asks you, make sure everyone knows you had nothing to do with it.'

'Thanks.'

FORTY-TWO

Lou Dell took the note as she had taken his previous ones and gave it to Willis, who walked down the hall, around the corner, and out of sight. He personally delivered it to His Honor, who at that moment was chatting on the phone, and anxious to hear the verdict. He heard verdicts all the time, but he had a hunch this one might have some pop to it. He felt sure he would one day preside over a grander civil trial, but one was hard to contemplate at the moment.

The note said: 'Judge Harkin, Could you arrange for a deputy to escort me from the courthouse as soon as we're dismissed? I'm scared. I'll explain later. Nicholas Easter.'

His Honor gave instructions to a deputy waiting outside his chambers, then strode purposefully through the door and into the courtroom, where the air seemed thick with trepidation. Lawyers, most of whom had been lounging around their offices not far away waiting for the call, were scurrying down the aisle, hustling to their seats, nerved up and wild-eyed. Spectators filtered in. It was almost eight o'clock.

'I have been informed that the jury has reached a verdict,' Harkin said loudly into his microphone, and he could see the lawyers shaking. 'Please bring in the jury.'

They filed in with solemn faces, something jurors always do. Regardless of what good news they bear for one side or the other, and regardless of how united they might be, their eyes are always downcast, causing both sides to instinctively sink low and begin plans for appeal.

Lou Dell took the form from Nicholas, gave it to His Honor, who somehow managed to examine it while remaining remarkably straight-faced. He gave not the slightest hint of the shattering news he was holding. The verdict shocked him beyond reason, but procedurally there was nothing he could do. It was technically in order. There would be motions to reduce it later, but he was handcuffed now. He refolded it, gave it back to Lou Dell, who walked it over to Nicholas. He was standing and ready for the announcement.

'Mr. Foreman, read the verdict.'

Nicholas unfolded his masterpiece, cleared his throat, glanced around quickly to see if Fitch was in the courtroom, and when he didn't see him, he read: 'We, the jury, find for the plaintiff, Celeste Wood, and award compensatory damages in the amount of two million dollars.'

This alone was a precedent. Wendall Rohr and his gang of trial lawyers breathed an enormous sigh of relief. They had just made history.

But the jury wasn't finished.

'And we, the jury, find for the plaintiff, Celeste Wood, and award punitive damages in the amount of four hundred million dollars.'

From a lawyer's point of view, the receiving of a verdict approaches an art form. One cannot flinch or twitch. One cannot look around for either solace or jubilation. One cannot grab one's client to celebrate or to comfort. One must sit perfectly still, frown hard at a legal pad upon which one is writing, and act as though one knew precisely what the verdict would be.

The art form was desecrated. Cable slumped as if shot in the stomach. His comrades stared at the jury box with mouths gaping, air rushing out, eyes squinted in utter disbelief. An 'Oh my god!' was heard from somewhere among the second-tier defense lawyers behind Cable.

Rohr was all teeth as he quickly put his arm around Celeste Wood, who had started crying. The other trial lawyers clutched each other with quiet congratulations. Oh, the thrill of victory, the prospect of splitting forty percent of this verdict.

Nicholas sat down and patted Loreen Duke on the leg. It was over, finally over.

Judge Harkin was suddenly all business, as if it were just another verdict. 'Now, ladies and gentlemen, I'm going to poll the jury. This means I will ask each of you individually if this is your verdict. I'll start with Ms. Loreen Duke. Please state clearly for the record whether or not you voted for this verdict.'

'I did,' she said proudly.

Some of the lawyers took notes. Some simply stared blankly into space.

'Mr. Easter? Did you vote in favor of this verdict?'

'I did.'

'Mrs. Dupree?'

'Yes sir. I did.'

'Mr. Savelle?'

'I did not.'

'Mr. Royce? Did you vote for this?'

'I did.'

'Ms. Weese?'

'I did.'

'Mr. Vu?'

'I did.'

'Mr. Lonnie Shaver?'

Lonnie half-stood, said loudly for the world to hear, 'No sir, Your Honor, I did not vote for this verdict, and I disagree with it entirely.'

'Thank you. Mrs. Rikki Coleman? Is this your verdict?'

'Yes sir.'

'Mrs. Gladys Card?'

'No sir.'

There suddenly arose a flicker of hope for Cable and Pynex and Fitch and the entire tobacco industry. Three jurors had now disclaimed the verdict. Only one more, and the jury would be sent back for more deliberations. Every trial judge could tell stories of juries whose verdicts disintegrated after they were delivered and while the polling took place. A verdict sounded much different in open court, with lawyers and clients watching, than it did only minutes earlier in the safety of the jury room.

But the slim prospect of a miracle was stamped out by the Poodle and Jerry. Both affirmed the verdict.

'Looks like the vote is nine to three,' His Honor said. 'Everything else appears to be in order. Anything, Mr. Rohr?'

Rohr simply shook his head. He could not thank the jury now, though he would've loved to jump over the railing and kiss their feet. He sat smugly in his seat, one heavy arm around Celeste Wood.

'Mr. Cable?'

'No sir,' Cable managed to say. Oh, the things he'd love to tell the jurors, the idiots.

The fact that Fitch was not in the courtroom worried Nicholas immensely. His absence meant he was out-side, somewhere in the dark, lurking and waiting. How much did Fitch know now? Probably too much. Nicholas was anxious to leave the courtroom, and get the hell out of town.

Harkin then began a windy thank-you, interspersed it with a rowsing dose of patriotism and civic duty, threw in every cliché he'd heard from the bench, warned them against talking to anybody about their deliberations and their verdict, said he could hold them in contempt of court if they breathed a word of what had happened in the jury room, and sent them away on their final journey to the motel to gather their things.

Fitch watched and listened from the viewing room next to his office. And he watched alone, the jury consultants having been fired hours earlier and sent back to Chicago.

He could snatch Easter, and this had been discussed at length with Swanson, who'd been told everything as soon as he arrived. But what good would it do? Easter wouldn't talk and they'd run the risk of a kidnapping charge. They had enough troubles without spending time in jail in Biloxi.

They decided to follow him, hoping he would lead them to the girl. Which, of course, posed another dilemma: What would they do with the girl if they found her? They couldn't report Marlee to the police. She'd made the magnificent decision to steal dirty money. What would Fitch tell the FBI in his sworn affidavit: that he gave her ten million dollars to deliver a verdict in a tobacco trial, and she had the nerve to double-cross him? Now would somebody please prosecute her?

Fitch was screwed at every turn.

He watched the video through the lens of Oliver McAdoo's hidden camera. The jurors stood, shuffled out, and the jury box was empty.

They gathered in the jury room to pick up books and magazines and knitting bags. Nicholas was in no mood for small talk. He slipped through the door, where Chuck, an old friend now, stopped him and told him the Sheriff was waiting outside.

Without a word to Lou Dell or Willis, or to any of the people he'd spent the last four weeks with, Nicholas hurriedly disappeared behind Chuck. They ducked out the back entrance, where the Sheriff himself was waiting behind the wheel of his big brown Ford.

'Judge said you needed some help,' the Sheriff said from behind the wheel.

476

'Yeah. Get on Forty-nine north. I'll show you where to go. And make sure we're not followed.'

'Okay. Who might be following you?'

'Bad guys.'

Chuck slammed the passenger door in the front, and they sped away. Nicholas took one last look at the jury room on the second floor. He saw Millie from the waist up, hugging Rikki Coleman.

'Don't you have things at the motel?' the Sheriff asked.

'Forget it. I'll get them later.'

The Sheriff radioed instructions for two cars to follow and make sure they were not being tailed. Twenty minutes later, as they raced through Gulfport, Nicholas began pointing this way and that, and the Sheriff stopped by the tennis court of a large apartment complex north of town. Nicholas said this was fine, and got out.

'You sure you're okay?' the Sheriff asked.

'I'm sure. I'll stay here with some friends. Thanks.'

'Call me if you need help.'

'Sure.'

Nicholas disappeared into the night, and watched from a corner as the patrol car left. He waited by the pool house, a vantage point that enabled him to see all traffic to and from the apartment complex. He saw nothing suspicious.

His getaway car was brand-new, a rental Marlee had left there two days ago, one of three now abandoned in various parking lots on the outskirts of Biloxi. He safely made the ninety-minute drive to Hattiesburg while watching his rear the entire way.

The Lear was waiting at the Hattiesburg airport. Nicholas locked the keys in the car, and walked nonchalantly into the small terminal.

Sometime after midnight, he breezed through customs

477

in George Town with fresh Canadian papers. There were no other passengers; the airport was practically deserted. Marlee met him by the baggage claim, and they embraced fiercely.

'Have you heard?' he asked. They stepped outside, where the humid air hit hard.

'Yeah, it's all over CNN,' she said. Was that the best you could do?' she asked with a laugh, and they kissed again.

She drove toward George Town, through the empty winding streets, around the modern bank buildings clustered near the pier. 'That's ours,' she said, pointing to the Royal Swiss Trust building.

'Nice.'

Later, they sat in the sand, at the edge of the water, splashing in the foam as the gentle waves broke across their feet. A few boats with dim lights inched along the horizon. The hotels and condos stood quiet behind them. They owned the beach for the moment.

And what a moment it was. Their four-year quest was now over. Their plans had finally worked, and to perfection. They'd dreamed of this night for so long, had been convinced countless times that it could never happen.

The hours drifted by.

They thought it best if Marcus the broker never laid eyes on Nicholas. There was an excellent chance authorities might ask questions later, and the less Marcus knew, the better. Marlee presented herself to the Royal Swiss Trust receptionist promptly at nine, and was escorted upstairs where Marcus was waiting with many questions he couldn't ask. He offered coffee, then closed his door.

'The shorting of Pynex seems to have been an excellent trade,' he said with a grin at his own talent for understatement.

478

'Seems so,' she said. 'Where will it open?'

'Good question. I've been on the phone to New York, and things are quite chaotic. The verdict has stunned everyone. Except you, I guess.' He wanted so badly to probe, but he knew there would be no answers. 'There's a chance it might not open. They could suspend trading for a day or two.'

She seemed to understand this perfectly. The coffee arrived. They sipped it as they reviewed yesterday's closings. At nine-thirty, Marcus slipped on his headset and focused on the two monitors on his side desk. 'The market is open,' he said, waiting.

Marlee listened intently while trying to appear calm. She and Nicholas wanted to make a quick killing, in and out, then be gone with the money to some faraway place they'd never seen before. She had to cover 160,000 shares of Pynex, stock she was anxious to unload.

'It's suspended,' Marcus said to his computer, and she flinched slightly. He punched digits and began a conversation with someone in New York. He mumbled numbers and points, then said to her, 'They're offering it at fifty, and there are no buyers. Yes or no?'

'No.'

Two minutes passed. His eyes never left the screen. 'It's on the board at forty-five. Yes or no?'

'No. What about the others?'

His fingers danced across the keyboard. 'Wow. Trellco is down thirteen to forty-three. Smith Greer down eleven to fifty-three and a quarter. ConPack down eight to twenty-five. It's a bloodbath. The entire industry is getting shelled.'

'Check Pynex.'

'Still falling. Forty-two, with a few small buyers.'

'Buy twenty thousand shares at forty-two,' she said, looking at her notes.

A few seconds passed before he said, 'Confirmed.

Up to forty-three. They're paying attention up there. I'd keep it under twenty thousand shares next time.'

Less commissions, the Marlee/Nicholas partnership had just made $740,000.

'Back down to forty-two.' he said.

'Buy twenty thousand shares at forty-one,' she said.

A minute later he said, 'Confirmed.'

Another $760,000 in profits.

'Steady at forty-one, now a half up,' he said like a robot. 'They saw your buy.'

'Is anybody else buying?' she asked.

'Not yet.'

'When will they start?'

'Who knows? But soon, I think. This company has too much cash to go under. Book value per share is around seventy. It's a steal at fifty. I'd tell all my clients to jump in now.'

She bought another twenty thousand shares at forty-one, then waited half an hour to buy twenty thousand at forty. When Trellco fell to forty, down sixteen, she bought twenty thousand shares, for a profit of $320,000.

The quick kill was happening. She borrowed a phone at ten-thirty and called Nicholas, who was glued to the TV, watching it all unfold on CNN. They had a crew in Biloxi trying to get interviews from Rohr and Cable and Harkin, from Gloria Lane or anybody who might know something. No one wanted to talk to them. Nicholas was also watching stock quotes on a financial news channel.

Pynex found its bottom an hour after it opened. Takers were found at thirty-eight, at which point Marlee dumped the remaining eighty thousand shares.

When Trellco found resistance at forty-one, she bought forty thousand shares. She was out of the Trellco business. With the bulk of her trades covered, and covered quite brilliantly, Marlee was less inclined to hang around and be greedy with the other stocks. She worked hard at being patient. She had rehearsed this plan many times, and the opportunity would never again be hers.

A few minutes before noon, with the market still in disarray, she covered the remaining shares of Smith Greer. Marcus removed his headset and wiped his forehead.

'Not a bad morning, Ms. MacRoland. You've netted over eight million, less commissions.' A printer hummed quietly on the desk, spewing out confirmations.

'I want the money wired to a bank in Zurich.'

'Our bank?'

'No.' She handed him a sheet of paper with wiring instructions.

'How much?' he asked.

'All of it, minus, of course, your commissions.'

'Certainly. I assume this is a priority.'

'Immediately, please.'

She packed quickly. He watched because he had nothing to pack, nothing but two golf shirts and a pair of jeans he'd purchased at a dive shop in the hotel. They promised each other new wardrobes at their next destination. Money would not be a factor.

They flew, first class, to Miami, where they waited two hours before boarding a flight to Amsterdam. The in-flight news service in first class featured none other than CNN and Financial News. They watched with great amusement as the verdict got covered in Biloxi while Wall Street ran in circles. Experts popped up everywhere. Law professors made fearless predictions about the future of tobacco liability. Stock analysts offered myriad opinions, each in sharp contrast to the preceding one. Judge Harkin had no comment. Cable could not be found. Rohr finally emerged from his

481

office and took full credit for the victory. No one knew of Rankin Fitch, which was a shame because Marlee wanted so badly to see his suffering face.

In hindsight, her timing was perfect. The market bottomed soon after it crashed, and by the end of the day Pynex was holding steady at forty-five.

From Amsterdam, they flew to Geneva, where they leased a hotel suite for a month.

FORTY-THREE

Fitch left Biloxi three days after the verdict. He returned to his home in Arlington and to his routine in Washington. Though his future as director of The Fund was in doubt, his anonymous little firm had plenty of non-tobacco work to keep it busy. Nothing, though, that paid like The Fund.

A week after the verdict, he met with Luther Vandemeer and D. Martin Jankle in New York, and confessed every detail of the deal with Marlee. It was not a pretty meeting.

He also conferred with a collection of ruthless New York lawyers on how best to attack the verdict. The fact that Easter had vanished immediately was grounds for suspicion. Herman Grimes had already agreed to release his medical records. There was no evidence of an imminent heart attack. He'd been fit and healthy until that morning. He remembered an odd taste to his coffee, then he was on the floor. Retired Colonel Frank Herrera had already given an affidavit in which he swore the unauthorized materials found under his bed were not placed there by him. He'd had no visitors. *Mogul* was not sold anywhere near the motel. The mystery surrounding the verdict swirled more each day.

The New York lawyers did not know about the Marlee deal, nor would they ever.

Cable had prepared and was almost ready to file a

motion requesting permission to interview the jurors, an idea Judge Harkin seemed to like. How else could they find out what had gone on in there? Lonnie Shaver was particularly anxious to tell all. He'd received his promotion and was ready to defend corporate America.

There was hope for the post-trial efforts. The appellate process would be long and arduous.

As for Rohr and the group of trial lawyers who'd funded the case, the future was filled with unbounded opportunity. A staff was organized just to handle the flood of calls from other lawyers and potential victims. An 800 number was implemented. Class actions were being considered.

Wall Street seemed more sympathetic to Rohr than to the tobacco industry. In the weeks following the verdict, Pynex couldn't top fifty, and the other three were down at least twenty percent. Antismoking groups openly predicted the bankruptcy and eventual demise of the tobacco companies.

Six weeks after he left Biloxi, Fitch was eating lunch alone in a tiny Indian diner near Dupont Circle in D.C. He huddled over a bowl of spicy soup, still wearing his overcoat because it was snowing outside and chilly inside.

She dropped in from nowhere, just appeared like an angel, the same way she'd emerged on the rooftop terrace of the St. Regis in New Orleans, over two months earlier. 'Hi, Fitch,' she said, and he dropped his spoon.

He glanced around the dark restaurant, saw nothing but small groups of Indians huddled over steaming bowls, not another spoken word of English within forty feet.

'What are you doing here?' he said without moving his lips. Her face was lined with the fur from her coat. He remembered how pretty she was. The hair seemed even shorter.

'Just dropped in to say hello.'

'You've said it.'

'And the money is being returned to you, even as we speak. I'm wiring it back to your account at Hanwa, in the Netherlands Antilles. All ten million, Fitch.'

He could think of no quick response to this. He was looking at the lovely face of the only person who'd ever beaten him. And she still had him guessing. 'How kind of you,' he said.

'I started to give it away, you know, like to some of those antismoking groups. But we decided against it.'

'We? How's Nicholas?'

'I'm sure you miss him.'

'Deeply.'

'He's fine.'

'So you're together?'

'Of course.'

'Thought you probably just took the money and ran from everybody, including him.'

'Come on, Fitch.'

'I don't want the money.'

'Great. Give it to the American Lung Association.'

'That's not my kinda charity. Why are you returning the money?'

'It's not mine.'

'So you've found ethics and morals, maybe even God.'

'Skip the lecture, Fitch. It sounds rather hollow coming from you. I never planned to keep the money. I just wanted to borrow it.'

'If you're gonna lie and cheat, why not go ahead and steal?'

'I'm not a thief. I lied and I cheated because that's what your client understands. Tell me, Fitch, did you find Gabrielle?'

'Yes, we did.'

'And did you find her parents?'

'We know where they are.'

'Do you understand now, Fitch?'

'It makes more sense, yes.'

'They were both wonderful people. They were intelligent and vigorous and they loved life. They both got hooked on cigarettes when they were in college, and I watched them fight the habit until they died. They hated themselves for smoking, but could never give it up. They died horrible deaths, Fitch. I watched them suffer and shrivel and gasp for breath until they couldn't breathe anymore. I was their only child, Fitch. Did your goons learn this?'

'Yes.'

'My mother died at home, on the sofa in the den because she couldn't walk to her bedroom. Just Mother and I.' She paused and glanced around. Fitch noticed her eyes were remarkably clear. Sad as it must have been, he could muster no sympathy.

'When did you set this plan in motion?' he asked, finally taking a spoonful of soup.

'Grad school. I studied finance, thought about law, then I dated a lawyer for a while and heard stories of tobacco litigation. The idea evolved.'

'A helluva plot.'

'Thanks, Fitch. Coming from you, that's a compliment.'

She pulled her gloves tighter as if she was ready to go. 'Just wanted to say hello, Fitch. And to make sure you know why it happened.'

'Are you finished with us?'

'No. We'll watch the appeal closely, and if your lawyers get too carried away attacking the verdict, then I've got copies of the wire transfers. Be careful, Fitch. We're kind of proud of that verdict, and we're always watching.'

She stood at the edge of the table. 'And remember, Fitch, next time you boys go to trial, we'll be there.'

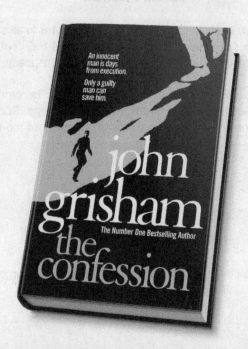

The Pelican Brief

John Grisham

Two Supreme Court Justices are dead. Their murders remain unsolved.

Darby Shaw, a brilliant and beautiful New Orleans legal student, draws up a speculative legal brief which links the deaths and uncovers an astonishing presidential conspiracy.

When her boyfriend is atomised in a car bomb, it becomes clear that somebody is intent on silencing Darby for good. Somebody who will stop at nothing to preserve the secrets of the Pelican Brief . . .

'Fast and furious'
Daily Telegraph

'A rattling good story'
New York Times

'I would highly recommend it . . . a real page-turner'
Frederick Forsyth, *Sunday Express*

arrow books